Praise for the Unwind Dystology

Unwind

★ "Gripping, brilliantly imagined futuristic thriller. . . . The issues raised could not be more provocative—the sanctity of life, the meaning of being human—while the delivery could hardly be more engrossing or better aimed to teens."
—*Publishers Weekly*, starred review

★ "A thought-provoking, well-paced read that will appeal widely."
—*School Library Journal*, starred review

"Well-written, this draws the readers into a world that is both familiar and strangely foreign, and generates feelings of horror, disturbance, disgust, and fear. As with classics such as *1984* and *Fahrenheit 451*, one can only hope that this vision of the future never becomes reality."—*Kirkus Reviews*

"Poignant, compelling, and ultimately terrifying, this book will enjoy popularity with a wide range of readers."—*VOYA*, 4Q4P

"Following in the footsteps of Jonathan Swift, Shusterman uncorks a Modest Proposal of his own to solve a Pro-Life/Pro-Choice dilemma . . . ingeniously developed cast and premise."—*Booklist*

UnWholly

"A breathless, unsettling read."—*Kirkus Reviews*

"Perfectly poised to catch the *Hunger Games* wave and based on an even more plausible dystopian scenario."—*Booklist*

"Thematically rich and packed with action, commentary, and consequences, this is a strong pick for dystopia fans that will also appeal to reluctant readers."
—*BCCB*

"Smart, intense, and thought provoking, this series will stick with readers."
—*VOYA*, 5Q4P

"Shusterman elegantly balances the strikingly different perspectives of the three main protagonists effectively, and these dissimilar approaches to life highlight the ways in which the larger world grapples with unwinding."—*Horn Book*

UnSouled

"Suspenseful . . . the overall premise is as hauntingly plausible as ever . . . electrifying."—*Booklist*

"It packs a punch and is an excellent addition to series."—*School Library Journal*

"Shusterman effectively balances the big-picture ethical musings with scenes of the teens simply being teens. . . . Join the ranks waiting for the next installment."—*Horn Book*

Also by Neal Shusterman

Visit the author at storyman.com and facebook.com/nealshusterman

Neal Shusterman

UnDivided

BOOK 4 OF THE UNWIND DYSTOLOGY

SIMON & SCHUSTER BFYR

New York   London   Toronto   Sydney   New Delhi

An imprint of Simon & Schuster Children's Publishing Division
1230 Avenue of the Americas, New York, New York 10020

Text copyright © 2014 by Neal Shusterman
Cover illustrations copyright © 2015 Luke Lucas
"Girl Smuggled into Britain to Have Her Organs Harvested"
© Steven Swinford / Telegraph Media Group Limited, 2013
"Belgium First Country to Allow Euthanasia for Children"
© David Harding / New York Daily News, December 14, 2013
"Body Art: Creations Made of Human Flesh, Blood & Bones"
© WebUrbanist, August 23, 2010
"3D Printing with Stem Cells Could Lead to Printable Organs"
© Amanda Kooser / CNET.com, February 5, 2013
"Anonymous Rallies Against Horrific, Abuse-Riddled 'Troubled Teen' Industry"
© Roy Klabin / PolicyMic.com, March 27, 2013

For information about special discounts for bulk purchases, please contact Simon &
Schuster Special Sales at 1-866-506-1949 or business@simonandschuster.com.
The Simon & Schuster Speakers Bureau can bring authors to your live event.
For more information or to book an event, contact the Simon & Schuster Speakers Bureau
at 1-866-248-3049 or visit our website at www.simonspeakers.com.
Also available in a SIMON & SCHUSTER BFYR hardcover edition
Book design by Hilary Zarycky based on a design by Al Cetta.
The text for this book is set in Fairfield.
Manufactured in the United States of America
First SIMON & SCHUSTER BFYR paperback edition November 2015
4 6 8 10 9 7 5 3
The Library of Congress has cataloged the hardcover edition as follows:
Shusterman, Neal.
UnDivided / Neal Shusterman.
pages cm.—(Unwind dystology ; 4)
Summary: Three teens band together in order to sway the government to repeal all rulings
in support of a procedure in which unwanted teenagers are captured and are unwound into
parts that can be reused for transplantation.
ISBN 978-1-4814-0975-9 (hc)
[1. Fugitives from justice—Fiction. 2. Revolutionaries—Fiction. 3. Science fiction.] I. Title.
PZ7.S55987Und 2014
[Fic]—dc23
2014003060
ISBN 978-1-4814-0976-6 (pbk)
ISBN 978-1-4814-0977-3 (eBook)

For my editor and friend, David Gale

ACKNOWLEDGMENTS

The Unwind Dystology has been an amazing journey! My editor, David Gale, and my publisher, Justin Chanda, have believed in these books from the beginning. Everyone at Simon & Schuster has been incredibly supportive, including Jon Anderson, Anne Zafian, Liz Kossnar, Paul Crichton, Katy Hershberger, Michelle Leo, Candace Greene, Anthony Parisi, Katrina Groover, Chava Wolin, and Chloë Foglia. My kids (who I would never dream of unwinding!), Brendan, Jarrod, Joelle, and Erin, have put up with book tours, and all the times Dad disappears into his own weird mind. I have the best kids ever! And I wouldn't have all the time I have to write, were it not for my assistants, Marcia Blanco and Barb Sobel. I also have the best "people" ever! My book agent, Andrea Brown; my foreign rights agent, Taryn Fagerness; my entertainment industry agents, Steve Fisher and Debbie Deuble-Hill; my manager, Trevor Engelson; and my contract attorneys, Shep Rosenman, Lee Rosenbaum, and Gia Paladino. I'd like to thank everyone striving to get *Unwind* made as a feature film: Julian Stone, Catherine Kimmel, Charlotte Stout, Marc Benardout, and Faber Dewar. I couldn't hope for better producers or friends. Thanks also to Robert Kulzer and Margo Klewans at Constantin Films, for your vision and passion for my work. Thanks to Michelle Knowlden, for her collaboration on "Unstrung," and upcoming short stories in the Unwind world; to Matthew Lurie, Symone Powell, Cimone Watson, Tyler Hotlzman, Annie Wilson, Meara McNitt, Matthew Setzekorn, and Natalie Sommors, for all your help on social media! And most importantly, I'd like to thank my fans, whose word of mouth has spread these books around the world. It is my hope that this conclusion is everything you've hoped for and more!

TO ALL OFFICERS AND FIELD AGENTS OF THE
JUVENILE AUTHORITY:

Our task is crucial, and the time short. Over the past few months a growing minority of delinquent youth have become a clear and present danger to public safety. Following is a reference sheet outlining how to engage different classes of incorrigible youth under our jurisdiction, as well as specific individuals high on our priority list.

DIVISIONAL RISKS

These are teens with a history of delinquent behavior, but whose parents, for whatever reason, have declined to sign an unwind order. They must be treated as any other citizen and may be tranq'd only in self-defense. Otherwise they are returned to their families if apprehended. Officers should gently encourage these families to seek a divisional solution.

FERALS

Incorrigible teenagers who have left home and have gone "feral" still have the rights of any other citizen. Ferals who prove themselves to be violent may be tranq'd with just cause. The feral may then be taken to detention centers until such time as parents can be found and notified, or until the law changes allowing for their unwinding without parental consent.

AWOLS

Unwind orders have been signed for all AWOLs before they escaped or evaded custody, which means that all of their rights have been revoked until they reach the age of seventeen (or the age of eighteen, if the Cap-17 law is overturned). AWOLs, therefore, are considered nothing more than a collection of parts, and may be treated as such. They are to be tranq'd on sight, and brought to the nearest harvest camp. Please strive, however, for a minimal amount of physical trauma in their capture, as the parts they contain have more value than their person.

CLAPPERS

By making their blood explosive, these nihilist terrorists present the greatest standing threat to public safety. While clappers can be of any age, they are almost always AWOLs, ferals, or divisional-risk youth. If faced with a clapper, remember to keep your distance, and to use approved ceramic bullets to neutralize the threat before the clapper can detonate. Ceramic bullets will take the clapper down without risk of explosion.

THE STORK BRIGADE

While statistics show that storks (i.e., babies abandoned on doorsteps) make up a disproportionately large percentage of Unwinds, it does not excuse the murderous rampage of Mason Starkey and his Stork Brigade. Rather, it validates the need for a stronger unwinding program. In order to protect harvest camps from Mason Starkey's ruthless attacks, we are increasing security, and upgrading weaponry at all harvest facilities. Should anyone encounter the Stork Brigade, do not engage. Instead, report any positive sighting to the nearest field office so that we can send in a swift aerial attack to take out the entire brigade.

CONNOR LASSITER AND RISA WARD

While it is believed that the "Akron AWOL," Connor Lassiter, is being given asylum by the Hopi tribe, we cannot ignore the possibility that it is merely a ruse, and he may be somewhere else entirely. It is possible that he has even returned to Ohio. Any officer who positively identifies Lassiter is charged with bringing him in, dead or alive. It is believed he may be traveling with Risa Ward, who, as you may remember, was given a new spine by Proactive Citizenry, one of the nation's leading charitable organizations, only to betray them and incite other teens to violence.

LEVI JEDEDIAH CALDER (AKA LEV GARRITY)

This tithe-turned-clapper violated the terms of his house arrest, and has been in hiding for several months. While it is commonly believed that the clapper organization blew up his residence in an attempt to kill him, it is our position that he staged that explosion himself, and that he is now working with the clappers.

CAMUS COMPRIX

While the rewinding of the unwound is not our immediate concern, we have been asked by Proactive Citizenry to be supportive of their efforts—especially in light of Risa Ward's betrayal. You are therefore to speak of Camus Comprix—and rewinding in general—in the most positive of terms. Whether you consider him to be a human being or not is irrelevant.

PARTS PIRATES

While the black market for Unwinds has increased in recent years, its success is directly related to our failure to catch and process AWOLs. It is our firm belief that with increased vigilance and greater federal funding, the number of AWOLs lost to parts pirates will drop, and the black-market cartels will fall.

THE CHANCEFOLK QUESTION

It has become increasingly evident that Native American Chancefolk tribes are working at cross-purposes to our objectives—particularly the Arápache, who have been known to give secret asylum to AWOL Unwinds on a regular basis. These so-called foster-fugitives are out of our jurisdiction as long as they remain on tribal land. Do not engage Chancefolk in any sort of direct conflict until such time that current treaties fall and military action is taken.

We are making great strides in bringing a lasting solution to the threats of violent youth. Through our efforts, the Anti-Divisional Resistance has collapsed. I believe we can look forward to a day free of fear from the juvenile sector, when our best and brightest youth can flourish like a tree that has been properly pruned. You, the agents and officers of the Juvenile Authority, are the ones who will make that happen. I thank you for your service.

Herman Sharply
Secretary of Juvenile Affairs

Part One

Sanctuaries of Purpose

*"If you're feeling like I feel, throw your fist
through the ceiling. . . ."*
—lyrics from "Burn It Down"
by AWOLNATION

1 · AWOL

A tranq tears past his head so close that his earlobe is skinned from the friction. A second tranq flies just beneath his armpit—he actually sees it flaring past—hitting the trash can in the alley ahead of him with a dull *clank*.

It's raining. The sky has torn loose with a late summer storm of near biblical proportions, but the storm is his best friend today because the relentless torrents hinder the Juvey-cops in pursuit. The sheets of rain make it harder for them to get a bead on him.

"Running will only make it worse for you, son," calls one of the Juvies.

He'd laugh at that if he could catch his breath. If he's caught, he'll be unwound; what could possibly be worse than that? And calling him "son"? How can a Juvey-cop have the nerve to call him "son" when the world no longer sees him as a child of the human race. As far as humanity is concerned, he's an object. A bag of biomatter ripe for salvage.

There are two, maybe three Juvey-cops chasing him. He won't turn to count them; when you're running for your life, desperate to remain undivided, it doesn't matter whether there's one, or ten, or a hundred Juvey-cops behind you. All that matters is that they're behind you—and that you run faster.

Another tranq whizzes past, but it's not as close as the others. The Juvies are getting sloppy in their aggravation. Good. He passes an overstuffed trash can and dumps it over, hoping to slow their pursuit even more. The alley seems to go on forever. He never remembered the streets of Detroit having

3

back alleys this long. The end finally comes into view maybe fifty yards ahead, and he's already visualizing freedom. He'll explode out of the alley into the city traffic. Maybe he'll cause a car accident, like the Akron AWOL. Maybe he'll find a tithe to use as a human shield like he did. Maybe he'll even pair up with a beautiful accomplice too. These thoughts push purpose into his bone-tired body, and speed into his strides. The Juvies fall farther behind, and now he has a spark of the AWOL's most valuable commodity: hope. It's something in short supply for those who have been deemed not worth the sum of their parts.

In an instant, however, that hope is eclipsed by the silhouettes of two more Juvey-cops blocking his exit from the alley. They've got him trapped. He turns to see the others closing in behind him. Unless he can sprout wings and fly, it's over for him.

Then, from a dark doorway beside him, he hears—

"Hey, you! Over here!"

Someone grabs his arm, pulling him in through an open door just as a volley of tranqs shoot past.

His mysterious savior closes the door, locking out the Juvies—but what good will that do? Being surrounded in a building is just as bad as being trapped in an alley.

"This way," says the guy who saved him. "Down here."

He leads him down rickety stairs to a dank basement. The AWOL takes a moment to size up his savior in the dim light. He seems to be three or four years older than him—eighteen, maybe even twenty. He's pale and thin, with dark stringy hair, and weak sideburns longing to be a beard, but failing to bridge the gap.

"Don't be scared," the guy says. "I'm an AWOL too."

Which seems unlikely, as he appears to be too old—on the other hand, kids who've been AWOL for a year or more tend to look older. It's as if time ticks by twice as quickly for them.

In the basement, there's a rusty sewer cap that's been

opened, and the dark hole, which couldn't be more than a foot wide, emits a malevolent odor.

"Down you go!" says the stringy-haired dude, as cheery as Santa about to go down the chimney.

"Are you kidding me?"

From upstairs comes the report of the door being kicked in, and suddenly that sewer hole doesn't seem like such a bad idea. He squeezes through, having to wiggle his hips and shoulders to fit. It feels like being swallowed by a snake. The stringy-haired dude slides in after him, then pulls the sewer cap closed, with a scrape of metal on concrete, sealing out the Juvies, without leaving a trace of where they went.

"They'll never find us down here," his strange savior says with a confidence that makes the AWOL believe him. The kid turns on a flashlight to illuminate the space around them. They're in a six-foot cylindrical sewer main that is wet with runoff from the storm, but doesn't seem to actually be in use. It still smells rank, but not as bad as it seemed from the other side.

"So whaddaya think?" the straggly-haired kid says. "It's an escape worthy of Connor Lassiter, right?"

"I don't think the Akron AWOL would climb into a sewer."

The kid grunts and leads them to a place where the sewer line is fractured, and they climb out into a concrete utility conduit that's hung with wires and lined with hot steam pipes, which make the air oppressive.

"So who are you?" the AWOL asks his rescuer.

"Name's Argent," he says, "Like 'sergeant' without the S." He holds out his hand for the AWOL to shake, then turns and leads the way down the steamy, narrow conduit. "This way, it's not far."

"Not far to where?"

"I got a pretty sweet setup. Hot food and a comfortable place to sleep."

"Sounds too good to be true."

"I know, doesn't it?" Argent offers him a smile almost as greasy as his hair.

"So what's your story? Why'd you risk your ass for me?"

Argent shrugs. "Isn't much of a risk when you know you've got 'em outsmarted," he says. "Anyway, I figure it's my civic duty. I escaped from a parts pirate a while back, now I help others less fortunate than myself. And it wasn't just any parts pirate I got away from—it was the ex-Juvey-cop who Connor Lassiter tranq'd with his own gun. He got drummed out of the force, and now he sells the kids he catches on the black market."

The AWOL reaches through his memory for the name. "That Neilson guy?"

"Nelson," Argent corrects, "Jasper T. Nelson. And I know Connor Lassiter too."

"Really," says the AWOL, dubiously.

"Oh, yeah—and he's a real piece of work. A total loser. I showed him hospitality like I'm showing you, and he did this to my face."

Only now does the AWOL see that the left half of Argent's face is badly damaged from wounds that are still healing.

"I'm supposed to believe that the Akron AWOL did that?"

Argent nods. "Yeah, when he was a guest in my storm cellar."

"Right." Obviously the guy is making all of this up, but the AWOL doesn't challenge him any further. Best not to bite the hand that's about to feed him.

"Just a little farther," says Argent. "You like steak?"

"Whenever I can get it."

Argent gestures to a breach in the concrete wall through which cool air spills, smelling like fresh mold, instead of old rot. "After you."

The AWOL climbs through to find himself in a cellar. There are other people here, but they're not moving. It takes a moment for him to register what he's seeing. Three teens lying on the ground, gagged and hog-tied.

"Hey, what the—"

But before he can finish the thought, Argent comes up behind him and puts him in a brutal choke hold that cuts off not just his windpipe, but all the blood to his brain. And the last thing that strikes the AWOL's mind before losing consciousness is the bleak realization that he's been swallowed by a snake after all.

2 · Argent

He's on top of the world. He's at the peak of his game. Things couldn't be going better for Argent Skinner, apprentice parts pirate, who's learning the trade from Jasper T. Nelson, the best there is.

Argent didn't land in Nelson's service under the best of circumstances, but he certainly has made the best of the circumstances he was given. He has proven himself so valuable that Nelson had no choice but to keep him on. The evidence of Argent's value is tied up in the U-Haul behind him.

The small van, a one-way rental, had replaced a rented car that they had left abandoned in a suburban Walmart parking lot. Argent doesn't worry that they'll be tracked down for these little bits of petty larceny, because Nelson is a true master of evading so-called justice and keeping under the radar. Having been a Juvey-cop for so many years, Nelson knows all the angles, all the ropes. He knows how to skate smoothly across the slick surface of the law.

Nelson is Argent's new hero. Connor Lassiter, the previous

object of Argent's hero worship, was a disappointment. Now both Argent and Nelson are united in hatred against the Akron AWOL—and such hatred can be as powerful a bonding force as love.

Argent turns around to take another look at the kids in the van behind him: four of them bound and gagged, practically gift wrapped for delivery. The AWOLs are all awake and squirming. Some cry, but silently and to themselves, because they don't want to incur Argent's wrath—which he has threatened to rain upon them several times. Of course, it's all blustering on Argent's part, because Nelson won't let him physically hurt them.

"Bruises reduce their market value," Nelson pointed out. "Divan does not like his fruit bruised. He's already going to be aggravated that he's getting a consolation offering from me, instead of the grand prize."

The grand prize, of course, is Connor Lassiter.

Nelson could tranq them into silence, but he won't. "I have to conserve," Nelson told Argent. "Tranqs are expensive."

However that doesn't seem to apply where Argent is concerned. Argent once tried to turn up the volume on the radio, and Nelson tranq'd him for it. Not for the first time either. Nelson seems to take great pleasure in rendering Argent unconscious. "It's like shocking a monkey to teach it not to take the banana," Nelson had said. The next song on the radio had been "Shock the Monkey." Argent is convinced that Nelson is psychic.

The prewar oldies station now plays Pearl Jam at the volume Nelson prefers: just loud enough to almost hear. Argent must constantly resist the impulse to turn up the annoyingly low music.

As Argent looks at the AWOLs in the back, the last kid that Argent caught locks eyes with him. He's a harsh-faced boy with gentle amber eyes that clash with the severity of his face. His eyes beg for something from Argent, but what? Release? Mercy? An explanation of why his life has come to this?

"Stop it!" Argent tells him. "Whatever you want, you're not gettin' it."

"Bff-foo," he mumbles through his gag.

"No bathroom stops!" Argent growls. "You'll hold it until we decide to stop—and don't give me those puppy-dog eyes unless you want 'em punched black-and-blue." Another idle threat, but the kid doesn't know that. The boy casts his eyes to the scuffed floor of the van in defeat, which cheers Argent up.

"Hey," Argent says to him. "Funny that we're in a U-Haul, because we're hauling *you*. Get it? Hauling *U*?"

"Do your lips ever stop flapping?" Nelson asks.

"Just having some fun." Argent has to admit that there's something very rewarding in talking to people who can't talk back. "Hey—I think you're gonna want this kid's eyes," Argent tells Nelson. "They're even nicer than the ones you got now."

And after an uncomfortable pause, Nelson says, "There's only one pair of eyes I want."

Even without Nelson telling him, Argent knows whose eyes he wants as his ultimate trophy. "You know, one of them's not even his," Argent points out. "Connor got stuck with a new eye along with his new arm."

"That doesn't matter," Nelson snaps. "It's not about whose eyes I *receive*; it's about whose eyes I *take*."

"Yeah, I get that. If you're seeing through his eyes it means he's not seeing through them anymore." Then Argent grins. "And besides, who wants a trophy on a shelf somewhere, when it can be right in your face. Get it? *In* your *face*?"

Nelson doesn't even offer him the courtesy of a groan. "I don't want to hear your voice anymore," Nelson says. "Just because you're a waste of life doesn't mean you have to be a waste of breath as well."

"Yeah? Well, this waste of life just caught four prime AWOLs for you to sell to your black-market buddy."

Nelson turns to him, revealing the good half of his face—the half that wasn't burned when he lay unconscious in the Arizona sun. Here is something else that bonds them beyond their shared hatred: They both have half of a face. Put Nelson's left half together with Argent's right, and you've got a whole. That proves they belong together as a team.

"He's not my buddy!" Nelson says. "Divan is the premier flesh trader in the western world. He even gives the Burmese Dah Zey a run for its money. He is a gentleman who appreciates formality, and when you meet him, you will treat him as such."

"Whatever," Argent says. Then he has to ask "So does this Divan guy treat Unwinds like the Dah Zey? Without anesthesia and stuff?"

The suggestion elicits groans and muffled sobs from the back, and Nelson throws Argent a searing glance. "Do I really need to tranq you again to get you to shut up?"

Argent, not caring for those little glimpses of death and the headaches that follow, zips his lips, determined to stay quiet for the duration.

Nelson tells him they're still not done.

"We'll catch one more AWOL before we bring them to Divan," he says. "If I'm not bringing him Lassiter, I want to show up with a full load." Then Nelson glances at Argent again. "I need to know that you'll make good on your promise once we arrive."

Argent swallows, suddenly feeling bound just as tightly as the kids in the back. "Of course," he says. "I'm a man of my word. I'll give you the tracking code the second we unload the 'merchandise.'"

Nelson nods, accepting it. "For your sake, you'd better hope that your sister's tracking chip is still active—and that she's still with Lassiter."

"She is," Argent tells him. "Grace is like a barnacle. Once she clings to a person, it takes an act of God to pull her off."

"Or a gun to the head," says Nelson.

It chills Argent to think about it. True, he's furious at Grace for siding with Connor over him, but would Connor kill her to get rid of her? After everything, Argent still doesn't see him as the type to do such a thing. Still, it's something he'd rather not think about, so he lets his thoughts drift to something more pleasant.

"So does this Divan guy have any kids? Like maybe a daughter my age?"

Nelson sighs, pulls out his tranq pistol, and fires a low-dose dart at Argent. The tranq dart hits him painfully in his Adam's apple. He pinches the little flag and pulls the thing out of his neck, but not before it delivers its full dose.

"That's coming out of your pay," Nelson says, which is a joke because Argent receives no pay from Nelson. He had made it clear it's an unpaid sort of internship. But that's okay. Even getting tranq'd is okay. Because life is good for Argent Skinner.

As he dives down toward tranq sleep, he takes comfort in the absolute knowledge that Connor Lassiter will soon be going down too—but unlike Argent, Connor will never be getting up.

3 · Connor

In a dusty corner of a cluttered antique shop on a weedy side street of Akron, Ohio, Connor Lassiter waits for the world to change before his eyes.

"I know it's here somewhere," Sonia says as she digs

through a pile of obsolete electronics. Connor wonders if the old woman was alive to witness the birth and the death of all that technology.

"Can I help?" Risa asks.

"I'm not an invalid!" Sonia responds.

It's a dizzying prospect to think that they are about to lay eyes upon *the* object on which the entire future hinges. The future of unwinding. The future of the Juvenile Authority's iron grip on kids like him. Then he looks over to Risa, who waits with the same electric anticipation. *Our future*, he thinks. It's been hard to consider the concept of tomorrow, when life has been all about surviving today.

Grace Skinner, sitting beside Risa, wrings her hands with friction-burn intensity. "Is it bigger than a bread box?" Grace asks.

"You'll see soon enough," Sonia says.

Connor has no idea what a bread box is, yet just like anyone who's ever played twenty questions, he knows its precise size. It's all he can do to keep from wringing his own hands too, as he waits for the device to be revealed.

When Sonia began to tell the tale of her husband, Connor thought he might, at best, get some information—clues as to why Proactive Citizenry was so afraid of not just the man, but the world's memory of him. Janson and Sonia Rheinschild, winners of the Nobel Prize for medicine, were erased from history. Connor thought Sonia might give him information. He never expected *this*!

"What if you invented a printer that could build living human organs?" Sonia said, after telling them of the disillusionment that ultimately took her husband's life. "And what if you sold the patent to the nation's largest medical manufacturer . . . and what if they took all of that work . . . and buried it? And took the plans and burned them? And took every printer and smashed it, and prevented anyone from ever knowing that the technology existed?"

Sonia trembled with such powerful fury as she spoke, she seemed much larger than her diminutive size—much more powerful than any of them.

"What if," Sonia said, "they made the solution to unwinding disappear because too many people have too much invested in keeping things exactly . . . the way . . . they are?"

It was Grace—"low-cortical" Grace—who figured out where this was leading.

"And what if there's still one organ printer left," she said, "hiding in the corner of an antique shop?"

The idea seemed to suck all the air out of the room. Connor actually gasped, and Risa gripped his hand, as if she needed to hold on to him to stave off her own mental vertigo.

Finally Sonia pulls forth a cardboard box that is about exactly the size of what Connor imagines a bread box would be. He makes room on a little round cherrywood table, and she sets the box down gently.

"You can take it out," Sonia says to him, a bit out of breath from her efforts.

Connor reaches in, gets his fingers around the dark object, then lifts it out of the box and sets it on the table.

"That's it?" says Grace, clearly disappointed. "It's just a printer."

"Exactly," says Sonia, with a smug sort of pride. "Earth-shaking technology doesn't arrive with bells and whistles. Those get added later."

The organ printer is small but deceptively heavy, packed with electronics tweaked for its peculiar purpose. To the eye, it is gunmetal gray and, as Grace already noted, entirely unremarkable. It looks like an ordinary printer that might have been manufactured before Connor was born, and the casing itself probably came from a standard printer.

"Like so many things in this world," Sonia tells them, "what matters is what's inside."

"Make it work," asks Grace, practically bouncing in her chair. "Make it print me out an eye, or something."

"Can't. The cartridge needs to be filled with pluripotent stem cells," Sonia explains. "Beyond that, I couldn't tell you much more. I'll be damned if I know how the thing does what it does; my forte was neurobiology, not electronics. Janson built it."

"We'll have to reverse engineer it," Risa says. "So it can be reproduced."

The small prototype has an output dish large enough to deliver the eye Grace requested—but clearly the technology could be applied to larger machines. The very idea sets Connor's mind reeling. "If every hospital could print organs and tissues for its patients, the whole system of unwinding collapses!"

Sonia leans back slowly shaking her head. "It won't happen that way," Sonia says. "It never does." She makes sure she looks at each of them as she talks, to make sure she drives the point home.

"There isn't one single thing that will end unwinding," she tells them. "It will take a hodgepodge of random events that come together in just the right way and at just the right time to remind society it's got a conscience." Then she gently pats the organ printer. "All these years I was afraid of putting it out there because if they were to destroy this one, there's no recourse. The technology dies with the machine. But now I think the time is right. Getting it out there won't solve everything, but it could be the lynchpin that holds together all those other events."

Then she smacks Connor so hard with her cane it could raise a welt. "God help me, but I think you're the ones to take charge of it. Janson's machine is your baby now. So go fix the world."

Connor immediately takes the secret artifact to the back room. He's always had an uncanny skill with mechanics, but this time, he doesn't even dare to open the casing for fear of doing something irreparable.

"We have to get this device into the right hands," says Connor. "Someone who knows what to do with it."

"And," points out Risa, "someone who isn't so tied to the current system that they'd rather destroy it than put it to use."

"Some trick that'll be," says Grace.

Sonia hobbles into the back room and catches the three of them still staring at the printer. "It's not a religious relic," she announces. "Get over it."

"Well, it is sacred in its own way," says Risa.

Sonia waves her hand dismissively. "Tools are neither demonic nor divine. It's all about who wields them." Then she points her cane to the old trunk, indicating it's time to descend into the shadows of her basement.

Grace pushes the trunk aside. She grunts as she does it. "What's in this thing anyway? Lead?"

Risa looks to Connor, and Connor looks away. They both know what's in there. He doubts even Risa knows how heavily it weighs on his heart. Much more heavily than the weight of the letters in the trunk. He wonders how many letters from how many kids are in there to make it weigh so much.

When the trunk is out of the way, Sonia rolls away the rug beneath it, revealing the trapdoor. Connor reaches down and lifts it up.

"I'm opening my store now," Sonia tells them. "Like it or not, I gotta make a living, so down you go. You know the drill. Mind the noise, and don't for once think you're too smart to be caught." Then she points to the printer. "And take that with you. I don't want some nosy-Nellie poking around back here and seeing it on display."

Connor has not been in Sonia's basement for almost two years. He came here on his second day AWOL. He had taken a tithe hostage, tranq'd a Juvey-cop with his own gun, and gotten caught up with an orphan girl who'd escaped from a bus headed to a harvest camp. What a mismatched band of fools they had been! Connor still feels the fool from time to time, but so much has changed, he can barely even remember the troubled kid he used to be. Now Lev—once an innocent kid brainwashed to want his own unwinding—was an old soul in a body that had stopped growing. Risa, who at first just scrambled to survive, had taken on Proactive Citizenry on national TV—but not before having her spine shattered, and then replaced against her will. And as for Connor—he had taken charge of the world's largest secret sanctuary for AWOL Unwinds . . . only to discover that it wasn't so secret after all. The memory of the Graveyard takedown is still a fresh wound in his soul. He had fought tooth and nail—valiantly, some might say—but in the end, the Juvenile authority won and sent hundreds of kids to harvest camp.

Kids just like the ones who now occupy Sonia's basement.

Connor knows it's crazy, but he feels he somehow let these kids down too, that day in the Graveyard. As he descends behind Risa, he feels apprehension and a vague kind of shame that just makes him angry. He's got nothing to be ashamed of. What happened at the Graveyard was beyond his control. And then there was Starkey, who double-crossed him and flew off with his storks in the only means of escape. No, Connor has nothing to be ashamed of . . . so why, as kids begin coming out of the basement shadows, can't he look any of them in the eye?

"Déjà vu?" asks Risa, when she hears him take a deep, shuddering breath.

"Something like that."

Risa, who has already spent a few weeks helping Sonia, knows all the players down here. She tries to smooth the way for Connor. The kids are either starstruck or threatened by his presence. The resident alpha—a tall meatless kid named Beau—is quick to urinate on his territory by saying, "So you're the Akron AWOL? I thought you'd look . . . healthier."

Connor's not quite sure what that means, and the kid probably isn't either. While Connor could make an enjoyable pastime of challenging Beau's bogus sense of testosterone supremacy, he decides it's not worth the effort.

"What's that you're holding?" asks an innocent-looking thirteen-year-old who reminds Connor a little bit of Lev, back in the days before Lev grew his hair long and got jaded.

"Just an old printer," says Connor. Grace chuckles at that, but doesn't speak of what she knows. Instead she goes around introducing herself and shaking hands, even with kids who would prefer not to shake hands with anyone.

"An old printer?" says Beau. "Like we need more junk down here."

"Yeah, well, it has sentimental value."

Beau *hmmph*s dismissively and saunters off. Connor suppresses the urge to stick out his foot and trip him.

Connor sets the printer down on a shelf, knowing if he treats it with too much care and attention, the smarter kids will figure something out. Right now, the fewer people who know about it, the better. At least until they can figure out a way to let *everyone* know about it.

"They're good kids," Risa tells Connor. "Of course, they've got issues, or they wouldn't be here."

Regardless of how much he loves Risa, he can't help but bristle a little. "I know how to deal with AWOLs. I've been doing it for a long time now."

Risa takes a moment to take an all-too-invasive look at him. "What's bothering you?" she asks.

And although he still hasn't gotten a handle on it himself, he finds that his gaze immediately goes to the shark tattooed on his arm. The last time he was in this basement, that arm was part of Roland. Risa catches that gaze and, as always, reads him better than he reads himself.

"Being down here might feel like we're back where we started—but we're not."

"I know," Connor admits. "But knowing that and feeling it are two different things. And there's a lot of . . . stuff . . . that being here brings back."

"Being here?" she asks. "Or being home?"

"Akron isn't home," he reminds her. "They might call me the Akron AWOL because it all went down here, but it's not home."

She smiles at him gently, and it melts at least some of his frustration. "You know, you never actually told me where home is for you."

He hesitates, as if saying it might bring it closer. He's not sure if he wants that or not. "Columbus," he finally tells her.

She considers it. "About an hour and a half from here?"

"About."

She nods. "The state home where I spent most of my life is much closer. And you know what? I couldn't care in the least."

And she walks away, leaving Connor unsure if her words were an attempt at commiseration, or a gentle slap in the face.

THE FOLLOWING IS A PAID POLITICAL ADVERTISEMENT

With all the confusing information out there, it's hard to know what to vote for. But not when it comes to Measure F—"the Prevention Initiative." Measure F is simple. It provides special funds to form a new arm of the Juvenile Authority that will monitor thousands of preteens who are at risk, offering counseling, treatment, and alternative options for their futures before they reach divisional age. What's more, Measure F won't cost taxpayers a dime! It will be fully funded by harvest camp proceeds.

Vote yes on Measure F. Isn't an ounce of prevention worth a pound of flesh?

—Sponsored by the Brighter Day Coalition

In Sonia's basement, it's hard to tell when night has fallen. There's a small window high up in a far back corner, but it's behind such a maze of junk, one has to strain to detect any light coming in through the frosted glass. The few clocks among the junk in the basement don't work, nor does the TV, and of the dozen kids down there, not a single one has a watch. Either they traded it for food before they landed here, or they were so used to using their phones as timepieces, they never had them. Phones, however, being traceable, are the first accessory ditched by the smart AWOL. Connor, of course, wasn't too smart his first night on the run. They tracked him by his phone, and he came within a hairsbreadth of getting caught. He wised up fast, though.

While everyone waits for Sonia to bring dinner—an event that never happens on any predictable schedule—Grace weaves the tale of the night before, getting more and more animated as she realizes she has the rapt attention of most of the kids.

"So we're upstairs in some lady's house, and I see these special-ops guys in black slinking across the lawn in the middle of the night," she says. "Prob'ly trained to kill. Hands are lethal weapons, that kind of thing." Connor cringes at her embellishments. The next time she tells it, they'll be dropping by helicopter.

"I hear them whispering and there's something in their words and the way they're speaking that makes me realize they're not after Connor or Risa or me—they're here for Camus Comprix! They want the rewind, and they don't even know that the rest of us are there!" She pauses for dramatic effect. "Suddenly they crash in through the back door, and they crash in through the front door, and we're all upstairs, and I tell Cam he's done for, but the rest of us don't have to be. Then I push Risa under the bed, and squeeze in after her, and Connor makes like he's asleep on the bed facedown, and they burst into the room, and tranq Connor and take Cam away, never realizing they just missed a chance at the Akron AWOL—and all because *I* figured it out!"

Some of the kids seem a bit dubious, and Connor feels its his responsibility to back Grace up. After all, credit where credit is due. "It's true," he tells them. "If Grace didn't lay it all on the table like that, I would have fought them, and probably would have been recognized and caught."

"But wait a second," says Jack, the Lev-ish kid. "Why would he let himself be taken without turning the rest of you in too? I mean, you guys are a big catch—he could probably cut himself a deal or something."

Grace grins way too broadly, and Connor knows what she's about to say. Now he wishes she'd never started this story.

"Because," says Grace, "Camus Comprix is in love with Risa!"

She lets her words hang in the air. Connor reflexively glances to Risa, but she won't meet his eye.

"But I don't get it," says another kid. "That whole media thing about them being a couple was fake, I thought."

Grace's grin doesn't slip an inch. "Not to Cam . . ."

It's Risa who finally puts an end to it. "Grace, enough. Okay?"

Grace deflates a bit, realizing that her moment in the spotlight is over. "Anyway," she says, without any of her previous dramatic flair, "that's what happened. Cam got caught, and we didn't."

"Wow," says Jack, "who'd have thought the rewind would be some sort of hero?"

"Hero?"

They all turn to see Beau, who was elsewhere in the basement, pretending not to listen, but apparently he had. "How many dozens of kids like us did it take to make one of him? There's nothing 'heroic' about him."

And Connor can't help but say, "I couldn't agree with you more."

Beau gives Connor a nod, finally finding himself and the Akron AWOL on common ground.

Later that evening, as everyone settles in for the night, Connor lays his bedroll next to Risa's in the same semiprivate nook where Risa slept their first time here. It's away from the other kids, and Connor shifts a tall bookcase to make it even more private. Risa watches him create their secluded nest, and doesn't bat an eye. Connor takes a deep breath of anticipation. This could well be the night where the stars of their relationship finally align. He's certainly imagined it long enough. He wonders if she has too. Connor tentatively lies down beside her. "Just like old times," he says.

"Yes, but the last time we were here, we were only pretending to be a couple to keep Roland's hands off of me."

He reaches out then, gently caressing her cheek with Roland's fingers. "And yet his hand is still all over you."

"Not all over," she says playfully. Then she rolls away, but grabs the offending arm as she does, wrapping it around herself

22

like a blanket, and pulling them into a tight spoon position, his chest to her back. The moment is electric, and they both know that anything is possible between them now. There's nothing to hold them back. Except this:

"I can't stop thinking about Cam," Risa says. "The way he sacrificed himself for us."

Connor's grafted arm pulls her tighter. He wishes it could be his own arm, but he's facing the wrong way for that. "Cam is the last thing on my mind."

"But after what he did for us, I feel like we need to . . . honor him somehow."

"I am," Connor says, smirking, although she can't see. "In fact, I'm saluting him right now—can't you tell?"

"Ha-ha."

In the silence, he can feel her heartbeat in his arm as he holds her. Her heartbeat in his chest pressed to her back. It's almost too much to bear. He wants to curse Cam for still being here between them, no matter how close they press. "So what do we owe him? Our eternal restraint?"

"No," Risa says, "Just . . . our hesitation."

Connor says nothing for a while. There are so many layers to his disappointment, but yet within that strata might there not be a vein of relief as well? He lets himself settle into the reality of what won't be happening tonight, setting his hope and desire at a distance, close enough that he's still aware of it, but far enough away so that it's not so tormenting.

"Okay," he tells her. "This night is for Cam. Let's hesitate our brains out."

She snickers gently, and they settle quietly into the night. Body heat and heartbeats until dawn.

Connor doesn't remember his dreams, only an amnesic sense that he had them, and that they were powerful. No nightmares—he's sure of that. They were dreams of fulfillment and empowerment, for that's how he feels as the faint, diffused light of morning touches upon the tiny basement window behind them.

To fall asleep, and to wake up with your arm around the only girl you've ever truly loved . . .

To know that the two of you have in your possession a device as earthshaking as a warhead . . .

To feel invincible, if only for a fleeting moment . . .

These things are enough to stop the world in its tracks and start it spinning in a new direction. At least that's how it feels to Connor. Until now he had been clinging to a threadbare hope, but now that hope feels full to bursting.

There's never been a moment in Connor's life that he could call perfect, but this moment, with his arm numb from being around Risa all night, and his sense of smell overwhelmed by the fragrance of her hair—this moment is the closest to perfection he's ever known. Even the shark seems to be smiling.

Such moments, however, never last for long.

Soon all the other kids are waking up. Beau moves the bookcase that gave them some level of privacy, claiming it was blocking the path to the bathroom, and the day begins. The kids down here have become creatures of routine, going about their business, or lack thereof, as if nothing has changed. Yet it has. They just don't know it. The world has just been turned upside down—or more accurately, it's been turned right side up after having been capsized for so long.

In a few minutes there's the *bang* of the trapdoor opening as Sonia arrives with breakfast, calling down for "some goddam help up here."

"Why don't you go help her," Risa suggests gently, for she knows that nothing short of a call to duty will peel Connor away from her.

Upstairs, Sonia has groceries enough to feed an army. Between Beau, Connor, and Grace, who is aggressively helpful today, the supplies are brought down in two trips, and Connor finds himself with nothing to carry the third time he comes up the stairs.

Today the trunk has been pushed off the trapdoor at a haphazard angle, impinging on a small plastic trash can that got in its way.

That trunk has been the elephant in the room since Connor arrived, although he hasn't dared to speak of its contents. Connor turns to see that Sonia has left to park her Suburban somewhere legal.

He's alone with the trunk.

Unable to resist its gravity, he kneels before it. It's a heavy, old thing. Antique to be sure. Old travel stickers adorn it, practically shellacked to the surface. Connor can't tell whether the old steamer trunk has actually been to those places, or if the stickers are merely decorations applied once it stopped travelling and became a piece of furniture.

He doesn't dare open it, but he knows what's inside.

Letters.

Hundreds of them.

Each one was written by an AWOL who'd been through Sonia's basement. Most wrote to their parents. They are missives of sorrow and disillusionment. Anger and the screaming question of "why?" *Why did you? How could you? When did things go so wrong?* Even the state wards, unloved but tolerated by the institution that raised them, found something to say to someone.

He wonders if Sonia ever sent his letter, or if it's still in there, buried among the other raging voices. He wonders what he would say to his parents now, and if it's any different from what he wrote. His letter began with how much he hated them for what they did, but by the time he reached the end, he was in tears, telling them that he loved them in spite of it. So much confusion. So much ambivalence. Just writing the letter helped him understand that—helped him to understand himself a bit more. Sonia had given him a gift that day, and the gift of the letter was in the writing, not in the sending. But still . . .

"I'd ask you to move the trunk back into place for me—but you've gotta be on the other side of the trapdoor before I do." Sonia raises her cane, pointing down the steep basement steps.

"Right. I'm going—don't use the cattle prod."

She doesn't whack him with her cane, but on his way down, she does tap him gently on the head with it to get his attention.

"Be good to her, Connor," Sonia says, gently. "And don't let Beau get to you. He just likes to be the big man."

"No worries."

He descends, and she closes the trapdoor above him. The basement smells like teen spirit, as the old prewar song goes. For a brief moment he has a flashback without words or images—just a swell of feeling—back to the first time he was herded down those steps two years ago. The invincibility he was feeling when he woke up is now tempered by the cold concentrate of that memory.

Risa's at her little first aid station tending to a girl's swollen, slightly bloody lip. "I bit my lip in my sleep—so?" the girl says, instantly on the defensive. "I have nightmares—so?"

Once the girl is tended to, Connor sits down in the treatment chair. "Doctor, I have a problem with my tongue," he says.

"And what might that be?" asks Risa cautiously.

"I can't keep it out of my girlfriend's ear."

She gives him the best *Oh, please* look he's ever seen, and says, "I'll call the Juvies to cut it out. I'm sure that'll take care of the problem."

"And it'll give some other poor soul a highly talented sensory organ."

She allows him the last laugh, studying him for a few moments.

"Tell me about Lev," she finally says.

He's a bit deflated to have the playfulness so totally squashed out of their conversation.

"What about him?" Connor asks.

"You said you were with him for a while. What's he like now?"

Connor shrugs, like it's nothing. "He's different."

"Good different, or bad different?

"Well, the last time you saw him, he was planning on blowing himself up—so anything is an improvement."

Another kid comes to Risa with what looks like a splinter in his finger, sees the two of them talking, and goes away to take care of it himself.

Connor knows he can't get out of this conversation, so he tells Risa what he can. "Lev's been through a lot since the harvest camp. You know that, right? Clappers tried to kill him. And that asshole Nelson captured him, but he got away."

"Nelson?" Risa says caught completely by surprise. "The Juvey-cop you tranq'd?"

"He's not a cop anymore. He's a parts pirate, and he's nuts. He's got it out for me and Lev. Probably you, too, if he could find you."

"Great," says Risa, "I'll add him to my list of people who want me dead."

Suddenly, with the specter of Nelson in the conversation, Connor finds bringing the conversation back to Lev is now a relief. "Anyway, Lev hasn't grown any—except for his hair. I don't like it. It's past his shoulders now."

"I worry about him," Risa says.

"Don't," Connor tells her. "He's safe on the Arápache reservation, communing with whatever it is that Chancefolk commune with."

27

"You don't sound too happy about that."

Connor sighs. When Connor and Grace left the Rez, Lev was filled with all of this crazy talk about getting the Arápache to take a stand against unwinding. As if they ever would. In some ways, he's just as naïve as the day Connor saved him from his tithing. "He says he wants to fight unwinding, but how can he do it from an isolationist reservation? The truth is, I think he just wants to disappear someplace safe."

"Well, if he's found peace, then I'm happy for him—and you should be too."

"I am," Connor admits. "Maybe I'm just jealous."

Risa smiles. "You wouldn't know what to do with peace if you had it."

Connor smiles right back at her. "I know exactly what I'd do." Then he leans in close to whisper, she leans in close to hear—and he licks her ear with precision enough to get him happily slapped. He thinks it might get her off the subject, but it doesn't.

"I miss Lev," she says. "He's kind of like a brother. I never had a brother—or at least not that I know of."

"I have a brother," Connor tells her. He doesn't know why he's chosen to volunteer this. He's never spoken of him to Risa. Mentioning his life before the unwind order somehow feels taboo. It's like conjuring ghosts.

"He's a few years younger than you, isn't he?" Risa asks.

"Three years younger."

"Right—now I remember," she says, which surprises him. But then he shouldn't be surprised at all. The whole life of the notorious Akron AWOL has been dissected by the media since the day he first got away.

"What's your brother's name?" Risa asks.

"Lucas," Connor tells her—and with the mention of the name comes a wave of emotion more powerful than he was prepared for. He feels regret, but also resentment, because

Lucas was the child their parents chose over Connor. He has to remind himself that it wasn't his brother's fault.

"Do you miss him?" Risa asks.

Connor shrugs uncomfortably. "He was a pain in the ass."

Risa grins. "That doesn't answer the question."

Connor meets her eyes, so beautifully green, and just as deep and expressive as their natural color.

"Yeah," Connor admits. "Sometimes." Back before Connor's parents gave up on him, he was constantly being compared to Lucas. Grades, sports—never mind that it was Connor who taught Lucas to play every sport. While Connor never had the dedication to stay on a team for a whole season, Lucas excelled, to their parents' enduring joy. And the more Lucas shone, the dimmer Connor's light seemed to them.

"I really don't want to talk about this," Connor tells her. And as easily as that, his old life and memories of his family are locked away just as securely as his letter to them is locked in Sonia's trunk.

4 · Lev

Lev is anything but at peace.

He's in the treetops again. It's the dead of night, but the night is alive. The forest canopy rolls like aquamarine clouds beneath a blue floodlight moon.

He's following the kinkajou again, that large-eyed monkey-like creature. Adorable but deadly. He now knows that it is his spirit he chases. It races before him through the highest branches of the dense rainforest, drawing him toward something resembling destiny, but not quite as fixed and fated. Not something inevitable, but something he *could* make real.

He dreams of the kinkajou, and this journey through the

trees, often. Each visit to this peculiar sanctuary of purpose feeds him and sustains him. It reminds him that there is a worthwhile goal to the things he drives himself to do.

The dreams are remarkably vivid, and he always remembers them. That, in and of itself, is a gift he's grateful for. It's not just the vibrancy of the sights that makes it so palpable, but the chirping, screeching, singing sounds of nocturnal life around him. The scent of the trees and the ground far below, so earthy, yet unearthly. The feel of the branches on his hands, feet, and tail. Yes, his tail, for he has caught up with the kinkajou now. He has become the creature, and becoming it makes him whole.

He knows what comes next. The edge of the forest, the edge of the world. But this time something's different. A feeling begins to well up inside of him. A foreboding that's way too familiar in his life, but unknown here, until now.

Something acrid wafts toward him now on the breeze. The stench of smoke. The soothing blue light around him is tainted to lavender then maroon. He turns behind him to see a forest fire that stretches like a blazing wall in the distance behind him. It's still perhaps a mile away, but it's consuming the trees with alarming speed.

The sounds of life become shrieks of warning and terror. Birds frantically take to the sky, but burst into flames before they can escape. Lev turns from the approaching firestorm, and leaps from branch to branch trying to outrun it. Branches appear before him exactly where he needs them to be, and he knows he could outrun whatever that fire is, were the forest canopy endless. But it's not.

Far too soon he comes to the place where the forest ends at a cliff that drops off into bottomless oblivion, and in the sky before him, just out of reach it seems, is the moon.

Bring it down, Lev.

He knows he can do it! If he leaps high enough, he can dig his claws into it and pull it from the sky. And when it falls, the shock wave it will create shall blow out the blaze like the breath of God blowing out a candle.

Lev gathers his courage as searing heat blooms against his back. He must have faith. He must not fail. On fire now, he leaps to the sky, and to his amazement he grasps the moon . . . but his claws don't dig deep enough to give him purchase.

It slips from his hands, and he falls, while behind him the fire consumes the last of the forest. He plummets from that world into an unfinished corner of the universe that not even dreams have reached.

Lev's teeth chatter uncontrollably and he shivers with the force of convulsions.

"Playing the castanets tonight, little brother?" says a figure standing over him. In the moment before time and place settle in his mind, he thinks this is one of his older sisters, and that he's home, a much younger, much more innocent child. But in an instant he knows it's not true. His sisters, along with the rest of his family, have disowned him. This is his Arápache sister, Una.

"If I could shut off the air conditioner I would, but like everything else in this lousy iMotel, it's automated, and for some reason the thermostat thinks it's ninety-two degrees."

Lev's too cold to speak yet. He clenches his teeth to stop from chattering, but is only partially successful.

Una grabs his blanket from where it has fallen on the floor, and covers him with it. Then she takes the bedspread and covers him with that as well.

"Thank you," he's finally able to squeak out.

"Is it just the cold, or do you have a fever?" she asks, then she feels his forehead. There's been no one for almost two years to feel his forehead for a fever. It brings him a wave of unwanted emotion, yet he can't be sure what that emotion is.

"Nope, no fever. You're just cold."

"Thanks again," he tells her. "I'm better now."

His chattering becomes intermittent, and eventually begins to fade, his body heat now held in by the covers. He marvels at how far his dream was from the real world, how the searing heat of the flames so quickly became the cold of a roadside motel room halfway between two nowheres. But then heat and cold are two sides of the same coin, aren't they? Either extreme is lethal. Lev closes his eyes, and tries to get back to the business of sleep, knowing his body needs as much rest as it can get for the days ahead.

In the morning, he awakes to the sound of a door closing. He thinks Una must have left—but no, she's been out and has just returned.

"Good morning," she says.

He grunts, still not having mustered enough energy to speak. The room is still cold, but with double covers, he feels warm.

Una holds up a McDonald's bag in either hand. "Your choice," she says, "heart attack or stroke?"

He yawns and sits up. "Don't tell me they were out of cancer . . ."

Una shakes her head. "Sorry, not served until after eleven thirty."

He takes the bag in her left hand and finds inside an Egg McSomething that tastes too good to be anything but deadly. Well, if it wants to kill him, it'll have to get in line behind the Juvenile Authority and the clappers and, of course, Nelson.

"What's the plan, little brother?" Una asks.

Lev gobbles down the rest of his breakfast.

"How far are we from Minneapolis?"

"About three hours."

Lev reaches over and pulls out of his backpack the pictures of the two parts pirates they're hunting. One is missing an ear, and the other is as ugly as a goat. "Do you need another look?"

"I've memorized every inch of those faces," Una says not even trying to hide her disgust at the thought of them. "But I'm still not thinking it'll make a difference. Minneapolis and St. Paul are big cities. It will be next to impossible to find two losers who don't want to be found."

Lev offers her the faintest of grins. "Who says they don't want to be found?"

Now Una sits on the bed next to his, regards him closely, and says again, "So what's the plan, little brother?"

Chandler Hennessey and Morton Fretwell. The two surviving parts pirates who infiltrated Arápache territory, and captured Lev and a bunch of younger kids in the woods.

It was Wil Tashi'ne—the love of Una's life—who saved them. He traded himself for Lev's life and the lives of the others, a trade the pirates took because he had something that would fetch them a very high price. Wil had talent. Talent in his hands, and in the parts of his brain that had mastered the guitar like few others. They took him, leaving Lev to deal with the consequences. He was helpless to stop Wil from sacrificing himself, and yet the Arápache blamed him. Lev was an outsider, like the parts pirates. He was a refugee from the same broken world. Even Una's feelings about him had a measure of ambivalence. "You're the harbinger of doom," she had told him. And she was right. Where Lev goes, terrible things always seem to follow. Yet still, he dreams he can break that pattern. It certainly would be easier than bringing down the moon.

Wil Tashi'ne's unwinding left a wound in the Arápache people that Lev knows he cannot mend, but perhaps he can soothe it. The scar will always be there, but if Lev has his way, he and Una will bring those flesh thieves back to face Arápache justice.

And then the Tribal Council will have to listen to him.

They will have to consider his plea to finally take a public stand against the Juvenile Authority.

Catching Hennessey and Fretwell won't quite bring down the moon, but if the Arápache—arguably the most influential Chancefolk tribe—can be brought into the battle against unwinding, it will be more than the moon that falls.

5 · Starkey

Mason Michael Starkey couldn't care less about what some Chancefolk tribe does or doesn't do. He doesn't need their pathetic support because he's taken his battle against unwinding right to the enemy, in the form of a gun muzzle rammed down the Juvenile Authority's throat. As far as he's concerned, anything less is for losers. Starkey knows he is poised for greatness. In fact, he's already achieved it. Now it's just a matter of degree.

"A little higher," he says. "Yes, right there."

He escaped with his storks from the Graveyard before the Juvies could capture them. He survived a plane crash. And now Starkey is a war hero. Never mind that no official war has been declared—he has declared it, and that's all that matters. If others out there choose to behave like this isn't a war, then they deserve what's coming to them.

"I'm not feeling it," he says. "A little harder."

Starkey is the savior of storks. He and his brigade of

unwanted babies who grew into unwanted kids have now grown into an army bursting with righteous rage against a system that would permanently silence them. Society would have them dismantled, their parts going to "serve humanity." Well, now humanity is getting a slightly different sort of service from them.

"You're not very good at this, are you?"

"I'm trying! I'm doing everything you say!"

Starkey lies facedown on a massage table in a room that used to be the executive office of a power plant. The plant was gutted years ago, leaving nothing but a rusty shell within a chain-link fence, miles away from anyplace anyone wants to be. It's a weedy corner of northern Mississippi, as overgrown and unloved as a place can be. The perfect hiding spot for an army of six hundred.

Starkey pushes himself up on one elbow. His masseuse, a pretty girl whose name he can't remember, looks away, too intimidated to meet his eye. "A good back massage should hurt as much as it soothes," Starkey tells her. "You have to work out the knots. You need to leave me loose and limber and ready for our next mission. Do you understand?"

The girl nods, overly obedient and too eager to please. "I think so."

"You said you've done this before."

"I know," she tells him. "I just wanted the chance . . ."

Starkey sighs. This is the way of things around him now. They climb over each other like rats to be close to him. To bask in his light. He can't blame them, really. He should applaud this girl for her ambition—but right now all he wants is a good massage.

"You can go," he tells her.

"I'm sorry . . ."

She lingers, and he contemplates the moment. Starkey knows he could take a detour with this afternoon and maybe get something other than a massage from this eager girl. Whatever he wants, he knows she will oblige . . . but the fact that he can have it so easily makes it so much less desirable.

"Just go," he tells her.

She slinks away, trying to do so quietly, but the rusty hinges on the door complain when she opens it. Rather than making the door squeal again, she leaves it open. Starkey can hear her clambering down the metal stairs, probably in tears at her failure to please him.

Alone now, he rolls his left shoulder and checks the bandage there. He took a bullet in the last harvest camp liberation. Well, not really. The bullet grazed him so slightly, it couldn't even be called a flesh wound. Yes, it drew blood, and yes, it will leave a scar, but as wounds go, on a scale of one to ten, this one is somewhere around one-point-five. Still the bandage makes it look worse, and so he wears a tank top that clearly displays the bandage on his upper arm for all the storks to see. Another war wound to go with the one farther down that same arm. His ruined hand, the hand he smashed to free himself from handcuffs back at the airplane graveyard. Smashing his hand saved him. It freed him to escape with the storks and start his war. Considering that he was once on the fast track to be unwound, giving up one hand seems like a bargain. Now he keeps it in a very expensive Louis Vuitton glove. That day at the Graveyard was early July, and now it's September. Less than three months have passed. Although it feels like a lifetime ago, his body measures the time properly, even if his mind doesn't. His broken hand still aches, still oozes, still requires a nice dose of painkillers every once in a while. It will never heal properly. He will never use that hand again, but it matters little. He has hundreds of other hands to do the work for him.

He looks out of the cracked, grimy windows that overlook the gutted power plant floor, now lined with bedrolls, folding tables, and the various necessities of the Stork Brigade's nomadic life.

"Keeping watch over your subjects?"

He turns to see Bam, his second-in-command, coming into the room, carrying a few newspapers.

"Some of the tabloids are now suggesting that you're Satan's spawn," she says. "A woman in Peoria claims she saw a jackal give birth to you."

Starkey laughs. "I've never even been to Peoria."

"That's okay," she says. "I don't think there are any jackals in Peoria either."

She drops the newspapers on the massage table. Starkey is pleased to find that he's on the first page of each one. He's seen his face on the newsfeeds and the public nimbus, but there's something very visceral about seeing his face in hard print.

"I must be doing something right, if the crazies think I'm as powerful as the Antichrist."

He leafs through the newspapers. The legitimate papers have more legitimate takes on him, but none of them are silent on the subject of Mason Michael Starkey. Experts try to psychoanalyze his motives. The Juvenile Authority goes rabid at the mention of his name, and in schools across the country, riots are breaking out, stork against nonstork. Everywhere, other kids like himself are demanding equal treatment in a world that would rather they just go away.

People call him a monster for lynching "innocent workers" at harvest camps. They call him a murderer for brutally executing doctors who perform unwindings. Let them call him whatever they want. Each label just adds to his growing legend.

"There's a new supply of ammo coming in today," he tells Bam. "Maybe some new guns, too." Then he watches her closely to see her response. Not what she says, but what she feels. Her body language. He can tell that she's bristling.

"If the clappers are going to supply weapons, maybe they

could teach these kids how to use them so they don't accidentally blow their own brains out."

That actually makes Starkey laugh. "They send kids out to blow themselves up for their cause," Starkey reminds her. "Do you really think they care if a few storks shoot themselves?"

"Maybe not," Bam says. "But *you* should care. They're *your* beloved storks."

This gives Starkey pause for thought, but he tries not to show it. "*Our* storks," he corrects.

"If you care about them as much as you say you do, you would take measures to protect them from themselves . . . and each other."

But Starkey knows what she's really thinking. *If you care about them, then you'll stop attacking harvest camps.*

"How many storks died in the last attack?" he asks.

Bam shrugs. "How should I know?"

"Because you do," Starkey says. A simple statement of fact. He knows she keeps track of such things to use against him, or maybe just to torture herself.

Bam holds eye contact, but her feigned ignorance fails her. "Seven," she says.

"And how many storks did we add to our numbers?" Starkey asks.

Bam clearly doesn't want to say, but he waits until she spits it out. "Ninety-three."

"Ninety-three storks . . . and two hundred seventy-five nonstorks freed from harvest camp hell. I think that's worth the seven lives we lost, don't you?"

She won't answer him.

"Don't you?" he demands.

Finally she casts her eyes out of the window, looking down on the hundreds of kids on the power plant floor. "Yes," she concedes.

"Then why are we having this argument?"

"We're not arguing," Bam says as she turns to go. "No one argues with you, Mason. There'd be no point."

As the sun begins to sink low, and the power plant's grime-covered windows begin to cast long shadows across the factory floor, Starkey descends to mingle among the masses. Many kids greet him; others are too intimidated to even look at him. He moves through the crowd of kids trouble-free. No one brings him their problems. This is yet another way he runs his ship differently than Connor ran the Graveyard. Connor was constantly inundated by daily minutia. Backed-up latrines, shortages on medical supplies, things like that. But here, kids know better than to waste Starkey's time. If they have a problem, they either live with it or take care of it themselves. He can't be bothered—he has a war to run.

With dinner fifteen minutes late, he checks their makeshift galley, where Hayden Upchurch and his food-prep team are all sweaty from moving industrial-size cans of processed ham.

"Hail, O mighty chief." Hayden says.

"Where's dinner?"

"We were waiting for the delivery from the 'applause department,' but apparently the clappers just sent guns and ammo, no food. So tonight we'll have to make do with SPAM."

Hayden seems far too pleased by the fact. "What are you smiling about? SPAM sucks."

"Are you kidding me? SPAM is my god. It's the only deity that can be eaten raw or fried. The stuff of Holy Communion."

The most annoying thing about Hayden is that Starkey can never tell if he's being disrespectful or just habitually sarcastic. For a while Hayden had been a problem, refusing to do the computer legwork Starkey needed to choose their targets. Lately, however, Hayden seems to have gotten with the program. Now that he's been demoted back to food service, he does his job with competent, if somewhat acerbic, cheer. Starkey still has no real trust of Hayden, but there's no one else who's organized enough to get food on the table three times a day for all six hundred of them. Hayden Upchurch is a necessary evil.

"You'll be serving in ten minutes, or I'll be looking for your replacement."

"Ultimatum acknowledged," Hayden says, and continues his work.

Starkey finds Bam in the weapons locker, unloading unmarked crates that were delivered in unmarked trucks. Their benefactors don't scrimp when it comes to giving them best of the best in artillery.

"What have we got?" Starkey asks.

"See for yourself," Bam says. "More assault rifles, sub-machine guns. And a whole bunch of Glocks. I guess they decided we need pistols for the littler kids."

Her voice drips with attitude, a kind of vitriolic sarcasm much darker than Hayden's. "Would you rather they go into a hostile environment unarmed?"

She doesn't answer the question, but when the kids helping her leave for dinner, Bam says, "Doesn't it bother you at all that we're being bankrolled and armed by the same people who fund the clapper movement?"

He rolls his eyes. He's never felt the slightest bit ambivalent about this. You never look a gift horse in the mouth, no matter where that gift horse has been. "C'mon—it's not like we're blowing ourselves up."

"Not yet. But who knows what they're going to ask in return for all they're giving us?"

"Has it occurred to you that the more they fund us, the less of their money goes to clappers?"

Bam laughs bitterly. "That's your best rationalization yet! 'Mason Starkey: saving the world from clappers one dollar at a time!'"

She goes out for dinner, leaving Starkey furious that she got the last word. In spite of being the undisputed master of his domain, Starkey always feels slightly diminished after going head-to-head with Bam. There's no question that she's been an asset—she's great at riding in his wake, keeping things running smoothly—but her insubordination has begun to cross the line, and that cannot be tolerated. Starkey knows he needs her for the next harvest camp takedown. But after that, there's room for change. There are plenty of qualified storks who could do the work Bam does. Kids he can truly trust, who won't second-guess him or give him snark.

The next harvest camp they're taking on is a big one. Lots of security. Lots of firepower. Who's to say if Bam will even make it back alive?

6 · Connor

Stagnation. It numbs him, dulls his senses and his response time. It saps his motivation. The task before them is so immense, he doesn't know where to start. Now that they have the printer, they need to make plans, but Sonia's basement is as it ever was, like a black hole drawing them back into the shut-in mentality of the safe-house AWOL. Risa tends to the various scrapes and medical woes, and does a good impersonation of a shrink for those kids who need someone to talk to, which is all of them, although not all of them are willing to talk. As for Connor, there are so many broken appliances, he finds his time is way too easily passed repairing them. It's easier than being proactive with the printer, because the world out there is a minefield. A single misstep and it's all over.

Proactive.

Connor knows while he's treading water, Proactive Citizenry is casting their formidable spells out there. More ads to mystify and befuddle the public. Are people really such sheep that they can be fooled? Maybe. Or maybe with so much conflicting media, people just shut down. Maybe that's the point. The movement to overthrow Cap-17 keeps gaining supporters. Measures calling for more harvest camps, and more ways to legally unwind "incorrigibles" keep gaining traction. The pundits are actually calling it the Starkey Factor. What's been obvious to Connor now has now been officially defined. Starkey and his storks spread more and more terror with every harvest camp they take down, but rather than dealing a blow to unwinding, those brutal, bloody attacks drive the public to embrace anything and anyone who promises to make the Starkeys of the world go away. Forever.

These relentless wheels turn in the outside world, but in Sonia's basement the days blend into nights, which blend back into days. It's hard not to be drawn into lethargy when your sanctuary is a timeless limbo.

"Sonia's been busy trying to find new safe houses for these kids," Risa explains, as if it's an excuse for doing nothing but waiting. "But the old network has fallen apart, and without the Graveyard, there's no destination anymore."

It was clear to Connor even before he left the Graveyard that the Anti-Divisional Resistance couldn't resist anything anymore. The ADR seems to have broken down completely. Key players in the resistance have been disappearing. Rumor has it that a number of them have been killed in "random" clapper attacks. It makes Connor wonder if the chaos and anarchy that clappers espouse have a deeper agenda that's anything but chaotic. And if *he's* wondering, there must be others who are too. Many others. But how does he find them . . . or, more to the point, how can he mobilize them to action?

"We're not going to save these kids by shuttling them around," he tells Risa. He can't help but look to the organ printer that sits so innocuously covered by a rag in the corner near where they sleep. There's the answer, but an answer means nothing if the world doesn't first hear the question.

They're going to need help. Help from the outside.

It's Grace, with her keen head for strategy, who gives them food for thought. "Of course, if you ask me, which you didn't," she says, "what ya gotta do is find someone connected in a wireless sort of way."

"A viral grassroots media kind of thing?"

43

"More like fertilizer to get those roots growing in a healthy kinda way," says Grace.

It immediately gets Connor thinking about Hayden. He'd be the first to call his "Radio Free Hayden" broadcasts fertilizer. After all, the range of his "station" never got beyond the boundaries of the airplane graveyard, but his little manifesto upon his arrest has become an iconic meme among the disenfranchised. If he broadcast now—or even shouted from the top of a building—people would listen. Unfortunately Connor has no idea where he is, or if he's even still alive.

When they bring the question of their next move with the organ printer to Sonia, she has the same advice every day.

"Sleep on it," Sonia tells them—and it's infuriating. Could it be that she's just as terrified as the rest of them about this powder keg on which they sit?

---

nest and alert the Authorities. Those AWOLs were captured, and now our daughter is safe."

"Our boy was a model student, a perfect son. We had no idea he was caught up with a Cuban cartel, dealing tobacco. Without Track-a-Teen® we would never have known in time to save him."

Remember, Parental Override is on the horizon. If you have a troubled child of unwinding age, Track-a-Teen® may be their last hope. Don't delay! With Track-a-Teen® peace of mind is just a download away!

Connor fixed the broken basement TV on his second day there. Beau insists it be tuned only to entertainment, and never the news.

"We know what's going on out there, and none of it's good," says Beau. "Better we should all laugh and try to forget for a little while."

Well, screw that. It's the one time when Connor flexes his muscles and refuses to get with the program. Beau is wise enough not to fight. Instead he permits it, using it to show what a magnanimous leader he is.

The news doesn't make anyone feel good—but as far as Connor is concerned, that's how it should be. When you're a prisoner of society, you shouldn't play at escape. At least until you really can escape it.

It's September now. Less than two months to election day, and the politicians who traditionally waffle on the unwinding issues are beginning to take sides that transcend all party lines, for the parties are divided. Connor watches a congressman on a Washington talk show speak of "the sociological necessity of unwinding undesirables."

Although the basement is warm, Connor notices that Risa crosses her arms as she watches, rubbing them like she's shielding herself from the wind. "I'll never understand how they're able to spin murder into social consciousness."

"It's not murder, didn't you know?" says Connor, and convincingly mimics the wholesome voice of a trustworthy announcer. "'It's the kindest thing we can do for troubled youth with biosystemic disunification disorder.'"

Grace, who seems to hear everything between him and Risa, just stares at him. "You're kidding. Right?"

If it were anyone else, Connor wouldn't justify the question with a response, but for Grace he winks, and she laughs in relief.

"We need to move on this," Connor says. They should be out of here seeking out the people who can actually use the printer—or at least trying to find out if it even works. He's taken the lead, but has yet to take action. It's not like him, and he wishes he knew what was holding him back.

"Move on what," Beau asks, adding his nose into the conversation. They've told none of the kids down in the basement about the printer because trust among AWOLs must be earned. There's no telling where these kids will ultimately end up and what bargains they'll strike to save their own lives.

"Lunch," says Connor. "Are you cooking today?"

Beau knows he's lying, but also doesn't push, probably because he also knows he won't get any information from Connor that Connor does not want to give. Better to avoid pushing than to push and fail. Beau chooses his battles well: only the ones he stands a good chance of winning. Connor actually finds that admirable; the kid doesn't waste his time in futile pursuits. He could actually be a decent leader if he ever gets over himself.

When Sonia comes down to deliver cold cuts and fairly stale bread for supper that night, Connor manages to talk to her alone, while Beau and the other kids are occupied scarfing down their sandwiches.

"You do realize that we need to get our hands on some of those stem cells you were talking about, and make sure the printer still works before we go public."

"Fine," says Sonia, glaring at him. "I'll pick some up at Walmart tomorrow." And when Connor doesn't back down, Sonia sighs. "You're right. But it won't be easy. There are only a few research universities in the Midwest that still do that sort of research. Major organizations won't fund it, because people think stem cell research has something to do with embryos, and people are terrified it might reignite Heartland War issues. Even the mention of it brings protests and negative publicity. Of course, adult pluripotent stem cells have nothing to do with embryonic stem cells, but facts never prevent the ignorant from jerking their knees into the groin of science."

Connor grins. "Well, once we get this thing to work, and into the right hands, we can redirect that knee, hitting the Juvenile Authority and Proactive Citizenry where it counts!"

"I hope I live to see that day," Sonia says, and pats him on the cheek like a grandmother might. Connor, usually a bit of a touch-me-not, finds it curiously comforting. "I'll find us a place that has a supply of cells," she tells him. "The tricky part will be getting them."

"What the hell are you doing? Stop that! Do you have any idea what those are?"

Sonia has left the trapdoor open a bit longer than usual to help air out the basement, which has gotten noticeably rank. Connor, who takes every chance available to escape the cage, has come upstairs to find Grace at the old steamer trunk. She's opened it and envelopes are spilling out everywhere.

"I'm sorry, I'm sorry, I didn't mean it, I didn't mean it!" Grace frantically tries to put them back in, but the trunk is so full, they just topple out again. It's like trying to get toothpaste back in the tube.

Connor immediately regrets having yelled at her. He kneels down beside her. "Calm down, Grace."

"I just wanted to see what was inside, and they all started falling out. I didn't mean it!"

"I know you didn't. It's all right. Go downstairs, and I'll take care of it."

Grace doesn't need a second invitation. "I gotta stop touching things. Curiosity killed the cat. I gotta stop touching things."

Grace bounds down the stairs away from the situation, leaving Connor once again alone with the trunk, only this time Pandora's box is wide open. He has no idea where Sonia is, and what she'd say if she saw it like this.

There are hundreds upon hundreds of envelopes, many more than were there when Connor deposited his. The envelopes are mostly white and eggshell, but there is also the occasional colored one, as if Sonia got bored and started giving out brighter stationery to the kids. Each envelope is addressed by hand.

Now that he's begun, Connor finds he can't stop himself. He begins riffling through the sea of envelopes looking for a familiar address, in familiar handwriting. His envelope was simple white, and is hard to dig out of this snowstorm of correspondence.

"You'll never find it in there," Sonia says, coming up behind him, as he's elbow-deep in the trunk.

He takes his hands out, feeling almost as guilty as Grace had, and sits back on the dusty floor. "Haven't you mailed any of them?"

"Not a one," Sonia says sadly. "Never had the heart to do it."

"Did any kids who survived come to take their letter back?"

"Not a one," Sonia says again. "Guess they had more pressing things to do. If any of them *did* survive."

"A lot of them did," Connor reassures her. "I know because I sent a lot of them on their way when they reached a safe age."

"*You* sent them?" says Sonia. "I guess I should ask what you've been up to all this time, but I figure you'd rather not talk about it."

Connor smiles. *She's got that right.*

"You're not mixed up with that awful Starkey person, are you?"

Connor grimaces and can't hold her gaze. "He's actually my fault. My own little wind-up psychopath."

"Hmmph," says Sonia, and mercifully doesn't ask for details. "You may have wound him up, but he's not following anyone's marching orders but his own. We all have our accidental monsters."

Connor looks back to the letter-filled trunk and finally understands why he's still here. What's been holding him back.

"Will you ever send them out?" he asks.

Sonia sits at her desk, leaning forward on her cane. "I suppose if the time is right to unveil the printer, the time might be right for a postal run." Then she pauses, checks to see that no one is coming up from the basement, and proceeds to read Connor's mind.

"But you don't want me to mail yours, do you?"

"No, I don't."

"Because you're thinking you might deliver it yourself."

Connor takes a deep breath and slowly lets it out. "Is that just me being self-destructive again?"

"I can't say . . . but it would seem to me that wanting to bring closure is anything but self-destructive."

He looks to the trunk one more time. "What's the use? Like you said, I'll never find it in there anyway."

"No, you won't." Then she opens her top desk drawer and pulls out a single envelope. "Because it's right here."

Had she pulled out a stick of dynamite, it couldn't have felt more dangerous.

"I went fishing for it the night you came back. I thought you might want it eventually."

She hands it to him. His handwriting. The address where he grew up. On the back is the ripple of dried saliva where he licked it closed two years ago. He cannot yet tell if this letter is an enemy or a friend.

But now that he's holding it in his hand, there's something he knows beyond the shadow of any doubt.

God help me . . . before this is all over, I'm going to face them. I'm going to confront my parents. . . .

Part Two

Here Be Dragons

From *The Telegraph*:

GIRL SMUGGLED INTO BRITAIN TO HAVE HER "ORGANS HARVESTED"

By Steven Swinford, Senior Political Correspondent
10:00 PM BST 18 Oct 2013

The first case of a child being trafficked to Britain in order to have their organs harvested has been uncovered.

The unnamed girl was brought to the UK from Somalia with the intention of removing her organs and selling them on to those desperate for a transplant. . . .

The case emerged in a government report which showed that the number of human trafficking victims in the UK has risen by more than 50 per cent last year and reached record levels. . . .

Child protection charities warned last night that criminal gangs were attempting to exploit the demand for organ transplants in Britain.

Bharti Patel, the chief executive of Ecpat UK, the child protection charity, said: "Traffickers are exploiting the demand for organs and the vulnerability of children. It's unlikely that a trafficker is going to take this risk and bring just one child into the UK. It is likely there was a group."

According to the World Health Organisation as many as 7,000 kidneys are illegally obtained by traffickers each year around the world.

While there is a black market for organs such as hearts, lungs and livers, kidneys are the most sought after organs because one can be removed from a patient without any ill effects.

The process involves a number of people including the recruiter who identifies the victim, the person who arranges their transport, the medical professionals who perform the operation and the salesman who trades the organ . . .

The full article can be found at: *http://www.telegraph. co.uk/news/uknews/crime/10390183/Girl-smuggled-into-Britain-to-have-her-organs-harvested.html*

7 · Sky Jockey

Trouble in the world, trouble at home. How can they expect a man to concentrate on his work with all this trouble? AWOLs wreaking havoc everywhere, clappers blowing things up—and then, of course, there's my daughter. I thought she was finally wising up, getting a good head on her shoulders—and now she does this? What is she thinking?

"Earth to Frank!" the foreman's voice booms over the intercom, startling him. "Are you on this freaking planet?"

"Yeah, I'm here. Are we ready?"

"Ready? We've been waiting here twiddling our thumbs. Start hoisting already!"

"Starting the hoist. Clear the area around the payload."

"The arm's clear. I'll alert the media."

Frank chuckles—because the foreman isn't making a joke; he is literally alerting the media. They're gathered around Liberty Island, cameras aimed upward at the statue, which is ensconced in construction scaffolding. It may be a momentous occasion to them, but to a crane operator, it's just another job.

What the hell is my daughter thinking? How could she date such an obvious loser? She's barely fourteen; what business does a fourteen-year-old from Queens have dating a sixteen-year-old delinquent from the Bronx?

"He's got a good heart," she tells me.

Fine. So rip it out and put it into another kid more deserving of her attention.

The cables go taut, and the new arm shifts on the barge, slowly, smoothly. This is not a job accomplished with cavalier speed. That's the best way to wind up with snapped cables, dead coworkers, and lawsuits. Lots of lawsuits. The arm begins to rise, as if being levitated by a magician. He mans the crane's controls, feeling the cables attached to the massive unwieldy object as if they're his own sinews and the crane itself is just an extension of his body.

The boyfriend is not too old to be unwound. Not yet. That freaking tool won't be seventeen for at least a few months. And then if they repeal the Cap-17 law, there's a whole year of potential unwinding tacked on to his miserable life. The problem is, the lowlife's parents won't do it. Of course they won't! They're probably druggies or worse. No supervision, no boundaries. If you don't raise a kid right, it turns into a weed that's gotta be torn out. The whole damn thing is their fault!

"Frank! Jesus! What's going on up there? Keep it steady!"

"I'm on it. It's the wind."

"So compensate! The last thing we need is the freaking arm lying crushed at the freaking base of the statue like a dead freaking whale!"

There are cameras mounted on the crane, on the ground, and on the statue itself to monitor the arm as it rises, but the monitors don't tell as clear a story as actually seeing the thing. Frank leans to the side, looking out of the huge glass windows of the sky crane, to see the arm twisting and torquing in the wind below. He adjusts the tension on the cables, like fiddling with a pair of venetian blinds, to get the torch and hand to take on a forty-five-degree angle. Now it rises with the torch slightly higher than the rest of the arm, and at this angle it catches the wind differently, rising more steadily. In a minute, it has risen past the height of the statue's base. Now he pulls it in, the cable dolly bringing it closer to the statue.

Breed a bum to a bum, you get a bum. What goes for horse racing goes for humans as well. The loser's parents are probably too stoned to even sign an unwind order. Sometimes these things can't be left to the parents. Especially when those parents shoulda been unwound themselves before they started to breed. It's good that they're talking about mandatory unwinding of juvenile undesirables. If the law passes, maybe the problem will take care of itself. And if it doesn't, I've got a cousin who knows a guy, who knows a guy, who could put me in touch with a parts pirate. Someone who'll come in, take the kid, and be done with it. The thing is, I know I don't have the guts to make the call.

"It's looking pretty from down here. How's it hanging, Frank?" And the foreman laughs. "How's it hanging!" Probably didn't even notice his own joke until after he said it.

"I could use a hand," Frank tells him, and the foreman laughs some more. Frank increases the angle to eighty degrees. The torch is almost upright now as it dangles from multiple sets of cables on the massive crane.

Without her right arm, the statue's been looking a bit like the Venus de Milo. Sullen and vaguely impotent. Not the vision of liberty the early immigrants saw before disembarking at nearby Ellis Island—but the original arm had to go. The copper shell and interior framework of the torch arm were simply too heavy and had grown too weak over the years. Rather than allowing the arm to succumb to metal fatigue in one storm or another, it was decided to replace the torch and arm with a lighter, sturdier alloy. Aluminum/titanium. Something like that. Only problem is that the replacement arm is silver-gray, not pale green. Supposedly, the brainiacs in the design office have a plan to paint it to match the rest of the statue, but that's not Frank's problem.

No, the snotbag dating my daughter is my problem. And my wife yells at me, like it's my fault. Like I can do something about it.

"Ya shoulda never let her have so much freedom, Frank. And what if she gets pregnant? What then?"

What? She'll stork it, that's what. Learn her lesson the hard way. Or she'll marry the imbecile. It's all the stuff of nightmares.

"Easy now!" calls the foreman. "Just kiss it into place, Frank."

Now he engages the laser guidance system and sits back. It's out of his hands now. Like the docking of a spacecraft, it's all computerized down to the millimeter with surgical precision. He watches on various screens as the arm docks into the notches cut into the copper folds of Miss Liberty's gown, with a deep but gentle clank, and a vibration he can feel in his bones. Applause from the whole construction crew.

Now the assembly team takes over—a group of shipbuilders—because at this stage, fastening the arm is more like attaching the bow of a ship. There'll be a week of welding, brazing, and molecular bonding to get the steel and copper to fuse to the new alloy. Again, not his problem. Tomorrow he's back to work on a luxury high-rise on the Upper West Side. A regular sky jockey running a simple crane, lifting I beams to the eighty-eighth floor. Low profile, low stress.

Now if he can only get rid of his daughter's imbecile boyfriend and lower the stress at home, he'll be in business.

8 · Cam

Camus Comprix is a very happy young man. Yet not.

Camus is a highly driven young man. But he's not certain he's the one driving.

He sits alone on a balcony overlooking the ocean, high on a Molokai bluff, pondering his existence, which began a few short months ago. Prior to that he was part of ninety-nine other kids, although he suspects the number is greater. Ninety-nine is a nice alliterative number. Good for the media. Good for publicity. When it comes to Cam, his whole "life" is about public spin, and he's yet to figure out why. Why is Proactive Citizenry putting so much money behind him? Why has the United States military "purchased" him like a piece of property? Valuable, yes, but property nonetheless. It used to bother him, but it doesn't anymore. For some reason.

He loves being on Molokai—perhaps because it is the unloved sibling of the Hawaiian island chain. Once a leper colony, now just a curiosity, it's the home of a huge compound owned and maintained by Proactive Citizenry. The cliffside mansion, Cam has learned, is only a part of the compound. Like everything else about the organization, its sphere of influence extends far beyond first impressions.

"You're not eating, Cam," Roberta says as she comes out to join him across the table. Roberta—his creator, or builder—whatever term one gives to the individual who conceived of you. Perhaps, then, it should be "mother," though he's loath to use the word.

"I was waiting for you." He looks at the unappetizing appetizer before him. "And anyway, I have too few fans of foie gras in my internal community. I'll wait for the prime rib."

"Suit yourself."

"If I could suture self, I wouldn't have needed you."

She gives him a weak *Ha-ha* roll of her eyes and begins to daintily manipulate the unpleasant-looking duck liver onto her crostini. As he recalls, to cultivate foie gras, ducks are force-fed until they're morbidly obese, and their livers swell to near-exploding. Such wonderful tricks the human race has learned! Cam returns his gaze to the sea.

"General Bodeker is preparing quite the welcome for you at West Point next week."

"No speeches I hope?"

"Only informal. Toasts at meet-and-greets. He'll be out in a few days to brief you on the details."

"Why can't the military just *tell* people things?" Cam says. "Why must they *brief*?"

"I thought you, of all people, would appreciate linguistic formality."

"Don't you mean 'you of *many* people'? It would be beyond hyperbolic to suggest I am made of all people."

Cam's impending West Point experience—his entire life, it seems—has been spelled out for him. He'll be whisked through officer training, all the while posing for photo ops, and becoming the "Face of the Modern American Military," whatever that means. He hated the idea at first, but he's had a pronounced change of heart.

He must admit, the formal dress uniform looks great on him. It makes him look important. Part of something greater than himself. He imagines all the high-level people he'll brush elbows with—not just as a novelty, but as a proud officer of the United States Marine Corps—for they said he could choose his branch, and he chose the Marines. He thinks of his glorious future, and he's overjoyed. Yet not.

He finally turns his gaze from the ocean. "Let's talk about the person you're making me forget. Let's talk about the girl"

Roberta finishes her foie gras, unfazed. "You know I won't discuss it, so why ask?"

"Because the closest I'll ever come to remembering is forcing you to remember."

Their server comes to take away the appetizers, and brings the prime rib. Cam finds he's hungry for it, but not hungry enough to start right away. "I can still feel the worm in my brain."

"It's not really a worm. It's just a clever bit of nanotechnology, and anything you're feeling is just in your imagination."

He begins to cut his meat, imagining how his piecemeal brain has been routed by the army of microscopic nanites crawling along his axons, leaping between dendrites, all tuned to seek out very specific memory patterns. The moment his conscious thought hits upon the targeted memory, it gets zapped. No mess, no bother. For the first few days after the procedure, Cam was plagued with that tip-of-the-tongue feeling, reaching for a name and a face he thought he remembered a moment ago, but was then gone. The feeling has lessened, but the nagging sense of absence has remained. Well, not entirely. Because the nanites are also designed to tweak his pleasure receptors whenever he thinks of anything relating to the military. It's been filling the gaps like spackle in a cracking plaster wall.

It's the peripheral things he still knows that make it so difficult to leave his past life behind. He knows he was in Akron. He remembers helping Connor Lassiter, but the details are fuzzy. Cam also knows he chose to become a hero to The Girl, rather than be a hero to Proactive Citizenry. He could have turned them all in and done the nation a great service that would insure his place in history . . . but The Girl would hate him for the rest of his life if he had done it. So he chose to be a hero to her in a way that would outshine anything that Connor had ever done. And then maybe . . . maybe . . . when she tired of the Akron AWOL, she would see the purity of what he had done for her. And The Girl would love him. Cam chose the long play and was willing to wait. But now, he can't remember her face, or her name, or anything about her. He never imagined she could be stolen from the inside out.

"Is the prime rib to your liking, Cam?"

"It's fine."

"Just fine?"

"It's excellent. Must you always make inquiries of my taste buds?"

Roberta sighs. "Cam, please, I don't want to fight. It's our last week together. I want it to be pleasant."

"You're not coming with me?" Not that he wants her to, but as his "handler" in all public matters, he had just assumed she would.

"No one wants a doting mother at West Point," she says.

That catches Cam by surprise. Apparently it catches Roberta by surprise as well. A slip she didn't intend to make. It's the first time she's ever actually used the *M* word. Cam always felt theirs was a distorted parental/child relationship, but use of the *M* word has always been an unspoken taboo.

Roberta clears her throat and dots her lips with her napkin. "Besides, there's too much work to do here once you're gone."

That piques Cam's interest. "What sort of work?"

"Nothing you need to concern yourself with."

He knew she would attempt deflection. The idea of her focusing her attentions elsewhere brings forth a wave of unexpected jealousy. "Will you be gathering choice parts for the new-and-improved me?"

Cam notices the way Roberta slices her meat. With smooth grace, the same way she answers the question. "You said it once yourself, Cam—you are the concept car. The perfect design. A pinnacle to strive for." She inserts a piece of meat in her mouth, chews, and swallows before she speaks again. "Rest assured, we can't improve on you, and won't even try. You are our star, and always will be."

"So, what then?"

"Extrapolate for yourself if you must, but my work is classified. Just as my work with you was classified. I won't discuss it."

"Yes," says Cam with a grin, "the expression 'eyes only' takes on a new meaning when you're surgically removing them from Unwinds."

"Cam, we're eating. That's far from appropriate luncheon conversation."

"Pardon my indiscretion."

Cam considers. Extrapolates. A concept car is impractical. *He*'s impractical. Not what the world needs.

Dessert comes, and their conversation lapses into the mundane, but the question remains in the back of his mind: If he's not what the world needs, then what *does* it need? Or what can Proactive Citizenry *make* it need?

At night, Cam's thoughts drift to Una. She is not The Girl. He knows that, but thinking of her tempers the feeling of absence in his brain. Una has never met The Girl. He knows this, because none of his thoughts of Una get scrambled, and when The Girl is attached to a memory it turns momentarily into static. Then, when he grasps the memory once more, The Girl has been surgically removed from it. He remembers conversations, but none of the gists. He remembers talking to someone, but in the memory, he's talking to a wall, or a hallway, or just off into blank space.

That doesn't happen when he thinks of Una, so there's some comfort in that. Una despises him, of course. How could she not? He has the hands of her one true love. Cam has the part of his brain that feels emotion, and can render it in the soulful sound of a guitar, but Cam is not, nor will he ever be, Wil Tashi'ne. And so she hates him with good reason.

As Cam lies on his plush bed in his plush bedroom, he fills his mind, with thoughts not just of Una, but of everyone that he has encountered since being rewound. The guards who tended to him before he understood what he was. General Bodeker and Senator Cobb, who saw in him something worth paying money for. The jealous Akron AWOL and the low-cortical girl he was traveling with. What was her name? Oh yes, Grace. Cam fills his mind with everyone that was a part of his brief life, hoping that their presence will outline the shape of The Girl—like light around a silhouette—making the shape of her absence crystal clear and in perfect focus.

Amazing that Proactive Citizenry truly believes purging his memory of the girl he loved would do anything but make him hate them even more than he already does. Incredible that they actually think that stimulating his pleasure centers at the thought of a military life would lead to anything but virulent resentment. Yes, now Cam longs for his future in the Marine Corps, but he absolutely despises the people who implanted that longing within him.

Not the people, but the person.

Roberta.

As far as Cam is concerned, Roberta *is* Proactive Citizenry. Bringing them down means bringing her down. In flames.

But of course she can't know that. For the time being, he must appear to be her perfect boy. He will shine like the idol they carefully designed him to be. The golden calf for all of humanity to worship. And it will be all the more rewarding to see the bewildered astonishment in Roberta's eyes when he tears it all down.

• • •

General Bodeker needs no entourage. He cuts an imposing figure without the requisite team of toadies. The air around him seems to congeal with his formidable presence. The flowers of the entry path, wilting in the Hawaiian humidity, seem drawn to tight attention at his passing.

He does have one gentleman trailing in his wake. His personal attaché. More formal military linguistics for his personal assistant—or, more accurately, his gofer, because the slim, vaguely nervous man sycophantically responds the the general's slightest need. He's redundant here, however, because at Proactive Citizenry's Molokai compound, there are servants so far up the wazoo, they need a trail of bread crumbs to find their way out.

Cam is in his crisp uniform when he greets the general at the entrance to the grand mansion. Roberta insisted he wear it. Cam doesn't mind; he loves the uniform. Even thinking about it triggers in him the kind of deep personal pleasure that borders on ecstasy in a most annoying way. It's just one more emotional response that's been tweaked by Roberta and her team of cognitive architects. Another reason to loathe her.

"Good day, Miss Griswold. And to you, Mr. Comprix," says the General, nodding to each of them in turn. The attaché shakes their hands, as if it is part of his job to save Bodeker the trouble.

"*Goede dag, Generaal,*" Cam says, his accent perfect. "*Ik ben blij je te zien.*"

The man is taken aback rather than impressed. "Is that Dutch?"

"Yes," Roberta answers for Cam. "He's been studying it— adding it to the many languages he already knows."

"I see."

"You are of Dutch descent, aren't you?" Cam asks. "I mean, your name is Dutch."

"Yes," says Bodeker. "'Descent' is the key word. My parents spoke the language, but I never learned it."

His demeanor is guarded. Decidedly off. Suddenly Cam feels like a child trying to impress an emotionally distant parent. He hates that he feels this way, but he can't help it.

"Would you like me to show you around the grounds?" Cam asks.

"Maybe later," Bodeker says dismissively, and then glances at his clean-cut, overeager attaché, who steps forward enthusiastically.

"*I'd* like a tour," he says.

The moment becomes awkward until Cam obliges. "Of course. Let's start with the garden." For a moment, Cam is thrown by the way Bodeker has pawned off Cam's attention to his lackey. It's only as he and the attaché leave for the grand tour that Cam glances back and catches how intently Bodeker speaks to Roberta—as if Cam is not the center of the general's attention at all.

NEW! The official Camus Comprix action figure!

He's a calculator!

He's a tutor!

He speaks ten thousand phrases in nine languages!

And he's authentically rewound!*

Eyes that track!

Realistic multicultural skintones!

Fully posable and programmable!

His seams glow in the dark!

Quantities are limited!

CLICK HERE TO ORDER!

*Guaranteed to be rewound from at least twenty other action figures.

The rest of the day goes smoothly. That is to say smooth like a slick veneer that has yet to dry. To the eye it appears as a fine glaze, but to the touch it is sticky and unpleasant.

The evening meal is a stilted affair of formality around a table too large for only four, in a dining room specifically designed for the wining and dining of high-muck-a-mucks such as the general.

"My compliments to your chef," Bodeker says, interrupting the silverware-sound-infused silence.

"Yes, yes, it's all delicious," says his attaché, as Cam knew he would, because he has an irritating habit of seconding anything the general says.

Through the meal's pleasantries, Cam senses an atonal undertone he can't put his finger on. Like when a single guitar string is slightly out of tune. Perhaps it has to do with The Girl he can't remember. Or perhaps it just has to do with him.

"I'm really looking forward to West Point," Cam says, fishing for a response from the general that he can gauge.

"Yes, well, I'm sure they're looking forward to you, too."

"Montresor!" Cam blurts out. He doesn't mean to, but those curious connections in his brain still spark out references now and then that he can't control.

"Pardon?" says the general.

"Uh—Mr. Montresor—our chef," Cam says covering as best he can. "I'll be sure to let him know his Chateaubriand is appreciated."

Roberta throws him a severe glance, but does not give him away. Perhaps because she knows exactly what his outburst meant. "Yes," she says, "his offerings are always beyond reproach." The general, not a man of literary prowess, accepts this at face value, and his attaché is too involved in attempts to spear his peas to sense the lie.

Bodeker leaves the following morning without saying good-bye—or at least without saying good-bye to Cam. Once he is gone, Cam walks the grounds alone, pausing on the back lawn, at the spot overlooking the sea where he and The Girl looked up at the stars. He gave her a lesson in astronomy, but of course the memory has him lying on the lawn alone, conjuring the stars for himself. This is how he knows she must have been a part of the memory. That he remembers speaking aloud to no one. Now no stars save the sun are visible in the morning light, but he doesn't need stars to string together constellations of meaning from the general's visit.

The day before, while Cam was obliged to give Bodeker's lackey a tour of the grounds, he had taken note of the general riding off in a golf cart with Roberta to a distant part of the compound. Cam is pretty sure they hadn't gone to explore the fields of cane and taro still cultivated by Proactive Citizenry, to maintain a semblance of normality. Cam is well aware that there are other buildings within the massive compound, hidden by heavy growth. He's never actually seen them, but he knows they're there.

He also knows that if he asks Roberta about them, she will dissemble as she always does. Deflection that borders on deception is her finest gavotte, and she dances so well it has become its own form of entertainment to Cam.

General Bodeker, however, is not so skilled. He wears his lies on his sleeve like the chevrons of his uniform.

Montresor, indeed! The king of insincerity; Poe's most despicable character, claiming friendship even as he seals Fortunato alive in a secret tomb. Is Cam then Fortunato? Watching the bricks of his own doom laid one upon another? Or maybe it's all in his imagination. After all, Cam's personality is a composite of Unwinds—paranoia must have run rampant in many of them. Still, he can't help but feel that it all comes down to Roberta's little side trip with the general yesterday. Wherever they went holds the answer to the general's cool and distant behavior. Perhaps it's time Cam got to know Proactive Citizenry's Molokai compound more intimately.

"Here be dragons," he says aloud, but there's no one else on the back lawn to hear him.

9 · Una

She hopes that she and Lev find Hennessey and Fretwell. She also hopes they don't. Because she knows if they do, she'll tear the two parts pirates to shreds. Not figuratively, but literally. She'll cut them up bit by bit, relishing their agony as they die. Does she have it in her to do such a thing? She nearly did it to Camus Comprix. She took a chain saw to him, and almost cut off those beautiful hands that had once been Wil's. She knows if she had done it, she would have forever regretted it, for Cam was as much a victim as Wil had been. He never asked to be rewound. Wil, on the other hand, chose to give himself up to save the others. He chose unwinding over the alternative. Had she taken Wil's hands back from Cam, it would have turned Una into a monster, and there would be no coming back from that.

But tearing apart these human vermin would be different. It would be just. It would be satisfying. Maybe.

Would Wil want her to do it, if it gave her some peace? Or would he want Lev's justice to prevail? Would he want the parts pirates captured and turned over to the Arápache Tribal Council? To bring them back alive would require incredible restraint and forbearance on Una's part. Even if she isn't callous enough to tear them apart, she has no qualms at all about shooting them dead.

So she hopes they find them. And she hopes they don't.

It's night in a seedy Minneapolis neighborhood. Perhaps not as seedy as other neighborhoods in other cities, but even

Minneapolis has armpits and nether regions. Una is necessarily alone, because even with his long hair, Lev is still highly recognizable.

"I wish I could go with you into these places," he said before she first put herself in harm's way.

"You couldn't anyway," she replied. "They're all bars, and you're underage."

Of course, at six months shy of her twenty-first birthday, Una is underage as well—but her ID says otherwise.

She walks into the third bar this evening—twelfth one since arriving in town. Her long black hair is pulled back with a colorful ribbon, the kind that Wil always would untie because he liked her hair to flow free. There is a pistol in her purse. Small and dainty, a little .22 caliber. She much prefers her rifle, but that's not exactly something you take with you into a bar. Even a sleazy one like this.

For three nights she has been trolling these gutter spots, where bad news meets more bad news and maybe gets lucky. But no luck for Una. She hasn't come across a single sign of the parts pirates she seeks.

This place—the What Ales Ya Saloon—has long faded from a glory that wasn't so glorious to begin with. Greasy booths where the dark leatherette seats are held together by matching duct tape. A linoleum floor that may have once been blue. Light low enough to rob what little color there is left to the place. The only thing sorrier than the establishment is the clientele, sparse and mostly sullen.

Una sits down at the bar, and the bartender, a man who's had some exceptional good looks bashed out of him by a hard life, comes over to her. Before she's asked, she shows him her ID, and flashes her medical alcohol license. Sometime around the Heartland War, they made alcohol a controlled substance. So now everyone has a medical alcohol license. Scalpers sell them on street corners, and you can even buy them from medical vending machines. So much for separating mankind from its favorite vice.

"What'll it be?" the bartender asks.

"A pint of Guinness."

He raises an eyebrow. "You're a gal after my own heart." He has a Texas twang to him that is out of place in Minnesota. Una offers him a pained grin that says *Just get me my beer.*

When he returns, she drinks it slowly, taking note of the people around her. There are two tattooed guys playing darts, not seeming to care about the drunks crossing their path as they launch their sharp projectiles. Deep in the dim booths are couples making deals she doesn't want to hear. Sitting with her at the bar is a predictable collection of lonely-hearts and career alcoholics. The one sitting at the far end of the bar pays for her drink without her permission, and gestures to her with a two-finger wave and a grinning display of yellow teeth that say it's Halloween all year. Una's response is to put her own cash on the bar when the bartender passes.

"Here," she says. "Give Skeleton Jack his money back."

The bartender, who must see exchanges like this on a regular basis, is happy to oblige with a chuckle. She doesn't know if he's pleased with her self-reliance, or just enjoying the drunk's misfortune in the matter.

When the bartender seems to have a free moment, she delicately broaches the subject that brought her here. "Maybe you could help me," she begins, trying to be more polite than she actually feels. "I'm looking for two gentlemen who make their living in the flesh trade."

The bartender laughs at that. "First time I ever heard parts pirates called 'gentlemen,'" he says. "Sorry to disappoint you, darlin', but parts pirates only brag to one another. They don't tell the likes of me their business."

Una ignores him and continues. "Their names are Hennessey and Fretwell." Then she watches the bartender for a "tell."

"Never heard of 'em," he says, then casually goes about his business of washing dirty glasses—but Una notices him washing a glass that was already clean. *Bingo!*

This is closest thing to a lead she's had in three days. Now it's all up to her. She must play this carefully. She wonders what this man is worried about. Is it that he just doesn't want to get mixed up in business that's not his? Does he think she's a Fed come to crack down on his patrons? Well, whatever the reason for his silence, perhaps she can appeal to his wallet.

"Too bad," she says. "I hear they're the go-to guys for a high-value catch."

The bartender doesn't meet her eye. "I wouldn't know anything about that."

"And," adds Una, "I was planning on a nice finder's fee for anyone who could put me in touch with them." Then she finishes her beer, pushes the empty glass in his direction, and puts a fifty beneath it.

He glances at the bill, but doesn't take it.

"Of course, that's just for making the introduction," Una says. "If I actually make the sale, there'll be a whole lot more."

He goes farther down the bar and serves a sad-looking woman a Tom Collins that Skeleton Jack will probably pay for. When the bartender returns, he's had enough time to think about the proposition. He takes Una's glass and the fifty, making it disappear like a magician. He glances around, then leans closer, speaking in a voice so low, she can hardly hear him.

"If it's the guys I'm thinking about, you probably won't run into them here," he says. "I don't know about Hennessey, but Fretwell spends his time hustling pool at the Iron Monarch Pub, down on Nicollet Avenue—but listen—he's a scummy guy, and that's a scummy place. You oughta think twice about this."

Una can't help but laugh at that. "You mean there's a place scummier than this?"

He's not offended by the observation, and remains dead serious. "Plenty of them," he says. "There are pits and there are snake pits. Lemme tell ya, *that* place has venom to spare."

Una shivers in spite of herself. "I can handle it," she says. She knows it's true, but the intensity in this man's eyes makes her doubt herself the slightest bit. She gets up from her barstool. "If a deal goes down, you'll be hearing from me," she tells him.

"I sincerely doubt that," he says with the resigned grin of a man who's been around the block—and in this neighborhood, that's saying something.

"Well," says Una, "worst-case scenario, you never see me again, and you're up fifty bucks."

He accepts her evaluation of their situation, offers her a "You take care, now," and she leaves to find a pit of vipers called the Iron Monarch.

10 · Fretwell

To say that Morton Fretwell is ugly as sin is a grave insult to sin. He knows this. He's had a lifetime to come to terms with it—twenty-nine years, to be exact. Fretwell's development took him through various comparative species. He began life as a bat-faced baby, grew into a coyote-faced boy, and finally matured into a goat-faced man.

But rather than lament his unprepossessing nature, he chose to embrace it—revel in it, even. His ugliness defines him—for what would he have without it? When he and Hennessey bagged that SlotMonger kid and sold him for a small fortune, Fretwell's share was enough to pick himself out some nice new facial features, if he wanted. He had considered it, but not for long. Instead he spent the money on some of the finer things in life that his face usually denied him. But now that money is gone, and it's back to the day-to-day of trolling the streets for Unwinds to sell to those who will pay.

As he plays pool alone in a corner of the Iron Monarch he notices the girl. Actually, he noticed her when she first came in, looking like a nice drink of water in the desert. But now he notices *her* noticing *him*.

She's young. Twenty-one, maybe younger. She's alone in a booth, and already there are vultures around the Monarch with their eyes on her. She has dark hair, tied tightly back. When she came in, he noticed how it fell all the way to her tailbone. Fretwell has a thing for girls with long hair.

She doesn't just notice him, she makes eye contact with him now. There may be the hint of a smile on her face, but he can't tell in the dim light of the bar.

There's an ethnic look about her. Hispanic, or maybe even SlotMonger—hard to tell. Either way, there's an untainted aura about her that makes it clear she doesn't belong here. Or at least doesn't belong here *yet*. Clearly she's a good girl who's "slumming it" and looking for low love. And it doesn't get lower than Morton Fretwell.

He breaks eye contact first, and handily sinks his next ball—a tough bank shot. The attention from this somewhat pretty girl improves his mojo. Girls who are actually looking for a guy like him are few and far between, so he's quick to make his move. He grabs a second cue stick, and saunters over to the booth where she sits.

"Name's Morty," he says "You play?"

"A little," she answers, stirring the swizzle stick of a drink that she doesn't seem to have touched.

He hands her the cue. "C'mon, I'll rack them up." She

hasn't told him her name yet. He's confident that she will. He leads her back to the pool table. He lets her break. She takes the stroke with confidence, and the balls scatter at the far end of the table with a hearty *crack*. You can tell a lot about a person by the way they play pool. This is a girl who knows what she wants. Fretwell is determined to learn exactly what that is.

"New in town?" he asks.

"Just passing through."

She smiles at him and he runs his tongue across his teeth, checking for pizza debris, before smiling back. Then he sinks the seven ball, claiming solids, but intentionally misses the next shot to give her a fighting chance.

"Where ya from?"

"Doesn't matter as much as where I'm going," she says playfully.

Fretwell willingly takes the bait. "And where might that be?"

She takes a shot and sinks the twelve ball. "Victory," she answers.

"Nice," he says with a grin. She misses her follow-up shot, and he puts her in her place by dropping three in a row. "Might have to work for it, though."

Her long ponytail swishes past him as she slides by to take her next shot. It makes him shiver. She still hasn't told him her name. Maybe that doesn't matter.

"Anything in particular bring you to the Iron Monarch?"

"Business," she says.

"What kind of business?"

She chalks her cue. "Your kind of business."

He decides he doesn't have to know her name. He puts his cue on the rack. "Wanna get out of here?"

"Lead the way."

He tries to reign in his enthusiasm. Must be cool about this. Must play into whatever image of him she has set in her mind. Bad boy with bad intentions but a smooth way about him. Yeah. He can be that. "Car's out back," he tells her, and she doesn't bat an eye, so he puts his arm around her and leads her out the back door, his mind already racing miles ahead.

Then just as the door swings shut behind them, everything changes so quickly his racing brain finds itself with neither road nor traction. Suddenly he's thrown back against the jagged brick wall of the alley with more force than a girl this size should be capable of. She has a gun pressed painfully into his neck now, just below his right ear, aimed upward. It's a small weapon, but when a pistol is aimed toward the center of your brain, size doesn't matter.

He doesn't dare move or resist. "Easy, there" is all he can offer up in the way of words. His mojo has abandoned him.

"Let's be clear about this," she says, in a voice far colder than she had in the bar. "When I said business, that's exactly what I meant, so if you ever touch me again, I will shoot off each of your fingers one by one. Got it?"

"Yeah, yeah," he says. He'd nod, but he's afraid the motion would push her trigger finger.

"Good. Now, as it happens, I've caught myself a nice little prize, and I was told that you have the best black-market connections."

He breathes a sigh of relief, realizing that he might actually survive this encounter. "Yeah, the best connections," he says a little too agreeable. "European, South American—even the Burmese Dah Zey."

"Good to know," she says. "As long as you have a clear line to the people who pay real money for one-of-a-kind goods, we'll have a very happy working relationship." She backs off a little, but keeps the gun aimed at him in case he bolts, which he's not planning on. For one, if he tries to run, she'll probably shoot. And also because Morty Fretwell's greed has begun to supplant his fear. What could she possible mean by "one-of-a-kind"?

He dares to ask the question, hoping it won't solicit a bullet to any part of his anatomy. "So . . . whatcha got?"

"Not what, but who," she says with a grin that's a little bit scary.

He involuntarily begins to lick his lips. There are only a handful of people she could be talking about—a handful of kids whose parts would be worth a fortune. If she's not bluffing, this could be the payday of paydays.

"So who is it?"

"You'll find out soon enough. Set up a meeting between you, me, and your earless friend."

This nervy thing has done her homework! "He's not earless," Fretwell says. "He's still got one left."

"Call him."

Fretwell pulls out his phone but hesitates, calculating himself important enough in this equation to have a little bit of bargaining power now.

"I won't call him till you tell me who you got."

She lets out a short exasperated huff. Then she says, "The clapper who didn't clap."

And suddenly Fretwell's fingers can't dial fast enough.

11 · Lev

It's a standard freight container. Eight feet wide, eight-and-a-half feet high, and forty feet deep. During the day it's a perpetual twilight inside, with pinpricks of light penetrating rust holes in the corners. It smells like sour milk with overtones of chemical waste. Lev thought there might be rats, but rats only frequent places where there's something to scavenge.

He's far too alive to be a morsel for the resident rodentia of the freight yard.

Lev's wrists are bound by sturdy cable ties to the far wall of the long container. Una had to buy hasps and attach them to the wall with epoxy because the wall had no inherent way to shackle him and make it look convincing. He had asked Una to give him a small cut with her pocketknife right at the base of his left thumb. Not deep enough to do any real damage, but enough to bloody up his wrist and the cable tie. He knows that small touches like that will lend authenticity and make their ruse seem real. They've also strategically placed various bits of junk they found in the freight yard around the container, to provide camouflage for Una's rifle, which is propped up in deep shadow against a rusted filing cabinet.

The hasps are a bit too low to make him look torturously bound when he's standing, but when he kneels, his hands are higher than his head in a position that looks painful, because it is. Little blond Jesus crucified in a big steel box. Letting his head fall completely slack completes the illusion.

"You look positively helpless," Una said when she stood back to look at him, "but still a little clean, even with the blood on your wrist."

So he squirmed and writhed, getting rust and grime all over his clothes, and kicked off a shoe to make it seem as if he'd lost it while struggling.

"I'll keep it up until I break a good sweat," he told her, which was not hard to do considering that the container was oppressively hot.

Una went to meet their marks, and Lev was left alone with the stench and his thoughts.

That was over an hour ago.

He's been alone in here for way too long.

It's after dark now. The half-light spilling through the

rust holes has given way to darkness as thick as tar. He has a moment of panic when he imagines the impossible—that the two parts pirates have killed Una. He wouldn't put it past them. That would truly leave Lev imprisoned here with no means of escape. If that happened, then this container would be his tomb. That's when the rats would come.

But no. He can't let himself think that way. Una will be back. All will go according to plan.

Unless it doesn't.

He shakes his head in the dark, banishing his anxious thoughts. With his arms secured so uncomfortably, he knows time feels like it's dragging much more slowly than it actually is. He remembers another time he was bound like this, and for much longer. Nelson had held him and Miracolina captive in an isolated cabin. He was bound to a bed frame with cable ties similar to the ones on his wrists now, only that time it was for real. Nelson had played Russian roulette with them; five bullets in his clip were tranqs, and the sixth was deadly. No way of knowing when the killer bullet would come up. He didn't fire at Lev, though—he shot Miracolina each time Lev gave Nelson an answer he didn't like, and each time she was tranq'd into unconsciousness once more.

In the silence of the steel container, Lev's mind now takes him to alternate realities. What if Nelson had killed Miracolina? What would Lev have done then? Would he have had the where-withal to escape, or would the burden of her death weigh so heavily upon him that it would have crippled him?

And where would Connor be now, if Lev never got free from Nelson? Dead or in prison, probably. Or in a harvest camp, waiting until one of the proposed laws passes that allows the unwinding of criminals.

But Miracolina survived and helped him get to the airplane graveyard. He rescued Connor from the Juvies *and* from Nelson.

He did good. He wishes he could tell Miracolina all the good he's done—but he has no idea where she is, or if she even escaped.

He still cares for Miracolina, and thinks about her often—but so much has transpired in the weeks since he last saw her, it feels like another lifetime. She had been a tithe, which means she might be unwound by now if she held to the ideals she had when they first met. Lev can only hope that his influence had eroded her dangerously self-sacrificing resolve, but there's no way to know. Maybe someday he will track her down and find out what happened to her, but personal curiosity is a luxury he can't afford right now. For the time being, Miracolina Roselli must remain on his list of "maybe somedays."

He hears a bolt thrown, and the creaking of heavy hinges. The doors at the front of the container open just enough to admit a streak of pale moonlight, and three figures enter. Lev slumps, feigning unconsciousness. Through his closed eyes, he registers the glow of a flashlight against his face.

"That's not him, look at his hair!"

"Hair grows, you imbecile."

He recognizes their voices right away: Fretwell, the lackluster one, and Hennessey, the one-eared ringleader with prep-school affectations. He was only in their company once, but those voices are burned into his auditory memory enough to make him fill with an angry chill. Lev opens his eyes, and lets his disgust and horror play out on his face, because it serves him to do so.

"I do believe this actually is Levi Calder," says Hennessey, leaning in to examine him.

"It's Garrity!" Lev grunts.

"Call yourself whatever you want," Hennessey says with an antagonistic grin, "but to the world, you'll always be Levi Calder, the tithe-turned-clapper."

Lev spits in his face because he's close enough, and because it gives Lev great satisfaction to do so—and to his surprise, Una steps in and smashes Lev across the face with a brutal backhanded slap that nearly spins his head around.

"Show respect to your new owners," Una says bitterly. He responds by spitting at her, too.

Una steps forward as if to hit him again, but Hennessey grabs her. "Enough," he says. "Didn't anyone ever teach you not to damage the merchandise?"

Una backs off, setting down her flashlight on the rusty filing cabinet, painting the space in harsh oblique shadow. She looks away just enough to give Lev a wink that the two men can't see. Lev just scowls at her, because that's something they *can* see. The slap, Lev knows, was key to their illusion, even if it felt painfully real. He wonders if, on any level, Una took some satisfaction from it.

Now it's Fretwell's turn to taunt. He moves in closer. "We never shoulda let you go that first time," he says. "Of course, that was before you were a clapper. You were nobody then."

"And he's nobody now," says Hennessey, then he turns to Una. "We'll give you five thousand for him, and not a penny more."

Una is outraged, and Lev is, to say the least, insulted.

"Are you kidding me?" Una shouts. "He's got to be worth at least ten times that!"

Hennessey crosses his arms. "Oh, please! Don't be obtuse. The boy's organs are damaged from the explosive solution—his growth is stunted, and he's probably sterile. We are purveyors in flesh, sweetie. His flesh has no intrinsic value."

Lev suppresses the urge to argue. His organs aren't perfect, but they do the job, and no, he won't grow, but the doctors never said anything about him being sterile. How dare they? But arguing for his own value won't help things.

"I'm not stupid," says Una. "There are collectors who would pay top dollar for a piece of the clapper who didn't clap."

Lev looks at them all with absolute disdain. "So I'm a collectible?"

"Not you, your parts!" says Fretwell, and laughs.

Hennessey throws a nasty glance in Fretwell's direction—a nonverbal chastising for getting in the way of his negotiation.

"Perhaps, and perhaps not," Hennessey says. "But collectors are fickle. Who's to say what they're willing to pay for." Then he grabs Lev by the chin, turning his head to the left and right, looking him over like a horse he's about to buy. "Seventy-five hundred cash. Final offer. If you don't like it, try to sell him yourself."

Una looks at the two men, suitably disgusted, then says, "Fine."

Hennessey gestures to Fretwell. "Cut him loose." Fretwell pulls out a knife and bends down to cut the tie on Lev's right hand, while Hennessey pulls out his billfold. The instant Lev's hand is free, he reaches behind him, grabbing a handheld tranq dart, and jabs it in Fretwell's neck.

"Holy freaking mother of—" And Fretwell collapses unconscious before completing the thought.

Una, with lightning speed, has already grabbed her rifle and has it trained on Hennessey's face. "One move," she says. "Go on, give me a reason."

But Hennessey is quick-thinking. He hurls the wad of money in Una's face and bolts. The distraction is just enough to give him a full second head start. The bills drop from her face and she aims her rifle.

"Una, no!"

She fires but misses, blowing a hole in the front door of the container just as Hennessey escapes.

"Damn it!" She races after him, and Lev tries to race after

her—only to realize in a most painful way that his left hand is still secured to the wall.

"Una!"

But she's gone, and he must resort to searching for Fretwell's knife that lies somewhere in the shadows.

12 · Una

Una's fast, but a man running for his life is faster. He's out of the freight yard in seconds, and Una knows if he slips too far out of her sight, he'll be gone for good. She will not allow that. Capturing one of them is not enough. Capturing them both would not be enough to make up for Wil's unwinding either, but it will come closer.

He has a gun. She's sure of it. She hasn't seen it but she knows that he must, for men like him always do. He could be up ahead waiting to ambush her, so her pursuit needs to be stealthy. It needs to be more of a stalk than a chase—but you can't stalk someone who already knows you're coming after him. Una slows herself down. Allows herself to think. Back on the Rez, Pivane taught her to hunt. She was good at it. If she sees this as a hunt, she will prevail.

The flat, soulless walls of the old industrial buildings just outside the freight yard might give Hennessey cover, but they also provide a nice blind for her. She stops near a corner, keeping in shadow against a wall, and she listens. He will be listening too. Waiting for a moment to break for freedom. So, then, what will he see as freedom?

Una thinks she knows.

One block over, the industrial zone ends at the Mississippi River, and less than a quarter mile downriver is a stone arch pedestrian bridge. It's no longer in use, it has no overhead streetlamps. If he can get across that bridge he could disappear into downtown Minneapolis. That bridge is his freedom.

Una makes her way toward the bridge as stealthily as she can. Then, hiding in the shadow of a mailbox that probably hasn't seen a letter in years, she waits.

Thirty seconds later he bolts from a side street, making a beeline toward that bridge. She knows she won't be able to intercept him if she runs, but she doesn't have to run. It might be dark, but she can see he has his gun out—an ostentatious silver thing that catches the moonlight nicely. Just as he gets on the bridge, she takes aim and fires low. He wails in pain and goes down. Now Una runs down to the bridge to see the damage. She can see him clearly in the faint footlights still speckling the bridge. The bullet got him in the left knee, rendering him virtually immobile. He fires at her, but his aim is off. She's on him quickly enough to kick the gun from his hand. Then she backs up and raises the rifle.

Panting, spitting, Hennessey pulls himself up against the stone railing.

"This is about that SlotMonger kid, isn't it!"

"He had a name!" growls Una, fingering the trigger, tempting herself to pull it. *Just give me a reason,* she said. But she has plenty of reasons already. "His name was Wil Tashi'ne. I want you to say it."

He looks down at his shredded knee, and grimaces. "What's the point? You're going to kill me anyway. So do it."

Could anything be more tempting than that invitation? "You have two choices," she tells the man. "You could try to get away, and I'll kill you. Or you could surrender and be brought in to face Arápache justice."

"How about a third choice?" he says . . . and without warning Hennessey hurls himself over the railing into the river. It's not the highest bridge. A man—even a wounded man—could easily survive the fall and escape. Una hadn't considered this alternative, and is furious at herself, until she hears a faint *thud* from far below.

When she looks over the side, she sees not water, but a rocky shore. Hennessey severely misjudged and hit a boulder. Now he has all the choices of a dead man.

Una hears approaching footsteps, and sees Lev coming onto the bridge.

"What happened? I heard gunshots. Where is he?" He glances at the blood on the ground. "You didn't!"

"*I* didn't. *He* did." And she draws his attention over the side of the bridge. Lev pulls out the flashlight and shines it down at the rocks, making the scene much clearer. Hennessey's spine is broken across the back of a sharp boulder just a few feet from the water's edge.

Lev lets off a shiver that Una can feel like a shock wave. She knows she should feel revulsion, too, but all she can feel is disappointment that she can no longer exact revenge from the man.

Together Una and Lev go down to the shoreline to confirm that Hennessey is dead. Then they bring his broken body to the water, turn him facedown, and push him off to be carried away by the current.

"At least we still have Fretwell," says Lev. "That will be enough."

"Enough for you to win over the Arápache people," Una agrees, "but is it enough to get the Tribal Council to take a stand against unwinding?"

"It'll get them to listen to me," Lev says. "Then it's up to me to convince them."

In spite of the fact that they did no killing today, they both have blood on their hands from dragging Hennessey's body to the water. They wash their hands in the river as best they can.

"C'mon, we'd better get back to Fretwell," says Lev. "I tied him up, but we should be on our way back to the Rez with him before his tranqs wear off."

Before they leave, Una takes one last look at the jagged boulder that claimed Hennessey's life. How mystical, and how perfect the universe is! That boulder was shorn from a mountain by a glacier maybe a hundred thousand years ago, and then carefully deposited here with patient intent, waiting all these years to break that criminal's spine in two. All things have a purpose. That's something both she and Lev can take comfort in.

13 · Hayden

Hayden Upchurch watches it grow like a cancer clinging to the walls of the decaying power plant: Starkey's lethal crusade. It's ugly and toxic, and it won't stop devouring all the good that's left in these kids until there's none left. Starkey will drag his Stork Brigade through his bloody war front until they are either dead from bullets taken in battle, or dead on the inside from the things they've seen and done. Hayden knows that these harvest camp attacks are pointless. The consequence of Starkey's war on unwinding will not be the glorious vindication of AWOLs and storks, but instead their damnation.

"This is Radio Free Hayden podcasting from somewhere dark and dingy that smells of ancient grease and more recent body odor. If anyone actually hears this podcast, I must first apologize that there's no visual of me. My bandwidth is the digital equivalent of a mule train. So instead, I've posted this wonderful Norman Rockwell image instead of a video. You'll note how the poor innocent ginger kid standing on the chair with his butt

hanging out is about to be tranq'd in the ass by the 'kindly country doctor.' I felt the image was somehow appropriate."

Rumor is that Starkey's benefactors will be supplying clappers for the next harvest camp attack. Will there be anyone left not terrified of kids like them once Starkey is done? Starkey wants that terror—he thrives on it. Yet how could he not realize that the many who might have once been sympathetic to the cause are now turning to the Juvenile Authority for an answer to the violence. The Juvies have an answer, all right: the blessed peace of division. The eternal rest of unwinding. *That* will be Mason Starkey's legacy—an end to resistance, an end to rebellion, the absolute silencing of the last generation that could derail the hellish train civilization has boarded.

"I'm sure you've seen my brilliant and heartfelt call for a new teen uprising. I have to admit that heatstroke and dehydration from hours trapped in a sweltering World War II bomber turned me into quite the prophet. I'm sure my parents must be proud. Or horrified. Or are bitterly arguing about whether they're proud or horrified, and have already hired lawyers to resolve the dispute."

Hayden's entire recording is in a whisper that sounds much more desperate than he wants it to sound, but he must be quiet. He can only sneak access to Starkey's "computer center" in the middle of the night. It's off in a room in the corner of the power plant, but there's no door, so it's open to the rest of the plant. He can hear the snoring of the kids, which means any of them who are awake could hear him if he speaks too loudly.

"What did I mean in my rant of solidarity? Well, there are uprisings and there are uprisings. I want to make it perfectly clear about the kind I'm talking about. I am NOT advocating taking the law into our own hands and blowing people

away, burning various and sundry vehicles, and being the kind of pissed-off 'incorrigibles' who make society think that, yeah, maybe unwinding is a good idea. There are certain people—and I'm not naming names—who think that violence furthers our cause. It doesn't. I'm also not calling for a flower-child sit-in, or a Gandhi-like hunger strike. Passive resistance only works if the truck's not willing to run you over—and this truck is. What we need is something in between. We need to be loud enough and forceful enough to be heard—but sane enough that people will listen. The Juvenile Authority would like us to believe that we have no support—but that's a lie. Even the polls show that the various unwind-related propositions and initiatives on this year's ballots, as well as the bills slithering through Capitol Hill, are far more marginal than the Juvies will admit. But violence will tip the scale against us."

Once he puts this podcast out there, there will be no turning back. No changing his mind. He will have shown his hand. Starkey could very well find out. He probably will, and pretty quickly, too. Will Starkey kill him for it, he wonders?

"So whether you're a stork, or an AWOL, or a kid frightened for your own future—or an adult scared for your kids' futures—we DO have an opportunity to deal unwinding a mortal blow. We just have to figure out how to do it. I wish I knew the answer, but I'm not brilliant enough to figure it out on my own. So I'm putting the call out to you. Any of you. All of you. What do YOU think we should do? Contact me at RadioFreeHayden@yahoo.com with your own brilliance. All ideas will be considered. Even the stupid ones. This is Hayden Upchurch signing off. Stay sane, and stay whole."

His finger hovers over the "send" button, and hovers some more. He can't seem to make his finger move, and he marvels at how one's entire life can come down to the pressing of a single button.

Then Hayden hears a noise. Something shuffling behind him, and he spins in his chair.

A *rat—please, God, let it be a rat!*

But it's no rat. It's Jeevan.

Hayden's heart misses a beat, then compensates with a powerful pump that he can feel pulse through his neck and into his eyeballs.

"Up late, Jeevan?" He tries to be nonchalant, but the kid's not buying it. Jeevan, at only fifteen, is Starkey's technology wunderkind—but back in the Graveyard, he used to do his magic for Hayden. So to whom is he more loyal? Hayden knows that Jeevan has been giving Starkey less than his best—working much less efficiently and skillfully than Hayden knows he can. It's a form of resistance, but being resistant and turning against the "Stork Lord" are two different things.

"I heard it," Jeevan says, taking a few steps closer. "I heard all of it."

Hayden takes a slow silent breath before he speaks. No point in mincing words now. "Are you going to tell Starkey?"

Jeevan doesn't answer. Instead he says, "We're going the day after tomorrow, did you know? The next harvest camp attack. There are kids betting on how many of us will get killed this time. Whoever gets closest to the actual death count wins. Unless they're one of the ones killed, of course. Then it goes to the next closest who actually survived."

"Did you bet?"

Jeevan shakes his head. "No. Because if I'm right, I'll somehow feel I was partially responsible." For a moment Jeevan seems much younger than fifteen. And much older at the same time. "Do you think that's stupid?"

"If it is, Jeeves, it's outweighed by a far greater stupidity than yours."

They both look at the computer screen and the Norman Rockwell image that seems simultaneously innocent and sinister. "The Juvies will find that podcast, you know," says Jeevan. "They won't be able to trace it, but they'll take it down before it has the chance to spread."

"I know," says Hayden. "But if just a handful of people hear it, I'll be happy."

"No, you won't. You want *everyone* to hear it. It's just not going to happen, though." Jeevan shivers a bit, and holds his arms. Only now does Hayden realize how cold the night has gotten. "You need to find a way to make it kill-proof," Jeevan says. "You know, make it reproduce and shift locations on the web so that they can't take it down."

"Kind of like digital Whac-a-Mole."

Jeevan takes a moment to process that. "Oh yeah, right. Whac-a-Mole. Funny."

"So . . . can you make that happen?"

"Maybe. Or maybe you need to do an old-fashioned radio broadcast. They can't shut that down until it's already out there."

The idea of a real broadcast is appealing to Hayden. The trick would be getting a signal that's far-reaching enough.

"You haven't uploaded it yet," Jeevan says.

Hayden shrugs. "Yeah, well, follow-through has always been my weak point."

Jeevan looks at the screen. Hayden is usually good at knowing what people are thinking, but tonight, he has no clue what's in Jeevan's head. Well, whatever he's thinking, it must resonate with Hayden's thoughts, because Jeevan reaches out and does what was so hard for Hayden. He clicks on "send."

They both watch in silence as the podcast uploads. In a few moments it's done. A click of a button to change the world, or end his life, or both.

14 · Groundskeeper

A gardener by trade, he took the job because it was a job. The pay was decent, there were good benefits, and it included room and board. "You'd be an idiot to turn it down," his wife had told him. "So what if it's at a harvest camp? I won't mind living there if you won't."

Without a degree in horticulture, a steady job at a well-funded institution was probably the best he could hope for.

"And anyway," as his wife had pointed out, "it's not like *you're* unwinding anyone."

That's true enough. In his five years working at Horse Creek Harvest Camp, he's had very little contact with the kids. The camp is too regimented for that. The Unwinds are always being efficiently shuttled from one activity to another. Sports activities to gauge their physical prowess and to build muscle mass so their parts will be more valuable. Intellectual and creative endeavors designed to measure, and improve upon, their mental skills. The Unwinds of Horse Creek are kept far too busy to notice a gardener.

The tithes, who have a little more freedom, will talk to him on occasion. "What kind of flowers are those?" they'll ask, their bright innocence in stark contrast to the other Unwinds whose desperation radiates from them like a toxic field. "They're pretty—did you plant them all yourself?" He'll always answer politely, but rarely will he look at them, because he knows their fate, even if it's a fate they accept. It's his own personal superstition: Don't look into the eyes of the doomed.

He's not the only gardener, but his skill and success with planting has earned him the distinction of head groundskeeper. Now he gets to pick and choose his tasks, and assign work to others. He takes care of the heavier planting: new trees and hedges, and the design of the larger, more impressive flower beds. He loves to plant those himself. The largest of these is right in front of the place the kids call the Chop Shop. He's particularly proud of this year's fall theme: pumpkins growing within the swirling colors of toad lilies, monkhood, and other autumn-blooming flowers.

"You should be proud of what you do," his wife tells him. "Your flower beds are the last bit of nature these kids will see before they're divided. It's your gift to them."

For this reason he takes great care to place every growing thing in the Chop Shop flower bed personally.

He's troubled by the recent added security measures and the influx of "protective personnel." These new guards are not just the typical camp security staff, but tactical teams supplied by the Juvenile Authority. They carry assault weapons and wear thick, bulletproof clothing. It's all very intimidating. He's heard of the recent attacks on harvest camps, but there are so many camps, and the others that were attacked are far away. What are the chances that their little camp in rural Oklahoma will be singled out of all the harvest camps for a Stork Brigade attack? As far as he's concerned, this paranoid security serves only to make everyone worried for no good reason.

He's with a coworker, shaping a dragon topiary, when the attack comes, destroying the tranquility of a bucolic day. He doesn't see the first explosion—and he feels it more than hears it. It comes as a shock wave that, had he not been kneeling behind the topiary, would have knocked him over backward. A chunk of concrete the size of a basketball tears a hole in the heart of the dragon, but not before tearing through his coworker. The groundskeeper throws himself to the ground, splattered with the blood of his dead comrade, and when he looks up, he sees that the administration building is gone. All that remains are jagged fragments of walls. Pieces of the building are still coming down all around the grounds of the camp.

Staff and Unwinds alike all run from the scene in a panic. A second blast takes out a guard tower designed to look like a rustic windmill. Shredded timber tears through everything and everyone in its way, and from behind it, where a steel-reinforced fence used to be, floods an army of kids wielding weapons the groundskeeper has never seen the likes of before. The air is now filled with the *blam-blam-blam* of repeating rifles, the earsplitting *rat-tat-tat-tat* of machine guns, and the mournful shriek of a shoulder-mounted rocket launcher delivering its deadly payload to the staff quarters. The rocket crashes through a corner window of a second-floor apartment—the nice one overlooking the gardens—and an instant later, all the windows of the building blow out in a fireball from the explosion within.

He suppresses a scream, hunkering down in the dense ivy at the base of the topiary. He knows if he's spotted he's a dead man—he knows if anyone happens to spray their weapon in his general direction, he'll be dead as well. All he can do is lie low, belly to the ground, trying to disappear into the greenery he so painstakingly planted.

The Juvenile Authority's SWAT team, for all their training and weaponry, are ill prepared for an assault of this magnitude. They raise their ballistic shields and try to advance on the marauding throng of kids, taking some of them down, but not many. Then, from out of the crowd of kids races a single unarmed girl running toward them with her hands up.

"Help me, help me! Don't shoot!" she cries.

The SWAT team holds their fire as she approaches, ready to shield her, and save her from the crossfire. Then, as she nears them, she swings her hands together.

The instant her hands touch, she's gone.

The explosion is so powerful it sends the entire SWAT

team flying like bowling pins, their bodies twisting and burning in the air.

Another unarmed kid, frail but determined, hurls himself, arms wide, at the side of the SWAT team's armored truck, and as soon as he connects with it, the explosion tears the truck in two, sending half of it cannoning through the front gate and the other half tearing through the Chop Shop garden.

"They've got clappers!" someone yells. "My God, they've got clappers!"

And now the groundskeeper knows this is about more than just freeing the Unwinds here. This is about exacting pounds of flesh from all those complicit in unwinding. There will be no mercy for him if he is caught. Never mind that all he did was beautify the grounds. *You watched hundreds of kids taken into the Chop Shop, and you did nothing*, the Stork Brigade will tell him. *You dined with the men and women who held the scalpels and you did nothing*, they will say. *You took a place of nightmares and hid it behind flowers*, and his only defense will be, *I was just doing my job*. For that, they will gun him down, or blow him to bits, or kick out the chair from under him. And all because he did nothing.

Don't move, you fool, he knows his wife would tell him. *Play dead until it's all over*. But he knows she won't be telling him anything anymore. Because one of the perks of being the head groundskeeper is getting that corner apartment on the second floor of the staff house. The nice one overlooking the gardens.

15 · Jeevan

"You need to see it, Jeevan. You need to be a part of it. As a member of the Stork Brigade, you have to share in the fight so you'll truly feel the power of what we're doing. So you'll get the importance of it."

This is how Starkey couched the news that Jeevan was to be a foot soldier in the attack on Horse Creek Harvest Camp. "Until now you've just been behind the scenes, in the background. But today you become a warrior, Jeevan. Today is your day."

"Yes, sir," was Jeevan's response, as was always his response to Starkey.

But when the first rocket takes out the administration building, and the storks around him begin firing their weapons at anything that moves in the smoke, Jeevan knows that he should never have allowed himself to be here. There are kids around him who are bloated by the power of their weapons, turned maniacal by Starkey's skillful stroking of their most violent sides. There are also those who hold their weapons reluctantly, knowing that this couldn't be right, no matter how wrong unwinding is—but they are swept along in the powerful current and don't know how to resist.

None of these other kids have been as close to Starkey as Jeevan has been. None of them have been part of the planning, or have witnessed his temper tantrums, or have seen behind the curtain of his eyes to know the show that goes on behind the show.

Starkey believes he is invincible. He believes he is more than just destined for greatness, but that greatness is owed to him, and every one of these "victories" makes him believe it more and more. *The Stork Lord.* Hayden's epithet is more on-target then even he realizes, for Starkey truly does see himself as royalty reaching for divinity. A chosen one with the pride and privilege of a god.

When you believe in yourself that strongly, it attracts the belief of others. The more storks believe in Starkey, the more they want to, and the more fervent that belief becomes. Jeevan was one of those. He would have died for Starkey in those first days. Now he finally realizes the blindness of that faith, just in time for him to actually die for it.

As Jeevan's team races into the fray, blasting weapons with enough recoil to blow them backward every time they pull the trigger, Jeevan prays only to survive.

"Today you are a warrior," Starkey told him, clapping him on the shoulder like a brother when he said it. But Jeevan knows the truth behind the words. *Now you are expendable* is what Starkey meant—because with the power and resources of the clapper movement behind him, Starkey no longer needs Jeevan to work his computer magic. All the hard-core hacking for this operation was done elsewhere, and on hardware far superior to anything they've had until now. Jeevan is a redundancy. And so today, he is a warrior.

The battle rages around him, so one-sided, he could almost laugh if bullets weren't flying past him, if people weren't dying left and right. The camp's beefed-up security force is no match for the Stork Brigade.

Jeevan's orders are to shoot anyone over seventeen. Like many others, though, he's just been firing high, letting loose a battle scream, so it seems like he's killing, when all he's really doing is making a lot of noise. He stays away from open spaces, where he's a target, and finds himself standing amid topiary hedges that have been shredded by explosions. Then he sees motion—someone crawling through the ivy. *Shoot anyone over seventeen.* Is Starkey watching? What if he is? What if he sees Jeevan failing in his new role as a foot soldier in the Stork Brigade? What will Starkey do when he decides Jeevan is entirely useless?

Jeevan aims his machine gun at the crawling man, but when the man sees it, he rises and hurls himself at Jeevan.

The machine gun tumbles to the ground. Desperately the two scramble for it in the ivy.

The man, a gardener, swings a pair of garden shears at Jeevan, the blades connecting above his left eye. Blood spills forth from the gash, much more blood than such a small gash should bring. It clouds his vision. Jeevan grabs the machine gun, but his hands are slick with blood. His fingers slip, and the gardener grabs it away from him. He stands over Jeevan in the snarl of ruined hedges, aiming at him, finger on the trigger, and Jeevan knows that he's made a crucial error. He should have shot the man without hesitation the moment he saw him—because it's kill or be killed. Starkey has left no room for anything in between.

The man wails in anguish. He tightens his finger on the trigger aimed right at Jeevan's face. Tightens. Tightens. Then he falls to his knees, dropping the machine gun. For a moment Jeevan thinks the man's been shot in the back, but he hasn't been. The gardener's wailing drops an octave into sobs.

Another explosion rocks a building to their right, and both Jeevan and the man drop down to their bellies in the ivy as pieces of glass, stone, and brick fly past them, shredding the topiary beyond all recognition. And lying there, blood still streaming into his eyes, Jeevan does something. He doesn't know what possesses him to do it, but he is so terrified, so disconnected, that he is driven to find some sort of connection. He reaches through the ivy and grabs the hand of the gardener, now caked in both mud and blood. He clasps the man's hand tightly. And the man clasps his back.

He can't see the gardener's face—leaves are in the way— but in the midst of this chaos that clasped hand is an oasis of comfort. For both of them.

"We're not all evil," the man says.

"Neither are we," Jeevan responds.

And they wait there in silence hiding in the ivy, hiding to stay alive, until the sounds of gunfire fade and Starkey, the triumphant general, enters the theater of battle to claim his victory.

16 · Bam

When the battle begins, Bam and her team of twenty-five storks are positioned at the camp's back entrance. Their view is of the loading dock behind the Chop Shop, where medical vans haul away coolers of life, ready to be transplanted to those deemed more deserving. Or at least those whose pocketbooks or insurance can afford new parts. A single van is parked by the loading dock today, ready for the next shipment.

Bam's team—"Marabou Squad," as Starkey has called them, since he insists on naming each assault team after some kind of stork—waits outside the electrified gate, hidden by a dense oak grove, its branches filled with the oversize leaves of late September, just beginning to yellow. They have explosives to take out the fence. Bam is determined not to use them.

When the explosions begin on the other side of the harvest camp. Bam's team gets anxious. They remove the safeties from their weapons—weapons that they've only been minimally trained to use. The slighter kids can barely hold them, much less use them.

"Put the safeties back on!" Bam orders.

A meek, wide-eyed girl named Bree looks at her, almost more terrified by her order than by what lay ahead. "But . . . if we keep them on—"

"You heard me!"

All around, Bam hears the *click*s of the weapons being returned to the safe position. She takes a deep breath. Another explosion from somewhere beyond the Chop Shop shakes the ground beneath their feet and dislodges a hail of acorns. From this angle, all they can see are trees and the loading dock. Debris flies over the Chop Shop, landing on the loading dock. Small chunks of concrete pummel the roof of the medical van.

"We should go in!" says Garson DeGrutte. He's a muscular kid with painfully piercing gray eyes and a jarhead haircut. Clearly he wanted to be a military boeuf, and must see the Stork Brigade as his chance to live out his dream. "We need to go in now!" Garson shouts.

"Quiet!" yells Bam. "We're the second wave."

That's a lie, of course. Starkey adheres to an "all in" strategy: Hold nothing in reserve. Do or die. But Bam is determined to save these kid's lives. Today that is her personal mission.

"Look!" Bree says, pointing.

People in medical whites and scrubs burst out of the back door of the Chop Shop. Surgeons, nurses—the people who do the actual unwinding. Bam feels a surge of hate rage within her as the medical staff desperately tries the doors of the van, but can't get in. Another explosion blows out some of the Chop Shop's windows. The medical staff abandons the van and runs toward the gate. One of them hits a remote, and the gate begins to open.

"We're in without wasting explosives!" says Garson. "Pretty smart, Bam."

"Just shut your freaking mouth!" Bam growls at him. She glances to see the safety is off his weapon again and she burns him a glare that makes him click the safety back in place.

The medical workers, about seven or eight of them, race out of the gate.

"You're just letting them go?" Garson asks, incredulous.

Bam locks eyes with him. "Do you want to go out there and gun them down?"

The question leaves Garson speechless. He looks at his weapon, as if really seeing it for the first time. Bam looks to the whole group. "How about the rest of you? Anyone who wants to go out there and murder them, be my guest."

There are no takers. Not a one.

So they stay hidden in the trees as the men and woman run past, panicked and out of breath, some crying—and then out of nowhere comes a kid that Bam doesn't know. He has black hair hanging in his eyes, bad acne, and is emaciated in a radiation-chic kind of way. He stands in the middle of the road, holding his hands apart and tilting his head back like a flower opening for the sun.

The running people see him, but they're so terrified of what they're running from, they don't even consider what they might be running toward. Just before they reach his position, the dark-haired boy swings his hands together in a single powerful stroke.

The force of the explosion throws Bam and her team to the ground. And when she gets up to look, the trees on either side of the road are on fire, there's a crater in the asphalt, and there's no one there anymore. No one at all.

The other storks are silent for a few stunned moments, listening to the sound of flames, settling debris, and gunfire from beyond the Chop Shop loading dock, trying to deny the charred smell that has just reached their nostrils.

"They were unwinders," Garson says, his voice shaky. "They deserved to die."

"Maybe," says Bree. "But I'm glad I wasn't the one who killed them."

Bam's team waits out the battle, making no move to join it, and no one argues anymore. Not even Garson who seems hateful of the whole situation, probably thinking himself a coward, and blaming Bam for it.

It is only when the battle is over that Bam leads her team past the smoking remains of the Chop Shop, and into the battle-torn grounds of Horse Creek Harvest Camp.

Starkey has already gathered the liberated Unwinds in a grassy common, now strewn with bodies and wreckage. "My name is Mason Michael Starkey," Bam hears him announce to the gathered Unwinds, "and I have just freed you."

The crowd is too shell-shocked to cheer their liberation. The scenes of death and destruction surpass anything Bam has seen before. It's worse than the carnage at the Graveyard. The harvest camp has been burned to the ground. There are no living adults visible. Bam doesn't know if any escaped Starkey's dark vengeance against the world.

"What's he going to do with the tithes?" asks Bree. Bam turns to see several armed storks guarding a cluster of tithes, who are in the process of being taken captive, since they aren't taking well to freedom.

"Who knows," Bam says. "Maybe he'll turn them into slaves. Maybe he'll put them in the stew."

"Gross," says one of her team members, a tousled-haired kid whose name Bam doesn't know. "You don't think he'd really do that, do you?"

The fact that the kid can ask that, as if it's a real possibility, tells Bam that she's not the only one who thinks Starkey is out of his freaking mind. Yes, he has a tight core of loyalists who seem to suckle all the vengeance and vitriol he can feed them—but how much doubt is there among the others? How much support would she have if she were to challenge his leadership? Probably just enough to get her and her coconspirators executed as traitors to the cause.

To her right she sees Jeevan stumbling out of a ruined hedge, his face bleeding. Bam looks down and tears out a pocket in her khakis, giving it to Jeevan to blot his bleeding forehead.

"Your team's looking well rested," Starkey says when he sees her. He offers Bam something that resembles a grin, but not quite.

"You're the one who told us to take the loading dock," she tells him coldly. "There wasn't much action there."

He has no comment to that. "Load up, ship out," he orders, and strides away.

There are nondescript trucks waiting just down the road. The drivers, all supplied by the clapper movement, will take varied routes to deliver them back to the power plant, many hundreds of miles from the scene of the crime.

Hayden, along with Starkey's little harem and all the other kids who did not take part in this attack, was left there to wait for a triumphant homecoming. Bam finds herself anxious to unburden on Hayden everything that happened here today. She must tell someone—must confess her feelings about it. How strange that Hayden has become her confessor.

Load up. Ship out.

The windowless truck that brought them here, and now takes them back, doesn't feel all that different from an unwind transport truck. The lack of control over her own freedom is every bit as oppressive as incarceration. Bam checks to make sure that all weapons are disarmed and piled in a corner of the truck as they begin their journey, so they don't become playthings. She listens to snippets of conversations around her. There aren't many.

"Do you think there are clappers who didn't clap and they're in the trucks?"

"I get carsick when I can't look out a window."

"Austin Lee! Did anyone see Austin Lee? Please someone tell me you've seen him!"

"Starkey says we're getting better. Next time will be easier."

Then, loud and defiant, Jeevan says, "I miss the Graveyard."

That brings silence from everyone. And now that he has their attention, Jeevan says, even more loudly, "I miss the way Connor did things." It is brave; it is foolhardy. Bam didn't know that Jeevan had it in him.

No one responds for a few moments. Then a voice from the back says, "So do I."

Bam waits to see if anyone one else voices an opinion, but no one does. Still, she can tell from many of their faces that they agree. They're just afraid to say so.

"Well," says Bam, "maybe it can be like that again."

She pushes it no further, because she knows that some of the kids in the truck are the kind that worship Starkey, which means word of this conversation will get back to him. Even now, Garson DeGrutte is eying her bitterly. She takes a deep breath, and lets it out, then tries to offer Jeevan a comforting smile, but there isn't much comfort in it, because she knows the next war may not be at a harvest camp at all.

17 · Argent

Many miles to the north, Argent Skinner continues to ride shotgun beside Jasper Nelson in a U-Haul van, having added a fifth AWOL to their catch. According to Nelson, five healthy AWOLs can bring twenty, maybe thirty thousand dollars. Although math was never Argent's forte, he's already figured that a haul like this once a week could bring one-point-five million in a year and still leave time for vacation.

Their destination is a Canadian border city called Sarnia, which has the dubious distinction of being the most polluted city in Canada, what with the remains of old petroleum companies and the Chemical Valley corporations that still spew mysterious waste into the water and air. Some might consider Divan Umarov to be part of Sarnia's pollution—but to Argent, the mysterious black-market dealer could be his personal savior.

"So, what do we call him?" Argent asks Nelson when they cross the bridge into Canada. "Does he have a title or anything?"

Nelson sighs, as if to telegraph how put out he is by the question. "I've heard people refer to him as a flesh lord, but he doesn't like that. He's a businessman. He calls himself an independent supplier of biological upgrades."

Argent laughs at that, and Nelson returns a frown that cancels out anything jovial. "He takes his profession very seriously. You'd be wise to do the same."

Divan is not there when they offload the five AWOLs at the Porsche dealership that serves as a front for his operation.

"He spends, now, much of his time 'camping,'" they are told by an employee of undefined eastern European background, whose English skills are marginal at best. Nelson explains that "camping" is code for time spent overseeing his harvest camp. It's a place that not even Nelson has ever seen.

"He flies in, he flies out," Nelson tells Argent. "It's not my business to know where he does his unwinding, as long as I get paid for the AWOLs I bring him." And although Argent has a curious streak, the last thing he'd ever want would be a tour of a black-market harvest camp.

"You will please be his guests at his private residence until he should return," they are told, and are given the keys to a dealership Porsche to make the drive. Argent's the one who grabs the keys from the man's hands, but gives them to Nelson, knowing the alternative would be getting tranq'd again. Shocking the monkey has apparently paid off.

"Sweet ride, but isn't he afraid we might steal it?" Argent

asks Nelson as they take to the road. Nelson laughs at the suggestion and doesn't dignify him with an answer.

The residence turns out to be a simple A-frame cabin on a wooded bluff overlooking Lake Huron, four hours north of Sarnia. The cabin appears unremarkable and indistinguishable from all the other woodsy A-frames in the area. Argent is profoundly disappointed.

"He lives in that thing? We drove all the way here for this?"

The first hint that things are not as they seem is the butler who greets them. Argent finds it odd that a structure this small would require a servant. Then, once they enter the "cabin," all of Argent's perceptions and assumptions take a dramatic shift.

The angular A of the cabin is very literally the tip of the iceberg, because its ever-widening base extends underground for three more stories, creating space within the structure at least ten times its appearance from the outside. Inconspicuous windows are carved into the stone of the bluff, giving the "cabin" a glorious view of the lake, and the décor could match the ritziest of mountain lodges. Everything's crafted from fine polished wood. The walls are festooned with the mounted heads of a tiger, a rhino, a polar bear, and a dozen other extinct species.

"So Divan hunts?" Argent asks the butler as they descend a grand staircase into the expansive living room.

The man turns up his nose, offended. "Hardly. He *collects*."

There are other staff members to round out the crew. A maid who seems to endlessly dust, and a chef about as intimidating as an executioner, but who prepares a dinner for them that tastes better than anything Argent has ever eaten. Never in his life has he experienced this kind of first-class treatment or seen this kind of wealth. He concludes that for Divan, business must be very good.

• • •

They are given the white-glove treatment for four days.

Four days of leisurely living with no sign of the master of the house. Nelson, who has, by and large, been able to avoid contact with Argent except for meals, now becomes increasingly impatient. Maybe even a little bit nervous.

"He knows I was coming—he's never kept me waiting for this long," Nelson comments over lunch. He's barely able to sit for the meal, pacing, looking out of the windows at the windswept lake.

"Maybe he's just busy. A guy like him's gotta prioritize, right?" But Argent knows what Nelson is thinking. Divan is punishing him for showing up without Connor Lassiter. *Well,* thinks Argent, *if hanging here is punishment, then make me suffer!*

Divan finally arrives later that day by seaplane. Argent watches through a window as the small craft pulls up to the simple wooden dock that extends from the base of the bluff. Like the outward appearance of the cabin, the plane is neither ostentatious nor extreme. It's similar to other seaplanes Argent has seen traversing the lake. Apparently the only conspicuous show of extravagance Divan allows himself is the fleet of cars, which he keeps parked in an underground garage—but even then, they're all Porsches, playing into his cover story.

Argent hurries off to brush his hair and change into some of the fresh clothes that have been supplied for him—dark slacks and starched button-down shirts. Not his style, but maybe his style needs some changing.

He returns to find himself late for Divan's entrance. Nelson stands in the grand living room already talking to him. The man has jet-black hair, a toned physique, and wears an expensive silk suit that seems not to have a single wrinkle from his travels. He is impressive, and Argent now wishes he'd had the good sense to put on a tie.

"Ah," says Divan when he sees him, "this must be the

young man you've been telling me about." Like most of his employees, there is something European in his accent that's not easy to place, although Divan's English is much better.

"Y . . . you've been talking about me?" Argent doesn't want to imagine what Nelson might have said. Divan holds out his hand to Argent, and Argent reaches out his own to shake— but Divan shifts his hand at the last instant, and Argent grabs it wrong, making the handshake awkward, and making Argent somehow feel less than worthy of the greeting. Divan does not seem like a man who does anything by mistake, and Argent wonders if Divan created the awkward grasp intentionally to keep him off-balance.

"I understand you helped to catch several AWOLs."

"Yes, sir," Argent says. "Actually, I didn't *help* catch them, I caught them, period." He glances at Nelson almost involuntarily, and Nelson gives him a lukewarm *no comment* sort of gaze.

"I'm learning quickly," Argent says, and, assessing that some brown-nosing might be in order, he adds, "I've got a good teacher."

"The best," Divan says, nodding toward Nelson. "Even if the Akron AWOL still eludes him." Divan takes a moment to let that sink in, and to size them both up. Then he says to Nelson, "Can I assume there's a story to the wounds on the left half of your face, and the right half of the boy's?"

"Two different stories," Argent chimes in, "but Connor Lassiter plays into both of them."

Nelson cracks his neck. Argent suspects that if Divan were not here, Nelson would tranq him for talking out of turn. "The only story that Divan needs to hear," says Nelson, "is the one about your sister's tracking chip."

Divan smiles. "It sounds like a story worth hearing."

But apparently he has no interest in hearing it now. Instead he goes off to freshen up for dinner, leaving Argent alone with

Nelson. Argent braces for some sort of verbal abuse.

"That went well, right?" says Argent. He figures Nelson will ignore him at best, but instead Nelson smiles.

"It will only get better."

And although Argent can deal with Nelson's frowns and reprimands, he finds Nelson's smile as disconcerting as his botched handshake with Divan.

For dinner there are lamb chops as large as rib eye steaks.

"Neoteny lamb," Divan explains, "genetically altered to grow as large as sheep while maintaining their early characteristics. The meat is flavorful and tender because although the lambs grow, they don't grow up." He digs a knife into a bloody-rare filet. "Much the opposite of your friend Lev," he says to Nelson. "Who I understand will age but not grow."

The mention of Lev's name has the desired effect. Nelson becomes stiff and prickly. Argent takes some pleasure in seeing Nelson under someone else's thumb.

"After I capture Lassiter," Nelson says, "I intend to find Lev Calder as well."

"One prize at a time, Jasper."

Argent waits to be asked about the tracking chip. He has resolved not to volunteer the information until he's asked, and even then he won't give it up without getting something substantial in return. After all, it's his only bargaining chip. They don't ask him at dinner, though. Not Divan, not Nelson. Then, after a creamy dessert that Argent can't pronounce, Divan goes off with Nelson to discuss business.

"We'll talk later," Divan tells Argent. "Until then, feel free to entertain yourself. Have you discovered the game room?"

"It's like my second home."

Divan seems pleased. "It's there for you to enjoy. I built it for my nephews, but they do not visit." And then a heavy sigh. "Alas, my family and I are a bit estranged."

"Because of . . . what you do?" Argent can't help but ask.

"No. Because of what I choose *not* to do. I've taken a path of greater integrity than they would prefer." And although Argent can't imagine what could possibly have less integrity than Divan's current profession, he explains no further, and Nelson's glare makes it clear it's better not to ask.

True to his word, Divan calls for Argent an hour later. They meet in his garden, a glass atrium attached to the cabin. It's surrounded by dense privet hedges to hide it from the outside world, and is temperature-controlled to protect the exotic plants contained within. Apparently Divan collects living things in addition to the dead ones that hang on the walls of his home. Argent imagines the plants must be vibrant and colorful during the day, but are now subdued by the deepening twilight.

"Come sit. I hope you like espresso."

A servant pours coffee as black as tar from a silver pot into small porcelain cups as Argent sits across from Divan. Argent knows it will keep him up all night, but he won't refuse anything Divan offers him.

"Congratulations are in order," Divan says. "I've been informed that the AWOLs you caught are top specimens. Bringing six Unwinds in one trip is a nice haul."

"Five—but next time it'll be at least six."

Divan rubs a bit of lemon rind around the outside of his cup. Argent does the same, just so he doesn't appear uncultured. The man takes his time then, discussing the subtle differences in espresso roasts and the best conditions for the beans' growth. He not so much beats around the bush as avoids it entirely, as if they have nothing more important to talk about. Argent's anxiety builds with every moment the subject of his sister is not broached. But he still will not be the one to broach it.

"My garden here is a bit of a paradox," Divan says. "I come here for peace and solitude, and yet in this garden, one is never alone."

Argent looks to see that the servant has left, so, in fact, they are alone. He assumes Divan is speaking in a philosophical way.

"So . . . ," Argent prompts, getting more anxious as their coffee talk meanders on, "is there something we're here to talk about?"

"The unintended consequences of our actions," Divan responds, as if he was patiently waiting to be asked the question. "Take, for example, the specimens in my garden. While many are natural cuttings taken from around the world, there are others that have a different origin." He pauses to take a slow sip from his small cup. "There was a rather nasty Internet hoax before the Heartland War—you might have heard of it. A thing called 'bonsai cats.' A website presented a method of potting a live cat in a jar, effectively turning it into a houseplant. According to the website, the poor creature would grow within the constraints of the jar, becoming accustomed to its peculiar circumstance. People, of course were outraged at the suggestion, and rightly so."

"Wait a second," says Argent, feeling as if he'd been asked a trick question. "I thought bonsai cats were real."

"Ah," says Divan. "That's the interesting part. You see, the concept was so thoroughly thought-out, and the instructions so precise, that people were intrigued—and what began as a sick joke became all too real." He finishes his espresso, puts the cup down on the saucer with a delicate *clink*, and zeroes his eyes on Argent in a way that makes him want to squirm. "That hideous practice of growing potted felines—do you know where it first took root as a commercial endeavor?"

"No."

"Burma," Divan tells him. "And as the black-market business grew, it shifted to something more profitable. The organization began to dabble in the illicit sale of human flesh."

Argent finally connects the dots. "The Burmese Dah Zey!"

"Precisely," says Divan.

Argent has been intrigued by the Burmese flesh market since he was a child. Their unwinding practices make everything else look tame. There are stories of how anesthesia is rarely used, if ever. Stories of how they only sell a part of you at a time. Today they'll take your hands, tomorrow your feet, the next day a lung, keeping you alive through all of it, down to the moment the last part of you, whatever it happens to be, is sold and shipped out. To be unwound on the Burmese Dah Zey is to die a hundred times before death truly takes root.

"And so," continues Divan, "what began as one man's Internet hoax not only became real, but evolved into the most heinous organization in the world. Here is a lesson to be learned: We must always be careful of the actions we take, for there are always unintended consequences. Sometimes they are serendipitous, other times they are appalling, but those consequences are always there. We must tread lightly in this world, Argent, until we are sure of foot."

"Are you sure of foot, sir?"

"Very."

Then he touches a button on a remote, bringing up the lights in the atrium. As the space illuminates, the plants grow bright and beautiful. Truly breathtaking. And there in the corners stand four large ceramic vases about five feet high. Argent noticed them before, but not what they contained. Protruding from the tops of the ceramic jars are four human heads. It only takes a moment for Argent to realize that they are alive, and the rest of their bodies are trapped within the ceramic vases, which taper so that the openings are like tight collars around the prisoners' necks. Argent gasps, both horrified and amazed.

Divan rises and gestures for Argent to do so as well. "Don't be afraid, they won't hurt you."

They are all male, with bronze skin and Asian features. Argent tentatively approaches the nearest one. The man eyes Argent with a sort of dull disinterest, a look that must be the residue of evaporated hope.

"These men were sent by the Dah Zey to kill me." Divan explains. "You see, I am the Dah Zey's only real competition, and so if they take me out, they control the world's black-market flesh supply. Once I caught these assassins, I followed the Dah Zey's own bonsai process as best I could with grown men, and sent the Dah Zey a nice thank-you note."

Then he grabs a bowl of small brown cubes from the table. Argent had thought they were sugar cubes. "Nutritional chews," Divan tells him. "I hired a dietitian to make sure I could provide them a healthy diet, appropriate for their unique condition." He brings a cube toward the potted assassin, and the man opens his mouth, allowing himself to be hand-fed by Divan. "They put up a fuss at first, but they adapted, as people do. There's a Zen-like peace to them now, don't you think? Like monks in perpetual meditation."

Divan goes from vase to vase. He talks to them gently as one might talk to a beloved pet. The men don't speak at all; they just wait to be fed. Argent wonders whether their vocal cords have been removed, or if it is simply that when you've been turned into a houseplant, you've got nothing left to say. Argent is relieved that Divan doesn't ask him to help feed the bonsai men.

"I have relatives who believe I should join with the Dah Zey," Divan says, with more than a little bitterness, "but I refuse to ever become the kind of monster who would subject children to the inhumane practices of the Dah Zey. Their way is not, nor will it ever be, my way." He keeps feeding his prize "plants" until the bowl of chews is empty. Argent finds his legs shaky and has to sit down. "This is a business, yes, but it must be humane," Divan insists. "More humane, even, than your Juvenile Authority, or the European Jugenpol, or the Chinese Láng-Få. This is my wish. It is, I believe, a battle worth fighting for."

"Why are you telling me all this?"

Divan sits across from him once more. "Well, you have something important to tell me, do you not? I feel it's only fair for me to share something important with you first. So we might be on even ground." Then he leans back and crosses his arms. "So, shall we discuss your sister?"

Argent had it all worked out. He was going to ask for money before giving away the code to access Grace's tracking chip. And maybe a car. He was going to ask for a supply contract with Divan so he could go out on his own as a parts pirate.

But Divan's openness—it changes everything. Argent knows he should be horrified by the four men ensconced around them, but instead, all he feels is admiration for Divan. The man didn't kill his enemies; he subdued them. He didn't give in to the evil methods of the Dah Zey; instead he set himself as the world's last defense against them. Argent realizes he can't make demands of this man. Only by his willingness to give, will Argent receive.

"R-O-N-A-E-L-E-one-two-one-five," Argent says. "It's Grace's middle name spelled backwards, and her birthday. Code that into the InStaTrac website, and if the chip is still active, it'll give you her location down to the inch. When you find her, I guarantee you'll find Connor."

Divan pulls out a pen and pad, writes the information down, then calls for a servant to come take it, instructing him to give it to Nelson immediately.

"Once we've got a location, Nelson and I should leave right away," Argent suggests.

"Ah, well—I'm afraid the unintended consequences of your own actions preclude that," Divan says. "I'm speaking of that picture you posted of yourself and Connor Lassiter."

Argent grimaces. He's done stupid things in his life, but that may have been the stupidest—but who could blame him: He was starstruck by being in the presence of his then-hero.

"Your actions resulted in alerting the world that Lassiter is still alive, and has made tracking him down a race between the Juvenile Authority and our friend Jasper. Then, of course, there's fact that you withheld this information about your sister from him, which he is very sore about. It makes a continued partnership between the two of you untenable."

Argent swallows hard. His hands shake a bit, and he tells himself it's because of the espresso.

"Fine, so I won't go with him. I'll go out alone—I'll bring you back tons of AWOLs. You saw how good I am at it, right? I could be one of your best suppliers!"

Divan sighs. "I'm sure you could be. However, my arrangement with Jasper makes that impossible as well."

"Wait—what arrangement?"

But the sympathetic look on Divan's face makes the truth all too clear. Whatever that arrangement is, it doesn't involve things ending well for Argent. He tries to rise—as if there were somewhere to run—but he can't get up. He can't even feel his legs. He tries to lift his arms, but they just hang scarecrow-limp by his side. It takes all his effort just to remain upright in the chair.

"Never trust espresso," Divan tells him. "Its bitter taste can mask a multitude of things. This time, it masked a powerful muscle relaxant—a natural compound—designed to calm you and ease your handling."

Argent glances to the dull-eyed bonsai over Divan's shoulder. "Are you going to make me one of them? I won't make a good potted boy," Argent pleads.

"Of course not," Divan says with compassion that must be well practiced. "That's only for my enemies. I do not see you as an enemy, Argent. You are, however, a commodity."

Argent loses the battle with gravity, and falls to the soft grass. Divan kneels beside him. "Your name means 'silver,' but sadly, as an Unwind, I suspect you'll be worth little more than brass."

And then something Divan had said when they first sat down comes back to him. Divan spoke of the six Unwinds that Argent provided. Argent is the sixth. Divan does not do anything by mistake.

Servants arrive to take Argent away. "Please," he says, his teeth locked and his voice beginning to slur. "Please . . ." But the only answer he receives are the dispassionate stares from the bonsai . . . and as he's carried off, Argent holds on to the last glimmer of light left to him. Whatever happens now, he knows he'll receive mercy. Divan is all about mercy.

Part Three

A Path to Penance

BELGIUM FIRST COUNTRY TO ALLOW EUTHANASIA FOR CHILDREN

By David Harding / *New York Daily News*

Saturday, December 14, 2013 2:43 PM

Belgium has voted to extend euthanasia laws to cover children.

The Belgian Senate backed the plan on Friday, which means the controversial law will now cover terminally ill children.

It means Belgium is the first country in the world to remove any age limits on euthanasia. The country first adopted euthanasia in 2002, but restricted it to those over 18. . . .

Any child seeking euthanasia under the law must understand what is meant by euthanasia and the decision must be agreed by their parents.

Their illness must also be terminal.

Belgium recorded over 1,400 cases of euthanasia in 2012. . . .

The full article can be found at: *http://www.nydaily-news.com/life-style/health/belgium-country-euthana-sia-children -article-1.1547809#ixzz2qur84gzr*

18 · Cam

Meals with Roberta on the veranda. Always so formal. Always so genteel. Always a reminder to Cam that he is forever beneath her thumb. Even when he's miles away at West Point, he knows he will still feel her manipulations. Her puppeteer's strings are woven through his mind just as effectively as the "worm" that makes him forget that which is truly important.

During breakfast, a few days before he's scheduled to leave, he asks her the question point-blank. The question that sits between them at every meal like a glass of poison that neither is willing to touch.

"What was her name?"

He doesn't expect an answer. He knows Roberta will evade.

"You're leaving for a grand new life soon. What's the point?"

"There's no point—I just want to hear you say it."

Roberta takes a small bite of her eggs Benedict and puts down the fork. "Even if I tell you, the nanites will break the synapses and rob the memory within seconds."

"Tell me anyway."

Roberta sighs, crosses her arms, and to Cam's amazement, says, "Her name was Risa Ward."

. . . but the moment the words are spoken, they're gone from his mind, leaving him to wonder if she had told him at all.

"What was her name?" he asks again.

"Risa Ward."

"What was her name?"

"Risa Ward."

"WHAT WAS HER NAME?!"

Roberta shakes her head in a belittling show of pity. "You see, it's no use. Best to spend your time thinking of your future, Cam, not the past."

He looks at his plate feeling anything but hungry. From deep within him comes a desperate whisper of a question. He can't even remember why he's asking it, but it must have some significance, mustn't it?

"What . . . was . . . her . . . name?"

"I have no idea what you're talking about." Roberta says. "Now finish up—we have a lot to do before you leave."

19 · Risa

The girl who Cam can't remember is running for her life.

It was a bad idea—actually, a whole series of them—that brought her to this circumstance. Only now does Risa comprehend how monumentally bad those ideas were, as she races from armed security guards in a massive research hospital complex. There are windows, but they only look out on other wings of the complex, so there's no way to get one's bearings. Risa is convinced they're running in circles, spiraling toward inevitable doom.

There was little choice but to go on this fool's mission.

If the organ printer arrived as stillborn technology when they made their grand play, then all their efforts will have been for naught. It was crucial that they find a way to test it, for only by demonstrating what it could do, would the world sit up and take notice.

"Making sure it works should have been *your* job," Connor pointed out to Sonia as they discussed it in a relatively private corner of her basement. "You've been sitting on the thing for thirty years—you could have checked that it worked before you brought us into it."

Sonia glared at him. "So sue me," she said, and then added, "Oh, that's right, you can't—because for the past two years you've had the legal status of a canned ham."

Connor matched her glare, dagger for dagger, until Sonia backed down. "I never thought I'd get the chance to bring it out again," she said, "so I never bothered."

"What changed?" Connor asked.

"You showed up."

Although Connor couldn't get why that should matter, Risa did. It's their notoriety that makes all the difference. They have become the royalty of AWOLs. Attach their names to something, and suddenly people listen, whether they want to or not.

"OSU Medical Center," Sonia said, "is one of the only research hospitals in the Midwest that does curative biological research. Everyone else is just trying to figure out better ways of using parts from Unwinds. Plenty of funding for that—but try to fund alternatives, and you get nothing but tumbleweeds."

"OSU? Connor said. "As in Ohio State University? As in, the one in Columbus?"

"You got a problem with that?" Sonia asked. Connor gave her no answer.

She went on to tell them of one rogue doctor who was still seeking cures for systemic diseases, the kind that can't be cured by transplantation. "And guess what's at the heart of that research?" Sonia asked mischievously. The answer, of course, was adult pluripotent stem cells—the very sort of cells needed for the printer.

They had to talk Sonia out of going after the cells herself. A few days before, she had twisted her ankle and bruised her hip in a fall that no one had seen, probably back at her home. She tried to downplay it, but clearly she'd been in pain ever since. She couldn't go, but someone had to.

They discussed the possibility of sending some of the kids from the basement to retrieve the biomatter, but they didn't discuss it for long. This batch of AWOLs wasn't exactly the secret-mission type. Risa hated to judge any AWOLs the way the world judged them, but these poor kids had none of the skill sets needed to pull it off, and a grab bag of personal issues that would do nothing but hinder them. The kids in Sonia's basement would be liabilities on this mission. All of them, that is, except for Beau. For all his cockiness, he was capable—but was he capable enough to pull this off? Risa didn't think so.

"I'll go," Risa offered. Bad idea number one.

"I'll go with you," Connor chimed in. Bad idea number two.

Sonia raged about it, insisting that they'd be recognized, and that, of all the people who *shouldn't* go, Connor and Risa topped the list. She was, of course, right.

"Well, *I* ain't going," Grace was quick to announce. "I've had quite enough excitement over the past few weeks, thank you very much." To Sonia's absolute chagrin, Grace had appointed herself as Sonia's personal caregiver, minding that she didn't fall again.

"I don't need a nursemaid!" Sonia kept telling her, which just doubled Grace's resolve.

Risa knew a team of two was iffy. They needed at least one more as a fail-safe. And so Risa suggested that Beau be added to team. Bad idea number three.

"Are you kidding me? You want to ask Beau to come?" Connor said back in the basement. He raised his eyebrows at Risa. "Beau? Really?" He was amused, and it ticked Risa off.

"We're going to have to interact out there—we need at least one face that people aren't currently wearing on T-shirts." Connor couldn't argue with that logic.

Beau, of course, was thrilled to be included, although he tried to feign being blasé. "I'll drive," he proclaimed.

"You'll sit in the back," Connor told him, then handed him an old GPS he had pulled from a bin of marginal technology in Sonia's shop. "We'll need you to navigate."

Risa had to grin at the way Connor put Beau in his place without making him lose face.

It was Sonia's idea to arm them all with tranq-loaded pistols. Risa couldn't stand the things, because they reminded her of the Juvies. She hated the idea of using the Juvenile Authority's weapon of choice.

"Tranqs are quick, effective, and leave no mess, and even a peripheral hit does the job," Sonia told her. "That's why the Juvies use them."

Risa was quick to remove the tranqs from Beau's gun when he wasn't looking. The last thing she or Connor wanted was a trigger-happy Beau.

That was this morning. Now as they run through the hospital complex, Beau insists he knows where he's going even though neither of them has a clue about the mazelike facility. The blueprint they studied in preparation was hopelessly out of date and didn't include the newer buildings, or renovations in the older ones.

It's Sunday, and the particular office wing they've barged into is full of empty waiting rooms with generic art prints on the walls. Another place that's not on the map they studied.

"This way!" Beau says, and although Risa's sure it's going to take them back where they've been, she goes along, because at this point, any direction seems as good as another. She can only hope that Connor, wherever he is, hasn't been caught.

Connor took a different passageway—one that theoretically leads to the research wing of the massive complex. They hadn't planned on splitting up, but Connor had already turned a corner when a hospital rent-a-cop spotted Risa and Beau. Since the guard hadn't seen Connor, it seemed the clear choice to Risa that she and Beau act as decoys, luring the somewhat hefty guard away. The trick is to stay far enough ahead not to be caught, but close enough so that the guard doesn't give up the chase and go for donuts in the cafeteria, maybe encountering Connor along the way. The guard, however, is determined, and soon he's joined by a slimmer, faster comrade. That's when things begin to get serious.

Risa and Beau come to a dead end in the radiology wing. A locked door. The only way out is the way they came. The moment they turn, the two guards come around the corner, and, seeing that the two kids are cornered, they slow down and get a little smug in anticipation of the capture.

"Gave us a good workout, didn'tcha!" the chubby one says, huffing and puffing.

"Put your hands where we can see them," says the slim one.

Risa turns to Beau and speaks under her breath. "We'll talk our way out of it," she says. "We haven't done anything but make them chase us. If they don't recognize me . . ."

As the guards get closer, Risa sees a determined look in Beau's eye, and his hand is still in the pocket of his hoodie.

"No one runs without a reason," says the chubby one. "My bet is that you're a couple of AWOLs, aren'tcha!"

"Hands where we can see them!" insists the other again, unsnapping the holster on his weapon.

So Beau pulls out his hand. And in his hand is a pistol. And he aims that pistol at the slim rent-a-cop. Bad idea number four.

Beau levels his pistol at the slim guard. Risa knows exactly how this will go down, and she can only hope that the rent-a-cops are armed with tranqs and not real bullets—but she doubts it. The instant the targeted guard sees the weapon in Beau's hand, he reaches for his own gun. So Beau pulls the trigger—

—and to Risa's amazement, Beau's pistol goes off! She hears the telltale *PFFFT!* of a tranq shot. It hits the guard in the shoulder, before he can raise his own gun—and in a second he's down on his knees, and in another second, he's falling facedown onto the institutionally carpeted floor, unconscious.

The other cop, who probably never actually had to draw a gun in his life, is fumbling with the holster, and Beau tranqs him right in the chest. The man lets out a squeak that sounds like "Pshaw," stumbles a bit like a dying diva, and falls back against the wall, sliding to the ground, out cold.

"C'mon," Beau says, "let's get out of here." He takes her hand and pulls her away from the scene. She's too flabbergasted to resist his grasp.

"But . . . but how . . . ?"

"You think I didn't know what you did? I wasn't coming in here with an empty gun!"

Risa finally pulls out of his grasp and turns around.

"What are you doing?"

"We can't just leave them there," she says. "Someone will find them. We need to hide them."

Beau goes back with her, and together they drag the men down the hall. Then, when a faint voice comes through one of the guard's earpieces, asking for the status of the "unsubs," Beau grabs it and says in a very convincing voice, "Ten-four. Just a couple of local ferals. They ran out a back door. Not our problem anymore."

"Amen to that," says the voice on the other end, and they've bought themselves at least ten minutes until someone wonders about the two guards' mysterious disappearance.

"Ten-four?" Risa asks. "Did you actually say ten-four?"

Beau shrugs. "It worked, didn't it?"

They put the thin guard inside a wooden toy box in a

deserted pediatric waiting room. The corpulent one fits nicely in the cabinet underneath a huge fish tank, ironically populated by puffer fish that somewhat resemble the man.

Now that the unconscious guards are safely tucked away, Risa begins to relax. There's an exhilaration to a narrow escape that Risa had almost forgotten. A physiological payoff to the adrenaline rush of danger.

Beau, feeling his own relief, begins to laugh. It makes Risa laugh in spite of herself, which makes Beau laugh even harder, pushing Risa toward an unwanted giggle fit that is suddenly silenced by Beau grabbing her and kissing her.

Her response is immediate and reflexive—although even if it wasn't a reflex, she's pretty sure she would have done the same thing. She pushes him off and pops him in the eye with such force that his neck snaps back and his head hits the fish tank with a *thud*, scattering puffer fish in all directions. Risa doesn't want to stay for whatever the aftermath will be—apologetic or angry, she doesn't care. She storms away.

"Risa, wait!"

Of all the things to deal with at this particular moment, why must she have to suffer the advances of yet another hormonal douche?

"Risa!"

She turns to him with fury and has to restrain herself from slugging him again. "Are you an idiot? Stop saying my name! They don't know who we are, and if there happens to be anyone in these offices who can hear you . . ."

"Sorry." His eye is already swelling. Good.

"If Connor had seen that, your face would look a whole lot worse!" she tells him.

"It was a spur-of-the-moment thing."

"Why is it that every loser with a penis feels the obligation to put moves on me?"

He looks at her like the answer is obvious. "Because you're Risa Ward," he says. "And whatever happens now, I'll go to my grave knowing that once—just once—I kissed the one and only Risa Ward."

"You'll go to your grave?" says Risa, still outrageously bitter about the whole thing. "That's just wishful thinking. More likely your memories will get ripped out and planted in someone else's head!"

"Maybe, maybe not," he tells her. Then he finally reaches up to touch his swelling eye. He doesn't seem angry that she hit him. It's as if the act was well worth the consequences.

Risa feels a buzz in her pocket and pulls out the old flip phone Sonia gave them. Such phones and the fading providers that serviced them were considered "retirement sector technology." They were perfect for communicating under the radar, because the network was too antiquated for the Juvies to bother with.

"*U OK?*" reads Connor's text.

She lets out a breath of relief to know that he hasn't been caught. "*YES, U?*" She texts back.

"*FOUND THE LAB,*" he texts. "*MEET U AT CAR.*"

And although she doesn't want to just leave him, she knows further wandering through the hospital will just jeopardize things.

"Is that him?" Beau asks. "What does he say?"

"He says you're a lousy kisser, and I have to agree."

Beau gives a halfhearted laugh, maybe thinking that she forgives him a little. Which she doesn't. She realizes she doesn't care enough to hate him or to forgive him.

"We'll take the nearest stairs down," Risa says, "then slip out a back way—just like you told them we did. We'll meet Connor at the car."

He nods, accepting the plan, but then he's got to go ask, "What if Connor doesn't show?"

"You want another black eye?" Risa says, and so he backs down from the question, and opens the stairwell door for her.

"Oh, and for the record, I'm not a loser," Beau tells her. "No matter what my unwind order says."

20 · Connor

The plan is simple. Plans can be simple when you're dealing with the human mechanics of an institution that has no reason to expect intrigue and subterfuge. The hospital personnel are more on the lookout for slippery floors that might lead to lawsuits than for AWOLs stealing biomatter. Why on earth would anyone want to do that?

When Risa and Beau were spotted by security, Risa made the right decision to lure security away. It wasn't like the guard had any idea who they were and what they were up to. Of course, Connor's instinct was to go after Risa, but he knew it would be the wrong thing to do. That could just result in all of them getting caught. He had to trust that Risa was clever enough to play a successful cat and mouse, even if Beau couldn't.

Connor now wanders down corridors in the wings that don't cater to inpatients. It's mostly deserted on a Sunday. He finds the research building, connected to the rest of the complex by a glass-enclosed skywalk—which would give the world a clear view of him, if anyone in the world was looking. If someone is, he'll know soon enough.

He finds the lab he's looking for in the basement. While the rest of the research building is richly appointed, the basement is utilitarian and institutional. Dimly lit corridors floored with puke-colored linoleum tiles. The low-rent district of an otherwise upscale facility. Apparently the rogue research team that insisted on playing with pointless cellular manipulation is kept out of sight as an embarrassment to medical science. Shunned as if they were studying the use of leeches and snake oil.

There seems to be barely any security down here. The lab has a lock with no alarm, and it's easily picked—and with security focused on Risa and Beau, the basement of the research building is as silent as a morgue, which is probably in another basement not too far away.

He takes a gamble and texts Risa that he's found the lab, and he'll meet them at the car. If she's been caught, that text will give him away to whoever caught her, but he has to have faith that she evaded the slow-moving guard that was in pursuit. He waits for an agonizing few moments until she texts back "*K*," then he releases his breath, not even realizing he had been holding it.

He opens the door of the lab and flicks on a light. It's a simple repository of specimens in glass-front refrigerators. There are racks of test tubes, and petri dishes growing questionable cultures. There are also specimens sealed in plastic stasis containers, and the sight of them makes Connor shudder. These are the same kind of containers that are used to transport unwound parts. Modern stasis containers can preserve living tissue almost indefinitely. It's one of the many unwind-related technologies that sprang up after the signing of the Unwind Accord.

Everything is labeled with numbered codes that mean nothing to Connor.

"Adult pluripotent stem cells," Sonia said. He knows he's in the right place, but things in this lab are labeled for the researchers, not for an intruder looking to steal something.

He has an expandable tote bag that he can load with as many specimens as he can fit. He decides to take only stasis containers—because specimens in test tubes and dishes probably won't survive any temperature change in transport. He fills his bag like the Grinch stealing Christmas—then suddenly the lab door opens, and he's caught red-handed with his hand in the biological cookie jar by a lab tech who is so shocked by Connor's unexpected presence that he drops the glass vials he's holding and they shatter on the ground.

"Don't move," says Connor, because clearly the man is going to bolt and probably call security. "I've got a gun." Connor reaches into his jacket pocket.

"N . . . no, you don't," says the nervous tech, calling his bluff.

So Connor pulls out his pistol, showing that he's not bluffing at all.

The guy gasps and begins to wheeze, reminding Connor of Emby, his old asthmatic friend.

It then occurs to Connor that this confrontation doesn't need to happen. As Sonia pointed out, tranqs aren't just for Juvies anymore. They can be an AWOL's best friend too.

"Sorry, man," Connor says, "but I've got to send you off to Tranqistan." And he pulls the trigger—only to find out that his gun isn't loaded. He looks at the weapon and realizes that this isn't the gun Sonia gave him at all. This is Beau's. The one that Risa emptied. *Crap.*

"Wait! I know who you are! You're the Akron AWOL!"

Double crap. "Don't be a moron! The Akron AWOL is hiding with the Hopi. Haven't you been watching the news?"

"Well, you're here, so the news is wrong. You're from around here, aren't you? They call you the Akron AWOL, but you lived in Columbus!"

What, does everyone in Columbus know that? Is his house like a freaking landmark now? "Shut the hell up, or I swear . . ." Connor considers knocking the guy out. He could certainly do it, but he waits to see how this unfolds before he takes such a drastic move.

The lab tech just looks at him, breathing uneasily, keeping his eyes locked on Connor. No movement on either of their parts. Then the man says, "You don't want those specimens—they're already differentiated. You want the ones at the far end."

Connor wasn't expecting this. "How do you know what I want?"

"There's only one thing the Akron AWOL would be looking for here," he says. "Pluripotent cells. To build organs. It won't make a difference, though. Organ-building technology was a total bust; all the research led nowhere."

Connor says nothing—but his silence telegraphs the truth.

"You know something, don't you?" the lab tech asks, and dares to take a step closer, excitement trumping caution. "You know something, or you wouldn't be here!"

Connor won't answer him or let on how troubled he is that his intentions are so transparent. "The door at the far end?"

He nods. Connor makes his way to the far end of the lab, keeping one eye on the lab tech as he removes the containers in his bag and refills it with containers pulled from the last cooler.

"One problem," the lab tech says. "Our biomaterial is monitored. If any of it goes missing, it gets reported. Our funding will probably get pulled."

Connor looks to the mess of broken glass by the front door. "What was in those?"

The tech looks over to the broken vials. "Biomatter." Then he nods and grins at Connor, catching on to his train of thought. "A whole lot of biomatter. I'll get hell for dropping that . . . and forgetting to measure how much was lost before I disposed of it."

"Yeah," says Connor, "too bad about that." And he finishes filling the bag. When he's done, he sees the lab tech has taken a position by the door, peering out of the little window like he's Connor's lookout.

"So," says Connor, "I was never here, right?"

The tech nods his agreement. "It's our secret . . . on one condition."

Connor doesn't like the sound that. He braces for some impossible request. "What?"

Then the tech timidly asks, "Can I . . . shake your hand?"

Connor laughs, so unexpected is the request. He's seen starstruck kids, but this guy is at least thirty. Then he sees that his laughter has embarrassed the man.

"Naah, forget it," the guy says. "It was stupid of me to ask."

"No, no, it's okay." Cautiously Connor approaches him, and holds out his hand. He shakes Connor's hand with his cold, damp one.

"A lot of folks don't like unwinding, but no one knows how to stop it, so they don't even try," the man says. And then he whispers, "But if you've got an idea—there are people ready to listen. Not everyone—but maybe enough."

"Thanks," Connor says, glad that he didn't tranq the guy—although he's still furious at Beau for switching guns.

Connor slips out, and the tech gets to cleaning the mess of broken vials on the floor, happily whistling to himself.

"A lot of people want to stop unwinding," the lab tech said. It's not the first time Connor has heard that. Maybe if he hears it enough, he might begin to believe it.

21 · Risa

The ride home from the hospital is a triumphant one. They play music that makes them feel cocooned in normality. Even though it's an illusion, Risa's happy for a respite from being "the one and only Risa Ward."

Connor tells her and Beau about the fanboy lab tech.

Connor seems to preen a bit in the light of it, but Risa has always found herself painfully out of her element when faced with such adulation. She never wanted to be some sort of counterculture heroine. All she wanted was to survive. She would have been happy to stay at Ohio State Home 23 playing piano, graduating with unremarkable grades, and then being dumped at eighteen into the grand mosh pit of mediocre mankind, like all other state wards. Maybe she could have gotten herself into community college, working her way through with some service job. She could have eventually become a concert pianist, or, more realistically, a keyboardist in some bar band. It wouldn't be ideal, but at least it would be a life. She could have eventually married the unremarkable guitar player and had some unremarkable kids, whom she would love dearly and would never even think of storking. But her unwind order severed all ties Risa had to the hope of a normal future.

Thoughts of a guitar player bring her musings around to Cam. Where is he now that Proactive Citizenry has him in their clutches again? Does she care? Should she care? What a mixed bag of connections she has. . . . It's as if her whole life has been rewound with the strangest bits and pieces of humanity, from Connor, to Cam, to Sonia, to Grace and all the odd acquaintances in between.

There's no telling what her life will be like a day from now, much less a year from now. That's the best argument for living in the moment, but how can you live in the moment when all you want is for the moment to end?

"You look sad," Connor comments. "You should be happy— for once we did something right."

Risa smiles. "We do a lot right," she tells him. "Why else would random people want to shake our hands?" *Or,* she thinks, *kiss us,* and she throws a chilly glance back to Beau in the backseat, who plays the air drums, completely oblivious.

Connor hasn't asked about Beau's black eye. Either he doesn't care, or he doesn't want to know. Risa wonders how many girls have thrown themselves at Connor in a similar way, and finds herself pleasantly jealous at the very idea. Pleasantly, because Risa has what those nameless girls could only grasp at: the Akron AWOL all to herself.

Maybe this is better than her dream of normal. Living a high-octane, on-the-edge sort of life has its perks. Namely, Connor.

"Hey, you know that Upchurch dude, right?" Beau asks between drum solos.

"Who?" asks Risa, having no clue what he's talking about.

"You know—Hayden Upchurch. The guy who gave the news a mouthful when he got caught at the Graveyard."

"Oh," says Risa. "Hayden." She had never known his last name—and by the look on Connor's face, he never had either. A lot of Unwinds tried to erase their last name in defiance of parents who tried to unwind them. In Hayden's case, he probably avoided it because it was so easily made fun of.

"What about him? Risa asks, looking nervously to Connor. "Did something happen to him?"

"No—he's just shooting off his mouth again."

The next song starts, and Connor turns the volume down. "How do you know that?"

"Back in the basement, Jake was fiddling with that old computer Sonia lets us use down there, and he says there was something up on the Web. He tried to find it again to show me, but it was gone. He said Upchurch was calling for a teen uprising, like he did when he got caught. I'm thinking it might happen." Beau considers it for a moment more. "If it does, I know a whole lot of kids—not just the kids at Sonia's, but kids back home, too—who'd follow me into battle."

"More likely off a cliff, like lemmings," Connor says.

"Careful," Beau warns, and he pulls out the pistol he had

taken from Connor, "or I might tranq you with your own gun, like you did to that Nelson guy."

Risa sees Connor's face go stony, and his knuckles whiten on the steering wheel. She touches Connor's leg to get him to relax. To remind him it's not worth it.

"Put that thing away," Risa orders Beau, "before you accidentally shoot yourself."

"Best thing that could happen," says Connor, with a deadpan delivery that could take the bounce out of a basketball. Then he softens. "But I'm glad to hear that Hayden's okay. That is, if it's true."

If Hayden's really AWOL again, hiding out somewhere and calling for kids to take matters into their own hands, Risa wonders how many will be moved to action. There are stories about the first uprising. "Feral" kids took violently to the streets after the school failures. They wreaked havoc coast to coast, spreading terror and fear enough to make unwinding sound like an answer to all their problems. Anger with no direction.

Once the Heartland War ended, no one really spoke about the days leading up to the Unwind Accord. Risa suspects it's more than just bad memories. If people don't think about it, then they can deny their complicity in ongoing institutional murder. *Well,* thinks Risa, *we'll make people remember . . . and we'll give them a path to penance.*

It's as they reach the outlying neighborhoods of Columbus that Connor veers out of their lane, nearly slamming into a pickup truck next to them. The guy leans on his horn, gives them the finger, and shouts curses at them that they can't hear but that are easily read on his lips.

"What was that about?" Risa asks, realizing that Connor was distracted when he veered out of their lane.

"Nothing!" snaps Connor. "Why does it have to be about anything?"

"I told you I should be the one driving," says Beau.

Risa drops it, sensing something in Connor that's best left alone—but the moment lingers long after they're past the road sign above the freeway that Connor was staring at with such intensity it nearly got them killed.

22 · Connor

He steps back and allows Sonia to transfer the biomatter from the stasis container to the printer. He doesn't want to touch it.

"The stuff of life," Sonia says as she pours the red, syrupy suspension into the printer reservoir. It's not exactly the most hygienic of transfers, but then, they're in the back room of a cluttered antique shop, not a laboratory.

"It looks like the Blob," Grace comments.

Connor recalls the old movie about a flesh-eating mass of gelatinous space-goo that devours the hapless residents of a town that very well could have been Akron. He watched it with his brother when they were little. Lucas kept hiding his face in Connor's shoulder so he didn't have to look. Like all his memories before the unwind order, it comes with a mix of feelings as amorphous as the Blob.

Risa takes Connor's hand. "I hope it's worth what we went through to get it."

It's just after dark, and it's the four of them: Connor, Risa, Sonia, and Grace. Beau was quickly dispatched by Sonia to resolve some sort of petty territorial dispute in the basement that arose in his absence. "It all goes to hell without you down there, Beau," Sonia told him. "I need you to take charge and bring things back to order." Connor turned away when she said it, because his grin might have given Beau a clue as to how easily he was being manipulated. Beau knew the goal of their mission, but not the purpose of the cells they retrieved.

"Injection for my hip," Sonia had told him, "so I don't need a hip replacement from some poor unlucky unwind."

He had accepted the explanation at face value, partly because it sounded plausible under the circumstances, but mostly because Sonia is an accomplished liar. Probably half of her success as an antiques dealer comes from the lies she tells about her merchandise. Not to mention her success in harboring fugitive kids.

With the magic blob safely in the printer, Sonia turns to them. "So who would like to do the honors?"

Connor, who is closest to the controls, hits the "on" button, hesitates for a breath, then hits the little green button labeled "print." The device clicks and whirrs to life, making them all jump just the tiniest bit. Could it be as simple as hitting the "print" button? He supposes the most advanced of technology all comes down to a human being hitting a button or throwing a switch.

"What's it gonna make?" Grace asks—a question that's on all of their minds.

Sonia shrugs. "Whatever Janson last programmed it to make."

Her eyes seem to lose some of their light for a moment as she struggles with the memory of her husband. He's been dead for maybe thirty years, but clearly their devotion ran deeper than time.

They watch as the printer head flies back and forth over a petri dish, laying down microscopic layers of cells. In a few minutes the pale ghost of a shape appears. Oblong, about three inches across.

Risa gets it first. "Is that . . . an ear?"

"I do believe it is," Sonia says.

There's something wonderful and terrifying about this. Like watching life emerging from the first primordial pool.

"So it works," Connor says, finding he doesn't have patience for the printing process. Sonia says nothing, holding judgment for the fifteen minutes it takes for the printer to complete its cycle. The sudden silence when it's done is just as jarring as when it first grinded to life.

Before them in the dish is, as Risa predicted, an ear.

"Can it hear us?" Grace asks, leaning forward. "Hello?" she says into it.

Connor gently grabs her shoulder and pulls her back.

"It's just a pinna," says Sonia. "The outside part of an ear. It has none of the functional parts of the organ."

"It doesn't look too healthy," Risa points out. She's right. It looks pale and slightly gray.

"Hmm . . ." Sonia pulls out her reading glasses, slips them on, and leans closer to observe the thing. "It has no blood supply. And we didn't prepare the cells to properly differentiate into skin and cartilage—but that doesn't matter. All that matters is that it does exactly what it was designed to do."

Then she reaches out, picks the ear up between her thumb and forefinger, and drops it into the stasis container, where it sinks into the thick green oxygenated gel. Connor closes the box, it seals, and the light indicating hibernation goes green. Now it will be preserved for however long it needs to be.

"We're going to have to get this to a place that can mass-produce it, right?" Connor says. "Some big medical manufacturer."

"Nope," says Grace. "Big is bad, big is bad." She furrows her brow and rings her hands as she looks at the stasis box. "Can't go too small, either. Kinda like Goldilocks, it's gotta be just right."

Sonia, who is rarely impressed by anything, is impressed by Grace's assessment. "A very good point. It needs to be a company that's hungry, but not so hungry that it carries no clout."

"And," adds Risa, "it has to be a company with no ties to Proactive Citizenry."

"Does such a thing even exist?" asks Connor.

"Don't know," says Sonia. "Wherever we go, it will be a gamble. The best we can do is better the odds."

The thought gives Connor an unexpected shiver that must be strong enough for Risa to feel because she looks to him. So much of his life these past few years has been a gamble. Somehow in spite of the odds, he's managed to come through it all in once piece. What felt like bad luck at the time ultimately became good fortune, as evidenced by his continued survival. Which means he's overdue for something truly unfortunate. He can't help but feel that no matter what he does, he's still just circling the drain. He silently curses his parents for pulling the plug on that drain to begin with. And with that anger comes a sorrow that he wishes he were strong enough to ignore.

"Something wrong?" Risa asks.

Connor withdraws his hand from hers. "Why do you always think something's wrong with me?"

"Because something always is," she says, a little miffed. "You're a streaming meme of things that are wrong."

"And you're not?"

Risa sighs. "I am too. Which is why it's so easy for me to know when something's bothering you."

"Well, this time, you're wrong." Connor gets up and goes to the trapdoor. The trunk is already pushed to the side, and the rug is rolled away, making an escape from Risa's inquisition easy. He reaches down to pull open the trap door, and Connor feels something being pulled from his back pocket.

He turns to see Risa holding his letter. THE letter. From the moment Sonia gave it to him, he's been keeping it in that pocket. He's taken it out several times, each time determined to tear it up, or burn it up, or otherwise dismiss it from his life, but each time it winds up back in his pocket, and each time he feels a little angrier, and a little weaker for it.

"What's this?" Risa asks.

Connor grabs it back from her. "If it were your business, I'd tell you about it, but it's not." He slips it back in his pocket, but she already saw who it was addressed to. She knows exactly what it is.

"You think I don't know what's been going on in your head? Why you almost crashed us when we were leaving Columbus?"

"That has nothing to do with anything!"

"It was your old neighborhood, wasn't it? And you're thinking of going back."

Connor finds he can't deny it. "What I'm thinking and what I'm doing are two different things, okay?"

Sonia struggles to her feet. "Keep your voices down!" she growls. "Do you want people in the street to hear you?"

Grace, a bit anxious at the storm brewing around her, slips past Connor in a hurry to remove herself from the equation. She grabs the printer. "I'll take this back downstairs and hide it again. No point leaving it out in the open."

Sonia tries to stop her—"Grace, wait!"—but she's not fast enough.

The printer's power cord, which is still plugged in, goes taut and the printer flies from Grace's hands.

They all leap for it. Risa is closest. She gets a hand on it, but her momentum only serves to slap it away. It tumbles toward the open trapdoor, bounces once on the edge, and falls through. The cord goes taut again. And the printer dangles in the hole for a painful instant before the plug pulls free from the outlet.

Connor dives for that cord, knowing it's the last chance to save it. He grasps it with both hands, but the cord is slick with spilled bioslime. It slips through his fingers, his hands close on empty air, and he hears with a deadly finality as horrific as a car crash their last hope for a sane future smashing to bits on the basement floor.

Grace is inconsolable.

"I'm sorry, I'm sorry, I didn't mean it, I'm sorry." She wails desperate apologies while her eyes let loose a typhoon of tears with no sign of clear skies any time soon. "I'm so stupid, I didn't mean it, I'm sorry, I'm sorry."

Risa does her best to comfort her. "You're not stupid, and it's not your fault, Grace." She rubs Grace's back that now hunches under the weight of their loss.

"It was, it was," wails Grace. "Argent always says I ruin everything."

"Risa's right, it's not your fault," Connor assures her. "You wouldn't have been in such a hurry to leave if Risa and I weren't fighting. We're the stupid ones."

Risa meets his eye, but Connor can't read her. Is that look an apology for having grabbed the letter from his pocket like the pin from a grenade? Or is she waiting for him to apologize for losing his temper? Or maybe that gaze is just mirroring his own look of defeat.

Connor has picked up all the pieces of the printer. He now has them laid out on a table before him in the basement. Broken plastic, twisted metal. Gears and belts. When Sonia saw the state it was in, she grunted, climbed back up the stairs, and went home. Connor suspects there'll be no dinner for them tonight as she privately mourns their loss. For longer than Connor's been alive, the thing has sat in a box in a corner of the antique shop. It took an instant for them to destroy it.

"What's the big deal?" asks Jack. "It's just some old printer." He, like the other kids in the basement, is totally oblivious, and bewildered by the sudden air of despair, even more potent than the usual air of despair that permeates Sonia's basement.

"It belonged to Sonia's husband," Connor tells him. "It has sentimental value."

"Right," says Beau. "Sentimental value." And he slowly draws a finger along the broken plastic casing, coating his fingertip with the bioslime he risked his life to retrieve. He holds that finger up to Connor as an accusation, and tries to stare Connor down. Connor coldly holds that glare, refusing to give him anything. Beau finally backs down and returns to his task of ruling the roost.

Grace, her face in her hands now, sobs more quietly, and Risa leaves her long enough to assess the damage with Connor.

"You can fix it, can't you?" Her voice has none of its usual confidence. It's not a question; it's a plea. "You're good at fixing things."

"This isn't a TV or a refrigerator," he tells her. "I have to know how something works before I can fix it."

"But you can try."

Before, Connor had been afraid to even open the casing to look inside. Now he picks up each of the pieces, rearranging them on the table, trying to get a feel for how it goes back together. "It looks like the printing cartridge and head are still intact," Connor tells her, although he can't even be sure of that. He holds up an electronic component. "This looks like a hard drive, and it's not broken either, which means it probably still has the software it needs to do what it does. It's mostly the mechanical parts that are broken."

"Mostly?"

"I can't be sure about anything, Risa. It's a machine. It's broken. That's all I know."

"Well, someone somewhere's got to know how to fix it."

The thought that comes to Connor next hits him with such grand and absurd unease, he doesn't know whether to laugh or puke.

"My father could fix it," he says.

Risa leans away, as if trying to escape the deadly gravity of the thought.

"I mean, I'm good at fixing stuff because he taught me."

Risa doesn't say anything for a long time. She lets Connor's words drift in the air, maybe hoping they'll hang themselves. Finally she says, "Congratulations. You've been looking for an excuse to go back there since the moment you arrived."

Connor opens his mouth to deny it, but hesitates, because on some level Risa is right. "It's . . . not that simple," he says.

"Did you forget that these are the people who tried to unwind you? How can you forgive them for that?"

"I can't! But what if they can't forgive themselves either? I'll never know unless I face them."

"Are you entirely delusional? What do you think they'll do—take you back into their home and pretend like these past two years never happened?"

"Of course not."

"Then what?"

"I don't know! All I know is that I feel as broken as this machine." He looks at the fragmented device on the table before him. He may be whole, but there are times he feels unwound in the deepest possible way. "I can fix myself, but part of that means facing my parents on my own terms."

Connor looks around, realizing that they've been raising their voices again, attracting the attention of other kids. The others pretend like they're not listening, but he knows they are. He lowers his voice to an ardent whisper.

"And it's not just my parents, it's my brother, too. I never thought I'd say this about the little snot, but I miss him, Risa. I miss him like you can't believe."

"Missing your brother is not a reason to forfeit your life!"

And then it occurs to Connor that not only can't Risa ever

understand—she can't even understand *why* she can't. She was raised in a state home. No parents. No family. There was no one who cared enough to love her *or* to hate her. No one whose lives were so focused on hers that they could be made either proud or furious by her actions. Even her unwind order was not signed out of impassioned desperation, as Connor's was. For Risa it was a product of indifference. The deepest, most personal wound of her life wasn't personal for those who inflicted it. She was a budget cut. Suddenly Connor finds himself feeling sorry for her because of the pain she'll never be able to feel.

"I put a lot of trust in your opinions, Risa," he tells her. "Most of the time you're right. But not this time."

She studies him, maybe looking for a crack into which she can inject some doubt. What she doesn't know is that he's all doubt—but that doesn't change his need to do this.

"What can I say that will talk you out of it?"

Connor just shakes his head. Even if he had an answer to her question, he wouldn't tell her. "I'll be careful. And if I can safely get to them, I'll feel them out, see where they stand. If time has turned them against unwinding, maybe they'll see helping us as a second chance. "

"They're unwinders, Connor. They'll always be unwinders."

"They were parents first."

Risa finally backs down, accepting it with mournful resignation. Funny, but Connor wasn't even sure he'd go until Risa challenged him. Now he's committed.

Risa stands up and suddenly the gulf between them feels immense. "When your parents turn you in to the Juvenile Authority—and they will—I will not shed a single tear for you, Connor Lassiter."

But that's a lie, because her tears have already started.

· · ·

"The house will be under surveillance," Sonia says. "Not as much as before—after all, thanks to that Starkey person, you're no longer public enemy number one—but the Juvies still want to take you out if they can."

"I'll be careful."

"You realize how much danger you're putting yourself in. You don't know what your parents have been told, or what they believe about you. They might even think you mean to kill them."

Connor shakes his head to scramble away the thought. Was it possible that his mother and father knew him so little to think he'd do that? But on the other hand, they must feel responsible for everything that's happened to him since signing that unwind order, and might think he'd want vengeance. Was there ever a time he would have taken their lives to avenge himself? No, there wasn't. And not just because of his brother. Even were he an only child, he wouldn't do it. Someone like Starkey might target his own family—but Connor is not Starkey.

Connor turns the letter over in his hands. "I need to do this, and I need to do it soon. Or I'll never have the nerve again."

"You'll have the nerve," Sonia assures him, "but not the need. There's a critical time for everything. I do believe you need to do this now, or forever hold your peace."

He knows the worst that could happen probably outweighs the best that could happen. Lev found that out, didn't he? He found out the hard way.

"My friend Lev—I'm sure you've heard of him—he saw his parents again. They disowned him."

"Then Lev's parents are assholes."

Connor guffaws in surprise. Not that he wouldn't expect that out of Sonia, but to be so blunt about it. After everything, it's refreshing.

"I never met the boy, or his parents, but I see kids like him every day." Sonia tells Connor. "Their world is shattered, and they're so desperate for validation that they'd blow themselves up to get it. Any parent who disowns that boy after what he did, and *didn't* do . . . doesn't deserve to have children at all, much less a child to give away."

Connor smiles, thinking of Lev. He was mad when Lev chose not to come here with him, but he was only mad for selfish reasons. "He saved my life," Connor tells Sonia. "Twice now. He's a pretty amazing kid."

"If you ever see him again, you should tell him that. After what his parents did, he needs to hear it, and never stop hearing it."

Connor promises Sonia—and himself—that he will. Then he looks down the stairs to the basement. He considers going down, but knows if he does, he'll find too many reasons not to go. To reassure himself—and to remind himself of his resolve—he pulls the letter out of his back pocket. The envelope is tattered and beginning to fall apart. He takes a deep breath and tears it open, pulling out the pages within. He had planned to read it, but he can't bring himself to do it, because he doesn't know what emotional acrobatics his own words might send him through.

When he looks up, Sonia is watching him to see what he'll do. "Do you need some time alone?" she asks.

He answers by folding the pages of the letter and slipping them back into his pocket. "They're only words," he says, and Sonia doesn't argue.

"If you get there and change your mind at the last minute, you can always mail that letter instead." Then she looks over at the trunk. "In the meantime, I think I'll get all these other letters stamped and in the mail. I've never felt the time was right to send them. But if the Akron AWOL is going home, maybe it's time for all of these kids to be heard too."

"Have Grace help you," Connor suggests. "She needs it. I'll try to be back as soon as I can. Even if it looks like they're willing to help, I won't bring them back here . . ." Then he swallows hard, forcing himself to admit the real possibility. ". . . just in case they're lying."

"Fair enough." Then Sonia takes a few steps closer to Connor, considering him like she might appraise an antique. "I hope this brings you some peace. We all need a moratorium on misery now and then."

"Moratorium. Right," says Connor.

Sonia regards him with the sort of mock contempt usually displayed by people his own age. "It means a temporary break."

"I knew that," says Connor, which he didn't.

Sonia shakes her head dismissively and sighs. "It's Sunday morning—do your parents go to church?" Until then Connor had no idea the day of the week.

"Only on holidays and when someone dies."

"Well," says Sonia, "let's hope nobody dies today."

23 · Lev

Hennessey is dead, and Fretwell will face justice. The unwinding of Wil Tashi'ne will be avenged. Lev couldn't ask for more.

Una calls ahead so the Rez is expecting them—and intends to play it for all it's worth. The Royal Gorge Bridge is closed to traffic for the transfer. A phalanx of guards is there as Morton Fretwell, the Arápache's public enemy number one, is taken from the trunk of Una and Lev's car and into police custody. They remove the gag and plastic ties restraining him, and place his hands and feet in steel restraints that seem like overkill for his ugly, emaciated frame.

Then he is walked across the bridge, in perhaps the greatest perp walk of all time. The Arápache are nothing if not dramatic.

"You and Una will lead the procession," Chal Tashi'ne told them over the phone. "It will be a public event, and the first thing the public will see coming over the bridge will be you."

Chal is not there when they arrive. Lev is not surprised. As an accomplished attorney for the tribe, Chal might put on a professional façade, but as Wil's father he couldn't bring himself to face the last living parts pirate responsible for his son's unwinding. At least not yet.

At the far end of the bridge is a large turnout of the Arápache people. Five hundred at least.

"Don't wave or smile or anything," Una tells Lev as they cross the bridge toward the crowd. "Show no emotion. This is a somber event."

"Don't you think I know that?" Lev responds. "I'm not an idiot."

"But you've never faced the Arápache as a hero. There are expectations. A demeanor that goes back a thousand years."

When they reach the end of the bridge, the cheers begin. Una was right to tell Lev how to comport himself, because he does have an urge to bask in glory. Then as they get closer, the cheers drop off and are replaced by boos and jeers. It takes a moment for Lev to realize that this communal vitriol is for Fretwell, who hobbles behind them, with multiple sets of guards on either side.

The crowd shouts epithets in both Arápache and in English, to make sure he understands the nature and level of their hatred. The crowd makes as if to push through the wall of guards holding them back, but Lev suspects it's also just for show. Yes, they want to tear him apart, but they won't. They want him to suffer, and suffering requires many more opportunities for public humiliation.

"You people suck," Fretwell shouts, which thrills the crowd because it allows them to hate him even more.

The chief of police comes over to check out Fretwell. Lev finds himself disappointed that the tribal chief isn't here, but perhaps he had his expectations too high. As the police chief assesses Fretwell, the parts pirate makes that familiar guttural sound, dredging phlegm from the back of his throat.

"Spit at him and you die right here, right now," says one of the guards holding him. Fretwell's Adam's apple bobs as he swallows the substantial loogie.

The police chief turns to Lev and Una, shaking both of their hands. "Well done," he says. Then Fretwell is put into a squad car, driven off, and the party ends. Lev can't hide his disappointment.

"What did you expect?" Una asks him. "A medal of honor? The key to the Rez?"

"I don't know," Lev tells her. "But something more than a handshake."

"Handshakes from the right people mean a lot around here."

And there are plenty of handshakes.

First from members of the crowd before they disperse. People of all ages come forward to shake Lev's hand, and offer words of thanks and congratulations—and Lev begins to realize this is what he needs more than official recognition. What he needs is grassroots acceptance from the Arápache people, one person, one handshake at a time. Only with that sort of support—support on a personal, visceral level—will he find himself the clout to be taken seriously by the Tribal Council.

In the days following Fretwell's arrest, Lev makes every effort to be as visible as possible in town.

At diners and restaurants, he is given his food for free. He accepts the generosity but leaves an even more generous tip. He is stopped on the street by families who want to take pictures with him. Children want the occasional autograph. He is gracious and accommodating to everyone who approaches him. He handles his own emotion with reserve, just as Una told him. The deportment of a warrior hero, sublimated to modern times.

"I don't understand you," says Elina Tashi'ne—Wil's mother, and a woman whom Lev has come to love like a mother too. "You came here to escape attention, and now you bathe in it like a pig in mud. Perhaps your spirit animal should be the hog instead of that monkey creature."

"A pig rolls in the mud for a reason," he points out. "I have a reason too." She knows that reason, but Lev knows she's also worried for him. "You are one boy. You can't expect yourself to move heaven and earth."

Maybe not. But he still dreams he can bring down the moon.

Morton Fretwell is convicted in a trial that lasts only one day, peopled by a jury that is hard-pressed to conceal its rancor. He is found guilty of kidnapping, conspiring to commit murder, and as an accessory to murder—for by Arápache law, unwinding and murder are one and the same. Then, in a move that is no surprise to anyone, rather than pronouncing a life sentence, the judge falls back on an old tradition.

"Let the aggrieved levy punishment on the convicted," the judge announces, which opens the door to whatever the Tashi'ne family wants to do to him, including putting his life to a most painful end.

"This is justice?" Fretwell cries as he's led back to the jailhouse after the verdict. "This is justice?" There are no ears sympathetic to his pleas.

The following day, Elina, Chal, and Pivane Tashi'ne come to face Fretwell, along with Una and Lev. While they were there in the courthouse, never once did Lev see them make eye contact, or even look directly at Fretwell. Perhaps because they were so sickened by him, or perhaps because it would make this moment today all the more meaningful.

Fretwell looks pathetic in his cell. Dirty, even in the clean beige jumpsuit of Arápache convicts.

While Pivane, Chal, and even Una stand back, Elina comes forward to look at him. Her face is a study of the true Arápache heroine. Lev is in awe of her presence as she regards Fretwell. It's enough to make the man stand in quivering respect.

"Are you being treated well?" Elina asks, always the doctor.

Fretwell nods.

She regards him for a good long time before she speaks again. "We have discussed the various options of your punishment for the kidnapping and murdering of our son."

"He ain't dead!" Fretwell insists. "All his parts is still alive—I can prove it."

Elina ignores him. "We have discussed it and have decided that your death at our hands would be meaningless."

Fretwell breathes a sigh of relief.

"Therefore," she continues, "you will be remanded to the Central Tribal Penitentiary. You will, for the rest of your life, be given nothing but bread and water. The minimum required for survival. You will be allowed nothing to entertain yourself. No contact with other human beings—so that you will be left with nothing but your thoughts until the end of your days."

Fretwell's eyes swell with horror. "Nothing? But you have to give me something. A Bible at least. Or a TV."

"You will have one thing," Elina says, then Chal reaches behind him and pulls out the object he has been concealing.

It's a rope.

He hands it to the guard in attendance, who then passes it through the bars of the cell to Fretwell.

"We offer you this mercy," Elina tells him, "that when your

existence becomes too awful to bear, with this rope, you may end it."

Fretwell grips the rope tightly in his hands and, looking down on it, bursts into tears. Satisfied, Lev, Una, and the Tashi'nes leave the room.

The following morning Fretwell is found dead, having hanged himself from the ceiling light fixture in his cell. His question is finally answered. This *is* justice.

Lev has no idea if anyone in the outside world will mourn the man. He finds his own heart hardened. Fretwell's capture, conviction, and sorry demise mean only one thing to Lev. An opportunity.

That very afternoon, Lev petitions the Tribal Council for an audience. He receives his summons a week later. Elina is surprised that they responded to him at all, but Chal is not.

"Legally, they have to respond to every petitioner," Chal points out.

"Yes, and they don't get to some petitioners for years," says Elina.

"Perhaps Lev's a little too large a public figure to keep on their plate."

The idea of Lev being a large public figure in spite of his size both tickles Lev and makes him uncomfortable.

Elina and Chal accompany him, although Lev would have preferred to go alone.

"No one should face the council without a lawyer and a doctor," Chal says as they make the drive to Council Square. Then he gives Lev a mischievous smile. "Besides, irritating the Tribal Council is part of my basic job description."

"Yes," says Elina, feigning irritation, "and it's kept you from being the tribe's attorney general."

"Thank God!" says Chal. "I'd rather be representing the

tribe's interests out there in the world than be stuck handling the tribe's piddling internal affairs."

Lev shifts the heavy backpack he holds on his lap. The Tashi'nes haven't asked what's inside. He'd tell them if they asked, but he knows they won't, if he hasn't offered to share it. They do know the nature of his petition, however.

"You don't need to do this," Elina tells him. "As long as you don't bring trouble on us, you can stay."

And that's the problem. Because trouble is *exactly* what Lev means to bring to the Arápache. Their minds and souls need to be as troubled as his.

The Arápache council chamber consists of chairs around a huge donut-shaped table made of fine reservation-grown oak. On the outside rim of the table sit the chief, several representatives from key clans of the tribe, and the elected tribal officials. Twice a week they meet for public forum to hear the suggestions, complaints, and petitions of the people.

The circular setting was designed to reflect tradition, but somewhere along the way it was decided that petitioners stand in the table's ten-foot donut hole, thus making it an intimidating process, because with eyes on you from every direction, one begins to feel like an ant beneath a magnifying glass.

According to Chal and Elina, the Tribal Council was unofficially aware of Lev's presence on the reservation long before he left to apprehend Wil's kidnappers, and they had unofficially chosen to look the other way. At the Tribal Council table, however, there will be no "other way" to look. Today Lev puts himself beneath the heat of the magnifying glass.

"I can't say this is wise," Elina tells him as they enter Tribal Hall, "but we'll stand with you because what you're doing is noble."

They can't stand with him, however. Each petitioner must

make his or her case alone. When it's his turn, Lev leaves
Elina and Chal to watch from the gallery above, striding alone
through a small gap in the O-shaped table, and into the center
of scrutiny.

As he steps into the circle, the elder members of the council posture and grunt in disapproval. Others are merely curious, and a few smirk at the prospect of being amused by the
sparks that will surely fly. Clearly they all recognize him and
know who he is. His reputation sails before him like his spirit
animal through the forest canopy.

The Arápache chief, while just a symbolic position these
days, is the voice of the council, and Dji Quanah, the reign-
ing chief, has mastered the wielding of imaginary power. He
has also embraced his traditional role. His clothes are carefully
chosen to be reminiscent of old-school tribal garb. His hair
is split into two long gray braids that fall on either side of his
face, framing a square jaw. If modern Arápache culture is a
marriage of the old and the new, Chief Quanah is the ancestral
bridegroom.

Chal warned Lev that in spite of the circle, he should
always address the chief. "He may not have the true power of
the elected officials, but things never go smoothly if you don't
pay the respect that's due him."

Lev holds eye contact with the chief for a solid five seconds, waiting for the chief to begin the proceedings.

"First, let me congratulate you on your role in bringing the
parts pirate to justice," Chief Quanah says. And with that formality out of the way, he says, "Now state your purpose here,"
already sounding put off.

"If it pleases the council, I have a petition." Lev hands
a single page to the chief, then gives copies to the others
assembled. He's a little clumsy and awkward about it, finding
it hard to overcome the intimidating petition process. There

are eighteen seats in total around the table, although only a dozen people are present today.

The chief puts on a pair of reading glasses and looks over the petition. "Who is this 'Mahpee Kinkajou'?" he asks. It's rhetorical—he knows, but wants Lev to say it.

"It's the name I've been given as an Arápache foster-fugitive. The kinkajou is my spirit animal."

The chief puts down the petition, having only skimmed it. "Never heard of it."

"Neither did I, until it found me."

"Your name is Levi," the chief states. "That is the name by which you will be addressed."

Lev doesn't argue, even though no one ever called him Levi but his parents. And now his parents don't call him anything. He clears his throat. "My petition is—"

But the chief doesn't let him finish. "Your petition is foolishness, and a waste of our time. We have *important* business here."

"Like what?" Lev says before he can filter himself. "A petition to name fire hydrants, and a noise complaint about a karaoke bar? I saw the list of today's 'important business.'"

That brings forth a half-stifled guffaw from one of the elected council members. The chief throws the councilman a glare, but seems a bit embarrassed himself by some of today's other petitions.

Lev takes the moment to forge forward, hoping he can get it out with only a minimum of verbal bumbling. He's certainly practiced it enough. "The Arápache nation is a powerful force, not just among Chancefolk, but in the larger world too. Your policy has been to look the other way when people take on a foster-fugitive AWOL. But looking the other way isn't good enough anymore. This petition urges the tribe to openly and officially accept kids trying to escape being unwound."

"Toward what end?" asks a woman to his right. He turns to

see a council member about Elina's age but with more worry lines in her forehead. "If we open our gates to AWOLs officially, we'll be inundated. It will be a nightmare!"

"No," says Lev, happy for the unintentional setup. "*This* is the nightmare." Then he reaches into his backpack and pulls out sets of bound printouts. Reams and reams of paper as heavy as phone books. He quickly hands them out to Chief Quanah and the council members all around him. "The names of the unwound are public record, so I was able to access them. In these pages are the names of everyone subjected to 'summary division' since the Unwind Accord was signed. You can't look at all of those names and not feel something."

"We never signed the Unwind Accord, and never will," says one of the elders. "Our consciences are clear—which is more than I can say for you." He points a crooked finger. "We took you in two years ago, and then what did you do? You became a clapper!"

"Only after this council cast me out!" Lev reminds him. It gives everyone pause for thought. Some of the council members leaf through the pages, shaking their hands sadly at the sheer volume of names. Others won't even look.

To his credit, the chief takes some time to flip through the pages before he says, "The tragedy of unwinding is beyond this council's control. And our relations with Washington are already strained, isn't that true, Chal?" The chief looks up to the gallery.

Chal stands to respond. "Tense, not strained," he offers.

"So why add even more tension by throwing down a gauntlet to the Juvenile Authority?"

And then from a councilman behind Lev, "If we do, other tribes might follow."

"And they might not," says the chief with a finality that leaves no room for contradiction.

"There are plenty of people who are against unwinding," Lev tells the council, no longer addressing just the chief as he was instructed, but turning a slow pirouette, making sure to make eye contact with every council member around him. "But a lot of people won't speak out because they're afraid to. What they need is something to rally behind. If the Arápache make a stand against unwinding by giving official sanctuary to AWOLs, you'll be amazed the friends you'll find out there."

"We're not looking for friends," shouts one of the elders, angry to the point of spraying spittle as he speaks. "After generations of being abused, all we want is to be left alone!"

"Enough!" shouts Chief Quanah. "We'll put it to a vote and end this once and for all."

"No!" Lev shouts. He knows this is too soon for a vote, but the chief, offended by this show of disrespect, leans forward and locks eyes with him.

"It is being put to a vote, and you shall abide by the result, boy. Is that understood?"

Lev casts his eyes downward, humbling himself, giving the chief the respect due him. "Yes, sir."

The chief raises his voice to a commanding volume. "All in favor of adopting the petition to publicly and officially open the reservation to all Unwinds seeking asylum, affirm with a show of hands."

Three hands go up. Then a fourth.

"All those opposed?"

Eight hands rise in opposition. And just like that, AWOL hope among the Arápache is lost.

"The petition fails," the chief says. "However, in light of extenuating circumstances, I move that we officially and publicly accept Levi Jedediah Calder-Garrity as a full-fledged child of the Arápache Nation."

"That's not what I asked for, sir."

"But it's what you've received, so be thankful for it."

Lev is admitted to the tribe by a unanimous show of hands. Then Chief Quanah instructs the council members to return the books of Unwind names to Lev.

"No, keep them," Lev says. "When the Cap-17 law falls, and when the Juvenile Authority starts unwinding kids without their parents' permission, you can add the new names by hand."

"We will do no such thing," says the chief, insisting on the last word, "because those things will never happen." Then he calls for the next petitioner.

The walls of Lev's room are undecorated. The furniture is well crafted but understated. The bedroom is just as it was when Lev came to the Tashi'ne home the first time, the same as when he returned six weeks ago. He now knows why he feels so at home here: His soul is a lot like these Spartan walls. He tried to fill the emptiness with the angry graffiti of the clapper, but it washed clean. He accepted being a shining god for the ex-tithes in the Cavenaugh mansion, but that chalky portrait wiped away. He tried to draw himself a hero by saving Connor's life, but even after he succeeded, he felt no glory, no sense of honorable completion. And he curses his parents for raising him to be a tithe—for no matter how he runs from that destiny, it is imprinted so deep in his psyche that he will never be free of it. He will never feel complete, for there will always be that unwanted, uncomprehending part of himself that can only be completed in his demise. Far worse than his parents disowning him was that: raising him to only find satisfaction in the negation of his own existence.

On the evening of the day Lev fails to change the world in council, Elina comes to his room. She rarely does that, for she is a woman who respects privacy and contemplative solitude. She finds him lying on his stomach atop his tightly made bed. His pillow is on the floor because he doesn't care enough to pick it up.

"Are you all right?" she asks. "You ate very little at dinner."

"I just want to sleep tonight," he tells her. "I'll eat tomorrow."

She lingers, sitting down in the desk chair. She picks up the pillow and puts it on the bed, and he turns to face the wall, hoping she'll just go away, but she doesn't.

"There were four votes for your petition," Elina reminds him. "A single vote would have been surprising, considering the council's resistance to taking a stand on unwinding. You may not realize it, but four votes is a veritable coup!"

"It doesn't change a thing. The petition failed. Period."

Elina sighs. "You're not yet fifteen, Lev, and you came within three votes of changing tribal policy. Surely that counts for something."

He turns to look at her now. "Horseshoes and hand grenades." And off her confused expression, he explains, "It's something Pastor Dan used to say. Those are the only two situations where being close counts."

She chuckles her understanding, and Lev turns away from her again.

"Perhaps in the morning you can go out with Pivane, and he can teach you to hunt. Or maybe you could help Una in the shop. If you asked, I'm sure she'd let you work with her to build her instruments."

"Is that it for me then? I go out hunting, or I become a luthier's apprentice?"

Now Elina's voice becomes chastising, and a little cold. "You came here because you longed for a simpler, safer way of living. Now you resent us for giving it to you?"

"I don't resent anyone . . . I just feel . . . I don't know . . . unfulfilled."

"Welcome to the human race," she tells him with a bit of rueful condescension. "You should learn to relish the hunger more than the feast, lest you become a glutton."

Lev groans, not having the strength or even the desire to parse the poignancy from yet another of Elina's pithy Arápache metaphors.

"A great man knows not only when he's called upon, but also when he's not," says Elina. "The truly great know how to accept and embrace a common life, just as much as the call to duty."

"Then I will never be great, will I?"

"Listen to you! You posture like a man, but you pout like a child." It's a scolding, but she says it with such warmth in her voice that Lev both appreciates it and finds it embarrassing.

"I've never been a child," he tells her with a sadness no one but he will ever truly understand. "I've been a tithe, a clapper, and a fugitive, but never a child."

"Then be one now, because you deserve it. Be a child, if only for one night."

The last person to suggest such a thing was Pastor Dan. The night before he was killed by an explosion that was meant for Lev.

Neither of them speak for a moment. If Elina is uncomfortable with the silence, she doesn't show it. Then she begins to gently rub his back and sing to him in Arápache. Her voice is sweet, if not entirely on key. Lev has learned enough of the language to know what the song is about. It's a lullaby, perhaps one she used to sing to Wil when he was very little. It speaks of the moon and the mountain. How the mountain pushes forth from the earth, reaching ever skyward in a vain attempt to grab the moon, but the mischievous moon keeps slipping behind the mountain's peak to hide, remaining forever unattainable. Lev thinks of the challenge of his animal spirit—to bring down the moon—and he wonders if Elina even realizes what she's singing. Not a lullaby, but a lament.

When she's done, Lev's eyes are closed, and he's slowed

his breathing to a gentle snuffle. Elina leaves, probably thinking he's asleep, but he's not. Lev will not sleep well tonight,
if he sleeps at all. As much as he thought he wanted it, he is
immune to a normal life and is addicted to a life of dangerous
sway. He *must* make a difference out there. He *must* satisfy the
hunger, elbowing himself a place at the feast.

The council dismissed his petition out of hand. Perhaps
petitions are too tame an approach. Perhaps what Lev needs is
a method that's more extreme. He's seen extreme. He's lived it.
He knows how to play with fire. Perhaps this time he can use
what he knows to serve his own ends, not someone else's.

He shares none of this with Elina, or Una, or with anyone
else on the reservation. But silently and alone, he begins to
plan.

Today he failed to change the world.

As for tomorrow, who can tell?

24 · Cam

Security at the Molokai complex is state-of-the-art and extreme.
No one gets into the compound who doesn't belong there. The
outside fences are electrified and tranq-charged. The gates boast
scanners that can sniff you and decode your DNA just as easily as tell your brand of deodorant. Only the best for Proactive Citizenry's bioresearch facility. Unfortunately, all security
systems are flawed and limited by the arrogance of whoever
designed it. In this case, the designers were arrogant enough
to think that they only needed to secure the place from people
on the outside. No one counts on a fox that's already inside the
fence.

Newly tweaked and effectively remotivated, Camus Comprix
is, for all intents and purposes, glitch-free. True, there may still be

some issues, but in a few short days Cam will be the problem of the US military, and his issues will go with him. General Bodeker has not only purchased his physical self, but his emotional self as well. Not just his presence but his problems, whatever they turn out to be.

Cam goes for a daily run on the expansive grounds of the compound, where sugarcane and taro root still grow right up to the edge of cliffs overlooking the sea. It's all still harvested and sold—Proactive Citizenry is all about employing local residents and paying them higher-than-standard wages to satisfy the organization's need to feel they are Forward-Thinking for Humanity®. Roberta, and everyone else who is a part of Proactive Citizenry, seem to believe in the good work they're doing. They also believe in getting extremely rich while doing it.

Cam doesn't run alone. He's not allowed. One of the guards, a particularly bouef one, always joins him. Safety in numbers. They weave along the path that runs at the edge of the fields that grow year round, harvested in staggered intervals. Some patches are clear-cut, others still green. As they move from a clear-cut area and into tall cane, Cam bursts into a sudden sprint, catching his jogging partner off guard. The path curves left, and as soon as he's out of the guard's view, Cam turns sharply, disappearing into the cane.

"Mr. Comprix!" he hears the guard shout. They all call him "Mister" here. Cam pushes on, knowing exactly where he's going, trying to keep from knocking down the cane and creating an obvious path. The stiff leaves whip at his face as he barrels through, stinging, but he doesn't care. For a moment he wonders if he's miscalculated, and if he'll come from the field into an unexpected ocean inlet, where he'd go flying off the edge of a cliff to his doom.

"Mr. Comprix!" No doubt his jogging companion is now talking into his ear piece, spreading the word that Cam is AWOL.

He comes to another path, a wider one, but crosses over it, into a thick copse of bamboo that grows much higher than the cane. The bamboo is dense and hard to push through. It's there for one reason—to create an environmentally aesthetic façade for the facility behind it. In other words, to hide it. The place doesn't appear on maps. It doesn't even show up in satellite photos, at least not the ones available to the public. From the outside it appears to be just a warehouse—the way a movie studio soundstage is a warehouse: a large hollow building that can be redesigned on the inside to be whatever is needed at the time.

There's no telling what Proactive Citizenry has tinkered and toyed with here. Perhaps this is where they began the great agave extinction by genetically engineering the agave-specific Cyan Snout weevil, but only after buying up massive quantities of tequila that now goes for thousands of dollars a bottle. Or maybe this is where they grafted new faces on people in the Witness Relocation Program—a lucrative government contract that they had for eight years until the program's budget was cut, making it no longer worthwhile. Or maybe this is where they did all that intensive research that brought about the cure for muscular dystrophy. While the third one was something Proactive Citizenry widely publicized, the first two Cam found unexpectedly while hacking their computer system.

From Cam's vantage point at the fence, he sees three FedEx trucks at the front entrance. Workers unload cargo. One of the drivers, in familiar purple-and-black shirt and shorts, hands a clipboard to none other than Roberta, who is there to sign for the delivery. Cam thinks it odd that Proactive Citizenry wouldn't use their own private delivery trucks to shuttle this cargo from the airport, but then maybe the CEO of FedEx is on Proactive Citizenry's board. After all, it's the preferred philanthropic organization of corporate America.

The more Cam considers it, the more he realizes it must be true. How ingenious! Why go to the mountain when you can use an existing infrastructure to move the mountain to you, one piece at a time?

Cam leaves, having seen what he needed to see. He heads back through the bamboo, takes a different route, cutting through the cane and taro, then onto the jogging path once more, completing his jog back to the house.

One of the ubiquitous guards stands there, not too pleased. "Found him," he says into his earpiece, then to Cam, "Where've you been?"

"Shortcut through the sugarcane. Bad idea, though, the stuff hurts." He wipes some blood from one of several small scratches on his face.

"Do us all a favor and stick to the path next time. We get crap every time you don't toe the line."

"Gotta make life interesting."

"Dull is fine by me."

As he goes up to take a shower, Cam considers what he had seen. Those could have been shipments of just about anything, except for one fact. The shipping containers were FedEx stasis packs. Refrigerated. Perfect for live organs, although they're not usually used for that. But then, Proactive Citizenry knows how to do things without raising red flags. A FedEx plane flies in and out of Molokai daily. How many parts, Cam wonders, are flowing into this complex every day? With so much going in, it's only a matter of time before things begin coming out. . . .

Roberta doesn't trust Cam the way she used to—but like the designers of the security system, she trusts herself and her own ability not to be outwitted. Herein lies the problem of building someone smarter than yourself—because even with the nanite "worm" selectively routing his memory, Cam has no problem duplicating the holographic digital signature of her security badge. That's easy. The hard part is finding a way to convince the security computer that Roberta is in two places at once, because an identity signature pinging from two separate locations is certain to trip an alarm. In the end, he takes a different tack, and instead convinces the server that today is, in fact, yesterday. Since no one told the computer that there's no such thing as time travel, it sees nothing out of the ordinary when history repeats itself in a different place.

The rear door of the secret facility—the factory hidden within the bamboo—opens as obediently as Ali Baba's cave to the correct "open sesame," now that he has cloned Roberta's badge.

Cam isn't sure whether it would help or hinder him to know why he's doing this. All he knows—and he knows this beyond a shadow of a doubt—is that The Girl whose love motivates him is worth it. The fact that he doesn't know who she is anymore is irrelevant: His pretweaked self knew, and he trusts *that* self more than he trusts himself now.

It's five thirty a.m. There are plenty of guards, but they're anything but quiet, and he can hide long before they pass by on their routine patrols. There are also plenty of security cameras, but he already has the monitors running happy little video loops of quiet little hallways. The place is his to explore.

Using Roberta's forged security card, he gains access into several rooms. They're all the same. Long wards lined with empty beds, perhaps fifty in each. It's in the fourth room he visits that he hits the jackpot.

In this room, the beds are occupied.

He had a suspicion of what he might see, but imagining it and seeing it are two different things.

In each bed is a rewind, like himself . . . and yet not like himself. Some still wear bandages, but others, whose healing is further along, have the bandages removed, so he can see their faces and much of their bodies. These rewinds bear none of the aesthetic grace that Cam does. They are sloppy and ugly, as if assembled with the perfunctory hand of a hack, or worse, an assembly line. There is no regard to symmetry, or to the balancing of skin tone. Seams cut at strange angles across each figure, and the scars are far worse than any scars Cam ever had. While his scars were treated to disappear over time, he suspects these will have no such treatment.

None of them have yet awakened. They are all in an induced state of preconsciousness—a sort of integration gestation. He suspects that they are being kept comatose much longer than Cam was, as their many parts heal themselves into living beings. This building is their womb, and Cam realizes that this is where he must have begun as well. As Cam walks down the aisle, looking to his left and right at these preconscious beings, he finds it hard to catch his breath, as if the oxygen has been sucked out of the room.

There is one thing they all share other than the commonality of their randomness. Each of them has a mark on the right ankle. At first he thinks they're tattoos, but when he looks closer he sees that they're actually seared into the skin. They're brands. And they say PROPERTY OF THE UNITED STATES MILITARY followed by a serial number. The one Cam examines is numbered 00042. The presence of three zeroes suggests they will eventually number in the tens of thousands.

I am the idea, thinks Cam, *but they are the reality*. And finally, he sees his place in all of this. He will be the face the world sees. The one they become comfortable with. The public image of the military rewind. He'll be an officer, lauded and honored, and as such, he will not only open the door, but also pave the way for an army of rewinds. Perhaps it will start small.

A special force called upon for a key maneuver somewhere in the world, for there are always American interests to protect somewhere, some violent insurgency that must be addressed. REWINDS SAVE THE DAY! the headlines will read. Just as people became complacent and comfortable with unwinding, they will do the same for rewinding. *What a fine thing*, people will say, *that the unwanted bits of humanity can be reformed and repurposed to serve the greater good.* Like the way unwanted pork parts can be ground and pressed and reformed into a tasty pimento loaf. Cam would be sick to his stomach, but he feels he doesn't have the right, because now, more than ever before, he truly has the sense that his stomach is not his own.

"Cam?"

He turns to see Roberta standing at the entrance. Good. He's glad she's here.

"You didn't have to sneak in here. I would have shown you, if you had asked." Which is, of course, a lie—she already told him her work was top secret. His instinct is to point an accusing finger for the blatant hubris of what she's done here, but instead, he plays his emotions close, hoping she doesn't see the bile collecting within him, and he tells her calmly, "I could have asked, but I wanted to see them on my own terms."

"And how do you feel about what you see?" She watches him closely, so he buries his fury and revulsion. Instead he allows only an acceptable amount of ambivalence to bubble to the surface. "I knew I wasn't the be-all and end-all of your work . . . but to see it is . . ."

"Distressing?"

"Sobering," he says. "And maybe a little enlightening." He looks to the closest rewind, who stirs slightly in preconscious slumber. "Was an army always your plan?"

"Certainly not!" she says, a bit insulted by the suggestion. "But even *my* dreams must give way to reality. It was the military who expressed an interest in what we could do, the military who could afford to fund it. So here we are."

And then Cam realizes that he's the one who made all this possible. He's the one who romanced General Bodeker and Senator Cobb. Of course, the military doesn't need rewinds who can speak nine languages, recite poetry, and play the guitar. It needs rewinds who follow orders. Nonentities who are legally considered "property," who don't need to be paid, and who have no rights.

"You look pensive." Roberta comes closer to get a good look at him. He doesn't flinch or crack in the least.

"I was thinking how brilliant it is."

"Really?"

"Soldiers who have no families to go back to? Whose entire identity begins with their military service? A stroke of genius! And I'll bet you can tweak them the way you tweaked me—to find their greatest satisfaction in their service."

Roberta smiles, but hesitantly. "I'm impressed that you've grasped the scope of this so quickly."

"It's . . . visionary," Cam tells her. "Perhaps one day I'll be the commanding officer of all my rewind brethren."

"Perhaps you will be."

He turns and walks casually to the door. Roberta walks beside him, watching him, always watching him. "Now that you know, you can put it to rest, and get on with your life. And it will be a glorious life, Cam. They need it to be. You must be seen as a prince among peasants, and General Bodeker knows that. You will want for nothing. You will be treated with respect. You will be happy."

And so he beams for her, to project the impression that he already is happy. Roberta once told him his eyes came from a boy who could melt a girl's heart with a single glance. She probably never considered how effectively they could be weaponized against her.

"It's dawn," Cam says. "I don't know about you, but I'm up for an early breakfast."

"Splendid. I'll let the kitchen know when we get back to the mansion."

As they leave, Cam turns to take one last look at the room full of preconscious rewinds.

These truly are my brothers and sisters, he thinks. *And they must never be allowed to be born.*

Part Four

This Lane Must Exit

HEADLINES . . .

National Geographic, May 4, 2014

SWAPPING YOUNG BLOOD FOR OLD
REVERSES AGING

http://news.nationalgeographic.com/news/2014/05/140504-swapping-
young-blood-for-old-reverses-aging/

BBC News–Scotland, June 24, 2014

WOMAN TO BE FIRST IN UK TO HAVE DOUBLE
HAND TRANSPLANT

http://www.bbc.com/news/uk-scotland-27999349

ABC News, September 25, 2013

DOCTORS GROW NOSE ON MAN'S FOREHEAD

http://abcnews.go.com/blogs/health/2013/09/25/doctors-grow-nose-on-
mans-forehead/

The Boston Globe, March 19, 2008

EX-DOCTOR CONFESSES TO STEALING BODY PARTS

http://www.boston.com/news/nation/articles/2008/03/19/ex_doctor_
confesses_to_stealing_body_parts/

The Huffington Post, July 6, 2013

HUMAN HEAD TRANSPLANTS NOW POSSIBLE, ITALIAN NEUROSCIENTIST SAYS

http://www.huffingtonpost.com/2013/07/06/head-transplant-ital-
ian-neuroscientist_n_3533391.html

25 · Starkey

Safe within the isolated power plant, Mason Michael Starkey luxuriates in his particular addiction. He knows he's a junkie now. The chemical receptors of his brain have tuned to the ecstasy of power. It pumps through his veins, feeding his body and spirit so that he thrives in the kind of glory he never dared to imagine in the days before his unwind order. He should thank his adoptive parents for signing it, and setting in motion the gears that have turned him into something far better than what he was. The wayward stork has now become for all storks the new symbol of liberty.

Especially now that the old one has seen better days.

"Did you hear? They're sending the Statue of Liberty's old arm on tour," Garson DeGrutte told him, "like they did with King Tut, and all that crap from the *Titanic*. Like people are gonna pay to see an old copper arm."

"People will," Starkey said, "because people are nuts. They'll hold on to bits of the past like they're still worth something." Then he looked Garson in the eye. "What would you rather have: shreds of the past or the whole of the future?"

"You know my answer!" Garson said.

As should be the answer of every member of the Stork Brigade. The future—Starkey's future—is like Fourth of July fireworks: bright and bold, loud and dramatic, but deadly for those in the trajectory of the blasts. The Juvenile Authority fears him, the world is talking about him, and with the shadowy support of the clappers, there is no limit to the heights to which his fireworks will soar. It's true that revolutionaries are always vilified by the societies they seek to take down, but history has a different perspective. History calls them freedom fighters, and freedom fighters have statues erected to them. Starkey is determined that his will be made of metals far finer than copper.

A team of mercenaries sent by the clappers now supervise weapons training because the storks' arsenal has gotten so complex and diverse. After all, a thirteen-year-old shouldn't use a handheld missile launcher without proper instruction. Starkey has conveniently forgotten that training was Bam's suggestion.

Starkey, who wants to know how to use each and every weapon, trains with his own private instructor. He doesn't want the storks to see his learning curve. They must think he already knows this stuff. That he's the consummate guerrilla.

As for everyone else, the storks are each assigned a specific weapon, and train on that weapon for four hours a day.

So far there has only been one mishap.

Starkey decides that a good stork should be rewarded, and Garson DeGrutte is a good stork. Trustworthy. Dedicated. He follows orders without question, and has the right attitude. For this reason, Garson deserves some of the perks of Starkey's power. So Starkey pays a visit to a girl named Abigail, whom Garson has been not-so-secretly pining over.

As it turns out, Abigail is the same girl who gave Starkey a lousy massage two weeks ago.

He finds her washing dishes, and with a single gesture dismisses everyone else at the bank of industrial sinks.

"Is there something you want, sir?" the girl asks timidly.

Starkey gives her his winning smile, and reaches up with his bad hand to brush back her hair, which has gone limp from the steamy dishwater. His gloved hand brushes her cheek as he does. She purses her lips as if the touch from his glove pains her. Or maybe terrifies her.

"Does it hurt?" she asks. "Your hand."

"Only when I think about it," he says, then gets to business. "I'm here to talk to you about one of the other storks."

She visibly relaxes. "Which one?"

"Garson DeGrutte. Do you like him?"

"No, not really."

"Well, he likes you."

She looks up at him, trying to figure where this is going. "He told you that?"

"He mentioned it. And he also mentioned that you told him off."

Abigail shrugs, but in a strained, uncomfortable way—as if shaking off a chill. "Like I said, I don't really like him."

Starkey reaches over and dries a plate with a dish towel. Abigail takes this as a cue to start doing the same. "Garson is a good fighter. A loyal stork. He deserves some happiness. He doesn't deserve to be rejected."

Abigail looks down at the plate in her hands. "So you want me to lie to him?"

"No! I want you to like him," Starkey says. "I certainly like him. He's a likeable guy."

She still won't look at him. "I can't feel things that I don't feel."

Starkey grabs her shoulder with his good hand—a gentle grasp with a squeeze just hard enough to tip the scale of persuasion. "Yes, you can."

Later that day, Garson is all smiles. Starkey doesn't have to ask why, for he knows that today Cupid was armed with a stainless steel crossbow.

While Garson now enjoys the fruits of Cupid's steel arrow, Starkey finds in his own love life that multiple piercings can be unpleasant.

"I didn't trip her, it was an accident!" Makayla yells.

"She's lying—she wants me to lose the baby! Admit it!" Emmalee screams.

"Go ahead, tear each other apart, we'll all be better off," says Kate-Lynn.

The three girls in Starkey's personal harem, once friends, now do nothing but fight. He thought they would see each other as sisters, but the glow they all seemed to share when he first chose them has degraded into a clawing competition. Starkey doesn't even want to consider how they'll behave toward one another once all three of his children are born. It's still so many months away, it doesn't feel real yet—but the battles between the girls are.

Perhaps it's the problem of three. Maybe adding a fourth to their number will settle the dynamic. On the other hand, maybe it's just best to just keep away from Makayla, Emmalee, and Kate-Lynn altogether.

He takes comfort in anticipating the end result. The girls are beautiful; his children will be beautiful. And, thanks to their father, they will be raised in a world better than the world that gave birth to him. And he will love them unconditionally . . . if he can just get past the girls he chose to be their mothers.

"She thinks she's better than me because she was the first, but mine will be the firstborn, you'll see."

"And it'll be a whining little turd like its mother."

Definitely a fourth. That's what Starkey decides is needed. After the next harvest camp attack he will choose. A redhead this time. He dyed his hair red for a time to evade the authorities. He liked the way it looked. It would be nice to have a child who comes by it naturally.

"The applause department"—as Hayden so blithely calls the organization behind the clapper movement—requests an audience with Starkey. Jeevan sets up an encrypted teleconference, although Starkey suspects that those in charge of clappers have massive layers of their own encryption. On-screen is the man with salt-and-pepper hair, more salt than pepper. The man in charge. It still seems odd to Starkey that the man at the heart of the clapper movement appears about as radical as the *Wall Street Journal*. Starkey has to remind himself that the man was once a teenager himself, although somehow Starkey can't imagine he was ever an outsider in any sense of the word.

The fact that he's contacting them directly, rather than through the usual series of intermediaries, concerns Starkey. The only other time Starkey saw the guy was when they sent in a team to abduct Starkey in his sleep. Starkey thought he had been captured by the Juvies, but their little helicopter trip was nothing more than a courtship ritual. That was when the force behind the clapper movement offered the Stork Brigade its full support. That's when the game changed. The man had declined to give him his name at the time, but a few weeks ago one of his underlings let slip that his name is Dandrich. Starkey knows better than to let on that he knows the man's name. Or at least not until it serves Starkey's interests.

"Hello, Mason. It's good to see you."

"Hi, yourself."

Like Starkey, the man is short in stature and wields power with professional proficiency. Even on a small computer screen there's something intimidating about him.

"You're well, I trust?" Dandrich says. Small talk. Why do people in suits always insist on small talk before going for the jugular? Starkey braces himself for bad news. Has their location been compromised? Or worse, are the clappers pulling their support? No—why would they do such a thing when the harvest camp liberations have been so successful? Thousands have been freed, unwinders have been punished, and fear has been struck into the hearts of millions. Surely they're happy with all of that.

"Yeah, I'm good. But I'm sure this isn't about my health. Why are we talking?"

Dandrich chuckles, amused, perhaps a little bit impressed by Starkey's directness. "Word has come down that you're considering an attack on Pensacola Shores Harvest Camp. Our analysts are advising against it."

Starkey leans back and takes a moment to reign in his annoyance. After all he's done, why can't they simply trust his judgment? "That's what you said about Horse Creek, but that place came down like a house of cards."

Dandrich never loses his poise. "Yes, in spite of the risks, you prevailed. Pensacola Shores, however, is a different matter. It's a maximum security camp for violent Unwinds and, as such, has many more layers of security. You simply don't have the manpower to succeed. In addition, it's on an isolated peninsula, and you could very easily be trapped, with no means of escape."

"That's why I requested boats."

Now Dandrich becomes a little hot under his stiff collar. "Even if we could provide them, an armada attacking from the Gulf of Mexico would be hard to conceal."

"Exactly," says Starkey. "And what could be more dramatic than an old-fashioned siege? You know— like the conquistadors! Not only would it be newsworthy, it would be . . . it would be . . ."

Dandrich finds the word for him. "Iconic."

"Yes! It would be iconic!"

"But at what cost? I assure you the battles of Waterloo and Little Bighorn were iconic, but only because of how completely Napoleon and Custer were defeated. The world remembers their failure."

"I won't fail."

But Dandrich ignores him. "We have determined that the

next harvest camp in your campaign should be Mousetail Divisional Academy, in central Tennessee."

"Are you kidding me? Mousetail is all tithes!"

"Which is why they won't be expecting it. You can continue your policy of executing the staff, and you won't add any new mouths to feed, because there won't be any storks. Let the tithes do whatever they want once you've liberated them. They can stay, they can run—either way it's not your problem. This will give you time to continue training the kids you have before you're saddled with more."

"That's not the way I do things! My instincts tell me to hit Pensacola, and I can't go against my instincts."

Dandrich leans closer. His face fills the screen. Starkey can practically feel the man's hand reaching through the ether and grasping Starkey's shoulder. A gentle grasp, but with enough pressure for Starkey to feel a subtle increase in the earth's gravity.

"Yes, you can," says Dandrich.

Starkey rages through the power plant, venting his indignation at anyone who crosses his path. He yells at Jeevan for not being aggressive enough during their last attack.

"You're a soldier now, not a computer nerd, so start acting like one!"

He rips into kids who are laughing while coming back from weapons training.

"Those things aren't toys, and this is no laughing matter!" He tells them to drop and give him twenty, and when they say, "Twenty what?" he storms off, too irritated to tell them.

Hayden strides past him with a nod, and he's so furious at the casual way Hayden saunters, he complains about yesterday's dinner, even though it was fine. "If you're in charge of food then do your freaking job!"

And Bam.

He's glad he doesn't encounter Bam until he's calmed down a bit, because he might do something he'd regret later. Bam has become a liability, but he can put her in her place. Although Garson DeGrutte doesn't know it yet, the reward for his loyalty isn't just getting the girl. Starkey's going to put him in charge of a team on their next mission—and Bam will be part of that team. She will have to take orders from Garson, and it will humble her. It will remind her who is in charge. And if it doesn't, he'll simply have to step things up with her. It's a shame, really. Bam had been so loyal for so long. But when loyalty runs out, so would any leader's tolerance.

He finds her in the weapons locker. In spite of her concerns about arming the storks, the weapons locker seems her favorite place to be. When she sees him, she doesn't come to crisp attention. She doesn't even stop assembling the weapon she's working on. She just glances up at him, then back down at her work.

"I heard about the call from Mr. Big. Do you have your orders?"

"*I* give the orders."

"Whatever." She wipes some sweat from her brow. "Is there something you want, Mason? Because I have to make sure these weapons are assembled correctly. Unless, of course, you'd rather go in with water balloons."

Starkey considers telling her about her demotion, but decides against it. Let her find out the day of the attack, when it will hit her hardest. Maybe it will make her mad enough to take out some harvest camp personnel for once.

"I came to tell you that I've changed my mind," he says. "We won't be going after Pensacola right now."

Bam finally stops what she's doing and gives him her full attention. "You have another place in mind?"

"We'll be going north instead. Mousetail Divisional Academy, in Tennessee."

"But isn't that place tithes-only? I thought you hated tithes."

Starkey frowns, feeling his anger rekindling toward Dandrich and his lack of faith. Well, maybe Starkey can turn this into an event just as iconic as he would have had in Pensacola.

"Tithes are filthy unwinding sympathizers," Starkey tells her. "Which is why, when we go in, our objective will be a little bit different." Then he takes a deep breath, hardening his resolve.

"'This time, we're not just taking out the staff. We're killing every last tithe as well."

26 · Podcast

"This is Radio Free Hayden, podcasting from a place that's toxic in more ways than one. I'm not myself today. I'm not in my happy place at all—which is why the image accompanying today's podcast is Dali's Persistence of Memory. *Time melting on a bleak landscape of doom. Yeah, that about sums it up.*

"Everything changes today. Or nothing changes. If things go right, and we find a way to stop what's about to happen, I'll be in a much better place than I am now. Hell, I might even play some music for your listening pleasure. And if things go wrong, then the next sound you hear will be a collective scream that may never end.

"I can't tell you the specifics, you'll just have to trust me that big things are brewing, and this stew promises to be lethal. So in the next couple of days, if you hear something more horrific than usual in your evening news, and you're faced with more dead kiddos than you're comfortable with, then you'll know that things did not go well.

"I suspect I'll be one of the casualties if we can't stop this particular speeding train, so you may never hear from me again.

And, in which case, I hope you'll dedicate our little uprising to my memory.

"And speaking of the uprising, I've been considering how it might go down. I know such an event needs some rallying point. A date, a time, a place. I've been thinking of maybe Monday, November first, in Washington—the day before Election Day. It somehow seems appropriate to me that Election Day falls so close to Halloween this year, considering some of the measures on the ballot. Voluntary unwinding for cash. Tossing the brains of criminals and unwinding the rest of them. The "three strikes" law that allows the Juvenile Authority to arrest and unwind teenage offenders without parental consent. It certainly feels to me like a trip through the haunted mansion, and not even that unwound witch's head in the crystal ball can predict where it's going to end.

"So that's my proposal. A challenge for anyone who opposes unwinding to gather on November first, in Washington, DC. That gives you three weeks to make it happen. And if I don't make it—maybe you can carve my name on some random memorial so the world knows I was here."

27 · Mousetail

The story, far too old to be corroborated by anyone living, is that when the old tannery burned down, it was so infested with mice that they all ran out at once to escape the fire. The massive pack of mice raced toward the nearby Tennessee River, landing in a flood of vermin that rivaled the plagues on Egypt. And so, henceforth, and likely forevermore, the place came to be known as Mousetail Landing.

In the spot where the tannery once stood is now a harvest camp so picturesque it is often the subject of watercolors painted by vacationers camping across the river. The closest thing to mice at Mousetail now are the mild-mannered boys and girls all dressed in white, who arrive the day after their thirteenth birthdays. Happy children, all bright-eyed and trusting that the staff will ease them into a divided state with kindness and a reverence for the sanctity of their sacrifice.

The cabins of Mousetail Divisional Academy are heated in the winter by induction floorboards and cooled in the summer by multizone circulation systems that keep each tithe's sleeping area at precisely the temperature the tithe prefers. Spectacular meals are supervised by a chef who once had his own TV show and served by graduates of the International Institute of Modern Butlers.

Tithes are accepted to Mousetail through a rigorous and competitive application process akin to that of the most exclusive universities. To be chosen for the academy is a source of pride for a tithe and his or her family—and to receive a Mousetail transplant is something bragged about in society's highest strata.

Until recently, the academy's front gate was not locked. In fact, there's a sign just inside the gate in bright yellow and red that reads THOSE WHO WISH TO LEAVE UNDIVIDED MAY EXIT HERE. Yet in fourteen years of operation, there have been only four tithes who went AWOL. One of them was later found frozen in the woods. He was buried in a highly visible and well-maintained tomb in the camp, testifying to the love and care that Mousetail provides its guests—even the AWOL ones. And it also stands as a reminder to other tithes that the wage of cowardice is death.

In recent weeks, by request of the Juvenile Authority, the gate has been locked, and the minimal security staff has been augmented by three additional armed guards. It's nowhere near the protection required for more likely targets of Mason Starkey's wrath: nonvoluntary harvest camps, where the campers don't actually want to be there.

The new security measures frighten the tithes, reminding them that there's evil out in the world—but they take comfort in knowing that it won't be coming for them. Very soon the evil of this world will no longer be their concern. In fact they are taught to pity the kind of ignorance that leads to violence against harvest camps.

The tithes of Mousetail Divisional Academy do not know and cannot see the dark thunderheads growing to the south. It is a tempest far more devastating than they dare imagine, which threatens to end them before the scalpel can.

On the night before the Stork Brigade's planned attack, the tithes take to their beds after gentle prayer and the brushing of teeth, never suspecting that judgment will soon rain upon them with ballistic intensity, unless an unexpected front moves in to quiet the storm.

28 · Starkey

He is abducted in the middle of the night. It's different from the time the clappers came for him. This time his attackers are of the stealth kind, rather than from the school of brute force. They sneak up to him instead of bludgeoning their way through the rank and file. Without a commotion to alert him, Starkey has no warning before the tranq bullet pierces his thigh. Not a tranq dart, which is kinder and gentler, but a full-payload chemical bullet that explodes like a bug on a windshield but only after penetrating deep into the epidermis. Tranq bullets hurt like hell, even if they don't do any real damage.

The pain jolts Starkey awake just long enough to register that he's been tranq'd, then he's swallowed by unconsciousness once more.

• • •

UnDivided

He's awakened sometime later by a slap to the face. A hard one. Then another, because the first slap didn't quite do the job. The third slap is purely gratuitous on the part of the assailant, whoever he is.

"Awake yet, stork boy?" says a man with tousled hair and a severe expression. "Or do you need another one?"

"Go to hell," Starkey grunts out. That summons forth another slap, this one backhanded and brutal. It would sting quite a lot if he weren't still numb from the tranqs. He feels blood on his face, though. The guy has a ring that cut Starkey's cheek.

"Whoever you are, you're a dead man," Starkey tells him, trying not to slur his words. "My storks will find you, kill you, and string you up as a warning for all the other idiots out there."

"Will they, now?" The man is amused. Sure of himself. This does not bode well for Starkey, and so Starkey takes a moment to measure the situation.

He's outside in the woods. It's chilly. Starkey can see only in scant grays and deep royal blues. It must be dawn. He's bound but not gagged, which means they want him to be able to talk. Negotiate perhaps. His attacker, however, is angry. Very angry.

"Let me go, and we'll pretend this never happened," Starkey suggests. He knows it won't work, but how the man responds will define Starkey's parameters.

The man's response is a swift kick to Starkey's ribs, and he feels at least two of them crack. Starkey falls to the side, moaning in pain that can't be quelled by the tranqs still in his system. He now knows his parameters. They're roughly the dimensions of a coffin.

"Don't break him," hisses a voice in the shadows. Barely a voice at all—more like the breathy rasp of ghost. Starkey sees a figure shift. The silhouette of a shoulder, but the rest is

183

obscured by a tree. "The less he's broken, the more he's worth."

The man backs off, but he doesn't seem any less angry. Although he's not all that big, not all that muscular, his simmering rage makes up for it. Starkey tries not to let the pain in his side drive him toward panic. There's never been a trap he hasn't been able to get out of. He escaped from the Juvey-rounders who came to unwind him, and killed one of them in the process. He escaped from the Graveyard, even though he had to shatter his own hand to do it. The lesson? He can escape from any situation . . . but he must be willing to do the unthinkable.

"Let me kill him!" says the brutal one, clearly the enforcer of this team. "Let me kill him and be done with it."

"Stick to the plan," rasps the voice in the shadows. "He's worth more to us alive."

Starkey tries to calculate how far he might be from safety. The growing light confirms that it's daybreak. They took him sometime during the night. He could be hours away from his storks, or just outside the gate of the abandoned power plant they've been calling home. The plant is on the banks of the Mississippi. He tries to listen for the river, but realizes that the river moves so slowly, you couldn't hear it if it were right behind you. You can smell it, though. He takes a deep whiff. The air does not have the unpleasant smell of organic decay married to chemical runoff that typifies the Mississippi. His panic begins bubbling to the surface again.

And this on what should be the day of his greatest harvest camp attack.

"What do you want?" he asks.

Finally the second assailant steps out of the shadows. There's a third one too. Shorter than the other two, lingering back. He holds something in his hand. Could be a weapon of some sort. While the enforcer's face is fully exposed, these other two wear black ski masks hiding their faces in wool-knit obscurity.

"Beg for your life," says the third assailant, with the same breathy hiss as the other masked kidnapper.

"I don't beg," announces Starkey, and his posturing is met with silence. As his arms are tied behind his back, he has to squirm up to a sitting position. "But I'm sure we can work this out."

"We know who you are," says the enforcer. "There's a reward on your head—dead or alive. I prefer dead."

Now he thinks he knows their play. They intend to turn him in for the reward—but they could have just kept him unconscious until they handed him over. They want him to make a better offer, and with the clapper movement behind him, he has the resources to do it.

"Name your price," Starkey says. "I pay better than the Juvenile Authority."

The enforcer seethes. "You think this is about money? We're not interested in yours, or the Juvies' money either."

Starkey wasn't expecting that.

The enforcer looks to the second assailant as if for permission. Number two, who is clearly in charge, nods. Starkey suspects that it's a woman, but the shadows are still too thick to be sure.

"The Burmese Dah Zey pays in more than just cash," the enforcer tells him. "It pays in respect. And career advancement."

Starkey's fear, which had just been gnawing at him, now clamps down, driving its teeth deep. His blood literally begins to feel cold within his body, like his veins are being caressed with ice. "You can't be serious."

But their solemn silence proves that they are. There's the black market, and then there's the Dah Zey.

Starkey tries to swallow, but finds his throat too dry.

"Okay . . . okay . . . we can work this out. You don't need to do this; we can work this out." Maybe he does beg after all.

"Too late for that," snaps the enforcer.

"No," rasps the whisperer. "Let him talk."

Starkey knows this will be the greatest escape act of his life, if he can pull it off. "I can supply you," he says.

"We don't need supplies," says the enforcer.

"That's not what I mean. If you free me, I can supply you with Unwinds to sell to the Dah Zey. They're AWOL storks marked for unwinding, so no one will miss them. Imagine that—a constant supply . . . and not just any kids—I'll give you the cream of the crop. The strongest, the healthiest, the smartest. I'll keep you flush for a long, long time, and get you that respect you were talking about."

They just stare at him for a moment. Then the enforcer says, "You would do that? Sacrifice the other storks to save yourself?"

Starkey nods without hesitation. "What you don't understand is that they need me. They need me more than they need each other."

Again, weighty silence as they consider it. Starkey wishes he could see their eyes better. He wishes he could see the expressions of the other two behind their ski masks.

"How many will you give us?" the whisperer asks, her voice still a toneless rasp.

"How many do you need?" Starkey forces a smile. "Ten percent? Like a tithing? That's right, they'll be like tithes!"

Starkey knows he's getting somewhere. As for the logistics, those can be worked out later. The consequences of this escape can be dealt with. The aftermath is always manageable. All that matters in the moment is the escape itself.

"How could you do that to them?" says the third one, and his whisper breaks, a bit of roundness coming into his timbre. In the back of Starkey's mind, that voice is familiar, but it's so far back in his mind, he doesn't register it yet.

"I can do it because it's the right thing to do!" Starkey insists. "The idea of a war is more important than any of its warriors. And I *am* the idea!" Then he looks away. "I don't expect you to understand that."

And suddenly the whispering woman isn't whispering anymore. "We understand a lot more than you think." Starkey realizes who she is the moment before she removes her ski mask.

"Bam?"

She turns to the third attacker. "Are we good, Jeevan?"

Jeevan removes his mask as well, then fiddles with the small object in his hand. "Yeah, we're good."

As the betrayal takes hold in his mind, Starkey finds his fear replaced by fury. He struggles against his bonds. He can escape from the ropes, but it will take time. He doesn't have time! He wants to tear free now, so he can tear them all apart.

"He should die now!" announces the enforcer, who now paces in the background. "If I still had my garden shears, I'd stab them through his heart right now!"

But apparently no one present has either the guts or the inclination to end his life. It's their weakness that will save him.

"There's been enough killing," Bam says. "Go wait for us in the car. We'll be there in a minute."

"Who the hell is that clown?" Starkey asks.

"That 'clown' is the head gardener at Horse Creek Harvest Camp," Jeevan tells him. "You blew up his wife last week. You're lucky he didn't blow your brains out just now."

Starkey turns to Bam, realizing that this is still a negotiation, just a very different one. "Bam, let's talk about this. You've made your point, so let's talk."

"I'll talk," she says. "And you'll listen." She's calm. Too calm for Starkey's taste. He much preferred when her anger was out of control. That anger is malleable. It can be shaped any way Starkey wants. But this cool calm is like Teflon. He knows anything he says will slide right off it.

"You're going to disappear, Mason," she tells him. "I don't care where you go, but you're going to perform a total vanishing act. You will not kill the tithes at Mousetail. You will never attack another harvest camp. You'll never fight for another 'cause,' and most of all, you'll stay far away from the Stork Brigade, from now until the end of time. Or at least until the end of your miserable life."

Starkey glares at her. "And why would I do that?"

"This is why." And she turns to Jeevan, who fiddles with the device in his hands that Starkey had mistaken for a weapon. It's not a weapon at all; it's a small recording device. Jeevan hits a button, and it projects a hologram—a miniaturized version of the spot they still stand in, in high definition, just as clear as the real thing. Starkey watches himself say:

"If you free me, I can supply you with Unwinds to sell to the Dah Zey. They're AWOL storks marked for unwinding, so no one will miss them."

Starkey finds he can't contain his anger. He thrashes, making his broken ribs resonate in pain. He practically dislocates his shoulders trying to pull out of the bonds. "You *bitch*! You made me say that. You made me make the deal!"

And yet Bam holds her Teflon calm. "No one made you do anything, Mason. We just gave you the rope; you're the one who hanged yourself with it."

Jeevan laughs at that. "Good one," he says. "Hanged himself."

"If you ever surface again anywhere," Bam says, "we'll play that recording for the storks. Not just our storks, but publicly for every stork out there. You'll go from being their savior to being seen as the self-serving egomaniac that you are."

"Self-serving? I did all of this for them! All of it." Starkey would kill them right now if he could. The traitors! He would execute them without the slightest hesitation. Can't they see what they're doing? They're killing a dream larger than all of them. How can storks ever hope to change their plight in the world without their leader?

He wants to scream with a wordless fury, but knows he must try as best he can to match Bam's detachment. He forces down his anger and says, "It's the small minds in this world that destroy everything. Don't be a small mind, Bam. You're smarter than that. You're *better* than that."

Bam smiles, and Starkey thinks that maybe she's finally beginning to see the wisdom of his words. Until she says, "You're so smooth, Mason. You can slide your way into getting what you want, and then convince everyone around you that it's what they want too. That was your best magic trick. You made everyone believe you were doing this for them—when it was all for the fame and fortune of Mason Michael Starkey."

"That's not true!"

"See how good the illusion is?" Bam says. "Even you believe it."

Starkey will not entertain this accusation. He cannot doubt himself, because doubt is his enemy. So he'll let Bam go on with her mindless lecture. Let her think what she wants to think. She's just jealous that she can never be him, or have him, or be in the same league as him. He is Mason Michael Starkey, the avenger of storks. No matter how hard Bam tries to take that away, the world will reward him for all the good he's done. He didn't do it for the fame, but he certainly deserves it.

"I'll never be a great leader," Bam tells him. "But knowing that already makes me a better leader than you. I just wish I could have figured that out sooner."

Starkey is exhausted struggling against his bonds. They're

looser now. He will escape. Not this moment, but soon. Ten minutes, twenty. The question is, will he go after Bam and Jeevan, or will he cave to their blackmail and go into hiding forever?

"You've heard our demands, and you know what will happen if you don't follow them," Bam says. "On the other hand, if you get with the program, we'll keep that recording to ourselves. I know how important it is for you to be seen as the hero. You get to keep that. It's more than you deserve. We'll tell the storks you were captured while scouting out Mousetail, and that will make you an instant martyr. What could be better?"

Mason has no strength to argue anymore. He feels sick to his stomach, and he knows it's not just from the tranqs. "Someone's going to make you pay for this."

"Maybe, but it won't be you." Then she turns to Jeevan, who pulls out a tranq gun—one of the nice ones the clappers provided. Probably the same one they tranq'd him with the first time.

"We can't take a chance you'll break free too soon," Bam tells him. "And once you do free yourself, if you're tempted to look for us at the power plant, don't bother. We'll all be gone from there long before you wake up."

Jeevan comes close to Starkey, aims, but he doesn't shoot just yet. Instead he suddenly spits in Starkey's face. "That's for all the people who died because of me," says Jeevan. "The people who died because of the things you made me do!"

Starkey smiles at him, and repeats what Bam said just a few moments ago. "I didn't make you do anything, Jeevan. I just gave you the rope."

Jeevan's response is a tranq blast right into the space between his broken ribs.

29 · Hayden

The waiting is unbearable, but Hayden cannot let it show, or it would arouse suspicion. He wanted to go with Bam and Jeevan— not that he doesn't trust them, but he knows that Starkey is a difficult force to overcome. He was crafty enough to get this far, mesmerizing hundreds of kids long past the point when they should have done their own reality checks. Who's to say if he might not Houdini his way out of the trap they've set for him?

Hayden still finds it amazing that Starkey managed to carve himself a cult, with few tools beyond communal anger and a fistful of personal magnetism. But on the other hand, there are plenty of historical precedents.

It's morning in the abandoned plant that's not so abandoned anymore now that it's home to almost seven hundred storks. Breakfast is in full swing. The kids eat in three shifts in the plant's basement, using folding chairs and tables that were here for them when they arrived—as were comfortable bed rolls—all courtesy of the "applause department." Very organized, this society of randomized violence. They've vowed to keep the storks safe, although Hayden suspects they're only safe until the applause department decides it's time to sacrifice them, just as they sacrifice all the other angry kids they recruit to serve the cause of mayhem. The storks won't blow themselves up, of course, but in the end, following Starkey off a cliff isn't all that different.

Everyone knows their next mission. Starkey made an announcement, and rallied the troops. He hasn't told them yet that their ultimate objective is the extermination of the Mousetail tithes. They may never know. The only reason Hayden knows is because Bam shared it with him. Hayden suspects Starkey has selected an elite team to do the dirty deed once the harvest camp has been taken down. Or maybe he plans on herding the tithes into a single building and doing it himself with a shoulder-mounted rocket launcher. They certainly have bunker busters that can do it in one fell swoop.

But that's tomorrow. It doesn't explain why Starkey isn't here today. Hayden knows why. After all, it was his plan. The storks, however, can't know the truth.

"He went with a special team to do some reconnaissance," Hayden tells the masses when people begin to question Starkey's absence. Most of the kids accept it, and are relieved because maybe it pushes their imminent attack on Mousetail back a day or two. Of course, there are some kids who are suspicious. Garson DeGrutte is full of questions.

"Why didn't he tell us? Why didn't the clappers do reconnaissance for us, isn't that their job?" And, of course, the question that's most on his mind, "Why didn't he take me?"

Hayden plays it cool with a shrug. "Who can read the mind of the master?" Hayden tells him. "And maybe he left you here because he wanted to give you more quality time with Abigail." And then, for the second half of his one-two punch, Hayden gets quiet and whispers. "You know, with Starkey off-site, that office he likes to hang out in is empty . . . and very private. . . ."

With that suggestion, all the blood leaves Garson's brain and goes other places, leaving him with no further questions. Hayden then quickly finds Abigail and assigns her to shuck the thousand ears of corn that showed up in their last shipment, ensuring that she'll have no time for Garson. Even when Garson joins her, frantically shucking corn to speed up the process, Hayden knows it will take all day. He suspects that Abigail would rather shuck Hayden's corn in the kitchen than Garson's in the office.

Hayden walks the floor all morning, taking in the conversations, or lack thereof, trying to get a bead on today's mood. A mob, he knows, can be as dysfunctional as a family, given a bad enough parent—and Starkey is as dysfunctional as they come. Perhaps that's part of the reason why so many of these kids have been willing to follow Starkey: He reminds them of home.

"These waffles suck," says a malcontent stork who said the same thing when they were getting watery powdered eggs that actually did suck. Now the applause department supplies them a much higher quality of food than they could get for themselves. But there are always the complainers.

"Sorry," Hayden tells him. "The seafood breakfast buffet is tomorrow. I'll make sure they save you some crab legs and caviar."

He gives Hayden the finger and continues to scarf down his waffle. Since arriving at the plant two weeks ago, Hayden has not only been in charge of inventory, he's overseeing food preparation as well, due to the fact that the former kid in charge of the kitchen died in the Horse Creek Harvest Camp attack. It seems all of Hayden's jobs of late have been the result of terminal vacation of post.

With each harvest camp takedown, the mood among the storks has become progressively more somber and volatile. There have been more threatening glares, more fights over nothing, more issues among kids who had plenty of issues already. The last attack brought a numbness and an indefinable throbbing like the ache of a phantom limb. There is a vacuum left behind by the dead that can't be filled by the new faces added to their numbers, and there's no way to predict the names and numbers of the casualties yet to come from their next mission.

Starkey still has his die-hard believers who try to compensate for the plunging morale by screaming and cheering the loudest when he tries to rally them to the fever pitch he feeds on, but their efforts are less and less effective.

"Where are they, Hayden?"

He turns to see a girl loudly dropping her plate into the bus bin next to her table with an angry clatter as the punctuation to her question—although clearly it's an accusation. This is one of the girls liberated from Cold Springs Harvest Camp, where the director convinced everyone that Hayden was working for the Juvies. Those kids still cling to the belief that Hayden is a traitor. The one saving grace of the haters is that they keep him on his toes, never allowing him to get too complacent or comfortable.

"Where are what?" asks Hayden. "The sausages, you mean? They're gone, but there's still plenty of bacon."

"Don't play dumb. You said Starkey went with a team, but I've been checking around, and the only ones not here are Starkey, Bam, and Jeevan. That's not the kind of team Starkey would take. If you ask me, I think you have something to do with their disappearance."

A few other kids have taken notice of this little confrontation. One kid meets eyes with Hayden, rolling his as if to say *I'm on your side—these Cold Springs kids are nuts.* As more and more are added to their numbers, the voices of the Cold Springs haters mean less and less. In spite of them, Hayden knows he can be a leader here if he wants to. Good thing he doesn't want to.

"Anyone with half a brain could see that Starkey needs an assault team leader to scope the place out, and a hacker to figure out how to foil the security system," Hayden tells her, "otherwise more of us could die in the attack." Hayden makes sure to emphasize the word "die." Which has the desired affect. Everyone at the accusational girl's table becomes uncomfortable, as if spiders have just crawled into their laps from beneath the table.

"Why do we have to attack another harvest camp?" asks

Elias Dean, one of the mouthier kids. "Haven't we done enough already?"

Hayden smiles. The fact that kids are voicing their reservations out loud is a very good sign. "Starkey says we'll keep it up until either the harvest camps are all gone, or *we're* all gone."

More spiders, at more tables. The kind that bite.

"One of these days they'll be ready for us," someone else mumbles, "and take us all out before we even get through the gate."

"Starkey's a genius and all," Elias says, "but it's a little much, don't you think?"

"Not my job to think, although I occasionally do," Hayden says. "I'm glad that you do too." And that's as far as Hayden will take it. God forbid he be accused of fomenting dissent.

The "reconnaissance team" returns at noon.

"They're back," announces a guard running in from his lookout at the rusty front gate of the plant. At first Hayden thinks the plan must have failed—or that maybe Bam and Jeevan scrubbed it, unable to go through with it. Maybe their accomplice, the gardener, never showed to make the capture feel authentic. But when Bam and Jeevan enter, Starkey is not with them—a fact that the lookout was not observant enough to notice.

"Where's Starkey?" comes the obvious question—not just from one stork, but from many, whispering the question to one another, not daring to ask Bam or Jeevan. The storks are afraid. They're hopeful. They're angry. They are filled with too many emotions to sort.

Hayden approaches Bam and Jeevan with caution, knowing he's being watched, knowing that all three of them are being measured in the moment.

"Don't tell me—you got stranded in a mountain pass, and

had to do like the Donner party," Hayden says. "If you ate Starkey, I hope you saved me some breast meat."

"You're not funny," Bam says, loudly enough for Hayden to know it's for show. "We were ambushed by parts pirates. We're lucky we're still in one piece." She hesitates as more kids drift into hearing range, drawn by the curious gravity of tragedy. "They recognized Starkey, so they tranq'd Jeevan and me, and left us there. When we came to, Starkey was gone. They took him."

No gasps, no cries, just silence. Jeevan tries to slip away, not wanting to be within this little center of attention, but Bam holds him tightly by the shoulder, preventing him from leaving.

"Starkey's gone?" asks one of the youngest, smallest storks—one whom Hayden recalls having trouble wielding his weapon at the last takedown.

"I'm sorry," says Bam. "There was nothing we could do."

And to Hayden's amazement, Bam's eyes begin to cloud with tears. Either she's far better at deception than Hayden ever gave her credit for, or at least part of her emotion is real.

"What do we do?" someone asks.

"We go on without him," Bam says with subtle authority. "Gather everyone on the turbine floor. We have decisions to make."

Word quickly spreads, and the somber sense of hopelessness lifts as everyone begins to grapple with the idea of a world without Starkey. The three girls in his personal harem alternate between comforting and sniping at one another. They are inconsolable, but they are the only ones. Even Garson DeGrutte and Starkey's other supporters have quickly overcome their grief, and are now promoting themselves, jockeying for a leadership position in the new hierarchy. But when Bam addresses the storks later that morning, she's a commanding presence that makes it clear who's in charge. No one has the audacity to challenge her authority. From here on in, all the jockeying will be for positions beneath her leadership.

She doesn't so much give a speech as tell everyone how it is. It's not a rallying hyperbole-filled war cry like Starkey might have delivered, just a bracing dose of harsh, heavy reality. She drives three key points home:

"We're a fugitive mob of unwanted kids with a price on our heads."

"Our friends, the clappers, are worse than our enemies."

"If we're going to stay whole and alive, we're going to have to stop taking down harvest camps, and disappear. Now."

And although there are some who bluster about vengeance, and what Starkey would want, those voices are weak and find no resonance among the storks. With Bam's declaration, their suicide run has ended, and their new mission is to live. Hard to argue with survival.

"Well done," Hayden tells her, catching her alone in one of the ammunition storerooms. "Are you going to tell me what really happened?"

"You know what happened. Your plan happened, and he fell right into it, just like you said he would."

Bam tells him about the video, carefully recorded and duplicated, and stashed in various virtual locations like defensive nukes, should Starkey launch an offensive.

"Are you really sure he won't just come right back here?" Bam asks.

Although nothing is ever 100 percent, Hayden is pretty sure. "In the battle between ego and vengeance, Starkey's ego wins. His image is more important than his need to get back at you. He might try, but not until he he's scrounged himself up a new murder of storks to follow him."

She gives him the sneering curl of her lip that feels less intimidating than it used to. "It pisses me off that you know him better than I do."

"I'm a savant when it comes to character judgment," he tells her. "For instance, most people wouldn't see anything in you besides attitude and a need for stronger deodorant, but I think you can handle the storks almost as well as Connor handled the Graveyard."

Bam gives him a halfhearted glare. "Can you ever give a compliment without also making it an insult?"

"No," he admits. "Not possible. It's the essence of my charm."

Bam turns to restack some of the weapons piled in the room, and Hayden helps her, checking to make sure that they are all unloaded and safeties are in place. Can't be too careful when it comes to deadly automatic firepower.

Bam pauses for a moment, looking at the weapons piled before them. "There's no question that power blew out Starkey's brain," Bam says, "but what he did . . . it wasn't all bad. We have more than five hundred kids who would have been unwound, and that doesn't even count the nonstorks we freed from those harvest camps."

Although Hayden isn't big on apologetics for tyrants, he offers her the benefit of a shrug. "Maybe in the big picture the end justifies the means, and maybe not. All I know for sure is that no one else is going to be hanged, shot, or otherwise executed for Mason Starkey's version of justice. And don't forget we just prevented a major massacre of innocent kids."

"Who will now be unwound on schedule," Bam reminds him.

"But not by us."

Several storks come into the storeroom to deposit their weapons. Bam thanks them, and they hurry out, relieved to make the guns someone else's problem. The plan is to keep only enough weapons for defense, should defense be needed. The rest will be left behind when they leave the power plant—and they'll have to leave soon. Once the bigwigs in the applause department know that Starkey is gone, it's anyone's guess what they'll do. Perhaps descend from the skies in a mass of unmarked helicopters and snuff them all. Hayden wouldn't put it past them.

"I've pegged Garson DeGrutte as my second-in-command, since you've made it clear you don't want the position," Bam says.

"You're kidding me!"

"He was a nuisance under Starkey, but he respects authority and follows orders. With Starkey out of the picture, I think he'll be an asset. And besides, we've got to keep him busy now that Abigail broke up with him."

Hayden laughs. "Shucking corn can kill any relationship." Then he finds himself getting uncharacteristically serious. "So what's next?" he asks, because his plan for the Stork Brigade only went so far as Starkey's removal.

"I have storks working on finding us somewhere safe," Bam tells him. "There are lots of places to hide. We'll find one, hunker down, and make it work."

"I wish you luck," Hayden tells her.

She eyes him with the old suspicion. "You're not coming with us?"

Hayden presents her with an overexaggerated sigh. "As much as I would enjoy being éminence gris to your striking figurehead, it's time I left for greener pastures. Actually, I've been considering setting out with a small crew of my own and reestablishing my broadcast radio show, since the podcasts keep being squelched by the Juvenile Authority a few hours after I post them."

Bam laughs at that. "Hayden, your broadcast never reached beyond the Graveyard, and even then, no one was listening but you."

"Yes, I do love to hear myself talk—but I think I can get a wider audience with the help of Jeevan and a few choice members of a special-ops team. We'll be the Verbal Strike Force. VSF, for short, because initials are always much more impressive."

Bam shakes her head. "You're an odd bird, Hayden."

"This coming from a stork named Bambi."

Bam offers him a genuine smile. Something he's rarely seen. "Call me that again," she says, "and I'll deck you."

30 · Starkey

It's night when he regains consciousness. The tranqs stole the whole day from him. He's shivering from a mild but constant rain and is near hypothermia, but he forces clarity to his thoughts. He knows his actions now are crucial if he's going to overcome this new dire circumstance. He borrows heat from his burning emotions to drag warmth into his body. The adrenaline of anger.

One would think that to be dethroned—to be torn from power—would bring unbearable humiliation . . . but not to Mason Michael Starkey. Perhaps because the core of his being has taken on a potent yin-yang of ambition swirled into righteous indignation. Those driving forces have become the essence of who he is, and they leave no room for humiliation. All Starkey can feel is fury at the betrayal, and a burning desire to reclaim the leadership that is rightfully his. The leadership he has earned. Treason is the highest crime of any culture, and he is determined to make the traitors pay.

He will lead the storks once more. Maybe not today, but soon. He'll have to bide his time. He has the money and the power of the clapper movement behind him, and he knows how to contact them, so he is not without hope, or friends. Dandrich gave him a phone number to use in case of emergency, and he can think of no emergency greater than this.

But first things first. Right now, he's got to get himself out of the cold. He must find some sort of shelter. In his darkest moments, he never dreamed he'd be thrust back into basic survival mode again. *They've taken everything away from me,* he thinks, but he strangles the thought before it can take hold. He despises those who feel sorry for themselves. He will not stoop so low.

He knows it won't be easy for him now. He's America's most wanted. There's nowhere he can go where he won't be recognized instantly. He'll be prey for anyone with a phone, looking to cash in on the huge reward being offered for his capture. Now the price on his head is far greater than the value his adoptive parents ever saw in him.

His future will all come down to a phone. The first one he sees will be either his salvation or his ruin depending on who gets to dial it first: him or the phone's owner, who will most certainly be calling the police.

Still dizzy from the tranqs, he makes his way through the woods to a highway, forcing his stiff legs to walk at a brisk pace, generating body heat, but still shivering with every step. A mile and a half up the road, he comes to a service area and hurries into the glorious warmth of a convenience store. He quickly sizes up the people there. A grisly looking clerk, a family deciding on snacks, and an old man in filthy jeans trying to scrounge up enough coins for a lottery ticket. No one looks at him as he slips into the bathroom and locks the door behind him. He sits on the toilet, fully clothed, too dehydrated to even pee, and gets his shivering under control. It takes longer than he thought it would, and finally the clerk bangs on the door.

"You okay in there, dude?"

"Yeah, I'll be out in a second."

He takes another minute, flexing the fingers of his good hand, and stands, noting that the last of his tranq vertigo has worn off. Then he steps back out into the convenience store, where another family argues about snacks, and a woman baffled by the coffee machine tries to figure out which is decaf and which is regular. The clerk is busy ringing up a fat man's gas, and Starkey gets down to business.

He goes outside, where the fat man's car waits, the gas hose still in the tank. Lo and behold, there's a phone plugged into a charger on the console inside. Starkey opens the door, but as he reaches for the phone, a kid in the shadows of the backseat yells, "Hey! Get outta here! Dad! Help!"

Starkey flinches, but it's too late to abort.

"Sorry, kid." He grabs the phone, disconnecting it from the charger, but the kid continues to scream, and the father bursts out of the shop.

Starkey curses himself for the clumsiness of the theft. As a magician, he always prided himself on his ability to slip things like watches, wallets, and phones in and out of pockets without being noticed. It's demoralizing to be so desperate that he must steal so inelegantly.

With the man taking chase, Starkey sprints into the dark brushy field behind the convenience store, continuing to run long after the cries of the kid and his furious but ponderously slow father can no longer be heard.

When he's sure he's too far away to be seen or followed, he checks the phone. For a moment, he thinks its interface is locked and he won't be able to use it, but luckily, the man was not expecting his phone to be taken from the safety of his vehicle. Starkey pulls up a dial screen and keys in the emergency number he'd been given. It rings twice, then a nondescript voice answers the phone with a standard, "Hello?"

"This is Mason Starkey," he says. "Something's happened. I need help."

He quickly explains the situation as best he can in a single breath. And calmly the voice on the other end of the line says, "Stay where you are. We'll come to you."

Following the instructions he's given, Starkey keeps the phone powered on, to be used as a homing beacon, and within an hour, a helicopter descends from the night sky like the proverbial stork to carry him to a place of greater safety.

Starkey has no idea where he's been taken. It's a city. That's all he knows. He's not so sophisticated as to know the silhouettes of a skyline at the earliest hint of dawn. All he knows for sure is that it's near a large body of water, and that it's colder than where he was, as evidenced by the blast of chilly air when they open the helicopter door and escort him from the rooftop heliport. It's a tall building, but not the tallest. Average, as far as skyscrapers go.

He knew the clapper movement was well funded and well organized, but to have such headquarters in plain sight gives Starkey pause for thought. In his own imagination, the clapper movement was far grittier and more counterculture. Hiding, perhaps in the dangerous backrooms of questionable clubs. That they have their own office building, however, is somehow more unsettling. The logo on the building—he saw it as the helicopter approached—is a simple design he did not recognize. It featured the initials "PC," which seem fairly generic and could stand for a great many things.

He's escorted down a flight of stairs and into an elevator by two men in dark suits with chests too well developed for them to be anything but security boeufs. The elevator takes him down to the thirty-seventh floor, and he's brought to a conference room with black leather chairs and a long table of blue marble. No one is present.

"Wait here," one of the guards says. "Someone will be along shortly."

The room has only one door, which the men lock as they

exit, leaving him alone. There are east-facing floor-to-ceiling windows, but they're made of the kind of frosted glass that diffuses light while denying a view. Translucent rather than transparent. The rising sun is little more than a golden haze.

He was alone in the helicopter, too. The pilot, sequestered in the cockpit, never spoke to him after letting him into the craft, other than to say, "Buckle in." The fact that they sent him a rescue craft so quickly, and that they've placed him in such a richly appointed room of their inner sanctum, tells Starkey that he's respected and valued. And yet, there's unease in him as diffuse and ill-defined as the light coming through the frosted windows.

No one comes.

After an hour, he tries, without luck, to jimmy the door lock using a paper clip he found on the floor. Despite his skill with locks, he can't pick this one.

"Hey!" he yells. "I'm still here in case you forgot! Someone get your ass over here and let me out!"

He begins pounding on the door, trying to create enough of a commotion that someone will come to shut him up. Nothing. It's as if the entire floor is deserted. Or maybe soundproof. Furious, he begins knocking over chairs, making a racket, but if, indeed, no one's there to hear him, all the sound and fury will signify nothing. Finally, not wanting to be found the author of this particular chaos, he sets the chairs back where he found them and, exhausted, sits down and cradles his head in his arms on the table. He falls asleep in moments.

He dreams of Bam. She's laughing at him. She's goading the others to laugh at him as well, and although he fires a machine gun at her, nothing comes out but flower petals and jelly beans and popcorn, and that just makes everyone laugh even more. Then Hayden grabs the machine gun away from

UnDivided

him and shoves the muzzle so far up his nose he can feel it in his brain. "That'll clear your sinuses," Hayden says, and the laughter all around feels like it can fill a stadium.

He's gently shaken awake by a hand on his shoulder and pulled mercifully out of the dream.

"Mr. Starkey?"

He looks up bleary eyed to see a well-groomed man with a tightly trimmed salt-and-pepper beard. Dandrich.

"About time," Starkey croaks.

"I gave orders that you be taken somewhere to rest until I arrived," he says kindly. "Orders, however, are often left to interpretation."

"Someone should be fired."

Dandrich considers it. "Or at least reprimanded. Be that as it may, I hope you got some rest. You must be exhausted from your triumphant efforts."

Starkey rolls the kink out of his neck while the man pours him a glass of water from a crystal pitcher that wasn't there before. "What is this place?"

Dandrich hands him the glass. "It's what is commonly called 'an undisclosed location'."

"It seems pretty disclosed to me if it's right in the middle of a city."

"It's not only AWOLs who can disappear in an urban environment, my friend," he says, sitting down casually beside Starkey. "To city dwellers, most buildings, no matter how large, are merely obstacles between home and office. In a city, convenience and anonymity go hand in hand. But we're not here to talk about our headquarters, are we?"

"There's a team of traitors." Starkey says, getting to the point. "We need to take them out if we're going to save the Stork Brigade."

Dandrich does not seem troubled. "A coup is always an

205

unfortunate thing. Unless, of course, you are the one staging it."

Starkey thinks of the coup he staged at the Graveyard. What goes around comes around, but the timing couldn't have been worse

"It's not a surprise that after the festivities at Horse Creek Harvest Camp, a number of storks would become disenchanted," his benefactor says.

"They invented an incriminating recording, but with your help I can convince everyone it's a fake. Send me back there with more firepower. I'll get control again, and rally them to the cause."

"No need." Dandrich says. "Your last few attacks have been so successful, we've decided that no further action on your part is needed."

"But what about Mousetail?"

"Unnecessary. It would be anticlimactic after what you did at Horse Creek. You were brilliant there," he says with a smile. Then his smile drifts neutral. "You were brilliant, but now you're done."

Starkey shakes his head. "There are still ninety-two harvest camps out there. You need me to take them down."

"Mason, you forget that it's not our purpose to take down every harvest camp."

Starkey stands up. "Well, it's *my* purpose!"

Now Dandrich's expression becomes icy. "We are not in the business of indulging adolescent power fantasies."

Even though the man is scrawny and at the weak end of middle age, Starkey finds himself intimidated by his unflinching gaze.

"So that's it? You're done with me? You're just going to cast me out into the street?"

Dandrich laughs at the suggestion, and his expression softens again. "No, of course not. We would never abandon someone as valuable as you. You can still serve our cause."

"To hell with your cause! What about *my* cause?"

"A wise general knows when his campaign has run its course." Then he raises his hands in broad sweeping gestures as he speaks. "Look at what you've done! Be satisfied that you made yourself the legend that you always dreamed you could be. That you freed hundreds of Unwinds. That you saved so many storks and struck a blow for what you believe."

Maybe he's right, but Starkey can't stand the thought that he was cast out, and now is being denied the right of vengeance. He slams his fist on the table. "They need to pay for what they've done!"

Dandrich never loses his cool. "They will. In time."

Starkey calms himself down. Patience was his strongest asset at the Graveyard. When did he lose it? He takes a deep breath, then another. If he can belay his thirst for revenge, it will be all the more satisfying and devastating when it comes. The betrayal has not undone his good work. He has to remember that. And in this strange organization that espouses the virtues of chaos and mayhem, he will find his place. Here, too, he will find ways of setting gears into motion, just as he did at the Graveyard.

"You've been the subject of much discussion," Dandrich says, "and we've decided that your greatest potential lies in our fund-raising division."

"Fund-raising?"

"There are people who would like to get to know you on a close, personal level," he says. "Important people. Some very wealthy, some very powerful."

"So . . . you're going to introduce me to these people?"

"Not personally, but I assure you, you will be in good hands." He opens the door, where two more beefy men in suits await. "My associates here will escort you to your new assignment." Then he shakes Starkey's hand. "Thank you for all you've done. I'm glad that our paths crossed, and that, for a time, our objectives complemented each other. Take care, Mason." And then he leaves Starkey with the two burly men, who lead him back to the elevator.

"Where am I going, if you don't mind me asking?" he asks the more intelligent-looking of the two guards as the elevator rises toward the rooftop heliport.

"Uh . . . from what I understand, you're going lots of places."

Which is fine with Starkey. He could get used to traveling in style.

31 · Grace

There are simply too many envelopes to mail for this to be a single postal excursion. Grace decides to make three trips—and not all to the same place. She plans multiple trips to multiple zip codes and finds an oversize unmarked shopping bag to carry them in—big enough and sturdy enough to get it done in three trips.

"Less suspicious this way," she tells Sonia. "So's if the postmaster general or something gets it into his head to trace all these letters back to a single place, they won't know where to look 'cept Akron in general, and Akron in general is big—not New York big, but big enough."

Sonia waves her hand. "Just get it done and don't talk my ear off." Which is fine with Grace, who likes being left to her own devices, as long as those devices don't have too much electronics, like that organ printer. She knows it will take her all day, but that's okay. It's something to do, something important, and it gets her out of the basement for a whole day.

Her first two sets of drops go off without a hitch. It's Sunday, so post offices are closed, but that hasn't stopped her from paying visits to various mailboxes in strategically random locations. By dusk, she's hit twelve mailboxes in three different zip codes.

It's while on her way back to empty out the trunk and mail the last batch of letters that things take a turn. It's already dusk, closer to the night side than the day, and she begins to think that the third batch will have to wait until tomorrow. The streetlights come on, making the dusk plunge into night—and there beneath a streetlight at the corner, just a few doors away from Sonia's shop, stands someone who looks familiar. Very familiar. She can see only his profile, but it's enough.

"Argie?" she says, before she can stop herself. "Argie, is that you?"

At first she's excited, but then she remembers how things were when she last saw her brother. He won't have forgiven her. Argent is not the forgiving type. As she gets closer, she can sense that there's something off about him. Something different in the way he carries himself, like it's not Argent at all . . . and yet clearly it's him. She only has to look at his face to know. . . .

Then he turns to her and smiles. "Hello, Grace."

And she begins to scream. Not because of what she sees but because of what she doesn't. She doesn't even feel the tranq dart hit her, because she's so committed to the scream. She's still screaming as her legs buckle beneath her and she hits the pavement. Still screaming as her peripheral vision fades. Still screaming as the tranqs drag her down into unconsciousness.

Because when he turned to look at her, Grace didn't see the other half of Argent's face. That other half was someone else entirely.

32 · Sonia

She's absorbed with her favorite playlist of prewar rock, and doesn't hear Grace's screams from just twenty yards down the street.

It's one song later—just after dark—that a man comes into the shop. Sonia takes out her earphones, immediately sizing up the man as a strange one. Strange in an unpleasant sort of way. She's been repositioning paintings so that they don't topple over every time some fool customer brushes up against them, and finds herself at a disadvantage being so far from her sales counter. She keeps a revolver beneath that counter. She only had to use it once, when a low-life thug demanded the cash in her register. She pulled out the revolver, and he headed for the hills. She didn't even have to use it. Right now, the man is standing between her and that revolver.

Putting down the picture she's holding, she tries to stand as straight as she can, considering her aggravated hip. "Can I help you?"

As he approaches, and comes into clearer focus, she sees what it is about him that's so disturbing. The left side of his face is that of a middle-aged man. But the right, from just above the jawline, is someone else's. Someone younger. Facial grafts are not entirely uncommon, but rarely do they preserve the integrity of the donor face. For whatever reason, this man intentionally took not just the skin, but the underlying bone structure of the donor as well. The sight of him is deeply unnerving, which was clearly his intent.

"I hope you *can* help me," he says, continuing to saunter toward her. "I'm looking for a very specific chair to complete a set. Solid frame, but a bit unbalanced. Firm, but overstuffed. That is to say, a little full of itself."

"Dining chairs are down aisle three," Sonia tells him, but she already knows he's not really looking for a chair.

"It won't be down aisle three," he says, holding her eye contact with two markedly mismatching eyes—one that clearly came with the grafted half of his face. "But I think it's here somewhere. The piece of flotsam I'm looking for goes by the name of Connor Lassiter."

"Hmph," says Sonia, keeping her poker face and pushing past him without any sense of urgency or terror. "Why would the Akron AWOL be in an antique shop? Wherever he is, I'm sure he has better things to do than polish my furniture."

"Perhaps I should ask Grace Skinner, then," he says. "Once she regains consciousness."

Now that he's behind her, and the counter is in front of her, she bolts toward it, but even with her cane, she can only move so fast.

Suddenly a gunshot rings out. The bullet hits her cane, splintering it to pieces, and she goes down sideways, hitting the hardwood floor. Pain explodes in her hip. She's sure that it's broken. What happens next comes with blinding speed, yet somehow in slow motion at the same time, her pain baffling the impetus of time.

She's dragged into the back room, and before she knows what has happened she finds herself slumped at her desk chair unable to move, her hip screaming in agony. He's used the chain from an old hanging lamp to secure her, wrapping it around her until it would take cable shears to free her.

Her attacker, with nothing but time on his hands now, saunters out into the shop again, whistling a tune she doesn't know. He locks the front door and returns, sitting on the edge of the old steamer trunk. *Did they hear the gunshot down below?*

Sonia wonders. *Are they smart enough to stay silent?* For it's not her life she's worried about; it's theirs.

"Now then," say both sides of the man's awful face, "let's talk about the friends we have in common."

33 · Nelson

With the infected, sun-scarred side of his face replaced, Jasper Thomas Nelson feels like a new man. Argent Skinner wasn't exactly a cooperative donor, of course.

"You said it yourself," he had told Argent before the undamaged side of the young man's face was harvested by Divan. "My left half and your right half make a whole." And although Argent insisted this is not what he meant, the complaints of a donor really don't matter.

Seeing the look on Grace Skinner's face when she saw him was an added perk. It will be even more rewarding to capture Lassiter's expression when they meet.

He had used a fast-acting, short-term tranq on Grace. Good thing, too. A stronger, slower tranq would have left her screaming long enough to attract plenty of attention. As it was, no one came to her aid. Nelson was able to throw her into a dense hedge, to keep her out of sight and out of mind. Then he proceeded to the antique shop where the tracking chip showed she was spending all of her time—that is, until today, when she went on an excursion all over Akron.

The moment he saw the old woman in the shop, Nelson read in her face a solid preview of all the things he needed to know. Lassiter is there, or has been there, or is hidden somewhere nearby—and Nelson is willing to wager that that stinking tithe-turned-clapper is here too. He doesn't know which will be more satisfying—taking the Akron AWOL to be unwound, or slowly killing Lev Calder for what he did at the Graveyard. Punishment for stealing Lassiter away from him, and leaving Nelson tranq'd by the side of the road for flesh-eating predators and the fiery eye of the Arizona sun.

Everything Nelson said to the old woman in the front room of her shop was to throw her off-balance, to probe her to see what she might unintentionally give away. Her reaction told him that he had hit a bull's-eye.

Now, here in the back room, he has her at his gentle mercy. All that remains is to extract the information he needs. This will certainly be easier than catching Lassiter at the airplane Graveyard. This will be a cakewalk, and after all he's been through, heaven knows, he deserves it.

34 · Sonia

This man is no Juvey-cop. He's not even a proper parts pirate. Sonia knows there is something fundamentally wrong with him. Something internally disfigured far worse than is revealed by his horrible face.

"If the media has it right, the triple threat has come together again," he says. "Connor Lassiter, Lev Calder, and Risa Ward. I'm hoping you can confirm that for me."

Sonia catches him eying the groceries stacked around the back room. She curses herself for not bringing them downstairs.

"Clearly, you're feeding a horde, and this is an ADR safe house. I didn't know there were any left."

Sonia says nothing. The trunk is on the rug, and the rug is smoothed out, leaving no hint that either has been moved. Not hint of the trapdoor beneath. He might suspect that she's harboring AWOLs, but he has no idea where.

When she doesn't answer him, he sighs and stands up, approaching her. "Don't assume I'm going to enjoy what I'm about to do," he says. "I do it only because it's necessary." Then he reaches out to her and presses his thumb against her broken left hip, with more force than anyone should be capable of delivering.

Beyond unbearable, the pain is unthinkable. She tries to bite it back, but it comes warbling out as a feeble wail between her gritted teeth. Dark worms squirm across her eyesight, threatening to overtake her, but then they recede to the periphery as he removes his thumb and backs away, assessing her. The pain remains and she feels weaker than she's ever felt. She wishes she could take the splintered end of her shattered cane and jam it through his stolen eye.

"Once again . . . Connor Lassiter."

Still Sonia says nothing. Let him kill her, she will still not speak. She thinks he may step forward again and cause her even more pain, but instead he turns to the trunk and, without the slightest hesitation, kicks it to the side, then flips back the rug to reveal the trapdoor beneath.

"Did you think I was stupid? I was a Juvey-Cop long enough to smell a hiding place the second I walk into a room. I wonder how many stinking AWOLs you have down there. Ten? Twenty?"

It's a far more effective tactic than pain as far as Sonia is concerned, and this bastard knows it. "Leave them alone! You're not here for them," Sonia reminds him.

"Indeed not." Now he sits on the edge of her desk, close to her. On her desk is a bowlful of old-fashioned cigarette lighters she was polishing and preparing to display in the shop. He pulls one out, silver with a red enameled rose, petals like flames.

"I truly pity you," he says. "You're the old woman who feeds the pigeons and allows them to propagate and spread disease." He flicks the lighter and watches the flame as it dances. "You're the misguided soul who lets rats overrun the city because you think they're an endangered species." He waves it before her, dangerously close, taunting, and she can do nothing about it. "You're certainly old enough to remember what it used to be like. People afraid to leave their homes for fear of feral teenagers, while other people suffered needlessly with everything from heart failure to lung cancer!" He flips the lighter closed, snuffing the flame, but doesn't put it down. "People like you baffle me. How could you not see the good in unwinding?"

And although Sonia does not want to dignify him with a response, she can't stop herself. "Those kids are human beings!"

"Were," he corrects. "Each has been deemed by society, and even by their own parents, to be worthless. What makes you think you know better?"

"Are you done?"

"That depends. Is Connor Lassiter down there with the rest of your pigeons?"

Sonia considers how she might respond, and decides that a half-truth may set them free.

"He's flown the coop. Here and gone. He won't stay anywhere for long."

"Then you won't mind if I check downstairs, will you?" He pockets the lighter and pulls out his gun—then a second pistol, checking the clips. One must be loaded with tranqs, the other with bullets. By the way in which he had shattered her cane, she knows those bullets are the deadly hollow-tipped kind. Miniature grenades exploding on contact. Her AWOLs won't stand a chance.

And then Sonia has a desperate idea.

"Connor left . . . but Lev Calder is here. I'll get him to come up . . . if you leave the rest of my AWOLs alone."

He smiles. "You see—that wasn't so hard. I had faith you could be reasoned with." He goes over to the trapdoor and reaches down toward it. "Be good," he tells Sonia. "And be convincing. If I leave here with Lev, I promise the rest of your brood will be safe." Then he pulls the trapdoor open and nods to Sonia.

"Lev!" she calls out. "Lev, can you come up? I need your help up here."

No response.

"You can do better than that," whispers the split-faced man.

"Lev! Get your ass up here!" Sonia calls, much louder. "I don't have all day." And Sonia closes her eyes, silently praying that those kids down there are smart enough to figure it out, and to do what needs to be done.

35 · Risa

Four minutes before the trapdoor opens, Risa hears a gunshot, and the sound of something—or someone—thudding to the floor. They all hear it, and it freezes them in the middle of whatever they're doing.

"Shh! Nobody move," says Beau. Then quieter: "And nobody talk."

Suddenly it's as if the floor beneath them—or, more accurately, the floor above them—has turned to ice that could fracture with the slightest shift of weight. The first thing that Risa does is reflexively look for Connor, then an instant later realizes he's not there. According to Sonia, he went to take care of "unfinished business," and although Sonia wouldn't say specifically, Risa knows what that business is. Just like the time he rescued Didi from the doorstep, Connor has impulsively chosen the wrong time to do the right thing. She curses him and prays for him at the same time, because at least he's away from here.

Everyone looks up, following the sound of something heavy being dragged from the shop and into the back room. Is it Sonia being dragged? Is it Grace? She was out taking care of "unfinished business" as well, wasn't she? What if one of them was shot? What if one of them is dead?

Beau turns off all the lights except for the single dim dangling one in the middle of the basement, because without it the darkness would be unbearable.

"What do we do?" asks Ellie, a girl who's always looking to Risa for guidance.

"Listen to Beau," she whispers. "Stay still, and stay quiet!"

Risa, however, is the first to break their terrified tableau, and looks for something she can use as a weapon. She finds a claw hammer. Other kids, seeing what she's doing, move quietly to find their own makeshift weapons.

Risa sees Beau eying the one window in the basement. It's a small thing positioned high up the wall, in a far corner. The glass is smudged with grease that makes it impossible to see out, or in.

"Never open that window," Sonia always told them. "You never know who will be in the alley out there." And just to make sure none of them was ever tempted, the window frame has been nailed shut.

Beau grabs the hammer from Risa, giving her a wrench instead. Risa nods her understanding, and Beau makes his way to window, taking the claw end of the hammer to the nails, trying to wrest them free from the wood.

While Beau works the window, Risa quietly makes her way to the stairs. A kid tries to stop her, but she gives him an evil enough eye to make him back away. She climbs the stairs to the dark recesses just beneath the trapdoor. She knows she'll have warning before that door is pulled open. She'll hear the sliding of the trunk.

Risa tilts her head, focusing all her attention on any sounds coming from upstairs. The violent noises of just a few moments ago have ended. Now there's just talking. A man in conversation with Sonia. Risa takes a deep breath of relief just to know that the old woman's still alive. She wants to go up there and help her, but there's nothing Risa can do; the trapdoor can only be opened from the other side. She looks down the stairs to see the kids all armed with various basement items: pipes, scissors, bricks, and boards.

And then Sonia screams.

It's muffled, but there's no denying that it's a scream of pain. Then the trunk is slid away. Risa feels more than hears it: a vibration in the wood of the stairs that resonates in her bones. She scrambles down to the bottom of the stairs, backing into shadows with everyone else.

Beau steps away from the basement window. He was able to remove only one nail. "This is it," he tells Risa "This is the end for all of us if we don't play this right."

She wants to challenge that fatalistic view—but she can't, because he's right. *Maybe Connor will come back just in time,* she thinks. *He'll see what's going on upstairs and do something about it.* After all, Connor does have a talent for falling smack in the middle of bad situations.

"Whatever it is, we'll fight," Beau says.

The trapdoor opens, shedding harsh yellow light from above down the stairs, so much brighter than the single dangling bulb. And then up above, Sonia says the strangest thing.

"Lev!" she calls out. "Lev, can you come up? I need your help up here."

It takes a moment for Risa to even process what she's said. Lev? Why would she be calling for Lev? Beau looks at her, shaking his head, not getting it either.

"Lev! Get your ass up here!" Sonia calls, much louder. "I don't have all day."

And then it dawns on Risa exactly what Sonia is doing. *I'm giving you the advantage,* Sonia is saying. *Something is horribly wrong, but I'm giving you the advantage. Take it!*

Risa searches the group, and zeroes in on Jack, the blond, mousy kid who could pass for Lev for a whole of five seconds. She grabs him, and his eyes go manga-wide in surprise.

"Tell her you'll be right up!"

"What?"

"Just tell her!"

Jack clears his throat and calls up the stairs. "Coming! I'll be right up." Then he looks at Risa, begging with his eyes, pleading, but Risa puts her hands on his shoulders. "You'll be fine," she tells him. "I promise. I'll be right behind you!"

Beau nods to her and signals to all the others to stay hidden in shadows, then he gets behind Risa. "You've got his back, and I've got yours," he says.

With Jack in the lead, they go up the stairs to face whatever is in store for them.

36 · Nelson

He has every intention of honoring their bargain. He is, after all, a man of conscience. A man of his word. As the boy he assumes is Lev comes up the stairs, Nelson allows himself a small moment to relish this half victory. He will tranq Lev, then he will take Lev to a place where no one will hear him scream, and he will make him divulge where Lassiter has gone, because he surely knows, even if the old woman doesn't. Then, once Nelson has the information he needs, he will kill Lev in a most painful way—one he has yet to devise, because vengeance is best when experienced creatively and in the moment.

"You called for me, ma'am?" the boy says—and when he turns to face Nelson, Nelson immediately realizes he's been duped—just as someone else coming up from below swings a wrench at his legs. Pain explodes in his shin the moment the wrench connects with it, and Nelson immediately realizes his mistake. Of course they would have known it was a ruse! They must have heard the gunshot. His pain is a measure of his miscalculation.

He reaches down to disarm the girl attacking him, but she pulls her arm back and swings again, this time catching the back of his hand. More pain, but Nelson can handle pain, and the damage isn't enough to impair him. The third time she swings, he succeeds in grabbing the wrench from the girl and hurling it away—but there's someone else coming up the stairs behind her, and he's swinging a hammer. Nelson deflects the blow, backs away, and kicks the trunk toward the hammer-wielding AWOL to block him, but the trunk flips open and dumps at least a hundred envelopes on the floor. The kid takes one step forward, and begins slipping on the envelopes like they're banana peels. It's just the opening Nelson needs. He thrusts his palm to the imbalanced kid's chest, and it sends him tumbling down the hole and into the basement. Nelson quickly kicks the trapdoor closed behind him, then tugs on a heavy bookshelf, which comes crashing down over the trapdoor, spilling its load of books. No one's coming up that way anymore.

Now it's just him, the girl, the blond kid, and the old woman, who's telling them to run, but they're not smart enough to save themselves. The girl scrambles on the floor for the wrench, and the blond kid is parrying toward Nelson with a letter opener he found on the desk. Nelson pulls out one of his guns, taking aim at the blond kid, because he's closest, and because Nelson is profoundly pissed off at the kid's lack of Lev-ness.

He meant to pull out the gun loaded with tranqs, but in the commotion, who could blame him for pulling the wrong gun?

He fires, and the kid's chest shreds into a screaming red Rorschach. Blood splatters everywhere. He's dead before he hits the floor.

"No!" yells the girl. "You bastard!"

It's in that moment, with Nelson holding his gun, and her ready to strike with the wrench, that he realizes who she is. In spite of the hair, in spite of the eye color, he recognizes her—and knows he'll have a new prize today. A very useful one. He wonders how much Risa Ward will be worth to Divan.

Risa comes toward him just as he reaches for his other gun with his free hand. She gets in a swing at his head. It connects with his ear. A solid strike, but survivable, just like all the other blows. He shoves the tranq gun into her gut and pulls the trigger, and she grunts as the tranq embeds deep. He holds her as she slips helplessly from consciousness, the wrench falling from her hand, thudding onto the floor.

Nelson gently eases her to the ground beside the dead boy. Then he turns to the old woman, who sobs from the chair to which she's chained. "Your fault," Nelson tells her. "Entirely your fault. That boy's life is on your head for lying to me!"

The woman can only sob.

Now that the battle is over, he assesses the damage from the wrench. His shin may be fractured. It's swelling and he can feel his pulse in it. His right ear is hot, and the back of his hand is turning purple and swelling. All in a day's work. The pain will be good for him. It will release endorphins. Make him more alert.

"Please go . . ." wails the woman. "Just go . . ."

And he will . . . but not until he finishes his business here.

There's a torn envelope on the desk and a cigarette lighter in his pocket. He notes that everything around the basement, from the felled bookshelf and its pile of books, to the stacks of paperwork on the desk, to the various wooden antiques—everything in this room—everything in this shop, in fact—is highly flammable.

He grabs the envelope, takes out the lighter, and flicks it until it releases its tiny controlled flame.

"Stop!" yells the woman through her tears. "I'll give you Lassiter! I'll give him to you if you stop this and let the others go!"

He hesitates. He knows this is just another game, but he's willing to play, if only to give him a moment to contemplate the severity of what he's about to do.

"God forgive me," she says. "God forgive me. . . ."

"At this moment," Nelson reminds her, "it's *my* forgiveness that you need."

She nods, unable to look at him, and that's how he knows she's going to tell him the truth. But will it be truth enough?

"He's in your hand," she says. "He's in your hand, and you don't even know it." Then she lowers her head in defeat, and perhaps some self-loathing.

Nelson has no idea what she means . . . until he looks at the empty envelope he's holding and reads the handwritten address:

Claire & Kirk Lassiter
3048 Rosenstock Road
Columbus, Ohio 43017

He looks down to the other envelopes on the ground, and he can tell by the handwriting that they were all written by kids.

"You had your AWOLs write letters to their parents?"

She nods.

"What a pointless thing to do."

She nods.

"And our friend Connor went to deliver his personally?"

Then she finally looks to him, and the hatred on her face is a thing to see: as powerful as a smoldering volcano. "You have what you need. Now get the hell out of here."

There have been many times in Jasper Nelson's life when choice was taken from him. He did not choose to be tranq'd that fateful day two years ago by Connor Lassiter. He did not choose to get hurled out of the Juvenile force in humiliation. He did not choose to lose his ordinary, respectable life. He does have a choice here however, and it's an awe-inspiring moment—because he knows his choice today will be a defining one.

He could walk away from here and go find Lassiter . . . or he could bring on a little suffering first.

In the end, his sense of social consciousness prevails. Because as a good citizen, isn't it his responsibility to help rid the world of vermin?

Nelson memorizes the address, sets the envelope on fire, then drops it on the pile of envelopes on the ground.

"No! What have you done! What have you done!" cries the old woman, as the fire takes and the flames begin to rise.

"Only what necessity and my conscience dictate," he tells her. Then he grabs Risa Ward's limp, unconscious body, and carries her out the back door without a stitch of remorse.

37 · Sonia

How could she have done it? How could she have been such a fool to think he would let them go once he had what he wanted? She gave up Connor for nothing. It didn't save the kids in the basement. It saved no one.

The flames climb to the curtains, and the stack of news-papers in the corner ignites as if it had been doused with gasoline. Sonia struggles against her chains but succeeds only in upending the chair. Her hip complains bitterly as she and the chair fall backward to the floor, just inches from the building inferno.

Sonia Rheinschild knows she will die. In truth, she's amazed she has survived this long, what with so many other ADR operatives killed in "random" clapper attacks. But to lose the kids in her basement is too much to bear. Poor Jack, lying there beside her, had it easy compared to what the others will now have to endure.

Then, as the heat builds around her, as the air grows inky black with smoke, she hears the most wonderful sound she's ever been blessed to hear. A sound that changes everything.

In that moment, her fears and regrets leave her. She smiles and begins to breathe deep, over and over again, resisting the urge to cough, willing her body to succumb to smoke inhala-tion so that she never has to feel the flames.

She will go to her husband now. She will join Janson in whatever place, or nonplace, all the living eventually go—and she will go there in peace . . .

. . . because the wonderful sound she heard from the base-ment below was the breaking of a window.

38 · Grace

Cold, confused, and covered with scratches, Grace crawls out of the prickly hedge. Her head spins, and she's terrified because for the first few moments, she can't fathom how she got there.

Maybe she was hit by a car and thrown into the bushes. Maybe she was mugged.

When her memory begins to return, she resists it, because even before it oozes to the surface, she senses it's going to be bad. And she's right.

She saw Argent, but it wasn't Argent, but it was. She screamed and passed out—perhaps from her shock, perhaps from something else. The sky is a bit darker now than when she lost consciousness. It's still late twilight, though. How long was she out? Ten minutes? Twenty?

Her attention is drawn to orange light ebbing and flowing in random surges. Something around the corner is on fire.

Fighting the weakness in her knees, she holds on to a streetlamp for balance, then turns the corner to find Sonia's shop on fire. Grace can feel the heat of the flames all the way across the street. She runs toward the burning building in a panic, but the shop's plate glass window explodes before she can even reach the curb. She's thrown back onto a manhole cover, its hard steel skinning her elbows.

People have come out into the street to watch—perhaps they want to help, but there's nothing to be done. All they can do is stand there with phones to their ears. A dozen simultaneous calls to 911.

"Sonia!" she calls as she gets to her feet, then turns to the onlookers. "Has anyone seen Sonia?"

They answer with helpless expressions.

"You're useless! All of ya!"

She tries to peer into the flames, but all she can see are antiques burning. Then out of the corner of her eye, she sees kids slipping out of the alley behind the shop. She hurries to the alley, to find it's the AWOLs from Sonia's basement, as she had hoped it would be.

"What happened? What happened?" she asks them.

"We don't know! We don't know!"

Farther down the alley, Beau pulls himself out of the broken basement window—he's the last one out. As Grace scans the gathering of kids, she can't find Connor, which means he hasn't returned from whatever secret mission Sonia had sent him on. But Risa isn't here either.

"Grace, you're alive!" says Beau, pleased by the fact. "We've gotta get out of here before the fire trucks arrive."

"Where's Risa? Where's Sonia?"

Beau shakes his head. "Dead," he tells her. "Some maniac. We tried to stop him, but we couldn't, and then he set the whole place on fire."

"A guy with a messed-up face?"

"You know him?"

"No, but I know his face. Or part of it."

Now the hollow wail of sirens comes to them over the treetops, distant but drawing closer—and as bad as this whole thing is, something occurs to Grace that makes it even worse.

"Where's the printer?"

Beau looks at her as blankly as the fire watchers had. "What? Why the hell do you care about that stupid thing now?"

He doesn't know! They never told anyone else how crucial it was, and so, without Risa or Connor there, there was no one to save it. Connor had said that the gears and mechanics and stuff were broken, but the important part—the *printing* part—was still okay. Maybe. But if it burns, there isn't even "maybe" anymore.

Beau grabs her arm. "Come with us, Grace. I'll find us a place to hide. We'll be okay, I swear it."

She gently pulls out of his grip. "You be smart with them, Beau. Run north, and maybe east, 'cause most people runnin' away run south or west. Be smart, and keep them whole, you hear?"

Beau nods, and Grace turns and, without looking back, runs down the alley toward the back of the burning building.

The heat is so intense, Grace can't even get near the back door. A few feet over, low to the ground, is that solitary window into the basement. Rather than spewing smoke, it's drawing in air, breathing in oxygen to feed the flames above.

She gets down on her knees and peers in, but can't see a thing—which means that there's no fire down there!

Not yet, anyway. It may be too late to save Sonia and Risa, and for all she knows, Connor is dead too. She may be the only one left who knows of the printer's existence.

Something heavy crashes in the shop. The flames crackle with nasty, vicious greed.

The window is so small, and she's such a big-boned girl, she's convinced there's no way she can fit through the window— but she has to try. How terrible it would be if everything were to be lost because the window is too small and she's too big. The odds are even money she'll fit, and even money she'll get to the printer before the floor above her collapses. That's a 25 percent chance. Lousy odds, but they get worse the longer she hesitates.

Shutting down her survival instinct, she dives headfirst into the little rectangular hole.

As she suspected, she gets only partway through. Her hips are caught by the rigid wood, so she wriggles and squirms. The heat around her head is unbearable. And now there's light. The angry fire spies her through the slats of wood up above, like sunlight sneaking through a closed blind.

She grabs a support beam and with all her might pulls on it, until she falls into the basement, cutting herself on broken window glass on the floor.

The air is almost entirely clear down here, because smoke only knows up—but the heat! She can feel the skin on her scalp blistering. She keeps as low as she can, rounding a corner, and there, in the place Connor left it, is the box filled with all the broken parts of the organ printer, waiting patiently for their chance to burn. *Ain't gonna happen.* She grabs the box, then opens the stasis container, which is too large to take, and digs into the thick green gel to pull out the slimy ear, shoving it into the pocket of her blouse. Then she heads with the ear and the box of printer parts, back to the small window.

Behind her, a support beam gives way and the remains of the shop up above drop to the basement. The flames, fed by the oxygen-rich air, leap forward, flooding the basement like water. Grace reaches the window, shoves the printer through, then begins the monumental task of getting out the way she came in.

There's no leverage outside. Nothing to grab on to. She's stuck halfway in, halfway out, and she can feel the flames on her feet, melting her shoes.

"No!" she screams in furious defiance. "I won't die this way! I won't, I won't, I won't!"

And suddenly her deliverance arrives in the form of a stranger grabbing her arms, and pulling. "I've got you!" he says. He tugs once, twice, three times. It's the fourth tug that dislodges her.

The second she's out, she kicks off her burning shoes, and the man helps to stamp out the fire at the cuffs of her jeans. She has no idea who he is—just a neighbor man—but she can't help herself from throwing her arms around him. "Thank you!"

The sound of sirens now fills the air, coming from many different directions.

"An ambulance will be here in a second," says the man. "Let me help you."

But Grace is already on her feet and gone with the box of printer parts clasped to her breast like a baby.

39 · Connor

"There are places you could go," Ariana told him, "and a guy as smart as you has a decent chance of surviving to eighteen."

He's back at the freeway overpass, on the ledge behind the exit sign. It was once his favorite escape spot/make-out spot/danger spot. This time, it feels like none of those things. And this time he's alone.

He has been to many of the "places" Ariana had referred to. None of them were as safe as he wished they'd be. He did survive to eighteen, though. That should be enough, but it's not. Twilight gives way to night as he nests there, on the overpass, gathering fortitude.

Ariana, a girl he thought he loved before he actually knew what love was, had promised to go with him when he kicked AWOL, but when he showed up at her door in the middle of the night, she wouldn't even step over the threshold. It was as if there was an invisible barrier between them that could not be breached. She was remorseful, but more than that, she seemed relieved to be on the other side of that door, still welcome in her own home. It made it painfully clear how truly alone he was.

Connor was angry at her that night, and he held on to that anger for a long time. Now, however, he's more angry at himself. Wanting her to join him in this seedy fugitive life was pure selfishness. If he truly cared for her, he would have protected her from it, rather than pull her into it.

So much has changed since then. Connor remembers hearing somewhere that it takes seven years for one's body to purge itself of all its biological matter and replace it. Every seven years, everyone is literally a new person. For Connor, he couldn't be more different after two years. It's as if he's been unwound and put back together again.

Will his parents recognize the change? Will they care? Perhaps they'll see a stranger at their door. Or maybe they'll be strangers to him. And then there's his brother, Lucas. Connor can't help but imagine him as the same thirteen-year-old he was. He won't be. What must it be like to be the younger brother of the notorious Akron AWOL. Lucas must despise him.

The journey here began well enough. Sonia didn't offer him her car, of course. They both knew he had to leave no ties to the antique shop, in case he got caught. Instead he stole a car that had small dunes of runoff mud wedged beneath the tires, a clear indication that it hadn't been moved for a while, and wouldn't be immediately missed. He could probably bring it back, park it in the same place and the owners wouldn't even know it was gone.

The drive from Akron to Columbus took less than two hours. That was the easy part. But actually going to his old front door—that was a different story.

The reconnaissance ride through his neighborhood earlier that afternoon was the first indication of how difficult this would be. Memories of his pre-AWOL life kept leaping out so vividly, he sometimes swerved the car as if they were actual obstacles in his path—just as he did when he retrieved the stem cells with Risa and Beau. What a waste that whole excursion will have been if they can't fix the printer. He can tell himself his reason for going home is to enlist his father's help in repairing it, but Risa was right, it's just an excuse. Still, if they've had the change of heart he dreams they've had, it wouldn't be out of the question.

When he drove through his neighborhood today, it looked remarkably the same. Somehow in his mind's eye, Connor imagined it would look vaguely postapocalyptic: overgrown, underwatered, and indefinably forlorn, as if somehow the entire suburb suffered without him. But no. The lawns and hedges were all trimmed to good-neighbor standards. He considered driving down Ariana's street, but decided against it. Some parts of the past need to stay exactly where they are.

When he finally turned onto his street, he had to keep both hands firmly on the wheel to keep them from shaking.

Home sweet home.

It looked perfectly inviting on the outside, even if the invitation was false. For a moment, it crossed his mind that his family might have moved—until he saw the LASITRI license plate on a shiny new Nissan coupe in the driveway. His brother's? No, Lucas would be fifteen now, still too young to have a license. Perhaps one of his parents downsized from a sedan, having one less son to take up space.

A window was open upstairs, and Connor could hear the riffs of an electric guitar. Only then did he remember that his brother was begging for one around the time their parents signed Connor's unwind order. The music bears none of the acoustic skills of Cam Comprix. It's raucously dissonant—just the kind of thing that would irritate their father. Good for Lucas.

Connor had driven by twice, scouring the street for hidden officers in unmarked cars, and found none. No one would still be on the lookout for him here, now that the Juvenile Authority is convinced that the Hopi are giving Connor political asylum halfway across the country.

He could easily have made his appearance then—there was no good reason to delay it—but he made this detour anyway as a stalling tactic.

He needed to weigh Risa's dire warnings about going home.

He needed to search his own heart to know if he really needs to risk this.

So he went to the ledge, like he had done so many times in the past when he needed to think.

The ledge is cramped and crisscrossed with the webs of oblivious spiders who have no concept of a world larger than this overpass. Funny, but all the time he spent here brooding over how unfair his life was—in the days before it actually became unfair—Connor never knew what the sign actually read on the other side. He found out that day he drove past it with Risa and Beau.

THIS LANE MUST EXIT.

Thinking about it makes him laugh, although he can't say exactly why.

It's dark out now. It's been dark for a while. If he's going to do this, he can't wait much longer. He wonders if they'll invite him in, and if they do, will he accept? He knows he has to keep the visit short, just in case they secretly call the police. He'll have to watch them. Keep them both in sight the whole time he's there. That is, if he goes in at all. He's still not beyond aborting the whole thing at the last minute.

Finally he pulls himself over the railing, leaving the ledge behind, and returns to the car, which he parked nearby. He takes his time starting it. He takes his time driving to his street. It's so unlike him to do anything slowly, but this act of return—it has such inertia, it's like pushing a boulder uphill. He can only hope it doesn't roll back to crush him.

Some lights are on in the house: the living room lights downstairs and in Lucas's room upstairs. The light is off in the room that had been his. He wonders what it is now. A sewing room? No that's stupid, his mother didn't sew. Maybe just storage for all the junk that always accumulates in the house. *Or maybe they left it like it was.* Is there actually a part of him that hopes that? He knows that's even less likely than a sewing room.

He passes the house, parks down the street, and pulls the

four pages of his letter out of his pocket. He read it several times while on the ledge to prepare himself for this moment. It didn't.

He walks past the driveway and turns down the little flagstone path to the front door. Anticipation speeds his heart and makes it feel as if it's rising in his chest, trying to escape.

Maybe he'll just hand them the letter and leave. Or maybe he'll talk to them. He doesn't yet know. It's the not knowing that makes it so hard—not knowing what they will do, but even worse, having no clue what he's going to do either.

But whatever happens, good or bad, it will bring closure. He knows it will.

He's halfway to the front door when a figure steps out of the shadows of the porch and stands directly in his path. Then suddenly, there's a sharp stinging in Connor's chest. He's down on the ground before he even realizes he's been shot with a tranq, and his vision goes blurry, so he can't even tell who his attacker is as he draws near. For a moment something about his face makes him think of Argent Skinner—but it's not Argent. Not by a long shot.

"How unceremonious," the man says. "This moment should be grander."

And Roland's fist, which holds the pages of the letter so tightly, relaxes, letting the pages fall free as Connor plunges into the chemical void.

40 · Mom

Claire Lassiter takes a moment from her exhausting task of maintaining appearances. She thought she heard something out front and it's giving her an odd sense of prescient anticipation, although she doesn't know why. It's nothing new. She jumps every time a pinecone falls on the roof, or a squirrel scuttles over the rain gutters. She's been so edgy for so long, she can't remember the last time she felt calm.

She definitely needs a vacation. They all do. But they won't take one. There are tickets for a vacation they never took in a drawer upstairs somewhere. They ought to just throw them away, but they don't. Funny how their lives have become all about inactivity.

A sound outside. Yes, there is definitely something happening on their front lawn. She strides to the door and opens it, expecting to see perhaps some of Lucas's friends. Or a dog that got off its leash. Or maybe . . . or maybe . . .

Or maybe nothing at all. There's no one there and nothing to see but some litter blowing across the lawn. She lingers for a moment daring the night to offer her something better, and when it doesn't, she gets anxious, as if standing there is somehow tempting fate. So she closes the door once more.

"What is it?" her husband asks. "Was someone at the door?"

"No," she tells him. "I thought I heard something. Probably just another pinecone rolling off the roof."

Meanwhile, in their front yard, several pieces of paper are taken by the breeze to be victimized by shrubs and sprinklers and tires, until nothing remains but illegible pulp, never to be read by anyone, ripe only for the bedding of bird nests and the harsh spinning whisk of tomorrow morning's street sweeper.

Part Five

Mouth of the Monster

BODY ART: CREATIONS MADE OF HUMAN FLESH, BLOOD & BONES

WebUrbanist article by "Steph," filed under Sculpture & Craft in the Art category. 8/23/2010

. . . The human body has been used as a canvas for all sorts of art, but perhaps more interesting and rare is the use of human body parts as artistic media. . . . These 12 artists have made human body art that is often controversial and sometimes surprisingly poignant.

Marc Quinn

If you're going to do a self-portrait, why not go all out and make a sculpture out of your own frozen blood? That's what sculptor Marc Quinn has done. . . . Quinn's 2006 version of 'Self' was purchased by the UK's National Portrait Gallery for over $465,000.

Andrew Krasnow

. . . [I]s Andrew Krasnow's controversial skin art really a sensitive reflection on human cruelty? The artist creates flags, lampshades, boots and other everyday items from the skin of people who donated their bodies to medical science. Krasnow says that each piece is a statement on America's ethics. . . .

Gunther Von Hagens

Perhaps no artist using actual human flesh as his chosen medium has gained such renown as Gunther Von Hagens, the man behind the "Body Worlds" exhibition of plasticized human corpses. But for all the outcry regarding Von Hagens' supposedly "disrespectful" usage of human bodies, there's just as much fascination. . . .

François Robert

François Robert's fascination with human bones started with an unusual discovery: an articulated human skeleton hidden inside a presumably empty locker that he purchased. Realizing the potential for artistic expression, Robert traded in the wired skeleton for a disarticulated one so that he could arrange the parts into shapes and designs. . . .

Anthony-Noel Kelly

British artist Anthony-Noel Kelly followed in the footsteps of many artists before him, including Michelangelo, when he closely studied human body parts for his work. But unlike those artists, Kelly illegally smuggled human remains from the Royal College of Surgeons and used them to cast sculptures in plaster and silver paint. Kelly was found guilty of this unusual crime in 1998 and spent nine months in jail. . . .

Tim Hawkinson

Tiny and delicate, almost diaphanous, this little bird skeleton at first seems remarkable simply because it is so well preserved despite the fragility of bird bones. But those aren't bones at all—they're the fingernail clippings of the artist. . . .

Wieki Somers

Seemingly carved from concrete, the sculptures of Wieki Somers look weighty and hyper-realistic despite their lack of color. But these everyday objects . . . are more organic than they appear—they're made from human ashes. . . . "We may offer Grandpa a second life as a useful rocking chair or even as a vacuum cleaner or a toaster," she told the *Herald Sun*. "Would we then become more attached to these products?"

Pictures and full article can be found at: *http://weburbanist.com/2010/08/23/body-art-creations-made-of-human-flesh-blood-bones/*

41 · Broadcast

Small bandwidth, tall antenna. Endless cornfields. Corn took over the Midwest. The entire heartland is now genetically engineered maize for the masses.

A team of five pull off a country road. They are armed with weapons originally supplied by the folks who supplied the folks, who pay for the folks, who run the folks behind clappers. Now those weapons are used at crosspurposes to what those wealthy suppliers intended. Whatever they intended.

The team of five always chooses its targets carefully. Small-time, old-fashioned radio stations broadcasting from a dump on a two-block main street, or better yet, in the middle of nowhere, like this one at the edge of a cornfield. The more isolated the better. By current calculation, it would take the local deputy about nine minutes at top speed, siren blaring, to get to this particular spot from the coffee shop where he's currently having breakfast.

They drive a stolen van not yet reported stolen. Only way to go. These trying times turn honest kids to crime, and criminals into murderers. Fortunately there are no true criminals in this bunch. Perhaps that's why they walk in through the front door, instead of sneaking in the back.

"A fine morning to you. I'm pleased to let you know that your coffee break begins early today!"

When you enter a minimally staffed establishment with guns that look like they've been ripped off the deck of a battleship, no one fights back. Whether the guns are actually armed is immaterial. In truth, one of them is, but that's only in case of dire emergency.

"My associate may be smaller than his weapon, but he's happy about it. Trigger-happy, that is, so I'd avoid sudden movements if I was you."

Even the armchair special-ops potatoes of the broadcast facility, who fancy themselves the heroes of every TV show they watch, are subdued into stunned silence. They put their hands up, mimicking the way they've seen it done by the nonspeaking extras.

"Kindly step into the storeroom—plenty of space for all. Grab a legal pad, if you like, and write a memoir of your harrowing experience at our ruthless hands."

Someone tries to surreptitiously dial a phone in his pocket. That's only to be expected.

"By all means, use your phones to call for help. Of course, we've blocked outgoing phone signals, but we wouldn't want to deny you your false sense of hope."

The intruders lock the radio station staff in the storeroom, and the staff makes the best of their time in the tight quarters. The station manager stews. A secretary cries. Others grab snacks from the shelf and nervously eat, pondering their own mortality.

With the staff locked safely away, the intruders take over the broadcast for a total of five minutes, linking into a radio grid, increasing its effective broadcast range by a thousand miles. Not bad for five AWOLs.

On their way out, they silently unlock the store room, something the station staff discovers about a minute later. They emerge like turtles from a shell to find the station empty of intruders, but still broadcasting. Not dead air, because no radio station should ever suffer the indignation of radio silence. Instead it broadcasts the same signature song Hayden's guerrilla broadcast team always leaves behind to mark their patronage. Lush tones croon slick on the airwaves.

"I've got you . . . under my skin. . . ."

42 · Lev

Days come and go on the Arápache reservation without much fanfare. It's not that life is simple, because where in a modern world can life be called simple anymore? But it is an unencumbered life. By choosing isolation, the Arápache have successfully protected themselves, remaining safe and sane in a world gone foul. As they are the wealthiest of tribal nations, there are those who call the Arápache Rez the ultimate gated community. They are not blind to the things that go on beyond the gate, but are certainly removed by several degrees.

Naturally any attempt to bring the world a few degrees closer would be met with powerful resistance. Yet Lev truly believed he could make a difference. After all he's been through, he still cannot come to terms with disappointment. He wonders if that keeps him human, or if it's a flaw in his character. Perhaps a dangerous one.

With the door locked, Lev stands before a bathroom mirror, in the Tashi'ne home, making eye contact with his reflection, trying to connect with some other version of himself. Who he was, or who he is, or who he might still be.

Kele pounds on the door, impatient as twelve-year-olds tend to be. "Lev, what are you still doing in there? I need in!"

"Go use the other bathroom."

"I can't!" whines Kele. "My toothbrush is in this one."

"Then use someone else's."

"That's gross."

Kele stomps away, and Lev gets back to the business at hand. The more he studies himself in the mirror, the less familiar his face seems, like pondering a word until the world loses all meaning.

Lev was always at his best when he had something to strive for. A clear-cut and discernible goal, where victory can be measured. Back in his innocent days, it was all about baseball. Catch the ball, hit the ball, and run. Even as a clapper he was an overachiever. A model representative of the cause. Until he chose not to detonate, that is.

With the granite intransigence of the Arápache Tribal Council, he knows he has lost his battle. The Arápache will not enter the war against unwinding. They will continue to object by merely closing it out, rather than taking it on.

Connor called him naïve, and he was right. After all he had been through, Lev was still foolish enough to believe that reason and resolve would prevail. "You are only one boy, with one voice," Elina told him after his defeat in the Tribal Council. "If you keep trying to be a choir, you'll lose that voice, and then who will hear you?"

She hugged him, but he did not return the gesture. He didn't want consolation. It was *his* anger, and he wanted to own it. He needed to, because he knew that from that anger something new might grow. Something more effective than a pointless petition.

In the days since, Lev has given it much thought—all his thought, really—and has come to a conclusion. What he needs is a new approach that depends on no one but himself. He's done relying on the help of others, because others are too likely to disappoint. He must, once and for all, take matters into his own hands.

So he examines himself in the mirror, searching for a new resolve, even deeper than before. The things written on Lev's face are too complex to read. But he knows he can simplify them.

He reaches down to the counter and picks up the pair of scissors he brought into the bathroom. Without hesitation, he shears off his ponytail, dropping it to the ground. What remains is a ragged straggly blond mop. Then he grabs a lock of hair as close to the roots as he can get, and he shears it off. Then he grabs another lock, doing it again and again, until the floor is covered with hair, and his head looks like a hayfield that has just been reaped.

Again Kele bangs on the door.

"Lev, I gotta get in!"

"Soon," Lev tells Kele. "I'll be done soon."

Lev puts down the scissors and lathers up the short, uneven stubble on his head. Then he picks up a razor.

These days it's mostly young Arápache men planning to leave the Rez that get themselves tattoos. Those who have decided to go out into a larger world but want to take with them a permanent reminder of where they came from. A symbol that they can display with pride.

There are only a few tattoo artists on the Rez, and only one with real talent. The rest are more paint-by-numbers types. Lev visits Jase Taza, the talented one. He waits outside the shop until the last of Jase's customers leaves.

Jase looks him over as he enters, not sure whether to be troubled or amused. "You're the Tashi'nes' foster-fugitive, aren't you? The one who caught that parts pirate, right?" he says.

Lev shakes his head. "Didn't you hear? I'm not a foster-fugitive anymore. I'm a full member of the tribe."

"Glad to hear it." Then he points to Lev's shaved head. "What happened to your hair?"

"It became unnecessary," Lev tells him. It's the answer he gave the Tashi'nes, and anyone else who asks. His shaved head had troubled Elina, as he knew it would, but she allowed him his choice.

"What can I do for you?" asks Jase.

Lev presents him several pages and explains what he

wants. Jase looks the pages over, then looks at Lev dubiously. "You can't be serious."

"Do I look like I'm joking?"

Jase looks at the pages over and over. "Are you sure you want this?"

"Positive."

"This much ink, all at once?"

"Yes."

"It's going to hurt. A lot."

Lev has already considered that. "It *should* hurt," he says. "It *needs* to hurt, or it doesn't mean anything."

Jase looks around his shop, pointing to his many original designs. "How about a nice eagle, or a bear instead? You're not Arápache-born, so you can choose your own spirit animal. Mountain lions look good in ink."

"I already have a spirit animal, and it's not what I want. I want this." He points to the pages in Jase's hand.

"It will take many hours over many days."

"That's fine."

"And you'll have to pay me for my time—I don't come cheap."

"I'll pay whatever it costs." The Tashi'nes gave Lev spending money, enough to last a while. It's more than enough to pay Jase for his talent and his time. After that, he won't need Arápache currency, because it's no good off of the Rez.

He hasn't told Elina and Chal that he's leaving. He hasn't told anyone, because anyone he tells will try to talk him out of it or, at the very least, try to discover where he's going. It's crucial that no one knows that.

He pulls the money from his wallet and flashes it before Jase. Like everywhere else in the world, money talks.

Their first session begins a few minutes later. He allows Jase full creative expression.

"Where do you want to start?"

"Start at the top and work your way down," Lev tells him. Then he leans back in the chair and closes his eyes, mentally preparing himself for the ordeal to come. . . .

43 · Risa

Risa wakes to the breathy drone of some machine—a hiss that's both muffled and loud at once. She's on a king-size bed in a bedroom finished in polished redwood and brass. She's dizzy. Queasy. She feels as if the bed itself is shifting beneath her but she knows it's only the tranqs.

"Take your time," says an unfamiliar male voice. "You've been tranq'd eight or nine times in succession. It will take you longer than usual to recover. Had it been me, I would have done it differently. I would have made it easier on you."

The man speaks with a pearly lilt and an Eastern European accent. Russian perhaps. No, not quite, but something close.

As her eyes begin to focus, she sees him standing across the room, adjusting his hair in a full-length mirror. Slender, dark hair, well dressed. Risa pulls her knees up protectively, wondering what has transpired during her lapse of consciousness.

He glances over at her, and reading her body language, he chuckles.

"Do not worry," he says. "No one has harmed you while you slept off the tranquilizers."

Her head feels full of foam—fizz with no substance. She can only ask the obvious question. "Where am I?"

"Lady Lucrezia," he answers. "My harvest camp."

She has enough of the pieces now to pull at least some of

it together. The man at the antique shop was a parts pirate, and she is now in the hands of a black marketer. The parts pirate killed Jack—whom Risa promised she'd protect—whom she put directly in harm's way. And what of Sonia?

"I'm in a harvest camp . . . ," she repeats, hoping to get more out of him.

"Yes, you and your friend Connor."

She was not expecting to hear that. She shakes her head, not wanting to believe it. "You're lying! Connor wasn't there!"

Her captor looks at her curiously. "No? I thought you were captured together. But then, Nelson didn't explain the specific circumstances when he left you both with me."

Nelson? Not the same Nelson . . . But as she thinks of the parts pirate, she realizes that she knew that face—or at least half of it. Suddenly the entire room seems to heave, moving one way while Risa's stomach moves another. Without warning she's retching over the edge of the bed onto the floor.

The foreigner sits beside her, gently rubbing her back, and she doesn't even have the strength to recoil from him. "My name is Divan, and no harm will come to you while you're in my care." He gives her club soda to sip from a minibar beside the bed. "So much to take in. No surprise there are things that can't be held down." He leaves her with the club soda. "I'll have someone come and clean it up, not to worry. In the meantime, I have business to attend to. Sleep, Risa. We'll talk again when you're up to it."

He goes to the door, but turns back just before he exits. "If you feel ill again, I find that looking out of a window helps."

Once he's gone, Risa moves across the bed, and reaches for a curtain. Pulling it back reveals a window, but not the sort she was expecting. It's an oval window, and beyond it clouds. Nothing but clouds.

44 · The Lady Lucrezia

Simply put, the Antonov AN-225 Mriya is the largest flying object ever built. The six engines of the massive cargo jet boast more horsepower than Napoleon's entire cavalry, and when people talk of moving mountains, this is the plane that could do it. Only two of them were ever built. The first is in a Ukrainian air museum. The second is owned by wealthy Chechen entrepreneur Divan Umarov. Currently he is in negotiations to acquire the other one.

From the outside it looks like a 747 with glandular problems, but standing inside the jet's cavernous cargo hold can be a religious experience, because it rises around you with the breathtaking drama of a cathedral, but can get about eight miles closer to heaven.

The interior of the *Lady Lucrezia*, as Divan christened her, bears no resemblance to its original hollow shell, however. It was meticulously redesigned to be both a lavish residence as well as a fully functioning harvest camp, landing only to take on fuel and fresh Unwinds from Divan's international network of parts pirates, as well as to offload the various and sundry products of unwinding, worth so much more than the kids themselves.

Lately, he's spent more time airborne. Considering the ruthlessness of his enemies, it's safer to stay mobile as much as possible, and the current cargo, rare as to be almost priceless, requires his personal attention. It is a feather in his cap that he caught Connor Lassiter before the American Juvenile Authority or the despicable Dah Zey. He will remain on board, closely overseeing his business until such time as Connor Lassiter is sold at auction and his parts distributed to satisfied customers.

45 · Risa

When Risa wakes again, she feels a bit stronger. Strong enough to explore and test her immediate surroundings. The bedroom is, of course, locked from the outside. A view from the window reveals that they are still at a high altitude, and it's the trailing end of twilight, or dawn—Risa has no concept of the actual time, or how many time zones they've flown through.

There is a small table across the room with food for her. Light fare: Danish and such. She eats in spite of her resistance to accept anything offered her.

When the black marketer returns, he's pleased to see she's eaten, which makes her just want to throw it all up in his face.

"I can give you the grand tour if you like," Divan offers.

"I'm a prisoner," she reminds him flatly. "Why would you give a prisoner a tour?"

"I do not have prisoners," he tells her. "I have guests."

"Is that what you call the kids you unwind? Guests?"

He sighs. "No, I don't call them anything. If I did, it would make my work all the more difficult, you see."

He holds out his hand to help her up, but she will not take it. "Is there a reason why I'm a 'guest,' and not one of them?"

He smiles. "You'll be pleased to know, Miss Ward, that the clients of mine who are interested in you are only interested in you *corpus totus*. That is, in your entirety. Isn't it nice to know that of all the souls on board, you are the only one worth more whole than divided?"

Somehow that doesn't give her much comfort. "What sorts of clients buy someone *corpus totus*?"

"Wealthy ones with a penchant toward collecting. There's

a Saudi prince in particular who's been obsessed with you. He's made overtures in the millions."

She tries to hide her revulsion. "Imagine that."

"Don't worry," Divan tells her. "I'm less motivated to make a deal than you might think."

He holds his hand out to her once more, and again she refuses to take it. She does stand up, however, and moves to the door.

"You'll find the tour very eye-opening, to say the least," Divan says, unlocking the door. "And on the way you can entertain yourself by scheming ways to escape, and ways to kill me."

She makes eye contact with him for the first time, a bit shocked, because that is exactly what she was thinking. The look he returns is much warmer than she wants it to be.

"Don't be so surprised," he says. "How could I *not* know what you'd be thinking right now?"

Aside from the constant drone of the engines and the occasional turbulence, it is hard to believe that all this is crammed into a single airplane. The bedroom opens up into a vaulted living area, its geometry determined by the plane's width and the dome of the fuselage. There are sofas, a dining table, and a multiscreened entertainment center.

"The kitchen and pantry are below," Divan says. "My chef is world-class."

At the far end of the room, dominating the space, is something Risa needs time to wrap her mind around. It's an instrument. A pipe organ—however, instead of gleaming brass pipes, this one has faces. Dozens of faces.

"Impressive, isn't it?" Divan says with pride. "I purchased it from a Brazilian artist, who has apparently made a career working in flesh. He claims his artwork is to protest unwinding, but I ask you, how much of a protest can it be if he uses the unwound for his art?"

Risa is drawn to the thing like a spectator to a car accident. She's seen this before. In a dream, she thought. A dream that kept recurring. Only now does she realize that the dream had a grounding in reality: something she once saw on TV, although she can't place exactly when.

"He calls it 'Orgão Orgânico.' The Organic Organ.'"

Each shaved head rests inert, symmetrically placed above the keyboard, on multiple levels, connected to it by tubes and ducts. It's the very definition of abomination. Risa finds it too grotesque to even trigger the proper emotion. Too horrifying to feel. Slowly she reaches forward and pushes down on a key.

And directly in front of her, a disembodied face opens its mouth and voices a perfect middle C.

Risa yelps and jumps back, right into Divan. He gently holds her by the shoulders, but she pulls free.

"Nothing to fear," he tells her. "I assure you the brains are elsewhere—probably helping rich Brazilian children to think better. Although the eyes do open from time to time, which can be disconcerting."

Finally Risa tries to voice her own opinion, and it's far from middle C. "This thing . . . this thing is . . ."

"Unthinkable—I know. Even I was taken aback when I first viewed it . . . and yet the more I looked at it, the more compelled I was to have it. Such lovely voices should be heard, yes? And I'm not without a sense of irony. The *Lady Lucrezia* is my *Nautilus*, and I, like the good captain Nemo, must have my organ."

Although Risa has turned away, she finds her gaze drawn back to it, compelled to look on it, terrified of the prospect that it might look back.

"Won't you play it?" he asks her. "I can't do it justice, and I understand you're quite the accomplished pianist."

"I'd cut off my hands before I touch that thing again. Get me away from it."

"Of course," says Divan, ever obliging, but noticeably disappointed. He directs her to a stairwell across the room. "The tour continues this way."

Risa can't get away from the Orgão Orgânico fast enough. Yet as Divan said, the image lingers, along with a strange compelling sensation, like standing on a high ledge and leaning over, tempting gravity to steal one's balance. As horrified as she is by the eighty-eight-faced monstrosity, she's more horrified by the thought that she might actually want to play it.

They leave the comfort of his flying chalet, moving to the nether regions of the behemoth aircraft, into corridors and gangways without polished wood or leather, only utilitarian aluminum and steel.

"The harvest camp takes up the front two-thirds of the *Lady Lucrezia*. You'll be impressed by the economy of space."

"Why?" she asks. "Why are you showing me all of this? What possible purpose could it serve?"

Divan pauses before a large door. "It is my belief that the sooner you get beyond your initial shock, the sooner you will reach a place of comfort."

"I'll never be comfortable with any of this."

He nods, perhaps accepting her statement, but not its validity. "If there's one thing I understand well, it is human nature," he says. "We are the pinnacle species, are we not? This is because we have a remarkable ability to adapt, not just physically, but emotionally. Psychologically." He reaches for the door handle. "You are a consummate survivor, Risa. I have every faith that you will adapt in glorious ways." Then he swings the door open.

Risa was, as part of her state home enrichment program, once taken to a factory that manufactured bowling balls, mainly because it was the only factory convenient enough to take state home kids. What impressed Risa most was the complete lack of human involvement. Machines did everything from extruding the rubber core, to polishing the outer layer, to drilling holes to computer-precise specifications.

The moment Risa crosses the threshold, she realizes that Divan does not run a harvest camp at all. He runs a factory.

There are no cheery dormitories, no high-energy counselors. Instead, there's a huge drum, at least twenty feet in diameter, lining the shell of the airplane, inset with more than a hundred niches. In those niches lie Unwinds, like bodies in a catacomb.

"Do not be deceived by appearances," Divan tells her. "They rest on beds of the highest-quality silk, and the machine tends to their every needs. They are kept well nourished and spotlessly clean."

"But they're unconscious."

"Semiconscious. They are administered a mild sedative that keeps them in a twilight state, perpetually at the moment between dreams and waking. It's very pleasant."

At the far end of the cylindrical space is a huge black box about the size of an old-world iron lung. Risa shuts her thought processes down before she can imagine its purpose.

"Where's Connor?"

"He's here," Divan tells her, gesturing vaguely to the chamber of Unwinds around them.

"I want to see him."

"Unwise. Another time, perhaps."

"You mean after he's been unwound."

"For your information, he will not be unwound for several days at least. Auctioning off the parts of the Akron AWOL is a major affair—it takes time to get all my ducks in a row."

She looks at the semiconscious Unwinds all around her

and finds herself feeling weak at the knees again, as she did when she still had tranqs in her system. Meanwhile, Divan strolls through the space with carefree confidence.

"The Burmese Dah Zey represents the darkest end of what you call the black market. Slow unwinding without anesthesia, and in unsanitary conditions. Deplorable! I, on the other hand, strive for something better. I give these Unwinds a quality of treatment finer than any officially sanctioned harvest camp. Comfortable repose, electrical stimulation that painlessly tones their muscles, and a continual sense of euphoria as they await their unwinding. Many world leaders have purchased parts from me, although they would never admit it. Including several from your country, I might add."

The drum suddenly comes to life, and begins to rotate around them, repositioning the Unwinds. A mechanical arm reaches over to check on one of them with the gentle care of a mother's touch.

"Is the tour over? If it's not, I don't care. I've seen enough."

Divan takes her back to the living area, and she casts her eyes away from the organ, although she catches its reflection in a mirror. When they reach her bedroom, someone's there making her bed. He begins to work faster when he sees them.

"Almost done, sir."

The man seems frail, and a bit fearful, as if he were caught doing something he shouldn't. He doesn't appear to be much older than Risa. When he turns to glance at her, she's taken aback by his appearance. Part of his face is missing, and in its place is a formfitting biobandage, a paler pink than actual skin, covering his eye socket and most of his right cheek. He looks somewhat like the Phantom of the Opera with only one eye. The left side of his face doesn't look much better, having several scars that seem somewhat fresh.

"Your henchman, I presume," Risa says.

Divan is actually insulted. "I am not so arch as to have henchmen. This is Skinner, my valet."

Risa gives up a bitter grin in spite of herself. "How appropriate that you call him Skinner."

"Mere serendipity," Divan says. "That's his actual name."

Skinner leaves quickly, obsequiously, closing the door behind him. Then it occurs to Risa that Skinner is also Grace's last name. Could this be the troublesome brother she kept talking about? The more she pictures the half of his face that she could see, the more she's convinced there's a resemblance.

"What do you want from me?" Risa asks Divan, although she's afraid to hear the answer.

"Something simple," he tells her. "At least for you. I wish you to play the Orgão Orgânico for me. I have no talent for it, and it begs to be played by one with the skill."

He lets the proposition hang in the air. Risa can't dare to imagine herself sitting before the thing.

"No matter how well I play, you'll tire of the music, and of me," Risa tells him. "What happens to me then?"

"If our arrangement proves no longer viable, I shall let you go."

"In how many pieces?"

Divan rolls his eyes at her skepticism. "Risa, I am not a bad man. My business may be unsavory, but I am not. Consider the cattle farmer who raises Kobe beef. Is he to be condemned because his stock must be slaughtered? Of course not! I am no different; I just provide a different nature of product . . . and I provide it in a manner far more humane." He begins to walk toward her. "Unlike my associate who captured you, I have been able to separate myself from my work."

She sidesteps, refusing to be made to back up, but still maintaining a safe distance between them.

"Your choices are simple," he tells her. "You can choose to stay here, or you can choose to be auctioned. Here, I can promise you peace, patience, and respect. Which is more than I can say for the Saudi prince."

The veiled threat has the desired affect, and in spite of herself, Risa feels a sense of claustrophobia closing in around her. Still, she pulls forth the courage to make her own proposition.

"I'll do what you want under one condition."

"Yes?"

"You let Connor go."

Divan claps his hands together, overjoyed. "Excellent! The mere fact that you've entered negotiations is a step in the right direction. Unfortunately, freeing Connor is not an option."

"In that case, you can go to hell."

Divan is not offended, only amused. "I'll give you time to reconsider. In the meantime, I have another high-profile Unwind to auction off."

Risa can't help but ask, "Who is it?"

"America's most wanted," he answers. "I paid Proactive Citizenry a small fortune for him, but the profit I'll make will be worth it. There are many people out there who would like to own a piece of Mason Michael Starkey."

46 · Argent

He must be smart. He must be shrewd. But more than anything else, he must be obedient.

"I pitied you," Divan told him after the good half of his face had been harvested and given to Nelson. "Anyone else would have unwound the rest of you, but it's rare that I feel true pity, so I chose to act on it."

Pity, however, was not accompanied by charity. Rather

than replacing the missing half of Argent's face, Divan had it patched with the biobandage, like spackle over damaged drywall.

"What you need is too expensive to give away for free," Divan had said. "But if you work for me for six months, you will earn your choice of faces from my supply. Then you can choose to either continue as my valet, or return to the life you led."

Although Argent didn't say it, he had no intention of ever returning to the life he had led. A new life, perhaps, in a new city, with a new face . . . but having settled in on the *Lady Lucrezia*, Argent's beginning to think his will to live will be so sapped in six months time, he'll choose to stay. He tries not to think about it; instead, he just busies himself doing his daily tasks, which consist of cleaning messes, washing clothes, and being Divan's audience for lectures about life. Divan loves nothing more than to hear himself pontificate, and Argent is the perfect audience because he never disagrees, nor does he ever have an opinion of his own. In fact he's come to see "lack of an opinion" as a key element of his job description.

The arrival of Connor Lassiter, however, has been a major monkey wrench in Argent's mental gear work.

Argent watched from a window as Nelson made the transfer right there on the runway. The sight of Nelson wearing the good half of Argent's face as his own was such a violation, it made Argent's loins feel weak. He thought he hated Connor for what he had done to him, but that pales in comparison to how much he hates Nelson.

He was afraid that Nelson would be invited on board along with his catch, but Divan didn't do that.

"Nelson is a fine parts pirate—perhaps the best," Divan told Argent, "but that doesn't mean I care for his company."

Even so, Divan promised to personally deliver him Connor's eyes. As the harvester is fully automated, members of Divan's staff rarely go inside—even the medic charged with caring for the kids awaiting unwinding rarely goes in, because the machine does all the work.

Lyle, the medic, doesn't know that Argent replaced his spare key with the spare key to Divan's private bath. Occasionally, when he knows the harvester isn't being monitored, Argent sneaks off with his pilfered key and goes down to look at the Unwinds there, imagining their stories, and what their lives were like. Imagining what it might be like to have one of their faces for his own. He's only three years beyond legal unwinding age, but feels so much older. It will be nice when he can get himself a youthful face again.

Today, however, when he comes to the harvester, he has a different objective.

While Divan lines up bidders from around the world on the screens of his entertainment center, Argent slips into the harvester, locates Connor within the cylindrical grid of Unwinds, and rotates the drum until he's right there beside Argent. Then Argent disconnects him from the machine's monitoring system, and shuts off the constant sedative drip that keeps him in that blissful semiconscious state.

"This is all your fault! You hear me?"

Connor's response is just some lazy, incoherent babbling, but that will pass.

"Nelson did this to me on the way to you. He would never have done it if you didn't do what you did first!" He smacks Connor hard enough to make him stir. "Why'd you have to do it? We coulda been a team!" He hits him harder this time. "We coulda done great things! Outlaws with style. But now I don't even get to have a face! Just a scarred mess on one side, and a whole lotta nothing on the other."

Then he grabs Connor and shakes him. "Where's my sister, damn it?"

Connor turns to face him, blinking, yawning, seeing him for the first time. "Argent?"

"Where's Gracie? If you let Nelson hurt her, I swear I'll kill you!"

Connor doesn't seem to process everything he's saying yet. "If you're here, I must be in hell," Connor says.

"Yeah, you could say that."

Connor tries to sit up and bumps his head on the roof of his narrow niche. Argent hopes it hurt.

"I woke you to tell you that you've been caught, and are gonna be unwound. Not that I care, but you deserve to know. Divan's got Risa, too, but by the looks of it she'll stay whole."

"Risa's here? He's got Risa? Who's Divan?"

Argent feels no need to repeat himself. He punches Connor in the side, hard. Connor is still too weak to defend himself, and that suits Argent just fine. "Thought you were so smart smashing my face like you did. Well, how smart are ya now, huh? *And where's my sister?*"

"Antique shop," mumbles Connor. "That's where I last saw her." Connor lifts his arms weakly. "What am I wearing? It feels like I'm covered in spiderweb."

"It's an iron microfiber bodysuit. Kind of like long underwear, but you can be unwound in it. We call them 'long divisions.'"

Suddenly the drum of Unwinds grinds into life on its own accord, and Connor is rotated away. It makes a quarter turn and stops, then a pair of mechanical arms unfold, and, like an old-fashioned jukebox choosing a record, they lift an unwind and place her on a short conveyor belt leading to the door of the unwinding chamber, a place that Argent hopes he never sees the inside of. Argent knows what comes next. She'll regain consciousness, find that she can't move, and she'll cry for help, but no one will answer. Then, once the machine deems she's fully conscious, the door of the unwinding chamber will open, and the conveyor belt will roll her in.

"They must be fully conscious, or it isn't unwinding," Divan once told him. "It must be painless and humane, but they must be aware of what's happening to them every step of the way." Argent once stood beside a kid, trying to calm him down. Telling him his parents really loved him after all, and all that kind of comforting crap, but the kid just panicked, and in the end went into the chamber just like the rest of them. Argent didn't try talking to any of them after that.

Once the drum comes to rest, Argent locates Connor again and manually rotates him back.

"What's happening?" Connor asks, speaking a little more clearly than he had just a few moments ago.

"Today's auction," Argent explains. "Four kids go on the block today—fewer than usual, but number four is where the big money is. Divan'll auction off the first three to get the bidders all hot for the main event—and it'll be the same for you, when it's your turn! You're even more screwed than I am now. I hope you like it!" Then he shoves Connor for good measure, starts the sedative drip, and leaves.

It never occurs to him that Connor is still awake enough to pull the IV out of his arm.

47 · Connor

The instant Argent is gone, Connor takes action—but even awake and alert, Connor can find no way to give himself an advantage, and no way out of the harvester in one piece. The door through which Argent came and went requires a key. Not a code, or key card, or anything defeatable by technology, but an actual old-fashioned key. Connor might as well be sealed in the Great Pyramid. As for the machine itself, it's a soulless thing. A black rectangular box suspended from spring-loaded support legs that absorb the unpredictable motion of air turbulence. The thing looks like a spider, a massive daddy longlegs. There's a control panel, but he can't figure out how to open it, much less access it.

"Help me! Help me, please! DO something!"

When the girl awaiting unwinding on the conveyor belt gets enough of her wits about her to understand at least part of what's happening, Connor tries to lift her from the steel sled she rests upon, but she doesn't budge. He realizes why when he gets too close, and his wrist becomes stuck to the steel. The sled is powerfully magnetized—and once that magnet is engaged, the "long divisions," as Argent called their iron fiber bodysuits, are locked in place more powerfully than if they had been chained there. It takes all his strength and leverage to free his wrist. In the end, he can only be a witness to the girl's end, as the belt starts rolling and she's drawn into the unwinding chamber. The door closes, and the soundproof walls of the machine silence her. There's a small round window on the side of the machine, but Connor can't bring himself to look into it. As if anyone would want to see what happens in there.

Fifteen minutes later stasis containers of various sizes begin to roll out of the other end of the chamber and are neatly stacked in the cargo hold by mechanical arms. Her unwinding is complete in forty-five minutes—far more quickly than in a standard Chop Shop. Could this be the future of unwinding? Will machines like this eventually be approved for legal use? The great barrel of Unwinds begins to turn—a wheel of fortune selecting the next unlucky winner.

"Hey! You're the Akron AWOL! You're him! You can save me! You have to save me!"

Connor watches the second kid go the way of the first. Again he tries to do something—*anything*—to stop the process, but the machine ignores him. Connor almost loses a hand himself when the unwinding chamber door nearly closes on it. The harvester doesn't seem to have a protocol at all for outside interference, or even awareness of it—and although a single security camera constantly sweeps the room, apparently no one's watching, because Connor's sure it's caught him once or twice, but no one has come to investigate. Security here is about as necessary as in a mausoleum. No one's getting in, and none of the residents will be causing problems.

"Á l'aide! Á l'aide! Je ne veux pas mourir!"

The next victim—a girl who doesn't even speak English—is pulled into the machine against all of Connor's attempts to save her. He knows it's futile even trying, but what else can he do? Then with the first three kids unwound, and the bidders primed, the final specimen of the day is plucked by the hydraulic arms from his niche, and placed before the mouth of the machine. At first Connor thinks what he's seeing must be a hallucination brought on by the drugs still in his system, but as he draws closer, there's no mistaking the face. It's Starkey.

Connor stands there numbly as Starkey regains full consciousness and looks at him much the same way Connor had looked at Argent. Not so much with disbelief, but with a curious detachment from reality.

"You?" Starkey says. "Where am I? Why are *you* here?"

But he's quick to figure out his predicament, and the moment he does, Connor turns from sworn enemy into savior. He begins pleading just like the others.

"Please, Connor! However much you hate me, you have to do something!"

Connor actually goes through the motions of trying to free him at first—but only for Starkey's benefit. He knows that he can't do a thing. If an escape artist like Starkey can't do it, what hope does Connor have? Based on what he's already seen, Connor knows Starkey has only five minutes before he's unwound, but there's nothing Connor can do other than stand beside him, keeping him final company. The helpless above the hopeless.

"Fund-raising!" Starkey wails. "The clappers told me I had a new job in their fund-raising division. How could I have been so stupid!"

He struggles, fighting the magnetic restraint just as the other kids did, and in tears he says, "All I wanted was to give storks a fighting chance! And revenge for all the mistreatment and unfairness. I did that, didn't I? I made a difference! Tell me that I made a difference!"

Connor considers how me might respond, and says, "You made people take notice."

If he could save Starkey, would he? Knowing all the death and destruction Starkey has caused? Knowing the maniacal direction his vendetta took? How his personal war actually furthered the cause of unwinding? If anyone deserves to be unwound, it's Starkey . . . and yet Connor would stop it if he could.

He puts a firm hand on Starkey's shoulder. "This is one escape you're not going to make, Mason. Try to relax. Use this time to prepare yourself."

"No! This can't be it! There's got to be a way out!"

"You're on a plane in the middle of God knows where!" yells Connor. "You are in front of a machine that can't be stopped. Use these last minutes to focus, Mason. Use what time you have left to put your life in order!"

And all at once Connor realizes he's not saying these words just to Starkey—he's saying them to himself as well. Conner thought that being awake would give him an advantage, but it has only emphasized how dire the situation is. He tries to tell himself he's been through worse, but there's an intuition as solid as the airframe carrying them across the sky that tells Connor he's not getting out in one piece. It's only a matter of time until he's the one lying before the mouth of the monster.

Starkey does calm himself. He closes his eyes, takes deep breaths, and then when he opens them again, there's a sense of resolve that wasn't there before.

"I know how you can keep me from being unwound," he says.

Connor shakes his head. "I told you, there's nothing I can do!"

"Yes, there is," Starkey tells him with steely certainty in his voice. "You can kill me."

Connor takes a step back and stares at Starkey, unable to respond.

"Kill me, Connor. I want you to. I *need* you to."

"I can't do that!"

"Yes you can!" Starkey insists. "Think about the Graveyard. Think about how I stole that plane. And I killed Trace Neuhauser—did you know that? I could have saved him, but I let him drown."

Connor grits his teeth. "Stop it, Starkey."

"Kill me for the things I've done, Connor! I know you think I deserve it, and I'd rather die by your hand than go into that machine!"

"What good will it do? You'll still go into that machine!"

"No, I won't. My body will go in, but I'll be gone. I'll be harvested, but I *won't* be unwound!"

Connor can't look at Starkey's pleading eyes anymore. He looks away and finds his gaze landing on the shark. The brutal, angry, predatory shark. Connor drops his gaze down to the habitual fist at the end of that same arm. He loosens the fingers, and clasps them again. He feels the strength in them.

"That's right, Connor. Make it fast—I won't resist."

Connor glances to the intake door of the machine. It could open at any moment. "Let me think!"

"No time! Do this for me. Please!"

Can cold-blooded murder be just? Could it be an act of compassion instead of cruelty? If he does this, will Connor ever be the same? If Starkey's alive, he'll be unwound. If he's dead, it will just be a harvest. Starkey's right—Connor has the power to prevent this from being an unwinding. It's a horrible power. But perhaps a necessary one.

"What if it were you?" Starkey asks. "What would *you* want?"

And when Connor thinks of it that way, his choice is clear. He'd never want to know what lies in store within that awful black box. He'd want to die first.

Before he can change his mind, Connor clamps Roland's hand on Starkey's throat. Starkey gasps slightly, but as he promised, he doesn't resist. Connor squeezes tighter . . . tighter . . . then, the instant he feels Starkey's windpipe close off, something entirely unexpected happens.

Roland's hand unclamps.

"Don't stop," hisses Starkey. "Don't stop now!"

Connor squeezes his fingers closed again around Starkey's neck. He holds it, feeling Starkey's pulse in the tips of his fingers—and again, his hand inexplicably releases. Connor starts gasping for air himself, not even realizing he was holding his breath along with Starkey.

"You're a coward!" Starkey wails. "You've always been a coward!"

"No," says Connor, "that's not it."

And finally it occurs to him what's wrong.

Roland tried to choke Connor with this same arm the day before he was unwound, but he couldn't do it.

Because Roland's not a killer.

Connor slowly looks from his right hand . . . to his left. His own hand. The one he was born with. That's the hand he brings to Starkey's throat. That's the hand that digs in until he feels Starkey's windpipe collapse beneath his fingers. That's the hand that is tenacious and determined enough to do what must be done.

Roland never had it in him to kill, thinks Connor. *But I do . . .*

It's harder than Connor could ever imagine. Tears cloud his eyes. "I'm sorry," he says. "I'm so sorry." He doesn't even know who he's apologizing to. He holds eye contact with Starkey, whose eyes begin to bulge and dart in physiological panic. His limbs quiver, his face deepens into bruise shades—yet even so, Starkey forces the corners of his mouth up in a faint grin of triumph.

Just a few moments more . . . just a few moments more . . .

Connor knows the exact moment Starkey dies. Not because he sees it in his eyes but because a vital signs transmitter on Starkey's ankle lets loose a piercing alarm. He pulls his hand from Starkey's throat and, hearing the outer door being unlocked, Connor leaps to the wall of Unwinds, climbs up to his niche, and vaults himself in just as the inner door opens.

First in is a medic, then the man who must be Divan. Connor watches the drama unfold from his perch, trying to slow his breathing so they can't hear him.

"How could this happen?" says Divan. "HOW COULD THIS HAPPEN?"

"I don't know," says the nervous medic. "A heart attack maybe? A congenital condition we didn't know about?"

"I've just auctioned him! Do you have any idea how much money I stand to lose? BRING HIM BACK! NOW!"

The medic scurries off and returns with a defibrillator. Five times he tries to revive Starkey, and although his chest arches with each blast of electricity, the end result is the same. Mason

Michael Starkey, the bloodthirsty Lord of Storks, is dead.

Through all the attempts to revive him, Divan paces, and after the final attempt, his fury resolves into direction. "All right, he's dead, but we can still harvest him."

"Not his brain," says the medic. "It will already have started breaking down."

"We'll assess its viability later—but even if we lose the brain, we can salvage everything else if we're fast enough. Set the machine to express mode, skip the anesthesia, and lower the temperature to thirty-six degrees."

The medic unlocks the control panel and makes the needed adjustments. Then, when the unwinding chamber door opens, Divan physically pushes Starkey's body inside, not waiting for the conveyor belt to do it for him.

The door on the unit closes, the process begins, and the two relax.

"Too bad," says the medic. "It's almost like he died to spite you."

"If it was intentional," says Divan, "then he had help." Divan raises his gaze to look at the Unwinds in the drum all around him.

Connor closes his eyes and remains absolutely still.

"Get back to the control room. I want you to check the telemetry on every Unwind here," Connor hears Divan say as they leave. "Find out if anyone's vital signs are unusually elevated."

They come for him ten minutes later. Three of them: the medic, some random crewman who looks nervous to even be there, and a silent chisel-faced boeuf who looks born to intimidate. Connor is prepared, or at least as prepared as he can be. Hiding near the door just out of view, he blasts them with a fire extinguisher as they enter, and grabs one of their weapons. A tranq gun. They're only armed with tranqs. He fires and manages to take down the nervous guy before the weapon is knocked from Connor's hands.

Then he dodges the grasp of the others, running for cover on the far side of the unwinding chamber, where the medical stasis coolers are stacked, ready for distribution. This fight is just for show, he knows. Escape is impossible, but if thrashing on the end of the line will give his captors grief, then it's well worth it.

The medic tries to lure him out with poorly delivered lies like, "Divan just wants to talk to you—there's nothing to be afraid of."

Connor doesn't even engage him in conversation. For a moment he has the mad thought of opening the hinged nose cone, which is right at the front of the unwinding chamber. It's a design feature that assumed a cargo of tanks, not teens. If he opens the nose cone in flight, it will suck them all out into the icy, airless void of thirty-seven thousand feet, and most certainly bring down the plane. The control switch is close enough—and he might do it too, if all the other kids weren't there in the harvester . . . and if Risa weren't some-where on board.

In the end, Connor is cornered, and they take him down, but not before Connor gets in a few good swings. His attackers don't fight back. Mustn't damage the merchandise. They don't tranq him either—maybe because they weren't entirely lying to him. Maybe Divan does want to talk to him, and talk now, rather than after a visit to Tranqistan.

They cinch his hands together with a cable tie—tight enough to do the job, but not tight enough to cut into his skin—and they take him out, stepping over the body of the tranq'd crewman, who, in a state of slumber, doesn't look nervous at all.

He's brought to a large, fancy room toward the rear of the jet, where Divan waits. There is a troubling collection of faces on the wall behind him, somehow adding a dark gravity to Divan's presence.

"Hello, Connor," he says with a calm he did not express upon Starkey's demise. "My name is—"

"I know who you are," Connor says, then covers by saying, "You're black-market scum, and that's all I need to know."

"Divan Umarov," he continues, ignoring Connor. "And you've been quite the irascible camper, haven't you? How on earth did you wake up?"

"His IV must have blown," says the medic, his eye almost swollen shut from Connor's punch. "The machine's supposed to alert us."

Behind Divan, Argent fumbles to clean a dining table, clearly too terrified for his own life to even make eye contact with Connor. Does he really think Connor will give him away for waking him, and lose the closest thing he has to an ally right now?

"Wait a second," says Connor, as if it's a total shock. "Is that Argent Skinner?" He looks at Argent with feigned incredulity. "What the hell is he doing here? And what happened to his face?"

"You shut up!" Argent says, playing into Connor's little theatrical, although a bit less convincingly. "I'm here because of you, so just shut up."

Divan apparently knows their unpleasant history together— as Connor hoped he would—and accepts that this is the first Connor is aware of Argent's presence on the plane. Argent's breath of relief would have been suspicious if anyone paid him the slightest bit of attention.

Divan looks Connor over. "Am I right in assuming that you dispatched Mason Starkey prior to his unwinding?" And when he doesn't answer Divan says, "Come now, don't you have anything to say?"

Connor shrugs and obliges. "Nice socks," he says with a satisfied smile.

Divan never breaks eye contact. "Indeed they are. Cervelt. New Zealand deer fiber, a bargain at a thousand dollars a pair." He returns Connor's smile, leaving Connor feeling far less satisfied.

"Skinner! Bring Connor something to drink. Lemonade."

Argent, dusting a piano keyboard flinches and hits a few of the keys. On the wall behind him three adjacent faces open their mouths and voice a dissonant chord. Connor swallows, and tries to convince his rational mind that he didn't just see that.

"I'll confess," says Divan, "I was hoping to spend perhaps a week to build hype among my customers for your auction . . . but now, in light of your interference with Mr. Starkey, I just want to be rid of you."

He gestures to the boeuf and the medic to take him away, and they step forward, grabbing him. "Where's Risa?" demands Connor. "I want to talk to her. If you're going to unwind me, at least let me say good-bye."

"Unwise," he says. "No need to compound her grief."

Argent brings the lemonade but is literally blindsided by a chair. Bumping into it, he drops the glass on the floor, which calls forth a long-suffering sigh from Divan.

"I'm sorry, sir! I'm sorry!"

"Apologize to Connor; it was his drink."

"I'm sorry, Connor."

"It's all good, Argent," Connor says. "All good." And he turns his head just enough to hide from Divan the wink he gives Argent.

Divan orders that Connor be not only restrained but kept in isolation.

"Should we now to tranq him?" asks the boeuf in something

269

resembling English, with an accent much stronger than Divan's.

"No," Divan tells him, "I can think of no greater punishment than leaving him alone with his own thoughts."

48 · Argent

In his twenty years on this earth, Argent Skinner could never connect his life's aspirations to anything real. As a child, he wanted to be a football star, but lacked the physique, so he lowered his expectations and became a vocal spectator. As an adolescent, he wanted to be a basketball star, and although he had some talent, he lacked the drive to see it through. So he lowered his expectations and accepted the chance to warm the bench for the one season he actually made the team.

It was more than two years after almost finishing high school that Connor Lassiter showed up in his checkout line. During that time, Argent had gotten no closer to his adult life goals than he ever got to his childhood goals. Argent wanted to be rich. He wanted to be respected. He wanted to be surrounded by beautiful women who adored him. But as with everything else, he lacked the vision required to manifest these things, so once more he lowered his expectations. Now all he wanted was a job that gave him enough money to keep his car running, and enough beer so he could hang out with other low-expectation friends and bad-mouth the types of people who got a piece of their dream.

Then Connor showed up, and Argent truly believed, if he could only win Connor over, he could hitch himself up to Connor's shooting star, and blast himself out of mediocrity.

It didn't work out.

Then Argent figured hitching himself up with a seasoned

parts pirate might provide him with a life of intrigue and purpose. After all, he'd already been doing some under-the-table dealing with groceries he'd been pilfering. That could be considered black-market experience, couldn't it? His hopes were high for a future in parts pirateering.

That didn't work out either.

And now he's here. He supposes there are worse things than being in domestic service to a wealthy flesh trader, and once Argent regains face, perhaps Divan will promote him to a less thankless position. But who is he kidding? He has watched Divan and knows how he operates. If Argent screws up badly, he'll be unceremoniously unwound. Otherwise, Divan will do the honorable thing and deliver what he promised Argent—but no more. He'll be left, after his indentured servitude, at some airport somewhere with a new face, a handshake, and the same lack of a future he began with.

How amazing, then, to think that his entire life could change with a single wink.

He was terrified when Connor was brought in to Divan, and was certain that Connor would point the finger at Argent for having woken him in the first place. After all, that's what Argent would have done: deflected the blame. Spread the misery. At first he didn't understand Connor's choice to protect him. He thought it might be a setup for something worse.

Then Connor winked at him as he was being led out, and the wink explained it all. Argent had dreamed of teaming up with the Akron AWOL. He thought there was no hope of that, but that wink says otherwise. It says that they aren't just a team, they're a *secret* team, and that's the best kind. In that instant, Argent went from a flesh dealer's valet to being the inside man! A high-level spy disguised as a flunky! *I need you, Argent*, that wink said. *I need you, and I'm trusting my life to you.*

In that wink, both Argent and his hero were redeemed.

Argent carries on his duties for the rest of the day with an uncharacteristic spring in his step, because he knows something that Divan doesn't. He's part of something even larger than this massive aircraft.

As much as Argent hated Connor Lassiter for ruining his face, now he loves him like a brother—and if Argent plays this right, his life, his story will be forever intertwined with Connor's. That's certainly enough for Argent to risk everything!

49 · Broadcast

"This is Radio Free Hayden on the air for your listening pleasure, broadcasting from somewhere where the farm smells are pungent.

"So much going on out there! Clappers and AWOLs and storks, oh my! We have heaping mounds of new intel to report on the Juvenile Authority, as well—such as, how their newly announced budget increases the size of their street force by twenty percent. That's the largest single peacetime law enforcement personnel spike in modern history. It makes you wonder if this is 'peacetime' at all.

"But enough about the Juvies, let's talk about Mason Michael Starkey, political dissident, freedom fighter, sociopathic mass murderer. Whatever you want to call him, and whatever your personal opinion of him, here are some objective facts for you.

"Fact number one: His last two missions before he vanished from sight were funded by the people who brought you self-destructive teenagers. Not run-of-the-mill ones, but the kind who actually blow themselves up. Yes, folks, Mason Starkey didn't just use clappers in his harvest camp attacks, he was funded by them.

"Fact number two: Public support for the Juvenile Authority

has actually increased since Starkey's harvest camp liberations. Imagine that. The more harvest camps he frees, the less the public wants free teenagers!

"Fact number three: This year there is a record number of measures on the ballot and bills in Washington to determine the future of unwinding. Do we unwind prisoners? Do we allow the voluntary unwinding of adults? Do we give the Juvenile Authority the right to unwind kids without parental permission? Those are just a handful of the issues we're being asked to make decisions on.

"So what does all that have to do with the price of parts in Paraguay? Well, we've all been laboring under the belief that clappers want to destabilize our world. Create chaos for chaos's sake. But they made a crucial mistake when they put their muscle behind Mason Starkey, because it tipped their hand. It gave us a glimpse of their true motives.

"Funny how the more frightened people are, the more they turn to the Juvenile Authority to solve the problem. 'Unwind the baddies!' 'Protect my children from those children.' 'Make the world safe for law-abiding citizens.'

"Y'know, if I wanted to make sure that the Juvenile Authority had greater and greater support, I would trick angry teenagers into blowing themselves up, and then blame the angry teenagers! No mess, no bother. Well, quite a lot of mess, but you get my point.

"I put this before you right here, right now: Clapping is not chaotic or random—it is a well-organized effort by the medical grafting industry to ensure the future of unwinding now and forever.

"If you don't believe me, look for it yourself. Follow the money. Who gets rich if the Juvenile Authority gets strong? In the long run, who profits from clapper attacks? The smoking guns

are hard to find, but they're out there—and if you find some-
thing, let us know at radiofreehayden@yahoo.com.

"Well, with the approach of distant sirens, I'm sorry to say
that our time together has run out, but here's a tune just right for
finger snapping, as we sign off until next week! And remember,
the truth will keep you whole!

"I've got you . . . under my skin. . . ."

50 · Lev

Denver Union Station. Eighteenth stop of the eastbound
Zephyr, one of the few transcontinental passenger trains still
running on a regular schedule. Lev pays for his ticket in cash.
The ticket agent spares him a glance, then double-takes and
shakes his head in clear disapproval. Still, the agent passes the
ticket through the little hole at the base of the glass window.
Only after leaving the line does Lev hear the agent say to the
next customer, "We get all types here."

There are Juvey-cops in the station. AWOLs always try to
take trains. They rarely make it on board. One Juvey eyes Lev
suspiciously and heads him off before he can get to the train.

"Can I please see some identification, son?"

"I've already been cleared by security. The Juvenile Authority doesn't have the right to ask for identification without prob-
able cause."

"Fine," says the Juvey-cop. "You can file a formal rights
violation complaint with the Juvenile Authority after you show
me your ID."

He pulls out his wallet and hands an ID card to the cop.
The ID has a new picture, reflecting how he looks now. The
cop studies it, clearly disappointed that he can't make an
instant arrest.

"Mahpee Kinkajou. Is that Navajo?"

Trick question. "Arápache. Doesn't it say so?"

"My mistake," the cop says, handing him back the ID. "Have a nice trip, Mr. Kinkajou." The cop knows better than to mess with him now. The Arápache are very litigious when it comes to their off-Rez youth being harassed by the authorities.

Lev glances at the officer's name tag. "I'll make sure to file that rights violation report when I get where I'm going, Officer Triplitt." Lev won't do it, but the officer deserves a little heartache.

Lev finds his train and gets on board, ignoring the glances and stares of strangers, although sometimes he stares back until the strangers are so uncomfortable, they look away. No one recognizes him. No one will. His new look guarantees that.

Passengers already settled in their seats glance his way as he moves down the aisle. One woman quickly deposits her purse in the empty seat beside her. "This one's taken," she says.

He passes through three coach cars until coming to one a little less crowded and finds a place where he can sit by himself. Across the aisle, however, is a girl who seems to have almost set up camp in the two seats she's commandeered. She has a cobalt-blue streak in her black hair, and fingernails in various unmatching colors. She's seventeen, maybe eighteen. Perhaps an AWOL who survived long enough to be legit, or a legit girl playing at nonconformity. One look at him, and she thinks she's found a kindred spirit.

"Hi," she says.

"Hi," he echoes.

A moment of awkward silence then she asks, "So who are they?"

He plays dumb. "Who are who?"

"Zachary Vazquez, Courtney Wright, Matthew Praver," she says, reading them right off of his forehead, "and all the rest."

He has no reason to lie to her. He had the names tattooed

275

there so that they could be seen. His days of hiding are over. "They're Unwinds," he tells her. "They had no one to mourn for them. But now they have me."

She nods in unconditional approval. "Very cool. Nervy, too. I like it." She shifts from the window seat to the aisle seat. "So are they everywhere?"

"They're head to toe," he tells her.

"Wow! How many names are there?"

"Three hundred and twelve," Lev says, and adds with a grin, "any more and it would look cluttered."

That makes her laugh. She ponders his face and his clean-shaven head, then says, "You know, your hair will eventually grow back. You'll have to keep shaving it if you want people to see the names."

"That won't be a problem."

The train pulls out, and she moves across the aisle to sit next to him. Taking his hands, she examines the many names on his forearms, hands, and fingers. He lets her, enjoying the positive attention as much as he enjoyed the negative attention from the disapprovers.

"I like the color choices, and the fact that you didn't spare your face. It was a bold choice."

"None of *them* were spared, so why should any part of me be?"

He made sure that there wouldn't be a single part of his body not covered by the names of the Unwound. His only regret is that there aren't more. Jase was right. So much ink so fast hurt to the point of tears, and several sleepless nights. Even now it hurts, but he bore the pain, and he'll bear it still. The simple lettering of the names in red, black, blue, and green looks like war paint from a distance. Only when you get close enough to see Lev's eyes do the patterns resolve into the names of the Unwound. Jase is a true artist.

"I think it's beautiful," says the girl with the cobalt streak. "Maybe I'll follow your lead." She looks at her right arm. "I could ink an Unwind right here. Just one, though. There are times when less is more."

"Sabrina Fansher," he suggests.

"Excuse me?"

"Sabrina Fansher. She would have been number three hundred and thirteen if I'd kept on going."

The girl frowns. "Who was she?"

"I wish I knew. All I have are their names."

She sighs. "Her memories are scattered to the wind. Sad beyond sad." Then she nods. "Sabrina Fansher it shall be."

She introduces herself as Amelia Sabatini—her Italian last name making him think of Miracolina. Then she asks him his name. He hesitates before he tells her, still not entirely used to his new alias. "Mahpee," he tells her. "Mahpee Kinkajou."

"Interesting name."

"It's a Chancefolk name. You can call me Mah."

"Better than Pee. Or Kinky." She giggles. He decides he likes her, which could be a problem. His plans do not leave room for friendship.

"How far are you going?" he asks her.

"Kansas City. How about you?"

"All the way to the end of the line."

"New York?"

"Or bust."

"Well, I hope you don't do that," Amelia says, giggling again, this time a bit nervously. "What's there in the Big Apple for you?"

Her questions are probing. Invasive. With each one he's liking her less and less. Instead of answering, he puts it back on her. "What's for you in Kansas City?"

"A sister who can stand me," Amelia says. "You have family

277

in New York? Friends? Are you running away there?" She waits for his answer. She will not get one.

"It's nice that you have someone in your life who can stand you," he says. "Not everyone has that."

Then he turns to look out of the window, and keeps looking out of the window until she's moved across the aisle again.

51 · Tarmac

There are more than three thousand abandoned airfields in the world. Some are the relics of war, abandoned during peacetime. Others were built to handle air traffic in places where the population has declined. Still others were built by misguided investors, banking on a growth boom that never arrived.

Of those three thousand airfields, about nine hundred are still viable. Of those nine hundred, about one hundred and fifty have long enough runways to accommodate a craft the size of the *Lady Lucrezia*. Of those hundred and fifty, twelve are regular stops for the *Lady*—and they are spread out on every populated continent.

Today's itinerary features northern Europe.

Six small private jets are already on the weedy tarmac of Denmark's Rom Airfield, lined up like chicks awaiting the return of the mother hen. It's a ritual repeated several times a month in each airfield, with no fear of government interference, thanks to some well-placed palm greasing.

Distribution is a procedure much simpler than the actual unwindings. The *Lady Lucrezia* lands, her hinged nose rises, opening her voluminous cargo hold, and the crates, already sorted to their various destinations are loaded upon the smaller craft, representing buyers anxiously awaiting their purchases.

No worldwide delivery service is more efficient. No business-man is prouder of his operation than Divan Umarov.

52 · Risa

She watches the off-loading activity from the guest room window, getting only a small glimpse of it. This is the third time they've landed since she's been conscious. The first two times had them on the ground for less than ten minutes before accelerating down the runway once more, and she imagines this will be the same. Divan dispatches his cargo even faster than he unwinds them.

She turns at the sound of someone at the door, expecting to see Divan. Maybe he sold her after all, and the buyer is wait-ing on the tarmac to appraise the merchandise. She wonders if a swift kick to the groin would diminish her value in the bulg-ing eyes of the recipient. Instead of Divan at the door, however, its Grace's half-faced brother.

"Unless you're here to spring me, I'm not interested."

"Can't do that," Argent says, "but I can take you to see Connor."

And suddenly Argent's her new best friend.

"Gotta be quiet, and gotta be quick," Argent tells her as he leads her out of the room, sounding a little bit like Grace. "Divan's outside supervising the off-load, but he'll be back in just a few minutes."

Argent leads her farther back in the plane to another guest bedroom almost as richly appointed as hers. At first appear-ance, Connor's merely tucked into a well-made bed, until she realizes those aren't blankets, but dozens of thick canvas straps wrapping around him, locked into steel screw eyes in the floor-boards, on either side of the bed. Those straps aren't just keep-ing him from escaping, they're keeping him from moving.

Yet in the midst of all this, Connor is still able to smile at her and say, "So I'm beginning to think this spa isn't what the brochure promised."

Risa swore to herself that she wouldn't let him see tears, but she doesn't know how long she can hold to that.

"We're getting you out of here," she says, kneeling to see how the bands are secured. "Argent, help me!"

But Argent doesn't move. "Can't do it," he says. "And even if we could get him loose, we won't be on the ground long enough to get him out."

"That's no reason not to try!"

"Risa, stop," Connor says quietly.

"If I had a sharp enough knife . . ."

"Risa, stop!" says Connor a little bit louder. "I need you to slow down and listen to me!"

But the tears she kept from her eyes seem to be flooding her thoughts instead, filling her with panic. "This isn't going to happen to you! I won't let it!" And she continues to fight against his bonds until Argent says, "I told you she'd be useless."

That, more than anything else, clears her mind enough to listen to what Connor has to say.

"I have a plan, Risa."

Risa takes a deep breath to calm herself. "Tell me. I'm listening."

"The plan is . . . you stay whole, and I get unwound."

"That's not a plan!" she yells.

"Shh!" Argent says. "The whole plane'll hear you!"

As if in response the whole plane shudders and emits a mechanical grinding.

"Risa, it *is* a plan. Not much of one, but at least it's something. Argent knows the details. He'll fill you in."

"The nose cone is closing!" Argent whines. "Divan will be back on board any second, if he isn't already. I can't be caught in here!"

But Risa can't leave yet. Not without saying those words
that come so hard, but mean more than anything now. The
words she fears she may never get to say again. "Connor, I—"

"Don't!" Connor's lower lip quivers. "Because if you say it,
it'll sound too much like a good-bye, and I don't think I could
take that."

And so Risa doesn't speak it aloud, but it's there between
them, more powerful than anything either of them can say.

She leans over, kisses him, then hurries to the door where
Argent waits, his half-face red with fright. It's just as they leave
that Connor breaks down and utters the words he couldn't
bear to hear himself.

"I love you, Risa," he says. "Every last part of me."

53 · Connor

"I hope you're hungry."

Connor cranes his neck to see Divan coming into the room
with a tray. Connor answers him with a glare.

"No, I suppose you're not," says Divan, "but I wish you to
have this meal anyway. And I wish you to enjoy it."

Divan sits in the room's only chair, depositing the tray on a
small desk and removing its silver dome, releasing a plume of
steam toward the ceiling.

"Fine," Connor says, "and then you won't be able to unwind
me for twenty-four hours, isn't that right? I can't be unwound
on a full stomach."

"Ah yes," says Divan, unrolling silverware from a napkin,
"the many rules and regulations of the Juvenile Authority. Well,
we do things differently here."

"I've noticed."

The room now smells rich with butter and garlic. Connor

finds his mouth watering in spite of himself, and he despises Divan even more for making his own senses rebel against him.

"Have you ever had lobster, Connor?"

"I thought they were extinct."

"There are still private farms if one knows where to find them."

Through the corner of his eye, Connor sees Divan perform surgery on a red shell, removing a fist-size lump of steaming white shellfish meat.

"You're going to have to free my hands if you want me to eat."

Divan chuckles slightly. "Freeing your hands would give you ideas, and ideas would give you hope in a hopeless situation. It would be cruel to give you hope at this point, so no, your hands remain as restrained as the rest of you." Divan cuts the meat, then with a small fork, he proceeds to push a piece of the lobster toward Connor's mouth. "I will feed you. Your only responsibility is to enjoy the experience."

Although Connor keeps his lips pursed, Divan patiently waits, with the fork just above his mouth, saying nothing, just waiting. Like the unwinding itself, Connor realizes this meal is inevitable. After a few minutes, he opens his mouth, and allows Divan to feed him the most expensive thing he's ever eaten.

"You need to understand I am not your enemy, Connor."

That's much harder for Connor to swallow than the lobster. "How do you figure?"

"Because in spite of what you cost me with Starkey, I have nothing in my heart but admiration for you. Nelson may have had a vendetta against you, but I do not. In fact, were you not worth so many millions to me, I would seriously consider releasing you."

The idea of Connor's unwound parts being worth millions is so unimaginable to him that he glances at Divan to see if he's making a joke. But Divan keeps a straight face as he lowers another piece of lobster to Connor's mouth.

"You seem surprised. You shouldn't be. You're a worldwide folk hero. In fact, your auction has garnered almost twice what I thought it would."

"So I've already been auctioned?"

"It was finalized an hour ago. And to buyers on every continent." And then Divan smiles, "The sun will never set on you, Connor Lassiter. Few people can say such a thing." Then he strokes Connor's hair like a doting parent. Connor turns his head, but that doesn't stop him.

"I said you could feed me. I didn't say you could touch me."

"Forgive me," Divan says, feeding him some vegetables that are all texture and garlic. "I feel a closeness to my Unwinds that I don't think you could understand. Do you know I occasionally sit beside them, comforting them as they're brought into the unwinding chamber? Mostly they're inconsolable. But once in a while they will look at me with eyes of acceptance and understanding. There are few things more gratifying."

"What about the others you auctioned today? Will the sun set on them?"

"Every Unwind divides differently," Divan explains. "There were five today, and all sold quickly." Then he adds. "The boy before you sold piece by piece to only three buyers. They'll be reselling, of course, but as long as they pay my price, what they do with the merchandise is their business."

Connor takes a deep, shuddering breath. He hopes Divan doesn't notice it. He doesn't—he's more interested in the meal, as he feeds Connor another chunk of chewy white pulp.

"How do you find the lobster?"

"Like shrimp with an attitude," Connor says, then adds, "but in the end, in spite of all its airs, it's nothing but a bottom-feeder."

Divan blots Connor's lips with a silk napkin. "Well, even we bottom-feeders have our place in the ecosystem."

Logically, Connor knows the longer the meal takes, and the longer he keeps Divan talking, the longer it is until he's unwound. Yet he finds his curiosity about Divan to be real. How can a man do what this man does and believe himself to be anything but Satan incarnate?

"I abhor violence, you know," Divan says. "I grew up surrounded by it. I come from a family of arms dealers. But when it came my turn, I determined to rechannel my legacy, shifting away from the making of death to the sustaining of life."

"You're still an arms dealer," says Connor. "And legs. And everything else."

Divan nods, no doubt having heard it before. "I'm glad you're able to keep your sense of humor in these penultimate moments." He feeds Connor again, blots his mouth again, and then folds the napkin with compulsive precision. "I want you to know that you don't have to worry about Risa. She will be well taken care of."

"Taken care of," Connor mocks. "Is that supposed to make me feel better? That you're taking care of her?"

"There are worse things."

To which Connor says, "Higher levels of hell are still hell."

Divan looks to the tray and puts the fork down. "Congratulations, Connor. You've cleaned your plate. Your mother would be proud."

Connor closes his eyes. *My mother. How many yards was I from the front door before I was taken? How close did I come to knowing whether she'd see me with anything but shame? Now I'll never know.*

When he opens his eyes again, Divan is leaning closer, a strange hint of an Unwind's desperation in his eyes. "I don't want you to think ill of me, Connor."

And of all the emotions Connor feels, anger is the one that rises to the surface. "Why would you care what I think? You're about to tear me apart and sell me. Do you think if I forgive you—if *any* of us forgive you—it makes you worthy of forgiveness? Sorry, it doesn't."

Divan leans away, his veneer of aloof sophistication replaced with a despair as cold and empty as the air outside. Connor sees it only for a moment, but he sees it all the same— and in that moment, he realizes he has something that this man can only grasp at but can never capture: self-respect.

"We're done here," Connor says, realizing it will hasten the inevitable, but finding that he honestly doesn't care anymore. "I'm tired of looking at you. Unwind me."

As Divan stands, his perfect posture and larger-than-life presence seem hobbled. He looks away from Connor, not even able to hold his gaze. "As you wish."

54 · Risa

An hour later, Risa sits before the Orgão Orgânico, with a Mozart étude playing in her head. Keeping her hands to her side, she clings to her last threads of hope, while behind her Divan reclines on a sofa, watching her. The plane shudders with a tremor of turbulence.

"Is it happening now?" she asks. She won't look at Divan. Nor will she look up at the accusation of faces before her. She looks only at the keys. Black and white in a world of unrelenting gray.

"He'll be in the chamber soon, if he's not already," Divan tells her. "Try not to think about it. Play something cheery."

Her voice is barely a whisper when she says, "No."

Divan sighs. "Such pointless resistance. This moral high ground of yours is nothing but quicksand."

"Then let it take me under."

"It won't. You won't let it—and you *will* play. Maybe not today, but tomorrow, or the day after that. Because it is in your nature to survive. You see, Risa, survival is a dance between our needs and our consciences. When the need is great enough, and the music loud enough, we can stomp conscience into the ground."

Risa closes her eyes. She knows the dance. She did it for Roberta at Proactive Citizenry when she agreed to speak out in favor of unwinding. Yes, Risa was blackmailed, and she did it to protect the kids at the Graveyard, but still she joined the dance.

"It's the way of the world," Divan continues. "Look at unwinding, society's grand gavotte of denial. There will, no doubt, come a time when people look to one another and say, *My God, what have we done?* But I don't believe it will happen any time soon. Until then, the dance must have music; the chorus must have its voice. Give it that voice, Risa. Play for me."

But Risa's fingers offer him nothing, and the Orgão Orgânico holds the obdurate, unyielding silence of the grave.

55 · UNIS

The black box is bright on the inside. So bright that Connor must squint, waiting for his eyes to adjust.

"Hello, **Con**nor **Las**siter. Welcome to your divisional experience! I am your fully automated Unwinding Intelli-System, but you can call me UNIS."

The voice is genderless. Guileless. UNIS truly wants to make this the happiest day of Connor's life.

"Before we get started, **Con**nor **Las**siter, I have a few questions to make this a smooth and positive transition into a divided state. First, let me confirm your comfort level. Please rate your current level of comfort on a scale of one to ten, ten being least uncomfortable."

Connor resolves to not give the machine the benefit of his response.

"I'm sorry, I didn't get that. Please rate your current level of comfort on a scale of one to ten, ten being least uncomfortable."

His heart races out of his control. He tries to calm it by reminding himself he's just one of many others to go this way. That he survived more than two years after the order to unwind him was signed. That's more than most can say.

"All right, I'll assume you're sufficiently comfortable. Within the next few moments you'll feel slight pricks on either side of your neck as I administer the anesthetized synthetic plasma to facilitate your division, and so that you do not suffer any pain. While I'm doing this, let's take the time to personalize your experience. I can project a variety of scenic vistas for you. Please choose from the following: mountain flyby, ocean tranquility, vibrant cityscape, or landmarks of the world."

He wants to deny the fear, but he can't. He thought he was stronger. He wishes he had someone to do for him what he did for Starkey. Take him out before UNIS could get its claws into him.

"Would you like me to repeat the choices? Please say yes or no."

"*Shut up!*" Connor yells, unable to control himself. "*Just shut the hell up!*"

"I'm sorry, that's not a valid response. Since you seem to be having trouble selecting, I'll select for you. Your choice is . . . landmarks of the world."

Images soar before him, changing with a slow, relentless rhythm. Mount Rushmore. The Eiffel Tower. Golden Gate

Bridge. The anesthesia blurs the line between what's part of him and what's not. The images invade his mind as if they're being projected inside his head.

"You may now begin to feel a flurry of activity in your extremities, most noticeably in your wrists, elbows, knees, and ankles. This is entirely normal, and no cause for alarm."

Great Wall of China. Rock of Gibraltar. Angkor Wat. *The sun never sets on Connor Lassiter. Thousands of miles between every part of me.* Western Wall. Leaning Tower. Niagara Falls. *Will I be going to those places? Not if I can help it.*

"I can also play your choice of musical genre. Please make your selection now, **Con**nor **Las***si*ter. You can say things like 'techno-dance' or 'prewar rock.'"

All hope is now with Argent, and with Risa.

Risa . . .

He holds on to the image of her, projecting it out, even as the world is projected in. Back in the room where Divan had him, he was bound so tightly to that bed, Connor couldn't touch her. He'd have given anything to have brushed her cheek one last time. He didn't care whether it was his hand or Roland's.

"Please make your musical selection now. . . ."

He knows that his life was a life worth living, and he lived it remarkably well these past two years, in spite of the bleak cards he was dealt. He knows what it means to save countless lives. He knows what it means to end a life. But more than anything he knows what it means to love. He has to believe he will take that with him, wherever it is he now goes, whether it be oblivion, or the proverbial "better place," or an impossible web of global destinations.

"All right, I can choose for you. Your musical genre is . . . twentieth-century disco."

He must leave the battle now. Let others take over for him. All this time he recoiled at being called the Akron AWOL. Now he embraces it, and in defiance of his unwinding, he shifts his identity from himself, to his legend. His absence will only make his presence greater.

"Won't you take me to . . . FunkyTOWN?"

Connor doesn't know what became of the organ printer. He can only hope that it will be repaired and find its way into the right hands. And that Cam will bring down Proactive Citizenry, and that Lev will find his peace. All the things worth hoping for. He's amazed that even here, in the bowels of the beast, he finds a way to hope.

"You may feel unsettled by a sudden inability to breathe. Do not be alarmed; the need for you to breathe is no longer required."

Perhaps it's the anesthesia, but a sense of calm begins to come over him. Instead of the despair of things slipping away, Connor feels the empowerment of letting things go.

"We will soon be ending the audiovisual portion of your experience. Let me take this opportunity to say what a pleasure it has been to serve you, **Con**nor **Las**s*i*ter, on your special day."

He stops imagining the parts of himself that he can no longer feel, and focuses on what he still can, living within each moment until the moment is gone. Until the beat of his heart is a memory. Until the memory is a memory. Until the core of all that he is, is split like an atom, releasing its energy into a waiting universe.

56 · REM.

Do the Unwound dream? There, in the chill twilight between being, and being part of another, does an Unwind's fragmented mind struggle to bridge the distance? To the Unwound, that distance must be greater than the space between stars.

Still, if they live, as the law insists they do, they must

dream just like everyone else. Many of the "traditional living" insist they don't dream, but that's only because they refuse to remember their own surreal worlds of rewound hopes, fears, and memories.

For Risa, the night that follows Connor's unwinding falls quickly due to the *Lady Lucrezia*'s eastward heading. Risa's dreams that night are fitful and fraught with despair. She dreams that she's having tea with Sonia in the middle of her shop, in the midst of earthquakes. Fragile porcelain figurines fall from their shelves and shatter, but Sonia pays no heed. Everywhere are age-old clocks of every shape and size, all of them ticking in anxious arrhythmia.

"They've unwound him," she tells Sonia between tremors. "They've unwound Connor."

"I know, dear, I know." Sonia's voice is sympathetic and comforting, but all of that comfort is swallowed by the pit of Risa's distress.

"Sometimes," says Sonia, "the random events I spoke of work against us, and there's nothing to be done."

"I have to get the printer!" Risa insists over the din of clocks and crashes. "It's what he would want."

"Not your concern anymore," Sonia tells her, "but rest assured, dear, I'll fight the good fight as long as I have air left in these lungs."

And Risa finds herself filled with an even deeper anguish, for she suddenly realizes that there *is* no air left in Sonia's lungs. She's already dead. Their attacker was not the kind of man to leave witnesses.

"Don't forget that Connor is still counting on you," dead Sonia reminds her. "It's all up to you and Grace's good-for-nothing brother. Connor had a plan. Come through for him!"

The ground shakes again. Chandeliers overhead tinkle,

threatening to plunge, and suddenly something else in the antique shop comes into focus. The eighty-eight faces of Divan's dread instrument now loom behind Sonia.

"Something the matter, dear?"

But before Risa can speak, all the eyes open in unison, to stare her down in mute accusation.

She bolts awake unable to catch her breath, finding herself alone in a dark airborne night, rife with turbulence.

Cam's dreams, usually more disjointed than the dreams of others, coalesce tonight out of the meaningless memory snippets of his internal community, into something almost tangible. Before him is a marble staircase that seems to have no end. He climbs it until reaching a temple, a gleaming white Parthenon, its pillars evenly spaced and perfectly carved. The whole structure seems to be of one piece, as if it were hewn right out of the stone of the mountain. Inside, larger than life, are golden statues to the gods of Proactive Citizenry, and there, at the far end, is a statue of Roberta.

"Lay yourself on my altar," she commands. "The blood of many must be spilled, and you, Cam, hold the blood of many." Her voice is so compelling, Cam doesn't know how much longer he can resist it.

Grace dreams that she's on the diving platform again—the one she refused to leap from as a child. Only this time, it's so high, she's at cruising altitude. Argent is down below, urging her to jump, but she can't because she has a baby in her arms. Someone storked her a baby. Why would someone do that to her? She nears the edge of the platform, and as she does, she realizes it's not a baby in her arms at all. She's holding the organ printer.

"Jump, Gracie," yells Argent, too far away to be seen. "You're ruining it for everybody."

And so, holding on to the printer, she leaps toward a pool so far below, it seems the size of a postage stamp.

Lev's dream is far simpler than any of the others on this night. He finds himself in the yellowing treetops of an urban park, above the park bench on which he actually sleeps. In his dream, he leaps weightless from limb to limb until there's nowhere left to go, because the trees give way to an expanse of water. So he holds tightly to the last tree, watching the light of the moon dance on the waters, his eyes drawn to the statue on its own little island in the harbor, knowing that dawn will come all too soon.

57 · Broadcast

"Friends, it is with deep, deep regret that I inform you that the Parental Override bill has just been passed by the House of Representatives, and is now on its way to the Senate, where it is also expected to pass. For those of you living under, hiding beneath, or being smashed in the head by a rock, this means that the Juvenile Authority is one step closer to being able to go into a home—any home—and round up anyone between their thirteenth and seventeenth birthdays, and have them unwound without parental consent. All they'll need to do is prove 'incorrigibility,' by a loose legal definition.

"The good news here—if any of this can be called good news—is that Parental Override is still just a bill. It still needs to pass in the Senate, and be signed into law by the president. But I assure you it will become the law of the land if we don't do something to stop it.

"Today I don't speak to the supporters of Parental Override. I don't speak to its opponents, either. I'm talking to those of you out there who are sitting silently, allowing this to happen. All of

you out there who know it's wrong, but are too terrified of clappers, and the angry kids on your corner, and maybe even your own kids to speak out against it. You think it's out of your hands, but that's not true! These things aren't happening because of some government conspiracy. I mean, sure, big-money interests are trying to push it through, but there's always big money lobbying for influence in Washington. That's nothing surprising, and nothing new. No, if this happens, we made it happen. We chose fear over hope. We chose to beat our children into submission. Is that the world you want to live in?

"The bill won't worm its way to a Senate vote until November, which means we will get a chance to have our say. Now, more than ever, we need to rally. Remember—we meet at dawn on Monday, November first—All Saints' Day—on the National Mall, between the Capitol building and the Washington Monument. Whether we have ten in our uprising, or ten thousand, we need to make our voices heard. Or the next time someone hears your voice, it might be in someone else's throat."

58 · Jersey Girl

The ferry to Liberty Island has not changed much in a hundred years. Newer boats, perhaps, but even the new ones look like something from a bygone era. There was talk about building a subway line underneath the bay that connected the great lady to the mainland, but, for once, sanity prevailed, the project was killed, and the statue remained accessible only by overcrowded, overpriced ferry. It remained a key rite of the New York tourist experience.

As in all high-profile locations, there are plenty of security measures in place—NYPD officers, Juvey-cops, and various rent-a-cops are all over Battery Park, where the ferries board, as well as on the ferries themselves, and, of course, on Liberty Island—but on the island, the NYPD is replaced by New Jersey police, since Miss Liberty is technically a part of the Garden State. It's something New Yorkers are in denial about—that Liberty Island is really part of New Jersey. Regardless, there is no shortage of intimidating firepower, because liberty is not protected by tranquilizers. Mostly it's protected by lethal ceramic bullets, the kind specially designed to kill clappers without blowing them up in the process.

For years there have been fears of a clapper attack on the statue, but so far they've left her alone. The authorities hypothesize that by maintaining the fear of a clapper attack, the movement is creating more terror than if they actually did blow it up. The truth is that Proactive Citizenry considers itself too patriotic to ever do something so heinous as to turn Miss Liberty into shrapnel.

There's always one protest or another on the island. People gather there for countless causes. Usually they're peaceful in nature. A few dozen people with banners and a bullhorn garnering a little media attention. The violent protesters know better than to bring their anger there. Violent folk tend to rage against the system in places that are less symbolic and more effective.

On a sunny day in early October, a boy with a shaved head and names tattooed all over his body boards the three o'clock ferry to Liberty Island.

59 · Lev

From Battery Park, she seems much smaller and farther away than he thought she would. The ferry ride is also much longer than he had thought.

He is asked to show his identification three times. Once in

Battery Park, once before boarding the ferry, and a third time on board. Each time the officer backs off upon seeing the ID is of Arápache origin. None of them want to invoke the wrath of the tribe.

As the ferry approaches, it circles Liberty Island, giving a nice 360-degree view of the statue. Photo ops for everyone. Lev has no camera to record the visit, but he takes in the view just like everyone else.

From the green copper folds of her flowing robes extends a brand-new aluminum/titanium arm, shining silver-gray in the bright sun and holding a new torch. The new arm and torch is half the weight of the old one. The plan, Lev had read, was to spray the new arm with a copper oxide paint so the arm would match the rest of her body. However, tests proved that the paint was flawed. It wouldn't bond with the alloy, and thus would quickly peel, leaving her arm looking like rotting flesh. It was decided to leave her arm with a stainless steel sheen until they could figure out a way to match it to the rest of her body, or until people got used to it the way it is. The alloy is designed to never rust, however, without the protective paint, the bolts holding the panels together are very susceptible to the corrosive sea air.

As Lev's ferry nears the island, he can see that those bolts already have begun to rust. Less than a month after installation, he can see discolored seams all the way up her arm, to her fingertips and to the torch. Engineers are probably hard at work trying to find a solution.

The ferry docks, leaving the excited tourists to explore the island and wait in the long line to climb inside the statue, all the way up to the crown, and to the new torch—something that was off-limits for many years, due to the old arm's instability. Lev joins the cattle march of tourists off the ferry.

"Nice body art, freak," says someone behind him, someone

who's protected by the anonymity of the crowd. Far too many people think they can get away with anything if they're protected by anonymous masses. Well, let them deride him. Let them despise him. He stopped caring what people thought of him a very long time ago. Or at least, what strangers thought.

There's a protest rally today in the shadow of Miss Liberty. Fifty or so people are rallying for Albanian rights. Lev's not quite sure who's taken the rights of Albanians away, but someone must have. A small news crew is present. The reporter, still prebroadcast, has a lackey spray her hair with some sort of industrial megahold mist so that it can resist the constant wind that rips across the island. The lackey keeps spraying until the reporter's hair has the rigidity of plastic.

There's a small stage for the rally's key speakers. Lev weaves through the crowd toward the stage.

He could be of no help to Connor. He was useless in his attempt to sway the Arápache council. But here, today, he will make his stand. He will make a difference. Today will be the culmination of all the forces at work in his life. He has neither fear nor anger. That's how he knows this is right. As he pushes through the crowds, he is reminded of the kinkajou of his dreams bounding through the rainforest canopy, with joyous purpose.

The stiff breeze is chilly, but still he removes his shirt, ignoring the rise of goose bumps as he reveals another hundred and sixty names on his shoulders, chest, and back. As he nears the stage, he kicks off his sneakers and unbuttons his jeans, taking a moment to slip them off without tripping. Now the people he pushes past notice that there's an illustrated kid stripping and heading toward the stage. No one knows what to make of it yet. Perhaps it's part of the protest.

By the time he reaches the stage, he's down to his underwear, and most, if not all, of the 312 names written on his body are exposed to the world, and to the camera crew, which has taken a sudden interest in him, filming him as he climbs to the stage. The Albanian rights speaker halts in midsentence. People in the audience laugh, or gasp, or mutter to one another . . . until Lev holds his hands out wide. He says nothing. Just holds out his hands . . . and swings them together.

The reaction is instantaneous. The crowd panics and begins to bolt.

He spreads his hands once more, and, like a bird beating its wings against the wind, he swings them together again, and again. People are screaming now, climbing over one another. They can't get away fast enough.

He keeps swinging his hands together—but nothing happens. Because there is nothing in his blood but blood. No chemicals, no explosives. He does not explode—but that doesn't stop the security forces from taking action, just as he knew they would.

The first gunshot blasts out from one of the Juvey-cops protecting the island. The ceramic bullet rips through the right side of Lev's chest, spinning him around. He doesn't know who fires the second and third shots, because they both hit him in the back. His knees buckle beneath him. He goes down. A fourth bullet hits him in the gut, and a fifth whizzes past his ear, missing, but that's all right, because the first four have done the job.

The world will know what happened here today. That an unarmed boy was shot in broad daylight before hundreds of witnesses. And when they learn who that boy was, it will stop everyone in their tracks for a long painful moment.

WHY, LEV, WHY? the headlines will read once more—only this time people will know the answer, and the answer shall be the names written on his flesh. Then people's fury will turn on the ones who shot him beneath the unblinking eyes of liberty. And his sacrifice will change the world.

With blood pouring from his wounds, he lies on his back, eyes wide from the pain, looking up at the sky. High above him, the torch of the great statue points toward the moon, a pale specter almost directly overhead.

He reaches for it, his fingers sticky with blood. It seems to swell as he focuses his fading attention on it.

And Lev is happy . . . because he knows he's finally grabbed the moon, and has pulled it from the sky.

60 · Mail

2162 letters were in Sonia's trunk. 751 of them were lost in the fire, but 1411 were stamped and mailed by Grace Skinner, then delivered dutifully by the postal service from coast to coast—because the AWOLs who passed through Sonia's basement over the years hailed from everywhere.

A woman in Astoria, Oregon, opens the letter with no return address, not recognizing the handwriting because it's been almost three years since her daughter found the unwind order and went AWOL.

She begins to read, and from the very first line, the woman knows who wrote it. As much as she wants to run from the room, she is glued to her kitchen chair, unable to stop reading. When she's done, she sits there in silence, not sure what to do next, but knowing she must do something.

A man in Montpelier, Vermont, arrives home before his wife today. He scans through the various bills and solicitations, until coming across a curious envelope, and he recognizes his son's handwriting—a son who was sent off for unwinding almost five years ago. Although the Juvenile Authority wouldn't officially admit it, the man and his wife found out that he escaped before arriving at his assigned harvest camp.

The man stands the envelope up against a vase in the dining room, and sits there staring at it a full ten minutes before summoning the nerve to open it.

When he first begins to read, he thinks the letter was written recently—but no, there's a date written on the first page. His son wrote this more than three years ago. He's still out there somewhere. Maybe. Afraid to come home? Refusing to come home? Or did they catch him after all? For a time, the man and his family had considered moving for fear that he'd return and exact retribution on them. How ashamed he now feels for even thinking that.

His wife will be home from work any minute now. Should he show her the letter? Should he show his daughter when she's home from swim practice? He doesn't even know if she remembers her brother.

Although there's no one in the room but the dog, he covers his eyes as he cries, shedding grief he's denied since the day they came to take his son away.

A couple in Iowa City sits by the fireplace, and the two share the task of opening mail that accumulated while they were traveling. The man comes across a seemingly innocuous letter. He opens it, begins reading, then suddenly stops, folds the letter, and puts it back in the envelope.

"What is it?" asks his wife, having seen the way he's suddenly gone pale.

"Nothing," he says. "Junk mail."

But she reads the truth in his face as clearly as if she had opened the letter herself. She knows there's only one thing to be done. "Throw it into the fire," she says.

And so he does, ending the matter once and for all.

. . .

In Indianapolis, the letter arrives on the very day a woman's divorce is final. She reads it, her hands unable to keep from shaking. She signed the unwind order after her son's awful fight with her husband—his stepfather. It took nearly two years for her to realize she had taken the wrong side of that fight. But this letter gives her hope. It means her son might still be whole, and out there somewhere. If he is, she'd welcome him back in a heartbeat, shark tattoo and all.

Of the various people touched by the 1411 letters, some remain coldhearted, or just in adamant denial—but more than a thousand find reading the words of their lost son or daughter to be a life-changing event. In a population of hundreds of millions, such a small number of people is a mere drop in the bucket . . . but enough drops can make any bucket overflow.

61 · Nelson

More than a dozen small private jets wait on the taxiway of a remote airfield outside of Calgary, Canada. This far north, the leaves have fully turned and are beginning to fall. The forest around the airstrip ripples fiery orange, yellow, and red as the wind passes through. Then the air falls still. The wind itself seems to anticipate the arrival of lot 4832: Connor Lassiter, divided.

Out of place among the sleek jets is a Porsche, whose driver watches as Divan's behemoth craft drops through the low-hanging clouds and toward the runway, looking massive even from far away.

Jasper Nelson anxiously awaits a fresh pair of eyes in the car that Divan gave him as a reward for capturing the Akron

AWOL. Let the rest of Connor Lassiter be dispersed to various billionaires around the world; Nelson is happy to possess his vision. He knows it will bring everything full circle. Once he's seeing the world through those eyes, he will be able to bring his life back from the septic fringe, to a respectable place at last. Today, the troublesome young man that was Connor Lassiter will go the way of turning forest leaves, but the long winter of Jasper Nelson's discontent will be made glorious summer once he has the sight of the boy who took his life away.

The plane lands with the gargantuan roar of airborne armageddon, and the moment it rolls to a halt, Divan's ground crew gets to work refueling, The side passenger hatch opens, and stairs fold out for Divan. This is only the second time Nelson has come to Divan's North American airfield. Either business is so brisk Divan must stay on top of it, or he has reasons not to stay in one place for too long. Divan makes his appearance a moment later, along with his harvest medic, who carries a small medical stasis cooler. They come directly to Nelson.

"Use them in good health, my friend," Divan tells him as the nose cone of the jet begins to grind open for the transfer of the remaining cargo. Even before it's fully raised, it becomes clear that something is very wrong.

A flood of kids bursts from the cargo hold, sprinting, running, limping in every direction. Not just a few, but dozens of them. All of them!

Suddenly Divan has more important things to do than bother with Nelson. He points to his bodyguard. "Stop them! Now!" The beefy man fumbles with his tranq gun, running and firing at the same time, missing as often as he takes one down. Tranqing AWOLs is not this man's job. But it is Nelson's.

"I've got this," Nelson tells Divan. He pulls out his own tranq pistol and takes aim. "I love a shooting gallery." Sure enough, every one of Nelson's shots hits its mark, and in ten seconds he's taken down ten kids—but there are simply too many for even Nelson to stop.

"Who is responsible for this?" Divan demands, and he runs to get more help from his staff. It's Nelson who sees the answer to that question. She's easy to spot, because of all the escaping kids, she's the only one who's not in a gray bodysuit. Risa Ward is up to her old tricks. But not for much longer.

Nelson ignores the others, taking aim at the prize.

Then just as he pulls the trigger, he's grabbed from behind. The shot flies wild as his attacker puts him in a skillful choke hold so tight that it cuts off blood to Nelson's brain. Darkness squirms in from his periphery, his legs buckle beneath him, and before he loses consciousness, he gets a brief glimpse of the face of his assailant.

And to his own personal horror, he sees it's barely a face at all.

62 · Argent

The medic still has no idea that Argent took his spare key to the harvester.

Divan has no idea that Argent knows the code to access the UNIS control panel, which he copied from a small notebook on Divan's nightstand.

Argent has found many times in life that people are never so clueless as when they think you're stupid.

Thirty minutes before the *Lady Lucrezia* landed, the medic left the cargo hold with a small stasis cooler labeled LOT 4832-EY-L/R. Argent couldn't help but snicker to himself. As a grocery checker, he knows better than anyone that labels are only as good as the idiot doing the labeling.

As the plane began its descent, Argent snuck into the harvester, knowing that even though the hapless medic basically lived his life at thirty-seven thousand feet, he was a nervous flier, and always buckled himself into a chair in the crew lounge. That gave Argent a window to do what he had to do—what Connor Lassiter would have done, were he not in a gazillion pieces. Argent shut off the sedation system to all the Unwinds and twisted the security camera to face the wall, just in case someone got the bright idea to monitor it. He waited for the first one to wake up, an umber kid whose eyes got a little buggy when he found out where he was and what was happening to him.

"When the rest wake up, keep 'em quiet," Argent said. "Don't let 'em freak out. Then, when that nose cone opens, run like it's the end of the world, because it will be if you don't."

Then he left the harvester, strapping himself in next to the medic like it was any other day.

But his job wasn't over yet.

As soon as the plane had landed and Divan had gone down to the tarmac, he unlocked Risa's room and led her to the harvester, telling her the same thing he'd told the umber kid. By then the entire hold was crawling with scared, wakeful kids, but Risa had a certain presence about her that kept them quiet and in control.

"What about Connor?" Risa asked him, but it was no time for questions.

"I've taken care of it—just trust me."

"That's the problem," Risa said. "I don't."

"Well, too freakin' bad."

He couldn't stay—any second, Divan would demand something from him. A glass of Pellegrino or sunscreen for his delicate complexion. Divan always wanted something.

"If you get free, and you see my sister," he told Risa, "tell her I saved you. She'll get a kick out of it."

"Wait—you're not coming with us?"

Argent left without answering the question, because the

answer was obvious. He'd made a deal with Divan. Six months for a face. He doesn't have to be Divan's best friend, he just has to stick to his end of the bargain—and as long as Argent plays dumb lackey, Divan will never suspect he was behind what happened today. For Argent Skinner, stupidity is the best camouflage.

And with the AWOLs all going AWOL, Divan doesn't even notice Argent putting Nelson in that choke hold.

63 · Divan

In his years in the flesh trade, Divan Umarov has had to face many nasty situations. Unsatisfied buyers with dangerous tempers. Unscrupulous competitors whom he's had to take out—and of course, the Dah Zey, who are a constant threat to his business and personal well-being. Through all of these things, Divan triumphed and managed to remain a gentleman. When it comes to handling adversity, Divan knows that calm objectivity will always save the day. He lost his temper when Starkey died, but he is determined not to be ruled by his emotions today.

He takes in the big picture. Kids running everywhere. His ground crew chasing them. Half of the kids are already over the fence.

"Let them go," Divan says. Then, louder: "LET THEM GO!"

His bodyguard turns to him confused.

"But they escape. . . ."

"Why chase silver," Divan says, "when we have gold to move?"

He turns to his valet, who watches the spectacle with one-eyed impotence. It's all Divan can do not to smack him. "Skinner!

Go help collect the ones we managed to tranq, and put them back in the hold. The rest are no longer our problem." Then he looks down to see Nelson in a heap on the ground. "What happened to him?"

"Don't know," says Skinner. "Must have been hit by a tranq."

Well, Nelson's not his problem either. "What are you waiting for?" he asks Skinner. "Get to work!"

Skinner bounds off, and Divan focuses his full attention on the real business of the day. He supervises the removal of the active stasis coolers, paying close attention to the ones marked LOT 4832. His big-ticket items. The various and sundry parts of Connor Lassiter.

Only when all the crates have been loaded onto their respective planes bound for their buyers does he relax. Skinner reports that nineteen out of one hundred and seventeen Unwinds were recovered, and are back inside. As for the lost Unwinds, it may sting in the moment, but it's barely a setback at all. One trip around the world, and his suppliers will fill up his harvester once more. Divan looks around. Everything seems to be in order. The smaller jets are lining up to take off, and although Nelson's car is still there, Nelson is nowhere to be seen. Divan doesn't trouble himself with it. His work is done here. He grasps Skinner on the shoulder. "Good work," he says. "Now please draw me a bath."

Skinner trots up the stairs dutifully, but before Divan gets in the plane he takes a moment to consider the events that have just transpired. This was clearly sabotage by the Dah Zey. No question about it. That means there's a traitor on his staff. As far as Divan is concerned, this is the last straw. If the Dah Zey want a war, they'll get one. He'll recruit a militia of skilled mercenaries and fight the Dah Zey to the death.

But in the meantime, Divan must deal with the traitor—

and he's pretty certain who it is. The medic was the only one with access to the harvester, both the day Starkey died and today. Divan prides himself on rewarding loyalty and hard work. Disloyalty and sabotage, however, must be met with swift and decisive action. No time to make a bonsai this time. And so before he boards the plane, he makes a request of his body-guard. "I need you to release the medic from my employment, effective immediately."

"Release from employment," repeats his guard. "Use tranq?"

"Tranqs," says Divan, "are for AWOLs and other naughty children. The medic requires something more permanent. What's our next stop, Korea? We'll pick up a new medic there."

Then Divan, who abhors violence, gets on the plane, happy to let his guard take care of business, as long as it's out of Divan's presence.

64 · Nelson

The choke hold knocked him out for a good twenty minutes. Now he's no longer on the airfield tarmac. Nor is he anywhere familiar at all. Nelson regains consciousness to find himself lying in a claustrophobic space larger than a coffin, but much, much worse.

"Hello, **Jack**ass **Dirt***bag*," says a perky computer voice. "Welcome to your divisional experience! I am your fully auto-mated Unwinding Intelli-System, but you can call me UNIS."

"No! It can't be!" He tries to lift his arms and legs, but they won't move. He seems to be wearing that same gunmetal-gray bodysuit the Unwinds wore. Only now does he realize it's made of metallic filaments, and he's magnetically fixed in place.

"Before we get started, **Jack**ass **Dirt***bag*, I have a few questions to make this a smooth and positive transition into a divided state."

"Is anybody out there! Somebody let me out of here!" He's able to tilt his neck just enough to see someone peering in through the small window of the unwinding chamber. "Divan, is that you? Help me, please!"

"First, let me confirm your comfort level," says UNIS. "Please rate your current level of comfort on a scale of one to ten, ten being least uncomfortable."

And then he realizes with more than a little dismay who the observer is.

"Argent!" he yells. "Argent, you can't do this!"

But Argent offers nothing but a stoic cyclops stare.

"I'm sorry, I didn't get that," says UNIS. "Please rate your current level of comfort on a scale of one to ten, ten being least uncomfortable."

"Argent, I'll do anything! I'll give you anything!" But Nelson knows what Argent wants. He wants the right half of his face back. Now.

"All right," says UNIS, "I'll assume you're sufficiently comfortable. I see that my controls are set for an express unwinding without the use of anesthetic plasma. That means we can begin right away!"

"What? What was that?" Adrenaline panic makes his whole body begin to quiver. "Wait. Stop! Halt!"

"I regret, **Jack**ass **Dirt***bag*, that without anesthesia, you shall be experiencing extreme discomfort, beginning with your wrists, elbows, ankles, and knees, then quickly moving inward. This is perfectly normal for the machine's current setting."

As the process begins, Nelson locks on Argent's impassive eye, and suddenly realizes that not only is Argent going to unwind him, but he's going to watch every last minute of it. And he's going to enjoy it.

"To take your mind off of your discomfort," says UNIS, "I can project a variety of scenic vistas for you. Please choose from the following: mountain flyby, ocean tranquility, vibrant cityscape, or landmarks of the world."

But all that comes from Nelson is a shrill, bloodcurdling wail.

"I'm sorry," says UNIS, "that's not a valid response."

65 · Broadcast

"This is Radio Free Hayden broadcasting live once more, until we get chased away from the station. Today I have something special to share with my listeners. This comes from an article in a major national newspaper. Other articles just like it popped up in print and online everywhere this morning. Of course, some papers buried the story on page twelve beside mattress sale ads, but kudos to those who ran it front page, with a nice headline, like this one:

ARÁPACHE TO GIVE ASYLUM TO UNWINDS

By a unanimous vote of the Arápache Tribal Council yesterday, the nation's wealthiest and most influential Chancefolk tribe has officially announced it will give protective sanctuary to all Unwinds seeking to remain whole. A spokesperson for the Juvenile Authority has stated that they do not recognize the tribe's right to grant sanctuary to AWOLs, and vows to retrieve any fugitive Unwinds from Arápache territory. Chal Tashi'ne, an

*attorney for the tribe, responded by saying, "Any incur-
sion by the Juvenile Authority on sovereign tribal land
shall be seen as an act of war against the Arápache people,
and will be met with deadly force.*

*"Regardless of what side you're on, you've got to admit it took
a lot of guts for a Chancefolk tribe to spin the wheel and go all
in. If the Juvenile Authority thinks a tribe of once-great warriors
is going to blink, they're in for a surprise.*

*"And so, this week's song—you know the one—goes out to
our Arápache friends. Hopefully, we'll see one or two of you at
our rally in November. But until then—*

"I've got you . . . under my skin. . . ."

66 · Cam

Pretty purple monkshood accents the ornamental gardens of
Proactive Citizenry's Molokai complex. The gardeners wear
gloves, not only to protect themselves from the thorns of the
rosebushes, but because of the monkshood, which they know
is chock-full of aconite, a deadly poison that shuts down the
respiratory system. It's the roots of the plant that are the most
dangerous, especially when boiled and distilled down into a
concentrated toxin.

Once more, Camus Comprix defeats the security system of
the Molokai complex by tapping the security computer on the
wrong shoulder and making it look the other way. It's night now.
Not too late, just about ten o'clock, but late enough that activity
in the medical research building is at a minimum. They never
figured out how he compromised the video surveillance system
that first time, so he does it again—now toward a different end.

He's delayed the signal by fifteen minutes. That's how long he has to do the job before anyone sees what's going on.

He slips into the ward of preconscious rewinds unobserved, carrying in his hands a bag with syringes and vials of his special aconite elixir. When it's injected directly into the port of their intravenous PICC lines, they'll die within a minute. Once he gets into a rhythm, he estimates it will take him twelve minutes to euthanize all fifty.

Cam thinks he has it all under control. He's sure his plan can't go wrong. But then he makes a crucial mistake. Rather than beginning at the far end of the chamber, where the freshest rewinds lie, still heavily bandaged and nowhere near consciousness, he begins closest to the door, where the bandages have been removed and the rewinds are further along. Much further along.

As he fills the first syringe with the deadly liquid, he happens to glance down at the rewind.

And the rewind is looking back.

He studies Cam with a kind of vigilant terror, like a rabbit a moment before it bolts. Cam is hypnotized by two entirely mismatched eyes. One green, the other so dark brown it's almost black. The lines of scars across his face are like the roads of an old city—random, and senseless. His hands—one sienna, one umber—test the bonds that tie him to the bed.

"The fly?" he says, pleading. "The fly? In the web? The fly?"

It would make no sense to most, but Cam knows the way a rewind thinks. He understands the strange connections its patchwork brain must make in order to communicate, leaping over the concrete, grasping only upon impressions. Metaphors. Of the many languages Cam knows, this one came first. The inner language of the rewound mind.

Cam knows the reference. An old movie. The head of a

man on the body of a fly. It said, "Help me," as it struggled in the spider's web. "Help me, help me," and then it was devoured.

"Yes," Cam tells him. "I'm here to help you. In a manner of speaking." He presses air out of the syringe, the muddy poison fluid squirting just a bit from the needle tip. He finds the injection port and readies himself to end this poor rewind's life.

"Hike in the woods," the rewind says. "I told you to wear long pants. Pink lotion everywhere."

"Yes, you're itching, but it's not poison ivy," Cam tells him. "I'm sorry that you itch all over. That's just the way it is."

Then a single tear forms in the rewind's darker eye, coursing down the rough ridge of a scar, until spilling into his ear. "Back of my jersey? Card in my wallet? There, on the birthday cake, in blue?"

"No!" says Cam, surprised by his own anger. "No, I don't know who you are. I can't tell you your name. No one can!" He finds his hand that holds the syringe is starting to quiver. Best to do it quick. End it now. So why is he waiting?

"The fly . . . the fly . . ."

And the desperation, the absolute helplessness in the rewind's eyes is too much for Cam to bear. Cam knows what must be done . . . but he can't do it. He can't do it. He pulls the syringe away, capping it, furious at his own compassion. *Does this mean I'm truly whole?* he wonders. *Is compassion a virtue of a soul?*

"It's all right," Cam says. "The spider won't get you."

The rewind's eyes get a little bit wider, not with fear, but with hope. "Slide into home? Run scores?"

"Yes," Cam tells him. "You're safe."

67 · Roberta

Sometimes we must kill our babies. It's a basic tenet of every creative or scientific endeavor. Become too attached to any single aspect of one's work, and one risks failure. Such is the result of not being able to see the forest for the trees.

Hope for Cam's future had been shaky since that troubling meeting they had with Cobb and Bodeker back in Washington. The one where Cam became violent—if not in action, then in thought—and although they appeared to accept the cover story of Cam being sequestered in Molokai this whole time, Roberta suspects there's a mole within the staff who informed the senator and general that Cam was AWOL.

"We've decided that it's too unstable for our purposes," Bodeker told her earlier today. He always refers to Cam as "it," which has always annoyed Roberta, but now she's beginning to understanding the practicality of his approach. "We'd prefer that our entire investment go into the reintegrated infantry." That's Bodeker's euphemism for the rewind army they've commissioned. Roberta's understanding is that this reintegrated infantry will be carefully introduced to the public as "Team Mozaic," an even more euphemistic term to offer up the rewinds in the most appealing light.

As for Cam, he was like a toe dipped into the hot water of a bath. The public was intrigued by him, dazzled even. Thanks to Cam, they've come to feel that the water is fine. Now all that remains is for the public to be eased into the bath in calculated measures, lest they balk at the heat. Skillfully spun, Team Mozaic will become an accepted facet of the military, without anyone realizing exactly how it happened.

"You are to be commended for your vision," Bodeker told

Roberta, "but Camus Comprix is no longer a part of our equation. Its job is done."

Roberta doesn't know why she feels such regret. It's the way of all things. The beta test must always give way to the final product. True, the final product has fewer bells and whistles, but that should not concern her. Accommodations must always be made.

And so, when security calls that evening to notify her that, once again, Cam has managed to break into the reintegration unit, her course of action becomes clear. She puts on a linen blazer—insanely heavy for the tropical heat, but it has an outer pocket that's deep enough to conceal any number of things. Roberta knows what must be done. By no means will this be easy, but it is necessary—and what kind of visionary would she be if she didn't take all the necessary steps to see her vision through?

Roberta arrives at the reintegration building to find several guards and med techs standing around the door to the rewind ward, practically twiddling their thumbs in embarrassment. They all back away from the door when they see her coming.

"What's the situation?" she asks.

"He's just sitting there," says one of the med techs, and off of her dubious expression, he says, "See for yourself."

She peers through the small window in the locked door. Sure enough, Cam is sitting on the floor in the middle of the long room, arms wrapped around his knees, rocking gently back and forth. She pulls out her key card.

"It's no use," says one of the guards. "He's locked everyone out."

Nevertheless, she swipes her card, and the lock disengages. "He's locked all of *you* out," she says. It's clear he's been waiting for her, and her alone. "Get back to your posts," she tells them. "I'll handle this." Reluctantly, the others leave, and she pushes open the door, cautiously stepping in.

The room is awash with the white noise of medical monitors, and the hissing ventilators of the fresher rewinds who are still intubated. The room smells of Betadine antiseptic, and the vague vinegary odor of bandages overdue to be changed. She must remember to crack the whip at the nurses and med techs.

"Cam?" she asks gently as she nears him. He gives no response. He doesn't even look up.

As she gets closer, she can see the bag beside him. There's a syringe on the ground with a cloudy liquid. The needle is capped. For a moment she fears the worst, and looks around at the rewinds. She doesn't spot any monitors that show distress, but perhaps he defeated the life-signs monitors, as well.

Then, as if reading her mind, he says, "I couldn't kill them. I came here to do it—but I couldn't."

She knows she has to be careful with him. Handle him with kid gloves. "Of course you couldn't," she says. "They're your spiritual siblings. Ending their lives would be akin to ending your own."

"Spiritual," he echoes. "I didn't realize that word was part of your lexicon."

"I don't deny the spark of life," she tells him. "But it's forever debatable what that spark is, and what it means."

"Yes, I suppose so." Finally he looks at her, his eyes red and pleading. "I know too many things that I don't want to know. Can you take them away, the way you took *her* away?"

"That depends on the nature of the things in question."

"I'm talking about Proactive Citizenry, and the truth about it," he tells her. "I broke into their computer network, and I know everything. I know that Proactive Citizenry controls the Juvenile Authority. And that they want to increase the scope of unwinding so all those condemned kids can be rewound into this army you're creating."

Roberta sighs. "We don't control the Juvenile Authority, we just have considerable influence."

"'We,'" says Cam. "So it's back to 'we' again. Not 'they.' You must be out of Proactive Purgatory."

"I've always been appreciated, Cam," she tells him. "My work speaks for itself. It always has."

"Does your work involve clappers?" he asks. "You're aware that Proactive Citizenry created them as well, aren't you?"

She knows denying it will only jam a wedge in their rapport, and right now she needs that rapport. She needs for him to trust her unconditionally. So she breaks with all protocol, and tells him the truth.

"First of all, that's not my department. And second, we didn't create them. Clappers were blowing themselves up long before we had anything to do with them. Proactive Citizenry merely gives them money and direction. We shape their violence toward a purpose—so that it serves the greater good."

He nods, accepting, if not entirely approving. "There certainly are historical precedents for manipulating the public through fear."

"I prefer to see it as opening people's eyes, so they continue to see the sense in unwinding."

Cam looks down again and shakes his head slowly. "I don't want my eyes opened—I want them closed. I don't want to *know* any of this. Please, can you tweak me again, Roberta? Can you give me a new worm to make it all go away?"

She kneels beside him and puts her arm around his shoulder, pulling him close. "Poor Camus—you're in such pain. We'll find a way to make that pain go away."

He rests his head on her shoulder. She can feel his relief.

It's as it should be. As it must be. "Thank you, Roberta. I know you'll take care of me."

She reaches into the pocket of her blazer. "Haven't I always?"

"I know you've been there for me," he says. "When my thoughts went astray, you fixed them. When I ran away, you found me and brought me home."

"And I'm here for you now," she says as she pulls out her pistol. The one she always keeps in her nightstand, but until now, has never needed to use.

"Promise me you'll fix it all."

"I promise, Cam," and she brings the muzzle of the gun to his forehead, knowing that this *will* fix it all. "I promise."

Then she pulls the trigger.

68 · Cam

Cam couldn't be sure where this would end until he saw the metallic flash of the gun when she pulled it from her pocket. Now, as she speaks calming words to him, and brings the pistol to his forehead, he closes his eyes. He suspected it might come to this, but he didn't want to believe it. Now he has no choice.

He's made his decision. He won't stop her. He won't resist. He allows her to complete her deadly intention.

The trigger engages.

The hammer releases.

It flies toward the chamber, and strikes it.

But instead of a gunshot comes a harmless *click*. Still, that tiny, impotent sound tears through Cam's brain just as effectively as a bullet. Roberta has failed him. He's not surprised, but he's deeply disappointed.

Before Roberta has a chance to react, he wrenches the gun from her hands.

"Do you really believe I'm such a pathetic wreck that I'd sit here and let you kill me?"

He stands up, and Roberta, off-balance in her murderous crouch, stumbles, breaking a heel before rising to face him.

"Your gun hasn't had real bullets since we got here. I made sure they'd be as false as you are."

"Cam, please—let me explain."

"You don't need to," he tells her. "Your actions speak louder than your lies—they always have. But there's something I need to explain to *you*." He waves the gun, using it to point around the room. "This room is full of surveillance cameras. If you'll notice, several of them have been repositioned to this very spot, providing various angles of what just transpired here. The rest are still positioned on the rewinds . . . and every single camera is currently streaming live to the public nimbus."

She gasps audibly. Roberta Griswold is speechless! It's so wonderful to see her speechless that Cam smiles, feeling every seam on his face tingle with triumph. "I've already confirmed that the feeds have been picked up by the media. Of course, it wouldn't do to have just silent video feeds. That's why I rigged your phone to stream audio as well. Everything you've just said—about Proactive Citizenry building this army—about how they fund and 'direct' clappers—it's all public knowledge now, being heard by thousands, maybe millions, as we speak. You wanted to reach the world with your work. Well, my dear sweet mother, you've just succeeded."

She opens and closes her mouth a few times, like a goldfish that has leapt out of its bowl. "I don't believe you," she finally says, but her voice is shaky. "You're not that underhanded!"

"I wasn't at first," he admits, "but I've learned from you." He looks to the rewinds on either side of them. "I couldn't bring myself to kill them, but they don't have to die to kill the program, do they?"

That's when her phone rings.

Cam winks at her. "The backlash is already starting. Go on, answer it—the call will stream live too, and I'm sure there's plenty of people tuned in who want to hear what your bosses have to say about all this."

She pulls out her phone and checks the number. Cam doesn't know who's calling, but whoever it is, it must terrify her, because she drops the phone and crushes it beneath her one good heel.

"End transmission," Cam says, with a raised eyebrow. "But that's all right, the damage has already been done." He takes a moment to eject the gun's clip and pulls from his pocket a fresh cartridge filled with real bullets. He snaps it in place with a *click* far more satisfying than the impotent sound of the hammer when the gun was to his forehead.

"Can you hear it crumbling, Roberta? Not just your work, but those alabaster pillars that hold up Proactive Citizenry— the ones you were all so arrogant to think could never fall? And all because of you. I can't even imagine what they'll do to you. Not just the public, but your associates in Proactive Citizenry."

Then he tosses the loaded pistol to her.

"But you're in luck. Those cameras are still streaming, which means the show's not over." Then he nods. No more gloating. Now he gives her a solemn acknowledgment of her final responsibility to the world, and to herself. "Give them a proper ending, Roberta."

Then he turns and strides to the door without looking back.

69 · Roberta

She watches him go, then just before he leaves, she aims the gun at the back of his head. She holds it steady . . . but doesn't fire. If she kills him now, it will only be worse for her.

So she lets him leave. The door closes, and she's alone.

No, not alone—because she's surrounded by the fruits of her labor. Fifty hideous rewinds that will now be a part of no army. There will be no careful introduction of them to the public—no spin doctors can repair this and make it look any less horrible than it is. The public will see their creation as an atrocity, not as an opportunity. These rewinds will be shunned, Roberta will be despised, and Proactive Citizenry will hang her out to dry, if they let her live at all.

Cam was right to give her the gun. It was an act of bitter mercy, because in one way or another her life is over.

And so, with the eyes of the world watching, Roberta Griswold drops to her knees, puts the muzzle of the gun to her temple . . .

. . . and holds it there.

Holds it there . . .

Holds it there . . .

Until she realizes it's no use. She can't summon the courage to pull that trigger. And that's how they find her when they finally come to take her away, kneeling with a gun to her head, consumed by waves of dread yet unable to save herself from a fate worse than death, which is surely coming for her like a tsunami across the sea.

70 · Grace

"My name is Grace Eleanor Skinner, but you can call me Miss Skinner, or Miss Grace, but the Miss is a must, because that's respect, and you gotta show me respect because of what I'm bringin' ya."

John Rifkin, vice president of sales, sits in a big leather office chair. Not so fancy a chair that it reeks of money, it just reeks of office. His desk is nice too, but she can tell it's been put together with an Allen wrench. These are all good things, as far as Grace is concerned. The company needs to be hungry. The company needs to be just right.

The man seems amused by her presence in his office. That's okay. They let her get as far as his office because the man's underlings thought it might be an entertaining moment in an otherwise dull day. They have no idea.

"So what's in the box, Miss Skinner?"

Grace carefully begins to take out the pieces and lay them in size order on the desk, from left to right. The man swivels in his chair, maintaining a slight grin. Maybe he's thinking this is a practical joke. That's fine, as long as he lets it play out.

"It looks like the broken parts of a printer—and an obsolete one at that," says John Rifkin, vice president of sales, using that condescending tone people reserve for children and low-cortical adults. "As I'm not a collector of such things, I think you may be in the wrong place."

"Nothing wrong about it. I came to your company because there are six companies bigger and more successful than yours that make medical machines. I looked it up."

John Rifkin, vice president of sales, seems slightly taken aback. "*You* looked it up?"

"Yes, I did. Also, unlike those other companies, Rifkin Medical Instruments has no ties to Proactive Citizenry."

"No, we don't. Which is probably why we're number seven," he says, irritated by his own admission.

"I also looked *you* up," continues Grace. "The company's got your name—Rifkin Medical Instruments—but someone without your name is now its president, which tells me you've got fangs for that job, and could use a boost up the ladder, am I right?"

Now he gets uncomfortable. "Who put you up to this? Is it Bob? It's Bob, isn't it?"

"There ain't no Bob, there's only me." Then she gestures to the array of parts before her. "This here is an organ printer. It's kind of unwound right now, but it's the real deal."

John Rifkin relaxes a bit, and offers her something of a superior smirk. "Miss Skinner, organ printing was debunked as a fraud years ago. It was a nice idea, but it didn't work."

"That's what they want you to think," she whispers. "But Janson Rheinschild knew better."

Suddenly he's sitting up straight, like a kindergartner on his first day of school. "Did you say Janson Rheinschild?"

"You heard of him?"

"My father did. The man was a genius, but he went crazy, didn't he?"

"Or he got driven that way. But not before he built this."

Now John Rifkin is interested. He begins tapping his pen on the table, finally considering that maybe Grace is worth taking seriously. "If Rheinschild built that, why do *you* have it?"

"Got it from his widow. Old woman in Ohio, ran an antique shop."

He grabs his phone.

"Don't bother, she's dead. Big fire. But of everything in her shop, I knew she wanted me to save this, so I did. And I'm here to give it to you."

He reaches for one of the parts, but hesitates, and asks, "May I?" Grace nods, and he gently picks up the printing part, turning it over in his hands to explore it from every angle. "And you say it once worked."

"Once that I saw, before I went and dropped the thing down the stairs." Then she pulls out from her pocket an object that will seal the deal. A small plastic bag containing a decomposing ear. "I watched it make that."

Rifkin looks at it in both awe and disgust, and reaches for the bag.

"Prolly shouldn't take it out here," Grace warns. "It didn't keep well."

He withdraws his hand, and just continues to stare at it.

"My bet is that you can fix the printer and make more of them. *A lot* more. In all shapes and sizes and colors."

Grace studies him as he studies the ear and the pieces, and even the empty box. For a businessman he doesn't have much of a poker face. She can see him calculating. "How much are you asking for it?"

"Maybe I'll just give it to you."

Then he takes a moment to look at her. He glances at the door as if someone might be watching, then comes around the table, sitting in a chair just next to her.

"Grace . . ."

"Miss Grace."

"Miss Grace . . . if this is what you say it is, you shouldn't just give it away. I'll tell you what: I'll give it to our research and development department, and if it's, as you say, 'the real deal,' I will give you a very fair price for it."

Grace leans back in her chair satisfied with him, but even more satisfied with herself. She grabs his hand and shakes it vigorously. "Congratulations, Mr. John Rifkin. You passed my test."

"Excuse me?"

"I woulda walked if you were sleazy enough to rip me off, but you didn't. That means your company deserves to shoot up to number one. And if you play your cards right, it will. You'll probably get to be the company's president, too." Then she pulls out her phone.

John Rifkin seems a bit flustered now. "Wait . . . who are you calling?"

"My lawyer," she tells him with a wink. "He's waitin' out-side to negotiate my deal."

71 · Broadcast

"This is Radio Free Hayden broadcasting from somewhere where we can see cows. Is it just me, or do those videos of the military rewinds in Hawaii make you want to hurl up all the organs you may have gotten from guys like me? In case you missed it, here's a little sound bite of what General Edward Bodeker, head of the project, had to say about it:"

"Team Mozaic is a pilot program to ascertain the via-bility of creating a military force without impacting the resources of society by using the glut of unallocated unwound parts."

"Damn, that's an impressive mission statement! Shortly after those words left his lips, he was hauled in for a court-martial, and the Pentagon released the following statement instead:"

"This unsanctioned venture was the product of General Bodeker working without the knowledge or consent of the United States military. There is no question that the parties involved, including General Bodeker and Sena-tor Barton Cobb, will be investigated and prosecuted to the fullest extent of the law."

"Booyaah! The shrapnel just keeps flying. The military has covered their tender parts through plausible denial, and blamed the whole thing on Bodeker—which may or may not be true—but at least they won't be looking for a few good rewound men. Kudos, though, to one good rewound man—Camus Comprix—for expos-ing this bad idea before it could take root. But what about the next bad idea? I can see it now, a whole rewound service class custom cut to do all those dirty little jobs no one else wants to do.

"If that's not the world you want to live in, then let's make some noise together! I'll see you on the National Mall on Monday, November first. But if you're at the mall, and not on the mall, well, maybe unwinding might be your best option. Signing off with everyone's favorite tune. And remember—the truth will keep you whole.

"I've got you . . . under my skin. . . ."

72 · Strangers

He's a thirty-five-year-old accountant. Ran track for UCLA, but has since developed the spare tire that comes with a sedentary profession. Now he runs a steady clip on the treadmill at his local gym beside strangers, never getting any closer to the palm trees outside the window.

"Crazy thing, isn't it?" says the runner on the next treadmill. "That poor kid."

"I hear ya," says the accountant, in between breaths, knowing exactly what the guy is referring to. "The way they . . . just shot him . . . down."

They're speaking, of course, about that tithe clapper kid, Levi something-or-other, who came out from under a rock just long enough to be blasted by trigger-happy cops. Half the TVs hanging above their heads in the gym are still reporting on it days after the actual event.

"If you ask me," says the stranger, "the whole Juvenile Authority oughta be investigated. Heads need to roll."

"I hear ya."

Even though only one of the three officers that shot him was a Juvey-cop, the Juvies are getting all the heat from it—and rightly so. Up above, the TVs show various protests in the wake of the shooting. Seems like people are protesting everywhere.

The accountant tries to catch his breath so he can ask his co-runner a question. "Did they finally give him those organs?"

"Are you kidding me? The Juvenile Authority is stupid, but not that stupid."

At first, to calm a furious public, the Juvies promised to give him the organs needed to save him—but, of course, it would be all unwound parts. It was like throwing gasoline on a fire. Give a kid who's protesting unwinding the parts of other kids? What were they thinking?

"Naah," says a runner on his other side. "They'll just keep him hooked up to all those machines until people forget, and then quietly unplug him. The bastards."

"I hear ya."

Although the accountant doesn't think people will forget it so quickly.

A woman sits on a commuter train heading into Chicago for yet another day of pointless meetings with self-important people who think they know all there is to know about real estate.

There's something odd happening on the train today, however. Something entirely unheard of on public transportation. People are talking. Not people who know one another either, but total strangers. In fact, a stranger sitting across from her looks up from his newspaper and says to anyone who's listening, "I never thought I'd say this, but I'm glad for yesterday's clapper attack downtown."

"Well, I can't exactly say I'm glad," says a woman who rides standing and holding a pole. "But I'm certainly not shedding any tears."

"And anyone who survived ought to go to prison for life," adds someone else.

The real estate agent finds, oddly, that she's compelled to join in. "I don't even think it was a real clapper attack—it was just made to look like one," she says. "There are plenty of people angry enough to want to blow Proactive Citizenry sky-high."

"That's right," says someone else. "And if Proactive Citizenry controls the clappers, why would they target their own headquarters? It must have been someone else!"

"Whoever did it oughta be given a medal," calls someone from the front of the train car.

"Well, violence is never justified," says the standing woman. "But what goes around comes around, I say."

The real estate agent has to agree. The way the supposed charity manipulated the Juvenile Authority, bought politicians, and pushed the public to support unwinding . . . Thank God it's all come to light before this year's elections! Unable to contain her own righteous rage, she turns to the intimidating man in a hoodie beside her, a person whose existence she would have ignored a few days ago. "Have you seen the images of those poor rewinds they were making in Hawaii?"

The man nods sadly. "Some people say they oughta be euthanized."

The suggestion makes the woman uncomfortable. "Don't they have rights? After all, they're human beings, aren't they?"

"The law says otherwise. . . ."

The real estate agent finds herself clutching her purse close to her, as if it might be taken away—but she knows it's not her purse she's worried about losing.

"Then the law needs to change," she says.

The construction worker's been unemployed for months now. He sits in a coffee shop scouring want ads. His first interview in weeks is that afternoon. It's with a company contracted to build a harvest camp in rural Alabama. He should be thrilled, but his feelings are mixed. Why do they even need to build another harvest camp? Didn't some company just announce that there's a way to grow all sorts of organs? If it's true, then why cut up kids? Even bad kids?

It's just a job, he tries to tell himself, *and I'll be gone long before any kid is actually unwound there.* And yet, to be a silent partner with the Juvenile Authority . . . A week ago he might have thought nothing of it, but now?

At the table next to him, an older man looks up from his laptop, shaking his head in disgust. "Incredible!" he says. The construction worker has no idea exactly which incredible thing he's speaking of—there are plenty to choose from these days. The man looks at him. "Been five years, give or take, that I've had this unwound liver here. But truth be told, if I had it to do all over again, I'd quit drinking and make do with the one I was born with."

The construction worker offers him an understanding nod, and takes a moment to consider his own options. Then he pulls out his phone and cancels his job interview. It might hurt today, but he knows he won't have any regrets five years down the line.

The accountant arrives home after his workout too late to say good night to his kids. He lingers at the door to their room, watching them sleep. He loves them dearly—not just his natural one, but the one who arrived by stork as well. The news and conversations of the day have gotten him thinking. He would never unwind his kids—but isn't that what every parent says when their children are still young? Will he think differently when they become defiant and irrational, making infuriating choices, the way most kids do at some point in their lives?

He senses a change in himself. An awakening of sorts, brought on by all the events around him.

Had it just been the boy who was shot . . .

Had it just been the discovery of those military rewinds . . .

Had it just been the announcement of the organ printer technology, which had apparently been suppressed for years . . .

Had it been any one of those things, it might have piqued his attention for a day or two, then he would have gone on with life as usual. But it wasn't just one thing, it was all of them at once—and as a number cruncher, he knows that numbers don't always "crunch." Sometimes they multiply, exponentiate, even. Taken together, these seemingly unrelated events have stirred in him something huge.

His wife comes up beside him, and he puts his arm around her. "Hey, isn't there supposed to be some sort of rally against unwinding in Washington in a few weeks?" he asks.

She looks at him, trying to gauge where this is coming from. "You're not thinking of going, are you?"

"No," he says. And then, "Maybe."

She hesitates, but only for a moment. "I'll come with you. My sister can watch the kids."

"I think they'd rather be unwound."

She punches him halfheartedly and gives him the warmest of smirks. "You're not funny." Then she goes off to prepare for bed.

The accountant lingers at his children's doorway a moment more, listening to the easy rhythm of their breathing, and something cold moves through him, like the passage of a ghost—but he knows that's not it. It's more like the portent of a future. A future that must never come to pass . . .

. . . and for the first time, he gives rise to a thought that is silently echoed in millions of homes that night.

My God . . . what have we done?

Part Six

The Right Arm of Liberty

3D PRINTING WITH STEM CELLS COULD LEAD TO PRINTABLE ORGANS

A potentially breakthrough 3D-printing process using human stem cells could be the precursor to printing organs from a patient's own cells.

by Amanda Kooser, February 5, 2013 4:31 PM PST

Some day in the future, when you need a kidney transplant, you may get a 3D-printed organ created just for you. If scientists are able to achieve that milestone, they may look back fondly at a breakthrough printing process pioneered by researchers at Heriot-Watt University in Scotland in collaboration with Roslin Cellab, a stem cell technology company.

The printer creates 3D spheroids using delicate embryonic cell cultures floating in a "bio ink" medium. They end up looking like little bubbles. Each droplet can contain as few as five stem cells. Basically, this comes down to the printer "ink" being stem cells rather than plastic or another material.

Dr. Will Shu is part of the research team working on the project. "In the longer term, we envisage the technology being further developed to create viable 3D organs for medical implantation from a patient's own cells, eliminating the need for organ donation, immune suppression, and the problem of transplant rejection," Shu said in a release from Heriot-Watt.

. . . The research results have just been published in Biofabrication under the title "Development of a valve-based cell printer for the formation of human embryonic stem cell spheroid aggregates."

. . . [i]t's applications like this that could really turn 3D printing into a world changer.

The full article can be found at: *http://news.cnet.com/8301-17938_105-57567789-1/3d-printing-with-stem-cells-could-lead-to-printable-organs/*

73 · Lev

There's a tube down his throat. It pumps air into him, then lets his diaphragm pump it out. His chest rises and falls in a regular rhythm. He's had this sensation for a while, but this is the first time he's aware enough to understand what it is. He's on a ventilator. He shouldn't be on a ventilator. A martyr to the cause can't survive, or he's not a martyr. Did he fail even in that?

He opens his eyes, and although he can only see a fraction of the space he's in, he knows exactly where he is. He knows because of the shape and design of the room—a large circular space with windows that let in what he suspects is early morning light, because the morning glories in the window boxes are wide to the sun. Around the circular room are multiple alcoves for patients, and the foot of everyone's bed faces a soothing fountain in the center of the room. He's in the intensive care unit of the Arápache medical lodge. For Lev, it seems all roads—even the road of death—lead back to the Rez.

He closes his eyes, counting the pulses of the ventilator until he's asleep again.

The next time he opens his eyes, the morning glories have closed, and the last person he was expecting to see is sitting beside him, reading a book. He watches her, not entirely sure he's not hallucinating. When she notices he's awake, she closes her book.

"Good! You're awake," says Miracolina Roselli. "That means I can be the first to officially inform you that you're an idiot."

Miracolina! The willing tithe he had saved from her own

331

unwinding. The girl he fell for in spite of how much she hated him—or maybe *because* of how much she hated him. The girl who, in the dark, claustrophobic confines of a Greyhound luggage compartment, offered him absolution for all that he had done. He was afraid to even think of her, for fear that she had been caught and unwound—but here she is!

He tries to talk, forgetting the ventilator. Instead he just coughs, and the machine beeps, registering a burst of erratic breathing.

"Look at you! I don't even recognize you with all those names tattooed on your face, and that peach-fuzz hair."

He weakly lifts his hand, putting his thumb and forefinger together in the universal *Let me write this down* gesture.

She sighs with feigned exasperation, and says "Hold on." She leaves the unit, and returns with a pad and pen "As they didn't shoot you in the head," Miracolina says, "I assume you still have enough brainpower to write legibly."

He takes the pen and pad and writes

Why am I alive?

She looks at the pad, gives him a beat of the stink eye, and says, "Oh right, it's all about *you*, isn't it. Never mind saying, 'Good to see you, Miracolina. I missed you. I'm glad *you're* alive.'"

He takes the pad back and writes all that, but of course it's too late.

"The most annoying part about the idiotic thing you did is that it worked," she tells him. "Suddenly people are seeing the Juvenile Authority as the enemy—but don't you think for a second that excuses you!"

He can tell Miracolina enjoys the fact that he can't talk back and that she can berate him freely.

"Just so you know, your stunt has cost you your liver, your pancreas, both of your kidneys, and both of your lungs."

Considering how many bullets tore into him, that sounds right—but wait . . . if he lost both of his lungs, how is he breathing? How is he still alive at all? There's only one way he could survive the loss of so many organs, and he begins to thrash in his bed in angry panic, then grabs the pen and writes in big block letters:

NO UNWOUND PARTS! TAKE THEM OUT!!

She looks at him with mock attitude, and says. "Sorry, suicide boy, but you did not receive *any* unwound parts. Charles Kovac from Montpelier, Vermont, offered up the one lung that's currently in your chest."

He raises his hand to write, but Miracolina stops him.

"Don't ask me who he is, because I have no idea. He's just some guy who would rather live his life with one lung than see you die." And she goes on. "A woman from Utah donated part of her liver, a guy in a car accident actually bequeathed you his pancreas with his dying words. And the day you were admitted to New York Hospital, half the city seemed to show up to donate blood."

Finally she offers him a smile, although he suspects it slipped though her defenses. "I don't know what it is, but people suddenly love you, Lev. Even looking like that."

He tries to smile around the ventilator tube but finds it too difficult.

"Anyway," she says, "everyone who donated part of themselves to save your life were total strangers, except for one."

Perhaps it's the medication he's on, or perhaps he truly is dense, but he doesn't figure it out until Miracolina stands, turns around, and raises her blouse to show a six-inch wound on the left side of her back. "I think giving you my left kidney buys me the right to tell you that you're an idiot," she says.

Yes, it does, Lev writes. **And yes, I am.**

. . .

The rest of the day becomes a receiving line. First comes Elina, who is, of course, his primary physician. When Miracolina leaves, Elina tells him that the girl has barely left his bedside since the day she arrived two weeks ago. "She offered her kidney, but only with a guarantee that she and her family could come to the Rez while you recover." And then Elina adds, "She's a sweet girl, although she tries not to show it."

Chal takes time out of an extremely hectic day to give him a legal briefing of sorts. He tells him that the Tribal Council revoted on his petition to officially give AWOLs sanctuary, and it passed. Now the tribe is threatening a veritable war against the Juvenile Authority. Lev would like to think that his failed attempt at martyrdom might have had something to do with it, but they made the decision a day before, when the Parental Override bill passed in Congress. Still, Lev was the one who planted the idea in their heads.

"One more thing," Chal tells him. "In order to get you back here to the Rez, we had to jump through some legal hoops. Elina and I had to become your official guardians. . . . The easiest way to do that was to adopt. I'm afraid you'll have to change your business cards," Chal jokes. "Because now you're Lev Tashi'ne."

"You certainly are building up the identities," says Elina.

Pivane comes and sits beside him in stoic silence for a while, then later in the afternoon, Una and Kele pay him a visit. They bring with them something Lev was never expecting to see. In truth, he was never expecting to see anything in this world again, but this is something he *really* wasn't expecting to see. It's a small furry creature clinging to Kele's shoulder. Its large, soulful eyes dart everywhere around the room, before making eye contact with Lev.

They've brought him a kinkajou.

"It was Kele's idea," says Una.

"Well, it's your spirit animal," Kele says, "and people do keep them as pets sometimes." Kele peels the kinkajou from his neck and puts it on the bed next to Lev, where it promptly climbs to his head, makes itself comfortable, and urinates.

"Oops!" Kele grabs the animal away, but it's too late. Lev finds that it actually raises his spirits, though. He'd laugh if he could.

I guess he's claimed me, Lev writes.

To which Una responds, "I think you claimed him first."

Elina, who enters the unit a moment later, is fit to be tied. "Take that out of here! What were you two thinking? Now we'll have to sterilize everything, bathe him again, and redress all of his wounds. Out! Everyone out!"

But before Una leaves, she says the oddest thing.

"Your new friend might not be welcome here, but I'll let you bring him to the wedding."

He has to run it through his mind again to make sure he heard her right.

What wedding? Lev writes.

"Mine," Una tells him, with a smile that speaks as much of sadness as it does of joy. "I'm marrying Wil."

74 · Co/nn/or

In another hospital bed a thousand miles away, Connor lies awake. He has no memory of waking, he just is. And he knows something is off. Not exactly wrong, just different. Very different.

A face looms before him, inspecting him. It's a face he knows. Old. Wizened. Stern. Perfect teeth. The admiral.

"About time you came out of it," the admiral says. "I was ready to tear the surgeons a new one for rewinding you into a vegetable."

It all goes in one ear, but doesn't exactly come out the

other—it just gets tangled inside. He knows what the admiral said, but has trouble grasping it again once he's done speaking.

"Can you talk?" the admiral asks. "Or did the cat get your tongue?" And he laughs at his own gallows humor.

Connor opens his mouth to speak, but it's as if his mouth is on upside down. He knows it's not—it couldn't be—but it feels that way. *Where am I?* Connor wants to ask, but his mind can't find the words. He closes his eyes, reaching through his mind, but all that comes to him is the image of a globe he remembers from his elementary school library. The name of the company that manufactured it was written in bold black letters across the Pacific Ocean. *Where am I?* Connor wants to ask, but what comes out instead is—

"Rand? McNally? Rand McNally?"

"I have no idea what you're talking about," the admiral says.

"Rand McNally!" He shuts his mouth, and grunts in frustration, shutting his eyes, trying to grasp what's happening to him. Another image comes to mind.

"Zoo . . . ," he says. Caged animals in a zoo. These are his thoughts and memories. All still there, but locked away from one another.

"You're babbling, boy."

"Babbling," he says. Well, at least he can mimic.

The admiral seems a bit troubled by Connor's responses, and that troubles Connor. "Damn it," the admiral yells to a nurse Connor didn't see in the room a moment ago. "I want the doctors in here. Now!"

One doctor comes in, then another. Connor doesn't see them, but hears them. Connor only processes part of what they say. Something about "a severe insult to his brain." And "nanites working internal repairs." And the word "patience" repeated several times. Connor wonders how a person's brain can be insulted.

When the admiral returns to Connor's bedside, he seems placated. "Well, if nothing else, you're certainly building up identities."

Connor gives him what he hopes is a questioning look. It must work, because the admiral explains.

"First, you were the Akron AWOL, then you were Robert Elvis Mullard at the Graveyard, and now you're Bryce Barlow." He pauses, clearly intending to confuse Connor, and further confusion is definitely not something he needs.

"That was the name on all forty-six of the boxes you came in. Bryce Barlow was the boy we purchased at auction, before your friend Argent played the old shell game, and switched all the labels."

Now it all comes back to Connor. He lets the understanding flow through him.

His own unwinding.

The cheery voice of UNIS.

And the plan. The crazy, harebrained, desperate plan.

Connor honestly didn't have much faith in it, because it had too many moving parts. Far too many things could go wrong. First, Risa had to contact the admiral—the only person they knew with money enough to actually enter Divan's auction. Then Argent had to find a way to get him into the auction with various false identities without arousing Divan's suspicion. Then the admiral had to win the bids on every piece of some other poor kid who'd just been unwound. As if all that wasn't difficult enough, Argent—who was not the sharpest tool in the shed—had to be counted on to switch the labels, which wasn't just a matter of changing tags; the stasis containers were all digitally coded. Lot 4832 had to be switched with lot 4831. Every single box.

And even if all that came together, there was no telling if *Connor* would. No one had ever tried to physically reassemble

337

an Unwind from his own parts. Connor would become the real-life "Humphrey Dunfee," in a way Harlan Dunfee never had.

"We had help, of course," the admiral explains. "I put together a top-notch surgical team that could make Connor out of Connor stew."

"Toothpaste back in the tube." Connor says.

The admiral is pleased that Connor has said something he understands. "Yeah, that's the long and short of it."

Connor finds his mind fixed on poor Bryce Barlow. There was no one to fight for his reintegration. No one to bring him back. What made Connor any more worth saving than him?

And what of Risa? Just because he's here, doesn't mean she freed herself from Divan.

"Piano!" he demands. "Wheelchair! Heartbeat! Kiss!" He grunts in frustration, bears down, feeling an ache in his brain, and triumphantly pulls out her name. "Risa!" He says. "Risa! Rand McNally Risa?"

And he hears quietly from somewhere across the room, "I'm here, Connor."

She's been here all along, keeping her distance. How awful must he look if she has to build up the courage to approach him? Or maybe she was just trying to get her emotions under control, because he can see that her eyes are moist. If there's one thing Risa hates it's for people to see her cry.

As Risa comes into view, the admiral moves away. Or maybe Connor's mind is only able to hold one of them in his awareness at once. *Insulted brain,* he thinks.

She takes his hand. It hurts, but he lets her take it. "I'm so happy you're awake. We were all worried. It's a miracle you're here."

"Miracle," he says. "Happy. Miracle."

"It's going to be hard at first. To move and to think. You'll need rehabilitation, but I know you'll be back to your old self in no time."

Old self, he thinks, and something hits him that brings on a sudden wave of anxiety. "Eating machine! Blood in the water! Amity Island!"

Risa shakes her head, nowhere near understanding him. So in spite of the pain, he raises his right arm, and finds what he's looking for:

The shark.

It's still there! Thank goodness it's still there! He doesn't know why, but the fact that it's still a part of him gives him great comfort.

He takes a deep breath of relief. "Fireplace," he says. "Cocoa. Blanket."

"Are you cold?

"No," he says, happy to have found the right word. It inspires him to hack through the thicket to find more words. "I'm warm. Safe. Grateful." The cages begin to fall in the zoo. His thoughts begin to free themselves.

Risa goes on to tell of the things that happened while he was "in transit," and how he's been in a two-week coma since his rewinding.

"Trick or treat," he says.

"Not quite," Risa tells him. "Another two weeks."

She tells him how she and Divan's other Unwinds were freed, but that Argent never made it out. She tells him how Divan's black-market auctions have mysteriously stopped. "We think he's focusing his attention on fighting the Burmese Dah Zey."

Connor considers that. "Godzilla," he says. "Godzilla versus Mothra."

"Indeed," says the admiral from somewhere out of his line

of sight. "Best way to save humanity is to turn the monsters against one another."

Risa tries to cheer him up by talking about Cam, and what he accomplished on his own. "He's a hero now!" Risa tells him. "He brought down Proactive Citizenry, just like he said he would—and that awful woman who blackmailed me is being tried for 'crimes against humanity.' They're actually calling her 'Madame Mengele,' and I can't think of anyone more deserving."

There's more, about Lev, who, as usual, almost died but didn't, and Grace, who made herself some sweet deal with the organ printer—and Hayden, who's called for a march on Washington—but Connor finds he can't hold on to the details, so he closes his eyes and lets her words wash over him like a healing spell.

He knows it won't always be like this. It will get better each day. Maybe not easier but better . . . and yet he senses that the mere act of having been unwound has taken something from him. No matter how much he heals, he'll always have a deep and abiding war wound. Now he knows what Cam must feel. Not so much an emptiness, but a gap between what was and what is, like air trapped between the seams of his soul. He tries to express it to Risa, but the only word that comes is—

"Hole . . ." He grips Risa's hand tighter. "Hole, Risa, hole . . ."

And she smiles. "Yes, Connor," she says. "You're whole. You're finally whole."

The Rifkin-Skinner Biobuilder® utilizes cutting-edge medical technology to actually print out custom organs—and the best thing about it is that it uses your own cultivated stem cells. Now I can rest easy knowing my heart is mine alone, and no one had to be unwound for it.

So if you're considering a transplant, or graft, please don't settle for old-fashioned unwound parts. Ask your doctor about the Rifkin-Skinner Biobuilder® today.

Say good-bye to unwinding, and hello to a you that's truly you!

75 · Gatherings

The granite and marble markers of history hold memories that can't be unwound, especially so, the monuments of Washington, DC. They have witnessed change and stagnation, glorious feats of justice, as well as shameful failures of democracy. Lincoln's and Jefferson's eyes have seen great strides in Martin Luther King's dream, and have welcomed him as he strides forward in stone between them. Yet those same unblinking eyes have seen Vietnam War protesters teargassed, and thousands tranq'd during the first teen uprising. None of these things can they forget any more than the war memorials can forget the names they so solemnly bear.

A gathering begins to form before those vigilant eyes during the last few days of October. Airlines scramble to add flights to their schedules, the metro is at constant capacity, and vehicular traffic within the capital ensures that walking is the fastest way to get anywhere aboveground.

The grassy expanse of the National Mall begins to speckle

with tents in a slow but relentless occupation days before the actual event, which, as it is scheduled for November first, has been dubbed by the media as the "All Saint's Uprising."

From Capitol Hill the portent couldn't be more ominous than the obsidian-dark wall of a thunderstorm rolling in from the Chesapeake Bay.

Far to the west, there is another, smaller gathering. This one on a commune outside of Omaha, Nebraska. The gathering is a wedding—a bittersweet one at best, because of the parties involved. Una Jacali will wed Wil Tashi'ne in the only way she can.

The Arápache council forbade it to be done on tribal land. The Tashi'nes, although they love Una dearly, could not support it either, and chose not to attend.

It was Lev who came to Una's aid, and suggested that a revival commune—a place dedicated to the virtual union of someone divided—would be openminded when it came to Una's concept of "divisional matrimony." And Lev knew just the guy to ask.

As it turned out, CyFi and his dads were more than happy to not only provide the venue, but also to track down the beneficiaries of Wil Tashi'ne's parts—a task much easier now that every last rabbit hole of Proactive Citizenry's database has been opened to public scrutiny.

Not all of Wil's parts would come, but enough agreed. Perhaps they agreed to come out of curiosity, or for the novelty, or just for the chance to meet Camus Comprix, who is expected to be among them. All told, there will be twenty-seven grooms, representing almost two-thirds of Wil Tashi'ne. That a number of the grooms will be women seems little more than par for the course.

"True, the course is about as surreal as an Escher staircase," one of CyFi's dads pointed out, "but what's life without a little vertigo?"

76 · Lev

"I gotta tell ya, Fry, you really did a number on yourself with those tattoos—and that fur hat just ain't working."

Lev peels the kinkajou from his head, where he often goes, but rarely pees anymore. Lev lets him cling to his shoulder instead. "First of all," Lev tells CyFi, "they're not numbers, they're names; and second, don't insult Mahpee, or he might claw your eyes out."

"What? Little umber Elmo got claws?"

Lev smiles. It's good to see CyFi again, even if it is under unusual circumstances. Of course, any circumstances are better than when they last saw each other.

"So, I hear you got a girlfriend," teases CyFi.

"Kind of, I think. It's a long-distance thing," Lev tells him. "She's gone back to Indiana with her family, but I'm still on the Rez in Colorado."

CyFi raises his eyebrows. "Could be worse, if you catch my drift."

The sun comes out from behind a stray cloud, lighting up the garden. As the day is unseasonably warm, it was decided to have the wedding outside, within the circle of stones at the garden's center, the participants within the circle, and the guests standing just outside of it. With no tradition for this sort of thing, rules and structure are all spur-of-the-moment. Right now all the "grooms" mill around the inner circle getting to know one another and asking logistical questions of the minister, who keeps offering up shrugs.

Then, just before the ceremony begins, Lev hears a familiar voice behind him.

"I swear, I can't leave you alone for five minutes without you doing something crazy."

He turns to see Connor standing behind him, and not just Connor but Risa as well. The sight of them takes his breath away, quite literally, and Lev starts coughing and gasping. It's the nuisance of having only one lung. Supposedly, Elina's getting one of those new machines on the Rez that can grow him a second one, so it won't always be like this.

"Whoa," says Connor, "I didn't mean to freak you into cardiac arrest."

"I'm okay, I'm okay," Lev says, finally catching his breath. But as he looks at Connor, he can see that he's got his own issues. He's walking with a cane, and even though he's wearing a sports coat, Lev can see seams on his wrists, along his neckline—and even along his jawline. He suspects there are many more beneath his clothes that Lev can't see.

"What happened?" Lev asks.

Connor shares a loaded glance with Risa, then says, "Let's just say I had a gardening accident."

Lev accepts it without further question, knowing that with Connor sometimes it's best not to probe. It suddenly occurs to Lev how long it's been since he, Connor, and Risa have been together—but in a way, it's the first time, because until today, they were never truly together. When Connor kidnapped him, Lev was a tithe, who ran from both of them the first chance he got. Then, when they met again at the Graveyard, Lev had already detached himself from everyone and everything. He was already a clapper. But now all three of them have come out of their own gardening accidents, and are truly in the same place. Wherever that is.

"Well, the important thing is that you're here," Lev says. And then he realizes something. "But . . . why are you here?"

"To see you, of course," Risa tells him. "Cyrus told me you'd be here." Then she turns to CyFi. "Hi, Cyrus. Good to see you again."

"Wait a second," says Lev. "You two know each other?"

But before Risa can answer, a guitar begins to play, and Lev gasps—almost going into a coughing fit again—because he recognizes the music right away. That's Wil playing! Lev turns to see Camus Comprix sitting in the center of the circle—one of the few grooms actually wearing a tuxedo. More so than ever, he expresses Wil's soulful music so perfectly, Lev could swear Wil is really there.

In a moment Una comes down from the main house, flowers and ribbons woven into her long hair and wearing a traditional native gown. She doesn't smile, but maintains an unreadable expression that speaks of more emotions than can possibly mix.

She enters the circle, and in front of the minister, Cam takes Una's hand. But when the time comes, it's someone else, a man with Wil's voice, who speaks the vows, and Una looks into the eyes of yet another when she says hers. And although she exchanges rings with Cam, when the minister says, "You may now kiss the bride," that honor goes to someone else entirely. Lev finds his internal compass spinning, and he wonders how something can be so beautiful and so horrible at the same time.

"That's going to be one crowded wedding bed," says Connor, and Lev can't help but laugh, but he quickly settles back toward somber. This commune, this wedding—it's all collateral damage from unwinding. Even if the impossible happens, and the Unwind Accord is overthrown, they'll all still be tallying the psychological cost for years to come.

"I wanted to show you this," Risa tells him as Una and her entourage of grooms lead the way to the main house for a small reception. Risa holds out her right arm to show that there's a name tattooed on her wrist.

"You too, huh?" It doesn't surprise him. It's become the thing to do. Everyone is getting the name of an Unwind inked on their right arms. The idea is that it's in a place where they will see it every single day. The running gag is that Washington politicians should get them tattooed in their colons.

"Is Bryce Barlow someone you knew?" Lev asks.

Risa looks dolefully at the name on her wrist. "Just like the names on you, he's a boy I'll never meet."

"Did you hear the latest?" Connor asks. "Someone's proposing they build a memorial out of the old arm of the Statue of Liberty, and engrave it with the names of everyone who's ever been unwound by the Juvenile Authority."

Lev shifts Mahpee on his shoulder and smiles at both Connor and Risa, trying to take a mental snapshot of this moment, so he can save it forever. "I hope they do," he says. "And I'm glad our names won't be on it."

77 · Cam

The groom who got the ring moves through the reception, listening to other people's conversations.

"If Parental Override passes the Senate, I hear the entire Tribal Congress is threatening to secede from the union—not just the Arápache," says a woman Cam thinks has Wil Tashi'ne's liver. "That's dozens of Chancefolk tribes. We could have a second Heartland War on our hands."

"It'll never happen," says the taller of CyFi's fathers. "The president has vowed to veto if it passes."

Several of the wedding participants—ones who share parts of Wil's cerebral cortex—bond over connected memories. Cam wonders if they have a grand feeling of Wil's presence among them. For Cam, with all of the anxiety of the day—slipping a ring on Una's hand, and her slipping a ring on his—he can't be sure what he feels. He knows he experiences Wil's presence every time he plays guitar, though. For him, that's enough.

He tries to join the meeting of the minds, but as always, the instant he enters the conversation, the whole focus shifts to him.

"I think it's great what you did, Camus. Can I call you Camus?"

"Those bastards at Proactive Citizenry really had it coming."

"That awful woman should be locked up for life."

He politely excuses himself and slips away, listening in on conversations, hoping they don't see him and shift their conversation to him. Once upon a time, all the attention might have swelled his head, but his head has been swollen and deflated so many times, he's become immune.

Connor, who's been eyeing him since the reception began, finally makes an approach, looking a little pained and awkward as he does. "Empathy," Connor says, then clears his throat. "What I mean to say is that I get it now, and I just wanted you to know."

Cam has no idea what "it" he gets, until Connor explains his run-in with a little kitchen gadget named UNIS, and his whole dicing/slicing/rewinding experience. And then Connor asks him a question that perhaps no one else would understand. No one but Cam.

Connor grabs his arm, and looks into his eyes. "How do you fill it?" Connor asks. "How do you fill the . . . the *space*?"

And to Cam's own amazement, he has an answer. "Bit by bit," he says, "and not alone."

Connor holds his arm for a moment more, letting that sink in, then walks away satisfied. In that moment, Cam realizes that he can't hold on to any of the hatred he had for Connor. Now he can only admire him. All context of their rivalry is gone. He wonders why he ever disliked him at all.

Cam had no idea that The Girl was here. How could he? Even if he saw her from a distance, he'd forget the moment he looked away. She comes to him as he's picking over the remains of the buffet, which was attacked as if by vultures the moment the ceremony was over.

"I wanted to thank you, Cam, for what you did for us that night in Akron."

He remembers the night. He remembers Grace and Connor, but—

As soon as Cam turns to her, seeing her point-blank, his brain begins to resonate itself into convulsions. It's so painful he has to look away. The agony of longing blends with the pain of the nanites doing their accursed job, and he has to hold on to the wall to keep his balance. This is how he knows who she must be.

"Cam, are you all right?"

"Yes, yes, I'm fine," he says, making sure to focus on a point on the wall above her shoulder, seeing her only faintly in his peripheral vision. Even then the pain is too great. In the end he has to turn away from her entirely.

"Cam, don't be this way. . . ."

"No," he says. "No, you don't understand. They made me . . . they made me . . ." But even as he tries to explain, his thoughts are scrambled to the point that he's not sure what he was going to say. He doesn't even know her name. How can he talk to her if he doesn't even know her name? So he closes his eyes, sorts the pieces, and tells her what he can, as best as he can.

"You are the reason for everything I did," he tells her, keeping his eyes closed. "But now I need a new reason."

Silence for a moment. And then she says, "I understand." Her voice is so sweet. And so painful.

"But . . . but . . ." He has to get this out, because he knows it's the only chance he'll ever get. "But I can still remember what it felt like . . . to love you."

He feels her give him a kiss on the cheek. And when he opens his eyes, she's gone, and he wonders why on earth he's standing by the buffet with his eyes closed.

The reception barely lasts an hour. The eyes are the first to leave, apparently having seen enough, and the other bits and pieces of Wil Tashi'ne are quick to follow. Through the whole reception, Una has been noticeably absent. Cam finds her sitting on the back steps of the main house alone, her ribboned hair pulled forward in an attempt to hide tears.

He sits beside her. His presence doesn't chase her away. That's a good sign.

"Was it everything you expected?" he asks her.

"What do *you* think?" she says bitterly.

"I think you're a very loyal, and a very stubborn, human being, Mrs. Una Tashi'ne."

Then he pulls something out of his pocket. "Which reminds me, I have something to show you." He hands her his Hawaiian driver's license. She looks at it, unimpressed.

"So you can drive. Big deal."

"It *is* a big deal. This is an official ID. After what happened on Molokai, the state legislature passed a special referendum declaring that I am officially a human being. So now I actually exist. At least in Hawaii. The rest of the world isn't so sure."

She hands it back to him. "You don't need a license to prove you exist. *I* know you exist."

"Thank you, Una," he says. "That means a lot to me." Although he's not sure if she believes him.

"So what will you do now?" she asks.

He shrugs. "Lots of things. I've been asked to play Carnegie Hall, and to be the grand marshal of the Rose Parade."

"So you're still the shining star."

"I guess, but now it's because of what I've done, not because of who I am. There's a big difference."

Una considers it. "You're right, there is."

"Of course, I don't have Roberta to organize things for me anymore. Now I have an agent—and she's almost as scary."

Una laughs, which makes Cam happy. If he can make her laugh on this strange mournful wedding day, that's half the battle. He takes a moment to look at the identical rings on their fingers. She sees him looking, and the moment becomes awkward.

"Anyway," says Cam. "I'm going back to Molokai for a while. It seems no one knows what to do with all those rewinds now that the whole property has been confiscated by the state. They need someone to be their advocate, and to help them integrate themselves, mind and body."

"You mean they're just going to leave them there?"

"No one wants to deal with them, no one wants to admit they exist, and the public made a huge outcry when someone suggested they be euthanized." Cam sighs. "Molokai was once a leper colony. It looks like the island will be holding to its tradition."

Then Cam pauses. *You fill the emptiness bit by bit,* he thinks, *and not alone.* He takes her hand, rolling her ring between his fingers, and when she doesn't pull away, he says, "I would like it very much if you came back to Molokai with me."

She takes a long look at him. "Why would I do that?"

"Because I asked?" he says. "Because you want to?"

"I put that ring on your hand. But I didn't marry the rest of you."

"I know," he tells her. "But the rest of me comes with the hand."

She smirks. "Not if I get my chain saw."

"Ah," says Cam. "The good old days."

Silence falls again, but it's not as awkward as it was a moment ago.

Una flips her hair back from her face. Her tears from before have almost dried. "What's it like on Molokai? Hot and muggy? What should I wear?"

"Does that mean you'll come?" Cam asks, a little too eager.

Instead of answering, she leans forward and kisses him. Then she runs her fingers through his multitextured hair, and with the faintest of smiles, she regards his admittedly irresistible eyes, and she gently whispers, "How I despise you, Camus Comprix."

Then she kisses him again.

78 · Connor

Once the grooms all leave and the residents of the Tyler Walker Revival Compound return to their business, the dusk is filled with the mild melancholy that follows any grand event.

"It's Halloween," CyFi notes, as he, Connor, Risa, and Lev help with cleanup in the main house. "So was today's wedding the trick, or the treat?"

"The best of both?" Risa suggests. She takes Connor's hand a little too firmly and he can't help but flinch from the pain. "Sorry," she says.

His seams are deep, and although the healing enhancers speed the process, there's no escaping the aches of being rewound.

Lev shifts his clingy kinkajou from his waist to his back as he approaches Connor. "So what was it like?" Lev asks. No one has dared to ask Connor that question. Lev, however, having been to the edge of his own existence too, is one of the few who have the right to ask.

"Like . . . breathing out and never stopping," Connor tells him. "While listening to disco."

"No, not the unwinding," Lev says. "What was it like to be divided?"

The only way Connor can see Lev anymore is to look right into his eyes. Otherwise all he sees are the names inked on his face. What he sees in those eyes is longing. A need to know so intense that Connor can't look away.

"Did you go into the light?" Lev asks. "Did you see the face of God?"

"I think you have to get through the door before you see that," Connor tells him. "Being divided is kind of like being storked on the welcome mat."

Lev considers it and nods. "Interesting. I believe the door would have opened if the master of the house knew you were there to stay."

Connor smiles. "It's good to believe that."

"What do you believe?" he asks.

As much as Connor wants to avoid the question, he wants to give Lev an answer that's true. "I believe I'm here," Connor tells him. "I'm here even though after what happened, I shouldn't be. There's got to be something to that, but right now I'm not going to unwind my brain again wondering what that something is. Let me think of water for a while before I have to think about it turning into wine, okay?"

He thinks Lev might smile at that, but he doesn't. "Fair enough," he says.

The kinkajou—a literal monkey on his back—now peers out from behind Lev with wide innocent eyes, but clings with claws that can kill. It reminds Connor that as much as Lev has changed, he'll always carry the wide-eyed tithe somewhere within him. As well as the clapper.

Una and Cam escort Lev back to the Rez before leaving for Molokai. Out in the front yard before they go, Risa hugs Lev so tightly, she actually lifts him off the ground. Then suddenly she gasps, and apologizes, realizing she might have hurt him. But instead Lev is smiling. He smiles so rarely that when he does, it holds such joy that Connor can feel it from five feet away. He hugs Lev a little more gently.

"This way you won't blow up, and I won't fall apart," Connor says. He finds his eyes welling up, and sees a tear on Lev's cheek roll over Justin Levitz, to Marla Mendoza, to Cedric Beck, and off his chin.

"Thank you for saving me, Lev," Connor says, barely able to get it out. Maybe he'll fall apart after all.

"You saved me first."

Connor shakes his head. "I used you as a human shield."

"You could have let me go once you got to the woods, but you didn't," Lev points out. "Because you didn't want me to go back. You didn't want me to be tithed."

Connor can't argue with that. He might have grabbed Lev out of desperation, but he held on to him out of compassion, although he really didn't know it at the time.

"Do you still have the scar from where I bit you?" Lev asks.

Connor looks to his right forearm. Of course the bite mark isn't there. "Sorry, the scar went with the arm." But he notices for the first time that the shark's teeth are almost exactly where the scar from Lev's bite would have been.

The kinkajou, apparently wanting some attention climbs from Lev's hip to his shoulder, and starts pulling at Lev's ear. He seems impatient for Lev to get on with his day. To get on with his life.

"Take care of him," Connor says.

"I will," Lev answers.

"I was talking to the monkey."

And Lev smiles, big and broad.

At the insistence of CyFi, Connor and Risa stay the night. The day has been hard on Connor's healing body, and as he lies in bed, Risa gently rubs all his wounds with a special healing ointment that Cam gave them before he left.

"An early Christmas gift," he said. "My second-favorite Proactive Citizenry product."

Connor had been dense enough to ask him what his first favorite was.

"Me, of course," Cam had answered.

The ointment is soothing. Warming. But it's not just the ointment; it's the touch of Risa's hands.

"Remember back at the Graveyard, when I would massage your legs?"

"It was the best part of my day," Risa says.

"Mine too."

With all his wounds gently massaged, he rolls to face her. She kisses him, he takes her into his arms, and his embrace holds not the slightest bit of hesitation. Whatever else is wrong with the world dissolves into down pillows and fine linen sheets, and he finds that Risa fills that space left within him from being pulled apart and put back together.

Connor stays awake late into the night with Risa in his arms, wishing he could unwind time, so he could experience this night from every possible angle—not just passing through the moment, but living in it.

He holds on to the feeling until morning, when the authorities come to take them away.

Part Seven

All Saints

ANONYMOUS RALLIES AGAINST HORRIFIC, ABUSE-RIDDLED "TROUBLED TEEN" INDUSTRY

By Roy Klabin, March 27, 2013 PolicyMic.com

A faction within the exceedingly diverse "Anonymous" online collective has begun targeting the Troubled Teen Industry—trying to expose cases of extreme child abuse, sexual misconduct, psychological torture, and even deaths, at various facilities which claim to "correct bad behavior."

The sales pitch is simple: "If your teen has emotional issues, abuses drugs, or is promiscuous, help is just a phone call away. Our programs promise to fix bad behavior by teaching your child life skills and building self-esteem." . . . Sometimes you get taken to these facilities in the middle of the night, grabbed from your bed by camp employees your parents have let into your home.

Exposure of the behavior modification industry is slowly gaining traction. . . . But it seems parents all over the country are still falling for the misleading assurances offered by these companies—even though every corporate site that promises sunshine and happiness has shadow sites full of survivor's horror stories.

. . . [i]n a world of webcams, victims can no longer be hidden away. . . . But there are places where no cell phones or Internet are permitted. Places isolated in the wilderness miles from any form of civilization, where children are taken to correct their behavior—and suffer a wide array of vicious torments.

#OpTTIAbuse represents hackers, activists, victims, parents, and survivors who are trying to expose horrific abuses being suffered by children across this country at various facilities hidden away from public scrutiny. . . .

Cases where children have died from mistreatment, medical neglect, or starvation have rarely led to any consequences. This is partly due to the lack of any regulatory oversight, as well some states not even requiring any licensing system for these programs to exist. . . .

The prison-like design of some of these facilities further limits the children's ability to report abuse. . . . The children rarely have access to telephones, and when they do utilize these connections, their conversations are watched carefully. If they were to say anything "negative" to their parents, like "I miss you, I want to come home" they would be punished for being "manipulative."

Anonymous groups continue to try and expose the survivor stories from within the system, but with limited attention from the press their success has been marginal. Some of the major companies involved have even managed to lobby and block reform on private residential "treatment" centers. . . .

The full article can be found at: *http://www.policymic.com/articles/31203/anonymous-rallies-against-horrific-abuse-riddled-troubled-teen-industry*

79 · Connor

The raid comes just after Connor and Risa shuffle down for breakfast. All is quiet, then out of nowhere, the house is flooded with a tactical unit that's beyond overkill. It happens so fast, Connor finds himself surrounded while still holding his cereal spoon. There's no time to panic, or to resist. Too many guns are drawn for him to count. He locks eyes with Risa across the table, who returns the same shocked gaze. He should have known it wasn't safe coming here. CyFi and his fathers might be trustworthy, but with all the wedding grooms, and the various parts of Tyler Walker living in the commune, someone was bound to turn them in for the reward.

"What took you so long?" he says to the gaggle of gunmen. They don't answer. They don't make a move to apprehend him. They just wait. Then in walks the man in the dark suit. For once, Connor wished these people could find a more inspired wardrobe.

"Looks like we've got a twofer!" says the suit. He gestures for his unit to lower their guns, which they do.

In response, Connor puts down his spoon. "I'll come peacefully if you leave her."

"Connor, don't you dare!" says Risa.

The suit stays focused on Connor. "You're not really in a negotiating position."

Then Risa leaps up and lunges for him.

"Risa, no!"

She's tranq'd by one of the gunmen before she gets halfway there, and is caught by another before she falls to the ground.

This is her way of making sure that wherever Connor goes, she goes. *Damn her!*

CyFi and his fathers are brought downstairs. The one who happens to be a lawyer argues over the violation of their rights.

"We don't have time for this," says the suit, then he turns to Connor. "You want a deal? How's this? You and sleeping beauty come peacefully, and *they* don't get arrested for harboring known fugitives."

And although Connor doesn't believe for an instant that they're going to leave CyFi and his dads alone, his only other option is to fight and get tranq'd like Risa. What chance would he have to negotiate for her then? Besides, there's something that he senses in this man. He's trying to be efficient, even a little nonchalant, but there's an uneasiness in him. The man in the suit is scared. Why is he scared?

They turn Connor around to handcuff him, pulling his arms behind his back. He grimaces. "Careful! My seams!"

"Your what?" the suit says. "Forget it, I don't want to know." He has them turn Connor around again, cuffing him in front instead of behind.

They lead him and carry Risa to a jet that's sitting in a weedy field across the road, without the benefit of anything resembling a runway. Connor had seen planes like this at the Graveyard.

"A Harrier Whisper-Bomber?"

"You know your machines," the suit says. "Workhorse of the Heartland War. Vertical takeoff and landing. Completely silent."

"Then Risa and I must be the bombs."

The suit shifts uncomfortably. "That remains to be seen."

They're loaded inside, the three of them in a forward compartment separate from the tactical team. The intimidating boeuf carrying Risa puts her down gently and actually takes the time to put on her seat belt.

"Will you be coming back with the beverage cart?" Connor asks as he leaves to join his comrades.

The jet rises like a helicopter, its engines emitting only the faintest whine, then the craft accelerates, heading into the rising sun. Risa, still unconscious, slumps limply in the seat beside Connor, her seat belt and Connor's shoulder the only things keeping her from falling. Across from them, the suit seems very pleased with himself. Connor considers how he might, even in handcuffs, throw the man out of the plane. But then the suit says:

"Congratulations—you're in the protective custody of the federal government. We've taken you as a precaution, just in case the bee in the Juvenile Authority's bonnet buzzes in your direction."

It takes a moment for Connor to replay that in his mind and process it. "Wait—you're not the Juvies?"

"If we were, you wouldn't be alive right now."

Connor's still not ready to buy. "If I'm in protective custody, why am I in handcuffs?"

The suit smirks. "Because I trust you even less than you trust me."

He introduces himself as Supervisory Special Agent Aragon, reflexively flashing his FBI badge, as if it means anything to Connor at this point.

"We are not the enemy," he says.

"That's what the enemy always says."

He regards Connor, studying him like maybe he wants the eyes that Nelson never got.

"Do you believe in democracy, Connor?"

Not the kind of question Connor was expecting. "I used to," Connor tells him. "I believe in the way it's *supposed* to work."

"It always works the way it's supposed to work," Aragon says. "A lot of bitching and moaning until somebody gets their way." Then he pulls out a tablet and strokes the screen until he finds whatever it is he's looking for. "As of this morning, forty-four percent of the American people are ready to reject the idea of unwinding."

"It's still not a majority."

Aragon raises his eyebrows. "That's only because you're not seeing the whole picture." Then he turns the tablet so Connor can see it. On-screen is a simple pie chart. "This morning, support for unwinding hit an all-time low of thirty-seven percent, with nineteen percent undecided. And I have news for you—that nineteen percent will ALWAYS be undecided. Which means, Connor, after all the bitching and moaning, it looks like you're the one who got his way." Aragon forces a smile and winks at him.

Connor has no faith in anyone who winks. "So it's that easy?"

"You of all people should know it wasn't easy at all."

He's right about that. The thought of all Connor has been through makes his seams begin to ache inside and out.

"A lot of people know you're not Mason Starkey—so, as psychotic as that bastard is, he did you a service. Now you're the lesser of two evils."

The thought of Starkey makes Connor want to lose what little cereal he got down before he was captured. "Starkey's dead," Connor tells Aragon. "I killed him."

He studies Connor, not sure if Connor is joking. "Really. How disappointing for all the people who wanted to do it themselves."

Risa stirs against his shoulder, but he suspects she'll be out for at least an hour or longer, depending on the strength of the tranqs. Connor shifts his shoulder awkwardly to keep her sitting upright, then holds out his hands to Aragon, hoping he'll take off the cuffs so Connor can hold Risa properly.

"They'll come off when they need to come off," Aragon

tells him, and once more Connor feels the man's tension. "You have no idea what's in front of you, do you?"

"I never know. Two weeks ago I was in forty pieces, and now I'm whole. Ten minutes ago I was sitting in a kitchen, and now I'm flying across the sky. Tell me I'm going to the moon, and I wouldn't be surprised."

"Oh, farther than that," says Aragon. "With Proactive Citizenry completely torpedoed, and organ printers on the horizon, everything changes. If you make it through today, you and Miss Ward will be your own constellations out there. And you'll be amazed how many friends in high places you'll suddenly have."

"I don't want those kinds of friends."

"Yes, you do, because there are still plenty of haters calling for your head. But the parasites can protect you from the carnivores."

It's too much to take in. He can feel it deep in his skull, as if the various lobes of his healing brain are trying to reject one another. "Who *are* you?"

"Like I said, I'm just your run-of-the-mill field officer with the FBI. But like everyone else, I aspire to bigger things."

"You're my first parasite."

Aragon gives him that annoying wink again. "Now you're catching on."

They hit some choppy air, and Connor glances out of a window to see that the ground has disappeared beneath a blanket of clouds.

Aragon checks his watch. "It's nine a.m. where we're going. We should get there by eleven."

"Where are we going?"

Aragon doesn't answer him right away. The fear that Connor sensed in him begins to rise to the surface. He wouldn't be surprised if the man began to sweat. "I don't know if you're aware, but the Arápache, along with every other Chancefolk tribe are prepared to declare war. Riots have broken out over unwinding in every major city. We're on the verge of something that could make the Heartland War look like a domestic spat."

"So where are we going?" Connor asks again.

Aragon takes a deep breath and removes Connor's handcuffs. "You're paying a visit to an old friend."

80 · Risa

She awakes in Connor's arms and for a moment she thinks things are as they should be . . . until her focus clears, and she sees where she is and remembers what happened. They've been caught, and yet Connor's arm is around her. He smiles when he sees she's awake. What could he possibly have to smile about?

"Almost there," says the man sitting across from them. The man who captured them. "Have a look."

She turns slowly, knowing the tranqs will make her suffer if she turns too fast, and peers out of the window.

The first thing she sees is the unmistakable white spire of the Washington Monument. She had thought they were in a plane, but the speed and trajectory of their approach is more like that of a helicopter—yet she doesn't hear the pulse of rotor blades. As they get closer, she realizes something isn't right. The grassy lawn of the National Mall, which extends east to the Capitol, and west to the Lincoln Memorial, should be green or, at worst, yellow this time of year. Instead it's filled with color and movement, like snow on an old-fashioned tube TV. It takes a few moments for her to realize that there are people crowding the two-mile-long park. Thousands upon thousands of people!

"Hayden's rally," Connor tells her.

"Hayden?" she says, still unable to stretch her mind around the entire National Mall. "*Our* Hayden?"

Connor introduces her to Agent Aragon, whose hand she is

not quite ready to shake, and quickly explains what's going on, but it's too much for Risa to hold on to so soon after coming out of sedation. Connor shows her a letter. At first she thinks it's the same letter he was carrying around in Sonia's shop—but it can't be. She looks a little closer and sees that it's stamped with an official-looking seal.

"The announcement will be made at noon," Aragon says. "But these people need to hear it now, and they need to hear it from both of you."

"Wait—what announcement?" Then she turns to Connor. "You're going to let this guy tell you what to say?"

"Don't worry, I already know what to say, with or without him," Connor tells her.

They veer around the Washington Monument, getting a little too close for Risa's comfort, then descend toward the far end of the crowded park, just short of the Capitol building.

Risa still feels a beat behind. "How can we land with all those people in the way?"

"Don't worry," Aragon says. "When a Whisper-Bomber comes down on you, you move."

As they descend, the scene becomes clearer. The crowd is tightly packed. Riot police are everywhere, shoulder to shoulder, waiting for the first sign of violence—and in a crowd this big, this fired up, it's bound to happen.

"My God, this isn't a rally," Risa says. "It's a powder keg."

"Which is why you're here," says Aragon. "To make everyone play nice."

Risa catches sight of a shirt that reads in bold letters WHERE ARE THEY? And it's not just one shirt—there are hundreds of them, and other sentiments just like it speckled throughout the crowd. Risa's mind begins to reel when she realizes who the shirts are talking about.

"There's a growing rumor that the Juvenile Authority has

both of you buried in unmarked graves," Aragon says. "You've got to show people that it's not true before they decide it's time to take vengeance."

"Looks like they'll have to get new shirts," says Connor.

When the door is opened, it becomes clear how they were able to land. Their vertical descent has dropped them right into the Capitol reflecting pool. Beyond the edge of the pool, the crowd tries to peer in to see who has just arrived. Connor gets up first, then turns to Aragon, who hasn't moved from his seat. "Aren't you coming?"

Aragon shakes his head. "If this is going to work, it has to be your show, not mine. Good luck."

Connor reaches his hand out to Risa, and although she's not ready to face the multitude, she takes his hand and steps down into the water.

"Damn, that's cold," says Connor.

The reaction of the crowd is immediate. "It's them!" "It's the Akron AWOL!" "It's Risa Ward!" The news relays through the crowd and down the length of the massive park like a wave of electricity. Did Risa say thousands? There must be more than a million here! It's not just teenagers, either. There are people of all ages, all races, probably from all over the nation.

Hayden comes wading across the reflecting pool toward them. "What an entrance! You are the only people I know who can arrive by deus ex machina and pull it off."

"Hayden, I have no idea what you're talking about," says Connor.

"As it should be." He quickly hugs them both. "I'm glad the reports of your deaths were greatly exaggerated." He leads them out of the pool and through the crowd, toward the Capitol steps. The crowd parts before them, still whispering their names with charged excitement. Some people actually reach out to touch them. A woman grabs Risa's blouse, nearly ripping it.

"Hands to yourselves," Hayden tells the reachers. "It might look like they walked on water, but the reflecting pool's only a foot deep."

There's a speaker at a podium toward the top of the Capitol steps calling for justice, fairness, transparency, and all the other things people demand but rarely get from their government. Risa hears his words being broadcast throughout the rally by audio systems that seem to have sprung up spontaneously. The speaker, Risa realizes, is none other than rock star Brick McDaniel—and there are more celebrities in line to speak.

"When I called for this," says Hayden, "I wasn't even sure anyone was listening."

At the base of the Capitol steps, a line of riot police blocks the way, and the crowd taunts them, daring them to attack. Risa feels like she's just stepped into a mousetrap that's about to spring. Doesn't Hayden see that? How can he be so enthusiastic?

"I haven't seen a single Juvie," Connor notes. Risa looks around to realize he's right. There's the riot police, street cops, heavily armed military boeufs in camo, even special service, but no Juvies.

"The word is Herman What's-His-Face—that lying tool who ran the Juvenile Authority—is out," Hayden tells them.

"Sharply was fired?" says Connor.

"Had his nuts handed to him, is more like it."

"He was Proactive Citizenry's favorite puppet." Risa says.

Hayden offers up his famous grin. "I thought I'd get arrested the moment I showed up, but the powers that be are all scrambling like AWOLs. No telling where they're going to land, but I hope they all splat like tomatoes."

As they reach the line of riot police, Hayden says, "Open sesame," and they actually let him pass, but close their ranks again and grip their weapons before Connor and Risa can get through.

"Uh, excuse me," Hayden says. "Can't you see who they are?"

One of the guards looks at Connor, then at Risa, and the moment he recognizes them, he pulls his gun from its holster. She doesn't know if it's loaded with tranqs or real bullets, but it doesn't matter. If he shoots them, the crowd will attack, and it will be a bloodbath. So she looks into the officer's angry eyes.

"Are you willing to be the man who starts the war?" she asks. "Or do you want to be the man who prevents it?"

Although the anger never leaves his face, it's caressed by a little humanity, and maybe a little bit of fear. He holds his position for a moment more, then steps aside to let them pass.

Climbing the Capitol steps is clearly difficult for Connor. He grimaces with every step, and Risa helps him as much as she can. When Brick McDaniel sees them approaching, he stops speaking midsentence and yields the microphone, a little bit awed. The entire crowd from the Capitol to the Lincoln Memorial falls silent in anticipation.

Risa stops a few steps short of the podium, hanging back with Hayden. "It's you they need to hear from," she tells Connor. "I've already been in the media spotlight. Now it's your turn."

"I can't do this alone," he says.

Risa smiles. "Does it look like you're alone?"

81 · Connor

Gripping the letter in his hand to the point of crumpling it, Connor approaches the podium, trying to keep himself from hyperventilating. He's never seen so many people in his life. He leans forward into the microphone.

"Hi . . . I'm Connor Lassiter."

His voice booms out over the crowd, and the collective cheer it brings forth nearly knocks him off his feet. It's a roar that echoes back from the Capitol behind him. It even seems to sway the trees. He imagines it surging forth along the Potomac, out into Chesapeake Bay, and across the Atlantic, where it can be heard around the world. And then he realizes it will be! Everything that happens here today will be seen and heard everywhere!

"I'm here to tell you that I'm alive. And so is Risa Ward." He pauses for more cheers, once more waiting for the crowd to settle before he says, "And there's something I need to tell you."

He looks down to the letter in his hands, then realizes he doesn't have to. He's read it so many times since Aragon gave it to him, he's memorized it. He had to—it was the only way he could convince himself it was real.

"I'm happy to announce that the president has just vetoed the Parental Override bill."

This time the cheer begins tentatively, but rises to a fever pitch. He doesn't wait for them to quiet down to continue. "And there's more. The president is also calling on the legislature to place a moratorium on unwinding. And to shutter the Chop Shops of all harvest camps until *every voice is heard!*" He feels his own voice gathering strength from the crowd, gathering strength from deep within himself. "*And we will stand here!*" Connor yells. "*In front of the Capitol! Until! They! Are!*"

The roar from the crowd is an earthquake rumbling up the steps. He can feel it vibrating in his feet, shaking the foundations of the great domed building behind him. He doesn't know if this is what Aragon wanted, but it's what Connor wants: the galvanizing of millions—not to wage acts of violence or revenge, but to hold their ground against the institutionalized murder that has defined a generation.

"Stand with me!" Connor commands. *"And I swear to you EVERYTHING WILL CHANGE!"*

Up above, the news helicopters circle, and down below, media crews broadcast his message into every home, every workplace, every newsfeed. And he knows for each soul here today, there are a thousand more that at this very moment are rising up to join them. Not a teen uprising as Hayden thought this would be, but the awakening of a nation from its darkest nightmare.

Then, amid the tumult of the crowd, Connor hears his name called. Not just by some random person, but by a familiar voice. A little deeper perhaps, a little older than he remembers, but a voice he can never forget. He looks down to the front of the crowd and sees a boy emerging. A boy almost as tall as him.

"Lucas?"

And behind him, Connor sees them. His mother. His father. Fighting their way forward in the crowd. They came to the rally. They didn't even know he'd be here, but they still came!

That's when people begin to recognize them. They realize that these are the people who signed the order to unwind the Akron AWOL.

And the crowd begins to turn.

"They're unwinders!" the mob yells. *"Unwind the unwinders!"*

As high as spirits were an instant ago, the energy flips into fury, and his parents are attacked.

"No!"

Connor bolts down the Capitol steps, ignoring the pain in his joints. The crowd around his parents has gone mad! He can't even see them anymore—they've been taken down in a lethal screaming scrum.

"Stop!"

But they can't hear him over their own rage.

The riot police move toward the crowd wielding their weapons. Connor breaks through their ranks and gets to the rioting mob first.

"Connor, stop them!" begs Lucas.

Connor runs past him and hurls himself into the tangle of bodies, pushing people away. When they see him, they back off one by one, until he's at the epicenter of the attack, and he finds them.

His parents lie on the ground, their clothes torn, their faces and bodies bloody.

But they're alive! They're still alive.

Connor grabs his mother and helps her to her feet. He reaches out to his father, who takes his hand and rises. The two of them look like refugees. Desperate. Alone against a force that outnumbers them. They look like AWOLs.

Around them the crowd still seethes, and the riot police are on the verge of attack. The powder keg is about to blow, and who knows how bad it will be once it does? Everything hinges on this moment.

Connor knows what he must do to defuse this. He knows what the crowd needs to see.

He throws his arms around both his mother and his father and holds them with all the strength he has. Lucas, pulled in by their gravity, joins them in this odd and awkward familial embrace, and for Connor it's as if the crowd and the police and the world have gone away. But he knows they haven't. They're all there, waiting to see how this hair-trigger reunion will end.

Connor's father, his lips close to Connor's ear, whispers, "Can you forgive us?"

And Connor realizes he doesn't have an answer. Right now the yes and the no of his own pie chart are overwhelmed by the part of him that's undecided.

"I'm doing this to save your lives," Connor tells him. But

he knows it's more than that. It's as if his embrace can rewind them—not into the family they once were, but into the one they may still have a chance to be. Connor knows he can't forgive them today; they will have to fight for his forgiveness. They will have to earn it. But if they all survive today, there will be time for that.

His father now sobs uncontrollably into Connor's shoulder, and his mother holds his gaze as if looking at him gives her strength. The crowd watches. The crowd waits. And the moment of crisis passes.

It is then that Connor realizes that Aragon was absolutely right. Connor has won. Which means they've all won.

"Can we go home now?" Lucas asks.

"Soon," Connor tells him gently. "Very soon."

And so, as the mob backs away to give them space . . . and as the riot police holster their weapons, standing down, and as Risa takes the podium, calming the crowd with a voice as soothing as a sonata, Connor Lassiter holds his family like he'll never let them go.

A Curriculum Guide to

UnDivided

Part of the Unwind Dystology
By Neal Shusterman

About the Book

Connor Lassiter and Risa Ward, reunited in *UnSouled*, are holed up in Sonia Reinschild's antique store as the novel begins. They hide there with Grace Skinner, who helped Connor escape from her brother, and a dozen AWOL Unwinds given refuge by Sonia as they have nowhere else to go.

The elderly Sonia, a research scientist before the war, gives Connor, Risa, and Grace a 3-D printer that can produce human organs. Invented by her late husband, this prototype is the only unit remaining after Proactive Citizenry destroyed the rest and suppressed the technology. The organ printer can render unwinding unnecessary—but only if the teens can find a company willing to mass-produce it.

Grace's brother, Argent Skinner, is meanwhile working closely with Jasper Nelson, former Juvey-cop turned "parts pirate." They capture teen AWOLs and sell them to Divan Umarov, a big-league black marketeer with his own private harvest camp. Divan convinces Argent to track down his sister, Grace; once they have her, they'll capture Connor, and the Akron AWOL's parts will be worth a fortune at auction.

At the same time, Lev Calder, given sanctuary by the Arápache, and Camus Camprix, the Rewind constructed by Proactive Citizenry, each have their own plans to end society's reliance on Unwinding: Lev hopes to convince the tribal council to declare the reservation a safe haven for AWOLs, and Cam plans to reveal what Proactive Citizenry and the military are really up to, as soon as he figures out what that is.

As the novel races toward the breathtaking conclusion of the series, obstacles loom: Mason Starkey's Stork Brigade is violently liberating harvest camps, spreading terror and amplifying society's call for more draconian unwinding laws; Lev fails to raise the consciousness of the tribe; Cam is held captive by Proactive Citizenry; Sonia's antique shop is burned to the ground; and Connor and Risa are trapped aboard Divan's airborne Harvest Camp, a radically modified jumbo jet, and there's no way out without being unwound. . . .

Discussion Questions

1. Early in the novel, Sonia tells Connor, "There isn't one single thing that will end unwinding. It will be a hodgepodge of random events that come together in just the right way and at just the right time to remind society it's got a conscience." What does she mean? What are some of the "random events" in the novel that will have to come together for unwinding to end?

2. Who is the character you most relate to in the story, and who is the one you find the most repugnant? Why? Now imagine yourself spending time with those characters in the world of *UnDivided*. What would you say to them?

3. The fourth book in a series poses many challenges for an author, including the need to remind readers about characters introduced and events dramatized in the previous books, without slowing down this story's forward momentum. Shusterman finds clever, often poignant ways to do this (such as when he reminds the reader about Cam's deep love for Risa in the context of Cam's inability to remember her name—thanks to nanotech particles inserted by his keepers that disrupt his thoughts whenever he thinks of her). Select a passage or two of backstory in this novel, and describe the technique(s) Shusterman used to weave the exposition in.

4. One of the novel's most powerful symbols is the disembodied arm of the Statue of Liberty. Describe how the arm, and other arms, are used throughout the novel, from an early scene where the statue's original copper limb is replaced by an aluminum/titanium alloy, to the final mention of the arm as a monument covered by the names of all the Unwinds.

5. The novel is, in large part, about the manipulation of society by powerful special interests, represented here by Proactive Citizenry. And yet, as one character explains, before unwinding, people were "afraid to leave their homes for fear of feral teenagers, while other people suffered needlessly with everything from heart failure to lung cancer." Describe some of the things Proactive Citizenry does to manipulate public opinion. And how complicit do you feel the society itself has been in its own manipulation?

6. During the course of the story, Connor, Risa, Lev, and others run into minor characters who do heroic things—for example, a scientist at a research facility who helps Conner instead of turning him in; a stranger who pulls Grace from a burning building; people who donate their organs to the survivor of a shooting. Who are some of the other everyday heroes mentioned in the book, and what do they do? What do you think the author is saying about human nature?

7. Even knowing that Mason Starkey's campaign of terror is increasing the public's support for unwinding, the reader experiences mixed feelings as Starkey's army violently attacks harvest camps, since those involved in unwinding innocent teens *should* pay for their crimes. How does the author exploit the reader's conflicted emotions to increase the tension in these scenes and, ultimately, create sympathy for Starkey?

8. Connor needs to see his parents and his little brother; Cam is "mothered" by Roberta; Lev is adopted by a literal tribe; Risa feels that the Unwinds are her extended family—the theme of belonging to a family runs strongly throughout *UnDivided*. List some other examples of families or characters who belong to family groups. How do some of these families affect the story?

The characters? What happens to these families at the end of the story? Which ones stay the same? Which ones change?

9. "The only thing necessary for the triumph of evil is for good men to do nothing."—Edmund Burke, eighteenth-century Irish statesmen. This sentiment is vividly dramatized throughout the novel, as in the scene told from the point of view of the head gardener at a harvest camp who plants trees while children are unwound. Discuss how other characters and/or scenes represent this concept, and describe how it plays out in the end: Do good men and women finally take action against the evil being done in their names?

10. "Do you believe in democracy?" Special Agent Aragon asks Connor near the end of the novel. "I believe in the way it's *supposed* to work," Connor replies, and Aragon says, "It always works the way it's supposed to work." What do you think Aragon means by this? What do you think Connor means? What do you think the author means?

11. Most of the major characters receive some form of justice, for good or ill, by the end of the story. Sometimes it's straightforward, sometimes it's delivered ironically. What do you think of the justice meted out to various characters in the novel: Argent? Starkey? Nelson? Divan? Lev? Cam? Conner? And others? Do you think justice was served in each case, or was the guilty party treated too harshly—or not harshly enough?

12. What do you think makes the conclusion of a book series satisfying? According to Neal Shusterman, concluding a book series "is not about having a happy ending, or wrapping up everything neatly. It's about creating a trajectory—a light at the end of the tunnel, with the knowledge that the characters can

get there, both internally, and externally." Do you agree with his description? Do you think Shusterman achieves that for the Unwind series? Why or why not?

Guide written by Eric Elfman, author and writing coach,
Big Sur Children's Writers Workshop.

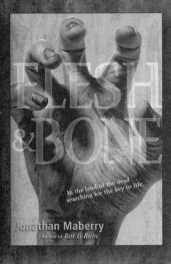

"Debut author Stefanie Gaither explores what happens when bleeding-edge science collides with the human experience. Highly recommended."
—Jonathan Maberry,
New York Times bestselling author of *Rot & Ruin* and editor of *V-Wars*

★ "A very engaging read and hard to put down until the last page."
—*VOYA*, starred review

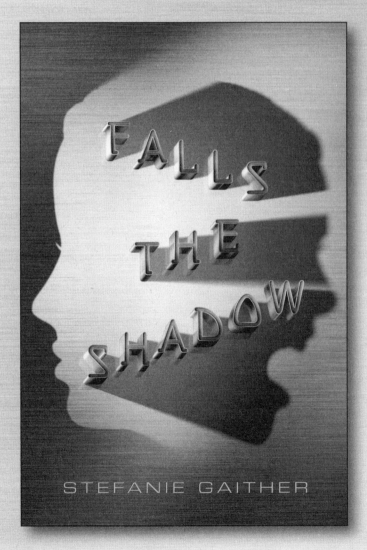

How far can you fall?

perfect

ruin

Lauren DeStefano
New York Times bestselling author
of the Chemical Garden Trilogy

burning

kingdoms

Lauren DeStefano
New York Times bestselling author
of the Chemical Garden Trilogy

Find out in the latest series by
Lauren DeStefano,
New York Times bestselling author of
the Chemical Garden Trilogy.